"This is Jihad, Pal.
There are no innocent bystanders, because in these
desperate hours, bystanders are not innocent."

—Mike Roselle,
Earth First Activist

 # prologue

"I am preparing the sweat lodge for the Ghost Dance. —Not the old Ghost Dance, which was supposed to roll up the white's Earth and bring back the Indian Earth underneath, but a new-old spirit. It is like raindrops making a tiny brook, many drops making a stream, many streams making a mighty river bursting all dams. We are the first raindrops."

— Henry Crow Dog

AFTER TEN YEARS OF SECOND THOUGHTS, A STRING OF FALSE PREGNAN-cies including the first that had rushed them to the altar and the last that had nearly ended in divorce, Ted's four-year-old—not to mention, the Portland cement of their marriage—Teddy Jr., sat between them in the front seat of the orange pick-up as it bounded down the familiar gravel road toward the river. It all but destroyed Ted the father to have to leave on these twelve-day trips. Being away from home for a week to two weeks at a time had worked when he and Samantha had been having problems instead of children. Now that he had a son, being a journeyman for the Corps had mutated from a job he loved into one he loathed.

Teddy Jr., sunburned and shirtless in Oshkosh overalls with a Cincinnati Reds baseball cap, squirmed under the seat belt between them. He knew what the black nylon bag in the back of the truck meant. He knew his Dad was leaving again. Except when he showed up ten or twelve days later, leaving was pretty much all that his Dad ever did. He looked out from under his red bangs through blondish eyelashes at Ted Sr. as if to say, even at four years old, that he knew he was getting the raw end of this deal being stuck at home with Mom. His dad ruffled his hair. "Learn to swim this summer, and you can come with me, Son."

His child's green eyes widened and for what had to be the first second in forty-eight months, he stopped squirming. "I will learn to swim," he said. "I sure will."

His son's determination made Ted's eyes water behind aviator-styled sunglasses. Watching his boy grow up in spurts, four days at a time, twice, maybe three times a month if he was lucky, was cheating him. He envied and resented Samantha all at once. She was the one who stayed home with Teddy in their doublewide situated down by the irrigation ditch on her parents' property. She didn't work outside the home, which meant he had to, and they couldn't even begin to make ends meet without the overtime that translated into even more time away from his son. Meanwhile, she and the boy did things together. They made cookies, invented games, fed her parents' farm animals and read stories. They really knew each other. Teddy Jr. was becoming a mama's boy and there wasn't much his father could do about it but wait for kindergarten to hopefully straighten him out.

The pick-up slowed to cross three sets of Burlington Northern railroad tracks and entered into the shadow thrown by ten grain silos, each about eight stories tall and not one of them more than a couple yards full this early in the year. Ted pushed his sunglasses to the top of his own red-haired head, whence nearly every one of his son's characteristics came. Never had a chip looked more like the original block or fallen a shorter distance from the tree. Their resemblance drew gasp and comment from complete strangers and after Austin Powers had hit the movie theaters, the joke among friends and family was that "Ted went and got himself a *Mini-Me*." It wasn't a particularly funny joke but this was Idaho and Ted lived in a trailer. Humor, like living, was pretty simple in these parts.

Ted couldn't fathom living anyplace else either. He watched the news, read newspapers, and listened to the radio while he was on the river. He knew how complicated and all-around-fucked-up the rest of the country was. He lived in Idaho but he wasn't ignorant, which is not to imply that Ted was an exception. It's just that aside from potatoes, Frank Church and maybe Ruby Ridge, the territory really hadn't produced anything nationally noteworthy in the last century to elevate its significance much beyond a pregnant pause during a geography quiz. That was okay by Ted. Places that boasted and bragged about how mighty they were became targets of envy if not revenge. In the absence of obscurity, targets can stand out and targets can be brought down. Nine out of nine and a half Americans couldn't tell you with any certainty where Idaho was located on a map or what states it bordered. After the events of last September, that suited Teddy DeHavlin and his young family just fine.

The year 2002 marked his ten-year anniversary with the U.S. Army Corps of Engineers. Out of high school in the late-Eighties, he had spent a year at Lewis-Clark College before swallowing the pitch of a U.S. Coast Guard Academy recruiter. Ted had never been outside the Pacific Northwest when he left home for the Academy in New London, Connecticut. In the middle of his academic degree he bailed on account of homesickness and begged a transfer back. He was assigned to U.S. Coast Guard Group Air Station Astoria. Excelling in marine navigation, he crewed the USCG Cutter *Cowslip*, which plied the infamous Columbia Bar, one of the most treacherous river mouths in the world. Before long, he began moonlighting as a River Pilot aiding barges and tankers in and out of the river. Astoria was close but it wasn't home so when he caught wind of a rumor the Army Corps of Engineers was looking for a Columbia River barge pilot based out of Lewiston, Ted pulled every string and called in every favor he had garnered to land the job.

His first night home, he met Samantha at an old hangout called The Wig-Wam. He'd rounded up a dozen high school and college friends to celebrate the new job. He had no intention of hooking-up. In fact, he knew the next months would be a proving ground for his career and purposely set about clearing his slate of any other distraction. Earlier in the day, he put a deposit down on a trailer home with money borrowed from his mother, who by this time had moved across the Snake River to Clarkston because she saw more on her monthly Social Security check in Washington State.

Ted had been only eleven when his father was killed in a cattle round-up accident. The horse he had been riding took a gopher hole and pitched him upside down into a barbed-wire fence that snapped his neck. Ted, the only son, had been conceived and groomed to inherit his father's modest ranch but the timing hadn't been right and his mother was forced to sell the ranch before Ted came of age.

Nineteen-year-old Samantha and a couple girlfriends had pledged earlier that afternoon to go out that evening with the sole purpose of landing husbands deploying whatever lures, techniques or traps necessary. The one who failed would be considered a dyke and might as well accept it. Samantha had not yet failed at anything. Never had a conclusion been more foregone.

Ted threw the Ford pick-up he'd named *Bruce* into park, leaving the engine to idle. Men with simple lives and uncluttered brains named everything from pick-ups to body parts and the actor Bruce Willis was more than an idol. He was the namesake of Ted's truck and Ted's penis respectively, which was a private nod to the often firmly held prophecy that the occasionally over-sexed Ted DeHavlin would *Die Hard*.

The goodbyes would be short, in fact, a peck on the cheek across the front seat and a kiss on his son's forehead, where the youngster's baseball cap nearly put Ted's eye out. Long goodbyes made things worse. He hopped out of the cab, leaving the door open for the change in drivers, grabbed his bag from the back and walked toward the docks without looking back.

"Daddy!" his son wailed, having squirmed out from under the seat belt and jumped from the open door while his mom was rounding the back of the truck. Ted glanced over his shoulder to see Teddy Jr. racing toward him. He lowered his bag off his shoulder and bent his knees to intercept the incoming red-haired missile. "I always miss you."

With that and a squeeze, Teddy Jr. turned and bounded off before his dad could navigate a sudden logjam of emotions to tell his son he always missed him, too.

"DUDE! I'VE BEEN WRITING FOR THIS CLOWN NEWSPAPER FOR THE PAST eight years. My name has always been Bret Meyer Brady. Every article, every byline, every time. It's who I am!" The red-faced reporter punctuated each word with a rolled-up copy of the offending paper dispatched by one hand into the other.

The production assistant didn't know what to say. The proof team had missed it. He missed it. Chances were that the readers of the 47,000 copies that had been trucked into circulation five hours earlier would miss it too, but this was a writer with a writer's ego. "I screwed up, Bret. What can I say?"

The battle-tested reporter bit his lower lip. In spite of all he'd been through—the corrupt politicians, a handful of corporate scams and the slippery fugitives he'd written about in a remarkable investigative journalism career about to span its first decade, not to mention the accompanying death threats and vandalism to his car, the graffiti warnings scribbled on the garage door of his home— it was going to be this miniscule typo on this day that would be his undoing.

"It's out there. We can't very well bring it back now," Bret fumed.

"Not unless you happen to know somebody at FDA that's willing to issue a recall." Brady was clearly not amused but the P.A. didn't know when to stop. "Random tests reveal toxic news-print off-gassing a not as yet identified nerve agent," he plotted the headline in the air between them. "Al Qaeda suspected…Papers yanked off stands and porches in the suburbs and trucked to an undisclosed location. *Register-Guard* reporter Bret Meyer Brady, never-ever in a million years to be confused with arch nemesis *Bret Brady Meyer*, is on the story from his ICU bed at Sacred Heart after apparently coming into contact with some of the toxins himself." The cocky assistant snatched the rolled paper from the reporter's hands and screamed, "HAZ-MAT!" holding the paper gingerly at arm's length.

"Amusing."

"Tell you what, I'll print you a single corrected edition for your scrapbook."

"Thank you."

Tantrum complete. The twenty-eight-year-old journalistic whiz kid hated to think of himself as a one-trick pony, but he'd followed one story, in fact, his own story, for nine and three-quarter years, and there was indeed a scrapbook, a meticulously kept journal that would one day be fodder for his non-fiction debut on the NYT Best Sellers List.

Ten years earlier, in 1992 and at the age of eighteen, *Bret Brady Meyer* had been brought up before the county magistrate of Lane County–Eugene on misdemeanor charges for damages sustained by a piece of logging equipment. Faced with the prospect of juvenile detention that would foreclose his opportunity to take advantage of a journalism scholarship he'd just received from Columbia, the plaintiff plea-bargained. Others took the fall. Others did the time. Meanwhile, Bret shuffled off to Buffalo…well, New York City, where he earned, in a quick four-year turn, an undergraduate degree in creative writing and a nearly simultaneous master's degree in journalism. All the while, the folks back home, those with a grudge, maybe those with a vendetta, had likely forgotten his involvement along with his name. But just in case someone remembered, Bret had legally changed the order of his three names from Bret Brady Meyer to Bret Meyer Brady to throw off anyone searching for him alphabetically. In his paranoid delirium, that was certain to keep his scent a secret.

The gist of the article in today's edition, now complete with an accidental reminder of the reformed criminal-journalist's real name, recapped with bullet points the "vandalistic achievements of the unscrupulously mischievous" Earth Liberation Front. It usually crossed Bret's mind at least a dozen times in a day that he was now old enough and had once been rebellious enough to have been considered one of ELF's founding hooligans. Had he not panicked and sold out a half dozen of his cohorts in the early Nineties, two of whom were still in prison for arson and conspiracy to commit, he could have very much found himself on the other side of the news-newsmaker divide.

He had reacted nimbly to metamorphose into a very talented messenger who was no longer the message, which he supposed made him no less culpable in this strangely symbiotic quest for public attention. Just knowing he and his former cohorts played two sides of the same coin proved a unifying bond. In a very real sense, Bret was still very much an operative for the Earth Liberation Front—its mouthpiece, its anointed spokesman. It was from this sense of importance and his perception of a shared mission to bring about an end to environmental destruction that Bret never really feared the threats he'd received over the years. He had strategically been quick to report them along with photos of the occasional vandalism to his property in order to write a little more separation into the equation in case he should ever sound or appear even remotely sympathetic, which of course he was. Between this reporting for the *Register-Guard* and ELF, there was not animosity, he reasoned, but mutual respect and undying trust in the cause. That's the way rose-colored glasses enabled Bret Meyer Brady to see it anyway.

"THAT FUCKER!" PRISONER #13797671 SLAMMED A CLOSED FIST ON the stainless steel table where the morning edition of Eugene's *Register-Guard* lay open to page A3.

Fifty feet away the guard assigned to library duty raised his crew-cut melon head from the *Sports Illustrated* he was pretending to read but lowered it again without ever opening his eyes. If the outburst had continued, he might have made a bigger effort but maybe not. It was early in the day and he still had another ten hours on this ticket. He craved the silence of the library and the better manners of the literate population who had earned the privilege to use it. On days like this, he reveled in the protection of the cream-painted stone walls that had kept his outside pressures out just as effectively as they had kept inside prisoners in since 1866. Not only was the guard hung over and screwdriver-good this time, but he had spent half the night writing a letter with no poetry to a lover he was now too afraid to face in person.

When Prisoner #13797671, known inside and out by the nickname of Libre, was satisfied that his outburst would not be met with reprimand, he decided to disregard the article's opening paragraph and see if the turncoat reporter had at least gotten the chronology correct. He continued reading.

October 14, 1996, Eugene: Locks glued, paint sprayed at a west Eugene McDonald's, a south Eugene Chevron gas station and the public relations office for Weyerhaeuser and Hyundai. –*Check*.

October 16, 1996, Grants Pass: Locks glued, paint sprayed at a McDonald's. –*Check.*

October 17, 1996, Cottage Grove and Myrtle Creek: Locks glued, slogans painted at McDonald's. –*Check.*

October 28, 1996, Detroit: Forest Service pick-up is torched at the Detroit Ranger District headquarters. $15,000 damage. –*Check.*

March 14, 1997, Willamette National Forest: Tree spiking at Robinson-Scott timber harvest site in McKenzie watershed. –*Check.*

July 21, 1997, Redmond: Fire at Cavel West meat-packing plant causes more than $1 million damage.

Prisoner #13797671 raised his head. That wasn't ELF. That one belonged to the Animal Liberation Front. He hadn't even known that one was going down when it made the papers. He continued down the list of considerable achievements.

November 29, 1997, Burns: Fire at BLM's wild horse corrals causes more than $450,000 in damage.

—ALF again. "Doofus!" he said out loud.

December 26, 1998, Medford: Fire at U.S. Forest Industries causes at least $700,000 in damage. –*Check.*

"Okay, now *Santa's* back in business," Libre whispered to himself. He and his grassroots network had long referred to the *Register-Guard* reporter as *Santa* since they pretty much always got whatever they asked for from that operative. The beauty of the relationship was that most times, they didn't even have to ask and they certainly didn't need to be good boys and girls either.

December 25, 1999, Monmouth: Fire causes $1 million in damage to Boise Cascade main office. –*Check.*

May 27, 2000: Failed arson attempt at Tyree Oil Co. No damage. –*Unfortunate, but Check.*

June 16, 2000: Fire damages two pick-ups at Romania truck dealership, causing $40,000 in damage. –*Check.*

September 6, 2000: Failed arson attempt at the West University Police substation causes minor damage. *–Check.*

January 1, 2001, Glendale: Fire at Superior Lumber Co. offices causes at least $400,000 in damage. *–Check.*

April 15, 2001, Portland: Fire at Ross Island Sand and Gravel destroys three trucks, causes $210,000 in damage. *–Kaa-ching! and Check.*

March 30, 2001: Fire destroys 35 SUVs at Romania truck dealership, causing $1 million in damage. *–Jackpot! and Check.*

Prisoner #13797671 rocked back on two legs of his chair. The chronology almost read like his personal C.V. but there were a few omissions. Someday, he might bother to correct the record at *The Register-Guard*, but for now, he'd let his pride simmer a spell. He got up from the table to return to his cell to take a shit. He passed by the guard's table.

"What's got you all riled up this morning?" the guard took time from his boredom to ask.

"Bullshit, that's what!" Libre slapped the newspaper on the desk under the guard's nose and made two short taps with his index finger on the article he'd been reading. He left the paper and a trace of breakfast gas behind in the library.

The guard read the first paragraph of the article aloud to himself. He hadn't been a particularly good reader in school but he had always compensated by being loud and confident. There was still another prisoner in the library, an older inmate not far from the guard's table, so he kept his reading volume down.

Long labeled a hotbed of eco-terrorism, even before last September, Eugene can now count itself renowned as the Pacific Northwest's official welcome mat for would-be eco-terrorists. For those seeking an intensive, seldom-busted boot camp for the defense of the environment—and apparently, according to one Libre Salazar, now an inmate at the Oregon State Pen in Salem, "we're talking nothing less spectacular than all-out Revolution, here"—Eugene is where they report for duty. During the past 18 years, in the Western states alone, at least 100 major acts of arson, bombings and sabotage have been claimed by spokespeople for the Earth Liberation Front, or ELF, as they prepare themselves and America for what's coming next. Maintaining a strategy of leaderless resistance, ELF proliferates by random, uncoordinated attacks against industry and machine designed to inflict damage on those profiting from the destruction and exploitation of the environment.

RUCKUS, an activist training organization with no physical address, offers passive resistance training courses in the Willamette and Siskiyou National Forests so often they wouldn't be blamed for attaching a mailbox to one of the trees they are defending.

Back in his cell, contending with foul air that never circulated anyway and after taking the mother of all dumps that could have been classified a terrorist act in itself, Libre sat down with watery eyes to pen the rebuttal that had been provoked by that reporter Brady and was by now surely expected of him by the readers of the *Register-Guard*.

AN OPEN LETTER TO THE READERS
OF THE *REGISTER-GUARD*

Those in Eugene who feared their town had become a hotbed for eco-terrorism activity may have been quick to over-react. Eugene was not a hotbed or a terrorist cell or home to a ring of eco-operatives. It was the address of one young man who now resides at 2605 State Street in Salem where he is serving out 22 years and 8 months for arson on a car dealership and an attempted arson of an oil truck. A mandatory minimum sentence of twenty-two years and eight months courtesy of Oregon's Ballot Measure 11 will ensure that this state prisoner won't be released until February 11 in the Year 2024. A lot will have changed by then. A lot has changed already.

Ninety days after he was sentenced and his prison term

had begun, real terrorists struck New York City, not with homemade Molotov cocktails but with firebombs made by Boeing. Imagine how the young man wasting the prime of his life in Oregon's State Pen must be dumbfounded to be incarcerated on par with such real terrorists. His nation has since gone to war once and seems to be itching to go again, imprisoned hundreds of would-be terrorists (just like him?) and American Citizens have exchanged their personal liberties and freedoms for a clamp-down Patriot Act and a brain-loose president who does nothing but lie to them. Times are crazy but at least the notorious terrorist from our hometown, who more than once tried to arrest our attention by sitting defiantly and passively in trees to protect what was left of our national forests, cannot "harm society" now, can he?

Meanwhile, politicians who make laws and declare wars are ordained and free to harm all of us, kill our sons and daughters and destroy our environment at will. An empire is swiftly headed for destruction when it begins to misapply terms like terrorist and anarchist and when it imprisons our superheroes and prophets.

Mine cannot be the only days that are numbered.
Libre Salazar, Prisoner #13797671

TED COULD RUN THE PRE-LAUNCH DRILLS IN HIS SLEEP. HE GLANCED AT the Citizen Promaster Cyber Aqualand NX Nitrox Dive Computer Watch on his wrist that Samantha had gotten for him last Christmas. The trucks weren't due from Dworshak National Fish Hatchery for another hour. He could take it easy this morning. He tossed his duffle bag on the deck near the pilot tower at the stern and, setting the countdown timer on his watch for forty minutes, he began the external inspection of the red-sided, gray-decked tandem barges belonging to the U.S. Army Corps of Engineers.

Ted loved that watch. He countdown timed practically everything from Teddy Jr. racing to the porch from the creek in front of their house to the passage times for each of the eight dam navigation locks he'd travel through during the next forty-eight hours to how fast he could masturbate *Willis*, usually out of boredom being the only crew member aboard and his own company for a dozen days if you didn't count the fifteen to twenty million salmon and steelhead juveniles that made the journey with him in any given year.

There were those that called it the *multimillion-dollar fish cruise*. On the surface it did seem a bit preposterous to barge fish that could swim, even to Ted DeHavlin, who quicker than the second hand on his fancy watch, regularly rose to the defense of the program. Not only was it his sole source of income and security, but for thirty years it had represented the only true hope for the survival of the salmon and steelhead species given the obstacles that had been placed in their migratory path. True that despite the millions of smolts Ted had delivered to the downstream side of Bonneville Dam in ten years' time, less than one percent actually managed to return to spawn. But Ted was convinced that one percent would have vanished long before now had it not been for Operation Fish Run.

According to *National Geographic*, in a feature it did on the Columbia River—Ted checked the calendar on his watch—almost a year ago, last April he recalled, complete with pictures of his barges too, this effort and numerous other recovery programs, so far costing around two billion dollars, had completely failed to rebuild and really couldn't make the claim to have saved the wild salmon runs. With over 250 dams erected within the 219,000-square-mile Columbia River Basin and with 14 dams on its main stem, the first 8 of which, between Portland and Lewiston, did a pretty efficient job of stopping upstream fish migration in its tracks, or rather fins, the species didn't have a prayer without Ted and his barges.

The fourth largest river in North America at over 1,200 miles in length from its headwaters in Alberta, Canada, to its mouth at Astoria, Oregon, was without equal the most engineered river in the world and as *National Geographic* had titled their feature a year ago, the Columbia was a river dammed. For all the hydropower and all the technological advances that helped settle the Pacific Northwest, plain and simple, the salmon had been fucked. Ted knew it. He wasn't responsible for the problem. But he was damn proud to be part of the solution, even if it only addressed one percent.

Then, in the middle of the pre-launch drill, something caught Ted's eye, out of place amid the high cylindrical aerators and massive water pumps on the front deck that would circulate the river water through the tanks, helping the smolt imprint on the smells and chemicals of the river along the route. He lifted his sunglasses for a better look and quickened his step.

"Hey there," he yelled as he scrambled onto the deck using the first hand ladder he came to. "Hey!" A small scattering of clothes and a pack encircled a lump inside a sleeping bag less than ten feet away from where he stopped on the deck. Ted's heart was drumming. The lump didn't stir. "Hey!" he shouted again. When that didn't work, he broke into a silent laugh and looked around as though he thought he might be on *Candid Camera* or something. This was so unusual he could honestly say it had never happened before. Human interaction in his job, unless it was over the radio, was rare. He moved closer. "This is government property," he threatened shallowly. He was no tough guy despite his size and the image he tried to cast. He was a river mariner and most often a victim of his own fabricated folklore. Again he smiled. It was a bit exciting really, like Christmas as a kid he thought, staring down a package you couldn't wait to open. "You are trespassing." That last part came out sounding more like a question.

A motorboat went speeding by, flat-out ignoring the no-wake zone established for this entire section of the Clearwater River as it flowed its last miles through the city of Lewiston before reaching its confluence with the Snake River. Looking across from the grain terminal where his barges loaded, Ted surveyed the city of 31,000 that rose steeply from the river bank at 738 feet above sea level to the Lewiston Orchards, which perched 2,000 feet above the wide valley floor at the edge of the city's limits.

Unlike the motorboat, the contents of the sleeping bag seemed to be in full compliance with the no-wake zone. Out of habit, Ted checked his wristwatch. His prep countdown was now out of sync but the rising sun and this unexpected pause warmed him in ways he found delightfully immobilizing. He knelt next to the bag and moved to gently grip what he took to be a shoulder. As he connected, the sleeping bag let out an enormously loud fart. Ted jumped back with a grimace. *That should smoke him out*, Ted thought to himself, trying to suppress his laughter. "He-y!" he said again, unable to keep the laughter from his voice.

All at once, the sleeping bag thrashed as its occupant struggled to emerge. "Jesus!" the young man exclaimed, gulping for fresh air.

Ted put a hand over his mouth to conceal his grin. "Uh, good morning," he managed.

The would-be stowaway looked up to where the voice had come from but was temporarily blinded by the morning sun's glare off the wristwatch. "Fuck! I've gotta whiz!" And with that introduction, he bounded naked out of the sleeping bag, hopped to the leeward side of the barge, his bare white ass to Ted, and unleashed a spillway that arched off the side of boat, caught the sun's morning kiss, and plunged into the river twenty feet below.

Ted could not stop grinning. He could not believe the events of his morning were unfolding like this. The hearty piss continued. Ted found himself hoping that anyone happening to look across the river from Lewiston at this moment didn't mistake this exhibitionist for him. Personally, he didn't see how that mistake could have been made, even at a distance. This guy appeared quite a bit shorter than Ted, which was pretty common given that Ted, at six-foot-three, usually towered over most folks. Ted was characteristically red-headed and stocky-fit, while the guy taking a leak off the side of his barge was dark-haired and almost sickly-lean, at least from his backside. Sure that he could maintain his composure now, Ted lowered his hand to cross his arms below his chest, while he waited for *Yosemite Sam* to run dry. Surely, minutes had already passed. Ted glanced down at his watch. Shit! He should have been timing this! Finally, Ted could tell the shake was in progress. He turned his gaze downriver toward Confluence Park.

"Now then," the Olympian cleared his throat and moved back to where Ted stood over the sleeping bag, "let me introduce myself properly."

Ted turned his head back to see the man moving toward him. In the snapshot his pride allowed his brain to process, the stranger was compact, every muscle on his chest and stomach defined even beneath a mat of dark body hair. Ted had honestly not been in a position to compare dicks since the Coast Guard Academy, and it's not that he'd made a hobby of it then but suddenly his bragging rights were being challenged. Soon enough, Ted focused on the hand that was being extended to him.

"My name's Sergio. Sergio Payne." Both men looked at the hand in a flash of mutual recognition that it had just handled the intruder's urinating penis. He had started to withdraw the hand and wave instead when Ted's long arm shot to grasp his hand and shake it.

"I'm Ted DeHavlin. You're on my boat," he paused to consider how much he needed to play the enforcer, "—illegally."

Sergio grinned, showing long white teeth characteristic of a Hollywood smile. "Yeah, about that…I wanted to talk to you about getting a lift to Portland, or as far as you're taking her."

"I can't," Ted fumbled, "I'm not allowed to, uh…it's government rules. I'm not allowed to transport passengers. I'm sorry," he thought to add.

"So make me one of your crew. Who's going to notice me anyway?"

"Uh, looking like that, you're liable to draw some attention." Ted tried to conceal a smile of his own by sucking in his upper lip.

"Right." Sergio seemed to realize for the first time that he was naked. "Right," he repeated, snatching a pair of boxer shorts near his feet. "Right." He continued dressing in yesterday's clothes, which consisted of a pair of army green cargo pants, a ratty-white Greenpeace T-shirt and a pair of Converse sneakers that must have been hand-me-downs at least a dozen times. He hand combed his naturally curly hair that just covered the collar of his T-shirt and contained it with a red baseball cap that he put on backwards. "There. Now I look just like you."

Ted allowed a burst of nervous air to break past his lips and just in case the grin that remained had miscommunicated anything, he quickly added, "I'm real sorry. I'd probably enjoy the company, but—"

"But you've got your government rules."

"That's right," Ted said nodding, relieved to be breaking through the awkwardness of the encounter. "I'm sure if you made your way through Clarkston on the other side of the river," he pointed past Confluence Park, "you could snag a ride on the highway heading toward Portland."

"No, of course. It's just that I try to stick to rivers whenever I can." Sergio began organizing his belongings. "I may not look like it naked, but I'm actually a trained chemist with a specialization in river morphology. Rivers are my gig, if you know what I mean."

Ted raised a hand to his chin as his forehead disappeared under red bangs. "Really? You look like you're about nineteen."

"Twenty-eight. Thanks." He folded his sleeping bag in half and began to roll from one end. Ted went down on one knee to hold the other end in place. "I teach at Portland State University. Spring Break ends this coming Sunday."

"Really, a chemist?"

"Yep." Sergio attached the sleeping bag to the frame of his pack before hoisting the whole contraption onto one shoulder.

From the other side of the railroad tracks, the sound of air compression brakes perforated the dusty morning silence. The hatchery trucks were arriving. Ted would need to scramble now in order to make his departure time, which had been calibrated with the navigation lock schedules of eight dams that he had downloaded from his laptop while Teddy Jr. fought for every last minute of his dad's attention.

"I have to get a move-on." The two moved toward the dock. "How'd ya get up here anyway?"

"Empty wheat barge I snagged at the Union Pacific Albina Yard in Portland a week ago." Sergio handed his pack to Ted, who had hopped onto the dock before him. "Thanks."

"Oh yeah? Who'd you come upriver with?"

"We never met, actually. Lots of places to stay unnoticed on an empty wheat barge." Sergio gave another Hollywood smile.

The three hatchery trucks lined up parallel to the tandem

barges and it took a minute for the dust they dispatched to move down the valley. Ted raised his sunglasses to the top of his head.

"Look, Sergio. If you hustle upriver to the dock in front of the grain elevators, a guy named Smitty should be getting close to shoving off with a full load. Don't be rude. Introduce yourself this time. Tell him we talked."

"I will. Thanks again."

"Sure thing," Ted said, watching the little explosions of dust set off by Sergio's Converse sneakers as he dashed up the road toward the elevators.

"'Morning, Jim!" Ted shouted to the first truck driver in the lineup as he punched the switch to activate the giant circulation pumps in the first barge.

"Heads-up!" the truck driver hollered as he extended the truck's giant vacuum arm over the rectangular hole in the deck that Ted revealed by pulling back and stacking the sun covers to one side. Ted grabbed the pull handle on the end of the metal tube to position it about two feet above the surface water in the tank. He moved a lever to the right and the contents of the truck began flushing through the tube and into the tank. He moved farther down the deck toward the bunkhouse, repeated the process with the second truck and began filling a second holding tank.

Next, Ted jogged toward the second barge, jumping the short chasm between the boats to open the lids on the first tank of the engine barge. The third truck was already in place and waiting. Ted gave a familiar wave to the last driver. He was Samantha's half-brother, Tom. He'd stood up for Ted at his wedding ten years ago and they probably exchanged ten words since. Samantha had always made the excuse for Tom that he had suffered some learning disabilities as a child and as a result didn't socialize well, but Ted believed that whatever bothered Tom was much closer to the surface. It was Ted who had gotten Tom the truck-driving job with the Corps. It was only part-time work but it seemed to suit Tom's needs and the Corps was happy. With the third tank filling, Ted gave another wave and Tom waved back without smiling.

Ted was off running for the wheelhouse to start the twin diesel engines idling. The 500hp behemoths needed to run a good twenty minutes before engaging the impellers. And then it was a clean hundred-yard dash back to the first tank to shut off the tube and swing it back to the truck before replacing the lids and starting the aerators on each of the frothy, fish-riddled tanks. Ted was sure he provided the morning's entertainment for the three truck drivers who sat in their rigs, guts hanging well over their laps, each of whom knew for dead certain that running even half of one barge's 196-foot long deck would bring on heart attacks. Ted was still an athlete at the age of thirty-two. He didn't mind showing that off.

"I don't know how you do it, Ted. I really don't." Jim, the first truck driver, could only shake his head and remember such stamina. "I'll see you in another couple weeks."

"See ya, Jim." Ted didn't have time to visit. He really couldn't hear him anyway over the vibration and noise of the engines now quickly pumping river water in and out of the six tanks on each barge. Ted knew each barge held just about 150,000 gallons of water and up to several million fish. They would take on even more passengers collected at each of the first four dams and by the time they reached the Columbia River, all twelve compartments would be at full capacity.

It was going to be a busy season. Drought years always were. This was only Ted's second run in a season that usually ran from April to October. With good weather, they'd started a little earlier this year and could be expected to run later too. In drought years, the Corps attempted to collect and carry all the Snake River fish it could. With water levels down and dams less willing to spill their reservoirs to aid the race to the ocean, barging really was the best option for the little guys. Ted got caught up in the urgency. He often felt he was driving a forty-foot-wide ambulance. He knew that neither the Lower Snake nor the Columbia River could even really be classified as rivers anymore. They had been turned into a string of connected reservoirs with a sluggish, sometimes undetectable downstream flow. The fish coming out of Hell's Canyon, the deepest canyon in North America, arrived in Lewiston-Clarkston, hit the slack water backed up behind Lower Granite Dam and became confused and crowded and prey for a host of predators. By the middle of summer during water shortages, the water temperature would often increase to the point the fish could no longer tolerate it and if they didn't move elsewhere they died. At least while the fish were swimming safe inside the Army Corps' fleet of eight red-hulled barges, the constantly circulating water kept the temperature cool during the all-expenses-paid, multimillion-dollar cruise.

"Welcome aboard," Ted often yelled into each of the hatches as he closed the lids and as the trucks were pulling away.

The captain looked at his wristwatch. It was time. He slipped the anchoring lines off their posts, grabbed his duffle bag at the base of the stern house and climbed the metal cheese grater steps until he was twenty-five feet above the deck, at the helm and with a commanding view. A couple dozen Kodak images of Teddy Jr., his *Mini-Me*, stared back at him from the ceiling and between the instruments in the panel. He engaged the engines and eased away from the loading pier, glancing over his shoulder. The Tidewater barge was just pulling away from the grain elevators about a mile upstream. Sunglasses back in place, Ted noted the Tidewater's draft was much deeper than his, indicating that it was already full and would move more slowly than his tethered vessels would at first. That advantage would lessen as he took on more passengers at each of the first several dams. He took a moment to program his wristwatch, setting alarms at every interval he calculated he should enter a navigation lock during the next forty-eight hours. This part was the contest for Ted. It had always been about precision with this mariner. That's how Ted DeHavlin knew he mastered a river and not the other way around.

In another five minutes, Ted and his fish had left Idaho's only seaport and had rounded Confluence Park, leaving the Clearwater for the Snake River and entering Washington State. Two rivers in two states in five minutes: Ted tapped his wristwatch for good luck and headed downstream grinning and on time.

39   44   42   121 47 41 **5** 46 30 53 116 17 48

B RET BRACED HIMSELF FOR HIS SO-CALLED DATE WITH ANNE, A NEXT-door neighbor, in fact the only other person he knew in the *Smart Growth*–inspired townhome complex. It had become a bit of a ritual between the two condo owners since shortly after he purchased his place. What it had become really was a bit of a pain in the ass, what with the age difference and an aching sense that he should have been dedicating his pre-midlife years dating a bit more frantically within his own generation, give or take a spread of five years. But their conversation always turned out to be more than stimulating and in the name of character-development for the novel he was going to pen someday, they met for dinner out once every month.

Anne Martondale was a retired X-ray technologist in her non-specified seventies. Originally from England, she had been in London during the war years that claimed her father and an older brother, which was apparently the excuse for her tough tea biscuit exterior and nearly impenetrable heart. And if that weren't enough to set the cement, after following her Yankee G.I. betrothed back to America to make a family for him, her war husband–turned–doctor–turned–hobby pilot had died in the mid-Seventies along with three of her four sons in a Thanksgiving Day plane crash after he had been forced to ditch his single-prop into the side of a mountain somewhere on the Olympic Peninsula. Her surviving son, Andrew, somehow went on to graduate high school despite the abrupt absence of two-thirds of his family but immediately chose to pursue his higher education in England where he, unlike his mother, had no memories.

Anne had been left high-centered on foreign land by the men in her life. No longer homebound by her gravitational pull they had retreated in three separate tides a thousand moons could not coax back. Just as Bret knew he could never replace one of them, he also knew he was cosmically obligated to their monthly check-in suppers, as she called them, because she had been brave enough or had become numb enough to trust again. And while he hadn't yet figured it out, Bret had the suspicion that he needed Anne much more than she needed him and that it might be she who was simply playing along.

Usually, one drove the other and they took turns picking restaurants with a rule they wouldn't patronize the same establishment twice in the same year even if that meant driving to the coast or up to Salem. All of that was tossed out the window today. The misprint of his name in the morning edition had left Bret in a foul mood for hours. Then came the phone call from the FBI Northwest Field Office just after he'd returned from a lunch hour he'd spent in the gym failing to manage his anger through cardio. By quitting time, he found himself in such an altered state he required familiarity and comfort and begged Anne for a few exceptions to their rules. They would meet at SweetWaters—a favorite restaurant equidistant from the *Register-Guard* offices on Chad Drive and Anne's townhouse next to his near College Hill. Baiting her with the bombshell-of-a-phone-call he'd received after lunch made the ol' Brit widow giddy-compliant. She absolutely adored it when they went covert.

The Valley River Inn was new-Eugene made to look old. Built in 1973 by a prominent local timber family, the hotel worked overtime to convey—as the brochure read—*a true feeling of Northwest casual elegance with towering wooden beams, warm and inviting fireplaces, lush gardens and artwork by Northwest artists.* Today, all it had to be for Bret was familiar.

They could have been meeting at Burger King and Anne would have been just as tickled. Where they ate made no difference to her as long as she got her monthly block of time with Bret. In her own mind, she hadn't been able to categorize her feelings for him in the past three years she'd known him. The age difference between them was enough to suggest a mother-son relationship and how could she be blamed for that, her cradles all but robbed as they were? But then there was also a shocking amount of sexual innuendo deployed for a woman her age, and a British one at that, which a more casual observer might well attribute to there being an unbalanced romantic, if not sexual, relationship between them. She didn't know what to make of her post-menopausal horniness but she knew she was addicted to Brett's company. Anne realized she was one needy biddy when it came to the one human being she broke her isolation embargo for, and while she never expected a balloon payment of his affections, she would take whatever installments he cared to make.

She looked up from her steaming cup of tea to spot the object of her affection entering the restaurant. She didn't care how eager she appeared. Contrary to her bloodline, she was not too proud. She raised a hand to signal him in order to get this date under way.

Bret tensed every muscle for the hug he'd learned to dread a full fifteen minutes before it happened. Anne was shorter by a head but it was her distended tummy that always pressed Brett in all the wrong places. It took unbelievable concentration to contain the cringe from becoming an asphalt-buckling, earthquaking shudder. He sucked in a giant breath. Anne squeezed with remarkable strength and immobilized him there.

"Hello, Anne," he expelled some air.

"Hello, my Dear." She gave an extended squeeze.

Where does her mutant strength come from, Bret wondered, counting the milliseconds to liberation. As much as he'd spent the past fifteen minutes self-coaching not to focus on where her belly connected with his own body, it was as though those were the only sensory nerves working within his entire six-foot system in that moment. At last, the release.

The two assumed opposing sides of the high-backed booth table. Bret disdained booth seating. Not only was it diner-gauche, it allowed no room for his legs to cultivate extension without trespass. He'd lodged this protest more than once but was not surprised to see his wishes overridden by someone keenly interested in the possibilities afforded by folding him into confined spaces. As if sensing his objection, Anne made the excuse that it was the only table with an unobstructed view of the Willamette River. Bret wished desperately to verify the claim but focused instead on the table top that divided them and concealed the midsection he didn't want to see and his own crotch, which had more than once drawn her unapologetic stare. He glanced at the river that flowed alongside the restaurant at a nice clip. With that, he could begin to relax.

"How have you been?" he asked politely, anxious to get to his news.

"I'm getting close to finishing my project, so I'm hardly sleeping. I imagine you may have noticed my lights burning at all hours."

He hadn't. "Pretty typical for you," he suggested. "So you're going to let me read it, now?" He knew the answer. She was guarded with her writing projects, but liked it when he groveled.

"It would leave you in the fetal position, my Dear." She sipped her tea. "While these writings are my inner thoughts, I wouldn't be able to begin to explain the details that support them unless you knew a great deal about quantum physics. It took me over two years to get a basic understanding of physics under my own belt before I could question the big guns in the only language they understand."

"Well, you use words in this thesis, don't you? I mean, it isn't some nonsensical string of mathematical equations, is it?"

"It's not a thesis," she snapped, rather defensively. "It is written in the format of a letter and much of it is far too personal and can only be understood by someone who knows where I am coming from."

"And these physicists you're sending this, uh, letter to—they know where you are coming from?" Bret opened his menu as the waitress approached. After exchanging the briefest of greetings, he lowered the menu. "What do you offer in a Pinot?" He was not a wine snob but had doubled as the *Register-Guard* food critic for several understaffed years.

"Certainly," she responded, clasping her hands as preface to her standard oration. "We've just uncorked a '97 Pinot Noir from the Beaux Frères Vineyards, if you'd like to try a glass. It's a dense ruby-purple color with exceptionally expressive aromatics that consist of smoke, black cherries, raspberries, and a touch of blackberry and cassis."

Bret considered the description. "And Beaux Frères is out of Newberg, isn't it?" The waitress nodded. "That's fine."

The waitress looked to his presumed mother. "And for you, Ma'am?"

"Let's see if he likes it, then perhaps we can get the bottle."

"Certainly," she said with a single nod and backed away from the table.

"I don't like her. She looks at me funny." Anne set her tea cup down with a clank.

"Looks at you funny, how?" Bret did not lift his head from the menu as he knew this would only encourage her. His wine choice called for a shift in strategy. He'd arrived with a bit of a craving for fresh seafood. Now, he wanted blood and promptly settled on the Oregon Country Natural Beef filet mignon. Anne had a way of stifling what would have otherwise been characterized as his vegetarian bent. Theirs was a meat and potatoes relationship. Anne conditionally selected the rack of lamb.

"And that comes with a mint sauce," she more stated than asked.

"I believe I can arrange for a mint jelly, yes," the waitress replied.

Bret rolled his eyes from behind a raised menu. They'd done

this comedy sketch before and it wasn't particularly funny. He could have lipped the words, "Jelly is not sauce, my Dear," as Anne spoke them across the table from him.

"I'll consult with the chef and let you know." As she walked away from the table, Bret could almost see twin impressions in the hair on the back of the waitress's head, where her unimpressed eyeballs must have just rolled to a rest.

"You know they'll simply water down the jelly," Bret teased.

"I know that."

And that was fine for Anne just as long as she'd made her preference known. Bret used to be that way too when he made an annoying habit of asking every restaurant if their salmon was wild or farmed. He hated the taste and texture of salmon and would never order it but that wasn't the point. Those were his heady enviro days. He was much more practical now.

He breathed the wine. He swirled it in the glass. He held the glass to the daylight to determine if he could see the river flowing through the other side. Satisfied, he indulged a sip. All the while, Anne's smile grew behind the hand that tried to conceal it. Americans who adopted an air of pretension amused her. She'd often thought Bret was trying too hard to be something he wasn't—like happy.

"What are you smiling about?" he was nearly accusatory, like smiling was not permitted. She maintained the silence. "So give me a synopsis of your project that isn't a thesis. Quantum mechanics, right?"

"All right," she lowered her hand. "Just to shut you up…none of life, as we know it, exists except as a perception of something that exists beneath our normal experience of life. The world as we know it, in space and time, emerges from the deep recesses of inner consciousness."

"That's the premise?"

"More like the keystone, but yes, in a nutshell."

"Okay, I get that." Bret was now content to let the anticipation build a little more before sharing his Big Bang of the day, so he humored her. "So this glass of pinot would not exist if I didn't have a perception of wine based on..." he stopped. He'd reiterated himself into a corner. "Okay, I don't get that."

Anne smiled. "You're a bright boy with enough things in your own head. Don't worry yourself about what's rattling around inside mine."

The waitress returned. "The chef will be preparing a mint sauce to accompany your lamb this evening."

Anne hesitated and then managed a curt *thank-you*. The waitress backed away from the table with a smile so fake it originated somewhere near her butt cheeks. She'd already watered down the jelly to a sauce consistency herself. *Some customers*, she thought to herself.

Bret gave Anne a big-eyed forehead scrunch.

"What?" she snapped back. She was in no mood to lay out her entire physics argument in a public restaurant. She knew Bret meant well, but she didn't want to jinx her theory by lending it a watered-down oratory. She thought of the mint sauce and smiled. "The reason I have the nerve to take on a world-renowned physicist is that I believe there is something deeper—much deeper—involved in the concept of the universe and its workings than the increasingly complicated and cold-blooded theories accepted thus far. They describe the universe like a BMW, as in terms of engine displacement, and torque and stroke, bore, et cetera." She leaned across the table. "Surely the universe encompasses something much more than their scientific points perceived only indirectly, through mathematical logic."

Bret felt the wine already going to his head. He adopted a posture that indicated he was still intrigued, paying attention even, but his brain had defaulted to unraveling the riddle of the telephone call he'd received earlier.

"Most of the progress in physics has taken place in the last two hundred years and although the technology it has produced is impressive, they seem to have come up against a wall which they cannot get beyond. I am convinced it is because there is a metaphysical or psychological component that has a very strong bearing on what happens next…something that causes the wave in Heisenberg's Uncertainty Principle to collapse."

"Heisenberg?"

"—The founder of quantum mechanics. He died in 1976." Anne took waitress-ing upon herself and poured him another glass of wine. "A central argument in physics is that nothing can travel faster than light. Well, something obviously can, unimpeded by time or distance."

"How so?"

"When my family was killed in the plane crash, I knew instantaneously that they were dead. It was 5:09 PM on the clock stove when I doubled over in my kitchen because I knew this without having to be told. The investigation later indicated that they went off Bellingham radar at 5:10 PM."

"And that is why all of this is so personal."

Anne nodded. "Psychologists are coming around a little to viewing the possibility. They call it stress telepathy but they still generally regard it with the same suspicion as physicists since according to current physics, it is impossible."

"Are you going to be able to prove your theory?"

"There is ongoing confusion, more like total incomprehension, which is to say nothing of resistance, around the concept that we— our inner consciousness or mind, which is not the same as brain which is conscious awareness—have something to do with what happens to us as individuals and what happens to us collectively." She stopped herself. She could read that she'd lost him.

Bret gave a grin. "You know the *Register-Guard* readers' poll says SweetWaters has the best Sunday brunch. We should try it sometime."

"I knew it would be too much for you. There have been times

when it has been too much for me, but I know I'm right and that I've stumbled onto something."

It was a cheap trick, but Bret reached for Anne's hand resting on the table. "May you one day enlighten the world like you enlighten me every time we get together."

"That sounds like a toast to me." She raised her glass. He released her hand to collect his glass. "Now, tell me about your day. Something's troubling you."

"'More of your telepathy? How spooky."

"Don't forget that I am a mother. A lot of that comes with the womb license."

"Well, my day got off to a grand start when my own paper scrambled the order of my names in my byline."

"I caught that."

"Of course you did. I have decided to let that be the straw. You know how fed up I've become with small-town reporting anyway. My friend Martin at *The Oregonian* has long told me I'm squandering my talents in Eugene."

Anne interrupted his closing argument. "Martin's not the only friend telling you that."

"Exactly. For the first few years, I treated this job as though I were working off my debt to society. I'd felt so damn lucky that I hadn't ended up like Libre...that I actually had a life to live and the freedom to live it, that I took the first job I was offered. I've been at odds ever since."

"So do something about it." Anne spoke frankly and with economy of words—something being British and over seventy afforded her.

Bret took a sip of wine. "I did. Sort of."

"Do tell, my Dear." Anne decided she wanted to try a little wine after all and poured a glass.

"No more than five minutes after I'd called Martin in Portland and asked him to put the wheels in motion at *The Oregonian*, I get a phone call. Except it isn't from *The Oregonian*. It's from the Portland field office of the FBI."

"The FBI?"

"Yeah, like they knew I was ready to snap or something."

"And you're surprised? They've probably maintained a file on you since you decided to turn somersaults for them a decade ago. Of course your phone at work is bugged. This is America!"

"Yeah, whatever. They have a new proposition they'd like me to consider. I'm driving to Portland in the morning for a meeting that I've been told is likely to turn into a full-fledged briefing. They've arranged overnight accommodations at the Vintage Plaza on their tab and everything."

"Why not just stay with your friend, Martin?"

"The Vintage Plaza...hello? Martin'll be begging to stay with me."

I N AN INSTANT, HE KNEW THE CORNDOG HAD BEEN A MISTAKE. WITH THE aggravating onset of middle-aged diabetes, he'd found his highs and lows to be uncannily unpredictable. For a fifty-something-year-old long-haul bus driver, whose life was already a circle tour of hell on ten wheels, diabetes and the accompanying hypoglycemic fits made for one schizophrenic devil behind the wheel.

Leaving Umatilla, he shifted into a higher gear and traveled at a nice clip through Irrigon. He'd reach the freeway in another ten minutes and that meant he could practically auto-pilot the rest of the leg into Portland. Being a Monday, the bus wasn't even half full when it left Spokane just before dawn. He glanced at his manifest clipped to the extendable table above the two gear shifts and counted four passengers that had boarded in the past two hundred miles. He wondered again about the passenger he had anticipated but who had failed to board in Lewiston-Clarkston. Perhaps he'd misread the email or remembered it wrong.

With only two more stops, The Dalles and Hood River, to go, he should have better anticipated his body and the host of after-affects the smuggled corndog would have as he sat for hours in the same position. A corndog, of all the snacks-on-the-fly available to him at the last fuel and passenger stop, would now sit in his gut and feel as though he'd swallowed it whole, stick and all. He took a swig from his water bottle and adjusted the sun visor.

He always envied his sleeping passengers through this dusty

stretch along the Columbia River. If it wasn't god-forsaken, it was definitely god-neglected. Had it not been for the river and its thousand and one diversions through pipe, pump, turbine and canal, these small towns of mostly Mexican migrant workers would have never found their place on a map in the first place. Certainly Meriwether Lewis and William Clark would have been forgiven had they left this stretch out of their journals entirely, to say nothing of what we've done with the place since.

In his lifetime, the Columbia had become one of the more fucked-up rivers in the world. This dubious distinction was not lost on the bus driver, who had devoted almost all his non-driving hours in the past twenty years to coordinating a region-wide campaign to remove the four dams on the lower Snake River between Clarkston and the confluence with the Columbia. He saw this effort as a respectable start to what he believed really needed to be done, which was to provide a river bypass at each of the four downriver dams to allow for the natural return of the annual Pacific salmon migrations to the upper reaches of the Snake and Salmon rivers, runs that had once numbered in the millions but had been systematically choked—just like the natural flow of the river—to about three percent of what it had been in Lewis and Clark's day.

When he thought about what the decisions and events of the last fifty years had done to the salmon that had been using the river for the past twenty centuries, it made him physically sick. He rubbed his belly with one hand. In all fairness, the corndog was not going to help matters. As he drove along the river that had been stopped nearly dead in its banks, he vowed to spend the next forty years of his life, if he was that lucky, doing everything in his power, legal or otherwise, to correct the damage that had been done in the previous fifty years.

His tummy rumbled. If he was going to be truly useful to society, he really needed to cut out the corndogs.

"R ED? MR. BRADY'S HERE FOR YOU." THE UNIT SECRETARY WAITED FOR his instructions.

The shooting star agent who had made regional bureau chief faster than anybody in his Academy class at Quantico pushed the speaker button on his phone. "Uh, Rich...can you let Mr. Brady know I'm running just about five minutes behind this morning? Oh, and Rich? Could you also let Floyd know that I've decided to run this first interview solo? I won't be needing him after all."

"Sure. Floyd's gone on a coffee run anyway. I think he forgot your meeting."

Typical, Red thought to himself, hitting the speaker button a second time. For at least the tenth time of practically every day with this outfit, Red Harvey wondered how the FBI accomplished anything. He arranged the notes and files on his desktop, then walked around his desk to sit in the chair that Bret Meyer Brady would occupy and he sized up the room of props from his perspective. Brady's FBI file was rearranged to be more prominently visible from the guest chair. The bureau chief walked to the window and opened the blinds. The office had a nice corner slice view of Tom McCall Park on the Willamette riverfront, but you had to walk right up to the glass to see it. He closed the blinds again. It didn't aid his case. Just like having Floyd in the room for added intimidation, Red decided he would have a better chance of getting this player for their team on his own.

After all, in his more junior years of service he'd already been where he was asking Brady to go. He'd been recruited years earlier under circumstances so similar it was freaky. He practically invented the modern deep cover procedure to infiltrate the environmental activist movement. He'd be there still if it weren't for Natalie Wesson, the investigative reporter for the *Seattle Times*, who had connected the dots between Red Harvey and the state pen inmate they called Libre. He'd gotten close to Libre by pretending to be sympathetic to the movement but then he slipped up. It was his fault the undercover program had to be temporarily scrapped. He shouldn't have trusted her. He shouldn't have confided in her. Hell, he shouldn't have fallen in love with her. She'd played him as an informant. She'd beaten him at his own game. He had been weak and being undercover had made him lonely. As sure as rain fell in the Pacific Northwest, there were whole new policies in the manual to help the next recruit avoid the same pitfalls.

Red opened one half of a tall closet next to the window. He preened a moment before a full-length mirror. That double-crossing bitch in Seattle was the real loser, he self-coached, toying with the gelled spikes of his red hair. He was a damn good-looking man. He didn't need Natalie Wesson to complete him. That was already so many years, a wife and two kids ago. He knew that it was a lie, but he thought it anyway: he didn't need anybody, really. His life had gone 180 degrees in a direction he could have never anticipated thanks to a reporter who had out-smarted and out-flirted him. The one that went into the stats column unrequited was understandably the hardest to overcome, which is why he hadn't.

He adjusted his tie and re-tucked his shirt. She was always popping into his head, usually when he was bored at work or home and especially when he played drum major for the *March of the What-ifs*. He growled at his reflection. He had long thought that if he could just create a set of circumstances under which she might be drawn back under his unquestionable magnetism, he could lead her on just enough to drop her flat on her heart, like she'd done to him; then he could move on with a bit of recovered dignity. Red Harvey was rough, perhaps a tad incomplete, but he was ready to do what he did best: compulsive collusion of the willing.

8

I T WAS ANOTHER GRAY AND OVERCAST TRADEMARK DAY IN THE EMERALD City. Elsewhere in America, spring was offering hints of summer, but not Seattle. No. Leaves had to practically be changing to fall colors before Seattle managed to squeeze in its one or two weeks of rationed summer. It shouldn't have bothered her anymore after living in these environs for a decade, but Natalie craved sunshine like a solar panel. The rains affected everything from her hair volume and complexion to her moods and diet. She was fucked up without sun and everyone paid for it.

A staffer pushed the mail cart past her cubicle and doubled back. He had this annoying habit of announcing the mail and adding editorial comments whenever the chance presented itself, like he was auditioning for a writing post. "Oh-h-h. Looks like another prison love letter! Look—" he held out the envelope. "He even wrote S.W.A.K. on the flap—what's that stand for? Hmmm, sealed with a krypto-lock?"

"Give me that!" Natalie snapped.

"What? That's how you discovered him, wasn't it? His neck locked to a piece of logging equipment." The staffer smiled devilishly. "You know what the rumor is in the mailroom, don't you?"

"I could only imagine," Natalie answered, rolling her eyes.

"That you milked your interview from your eco-terrorist by agreeing to some weird game of strip poker. That he told you a detail or turned over someone's name for every piece of clothing you removed."

"Really?" she feigned mild interest, mostly to see how far he'd take it. It wasn't unusual for her co-workers to come on to her by talking dirty in third person extrapolative. It was such a common occurrence Natalie wondered what it was about her demeanor that invited it.

"Yup. Then you got him all hot and bothered and you raped him on the spot with him pinned and immobilized against the logging truck."

"I raped him?"

The staffer grinned. "Are you confessing, then?"

"Get out of here!" Natalie's arm shot nearly out of its socket as she pointed for him to leave. She knew the source of the rumor. Months ago one of these letters from Libre had been delivered to her cubicle already opened. She'd demanded an investigation but after a week of internal review she was told all indications were that the envelope had arrived at the newspaper that way.

The staffer pushed the cart away and suddenly stopped. "Oh, and your editor wants you to have a look at this," he said before tossing a folded section of a newspaper onto her lap.

She recognized the masthead. It was the *Eugene Register-Guard*. Her editor had circled a front page article with a red Sharpie, written by none other than Bret Meyer Brady, about, and this was no surprise either, the Earth Liberation Front. He seemed to have hung his personal career on an ability to trump every other newspaper on the West Coast when it came to breaking stories about the "new terrorists." The story had always been there. ELF was nothing new, nothing she hadn't herself reported on for years, but Brady had taken full advantage of the terrorist state that permeated the national psyche since last September by focusing on the enemy within. In fact, ELF seemed to be all the Eugene reporter was able to write about. Brady was purported to have once been a member within its ranks and it was highly suspect, among her colleagues throughout the Northwest, that Brady was still being used as the organization's mouthpiece.

She'd never met the reporter-with-three-names though they'd spoken by phone once or twice to verify and share facts. She assumed he would be sent to Washington D.C. for the upcoming House of Representatives Oversight Hearing on Eco-terrorism and Lawlessness on the National Forests in June. Dry as the proceedings would be, she'd actually begged her editor for the assignment; he in turn responded with a laundry list of shit features for her to pen in the meantime. So intrigued was she by the possibility of meeting her reporting nemesis that she signed on to her editor's bidding despite loathing feature writing, fully considering it prostitution under any circumstances.

The staffer from the mailroom gave her the creeps. There was no doubt about that. He always treated her as though any minute he was going to formalize the terms of some blackmail scheme that he and his fellow-postal nerds had dreamt up to give them something to whack-off to in the basement.

Tucked inside her cubicle, she gingerly opened the envelope from Prisoner #13797671. As usual, the handwritten letter on lined notebook paper began with the standard *when are you coming to Salem to visit me?* She'd never completely ruled it out—going to Salem to see him, that is. The dirty notion of a prison pen pal happened to appeal to her rather stunted cosmopolitan fantasies even though she'd been advised not to encourage him. While others suggested he might be stalking her from his cell, that she should be careful, that she'd be wise to file charges of harassment, she balked. How could she press charges after all?

She'd answered every one of his letters.

JUST AS SOON AS HE'D TAKEN FIRST POSITION AND TETHERED THE BARGES in the locks at Ice Harbor Dam, his fourth dam and—he checked his wristwatch—just barely seventeen hours out of Lewiston, Ted scrambled up to the pilot house to grab his water-testing gear. One of his gauges indicated a troubling chemical imbalance with the water in the first hold. He glanced at his watch. Lockage at Ice Harbor usually took a total of fifty minutes from open gate to open gate. It only took twenty-four minutes and a 43-million-gallon water exchange to empty the 103-foot lift.

He glanced back into the floodlit night. He could make out a Tidewater barge that was tucking in behind him and would tie to his bow. The upstream gate was only now starting to close. He set his stop watch for twenty-four minutes and hoped the gauge was somehow malfunctioning.

Ten minutes later, Ted had his answer. In the first holding tank starboard aft, the depleted oxygen, or DO as it was normally abbreviated, was reading dangerously low. If he didn't get that corrected in the next thirty minutes, he could lose the whole tank and half a million fish. He could already see a larger than usual number of *morts* floating sideways and upside down for this soon in the journey. Overcrowding was the problem, especially during these spring trips when the pressure to move hatchery fish down-river always flew beyond practical. He would have to pump oxygen into the tank and fast. He sprang to the deck-side compressor and unstrapped the heavy rubber transit cables that secured it in place. Next he moved the diesel generator into position and connected the compressor to it, attaching a substantial air hose to its output nozzle. He stood to get the proper angle and torque over the starter pull cord on the compressor and gave three tugs in rapid succession. Nothing. Two more jerks and the cord snapped, sending Ted onto his ass in a cyclone of cuss words. There was a second compressor but it was near the pilot house on the port quarter of the other barge. It would be a nightmare to struggle with it alone.

Ted wiped his forehead, having worked up a sweat. There was no time to lament. His long legs quickly made short the distance between the barges and while he unfastened the cables on the second compressor, he hollered over his shoulder. "Hey, Tidewater!" There was no response. Ted straightened his posture, took a few steps toward the stern, cupped his hands and yelled again. "Tidewater!" His voice was like a racquetball smashing the opposing concrete walls of the locks. Ted looked down at his watch. It was twenty minutes before midnight. The Tidewater's captain was probably trying to catch a nap. He was losing time. He returned to the compressor and yanked it out of the sheet metal rails that had been welded onto the deck to keep equipment from rolling.

"That you, Ted?" A man's voice barreled from the tugboat wheelhouse.

Ted's eyes strained the distance. "Yeah. Stu? Say, can you give a hand?"

In another minute, the silhouette of a man was making its way along the port side of the Tidewater, using the wet concrete wall of the navigation locks to steady his pace. Ted had aligned the compressor in the direction it needed to go and when he looked back, the man from the Tidewater had leapt onto his barge. But it wasn't Stu.

"Hey there, Stranger. Captain Stewart says you needed some help."

Ted recognized the ratty Greenpeace T-shirt. Then the kid smiled and Ted accepted him aboard. "Sergio, right?"

"That's right. What's the problem?"

Ted licked his lower lip and raised the bill of his baseball cap. "I've got an oxygen problem in the front tank of the forward barge. I need a hand getting this compressor up there."

Sergio put his two hands on the back of the compressor's cylinder and prepared to push. The two were off in a clanging racket that magnified in the concrete corridor only eighty-six feet wide. The barges were already lowering in the locks as water steadily drained from the hold. For once, Ted didn't need to look at his watch. He could tell from the water line higher up on the wall that they were already fifteen minutes into the transition. They'd start losing fish, by his calculations, in the next twenty minutes.

The clanging stopped as the two lifted the compressor between the barges. Ted spoke first. "Funny running into you again."

"Is it funny?" Sergio asked.

Ted smiled and the clanging started again. When they reached the tank with the hatch removed, Sergio sized up the situation in an instant. "Your water's losing oxygen. There are too many fish in there."

"The water is supposed to circulate with the water on the outside of the barge. There must be something wrong with the pumps." Ted positioned the generator and started pulling on the starter cord. With the second pull, the engine turned over and with a few sputters and a poof of black smoke, the rhythm steadied. Ted plugged in the compressor and flicked a switch. A higher pitch whirr kicked in and bubbles appeared around the hose that had been plunged into the tank.

Sergio yelled to be heard above the machines. "Do you have any soda ash onboard?"

"Soda what?"

"Sodium carbonate—soda ash? You know it?"

Ted's face scrunched into a question mark. "I have soda ash, yes. But that's to lower the pH in the water."

"That's right. Sodium carbonate is a chemical compound that

happens to be made up of sodium and carbon bonded with three molecules of oxygen. And because it's soluble in water, it is one of the fastest ways to introduce oxygen into your fish tank." Sergio waited a moment for the blank stare on the redhead's face to register comprehension. "So do you have any or what?"

"Jesus. How do you know this stuff? I'll get it."

Sergio yelled after him. "And a big bucket to dilute it in."

Ten minutes later, by Ted's fancy watch, the crisis had been averted for the moment. With the arrival of daylight in a couple more hours, Ted would need to make a dive to check the intake pipe on that tank for obstruction. That meant applying to the Corps for a schedule variance and permission to idle tethered below the dam until the dive could be completed. If the dive failed to correct the problem, his only other option was to release the contents of the tank starboard bow and let the fish fend for themselves. The way he looked at it, at the very least he'd gotten them through the first four dams. The final four were up to them and Nature.

B RET WAS NO DUMMY. HE KNEW THAT IF YOU WERE AN ADULT CITIZEN OF the United States, or if, after 1996, you had ever applied for credit, then you had an FBI file. It was in '96 that the FBI began spending millions with ChoicePoint Inc. to buy information on virtually all adults living in the United States with any credit or public record history. ChoicePoint, formerly a part of credit-reporting company Equifax, was a database compiler selling personal information for a profit. Using Social Security numbers as the key identifier, ChoicePoint compiled dossiers on citizens from credit reports, and from public records such as court files, property tax documents, business incorporation filings, and professional license applications. ChoicePoint aggregated this up-to-date information and sold it for pennies on the dollar to the FBI.

Bret also knew that his own file had been intentionally angled on the desktop to snag his attention and trigger his adrenaline, and because he regularly applied to see his file under the Freedom of Information Act, he knew his particular file contained more than a copy of the deed to his townhouse and his driver's license expiration date. What's more, because the file in front of him was a bit anorexic, unless it contained microfiche, it was nothing more than a lame decoy. Bret leaned back in his chair as though he'd just been handed the correct question for Final Jeopardy: What is intimidation?

"Mr. Meyer, I don't have to tell you that this conversation is classified and doesn't leave this room."

"Brady," he corrected him. "The last name's Brady. It was legally changed nearly ten years ago so you might want to update your file there." The smirk came naturally as though it was part of the grammatical punctuation of his statement.

"No, of course." Red moved a few files with his forearm to conceal the file heading error. "I'll get right to the point, Bret." The bureau chief always managed to somehow get himself tangled up in tactics. He couldn't seem to get the knack of sticking with one tactic no matter how deep he had to take it. Within five minutes, his approach was generally a dizzying hybrid of differing measures of intimidation, honesty and distraction. It's the reason he had stopped conducting interviews and interrogations with a witnessing partner. The jabs and barbs his unique style drew from colleagues and underlings were better left unfed. He walked to the window and opened the blinds. "Some of our good work combating eco-terrorism was compromised by a Seattle reporter last year and we had to withdraw one of our assets. We'd like to send you into deep cover as a replacement."

Bret hadn't seen that coming and had to hand it to the agent who had successfully sprung the element of surprise. Not an original tactic but an effective one nonetheless. Of course, he had no interest in working for the Bureau but he did wonder how much they might be willing to pay.

"Don't you think I'm getting too old and too jaded for this type of an assignment? I'm not exactly loved by the environmental movement." Bret was launching a self-disqualifying tactic of his own.

"I think you underestimate your intrinsic value to the eco-uh-activists." Red managed to catch himself before he said the *terrorist* word in mixed company. "And your age figures nicely into a new theory, call it a hunch, we've been trying to pin down. I think you'll agree that eco-activists have been characterized, almost stereotyped, as disenfranchised youth, a Gen X fringe group bucking the system trying to usher in elements of an anarchist state that brings about a collapse of some of the principal tenets of our democracy."

"Uh, o-kay…if you say so," Bret raised an eyebrow to indicate how farfetched he found the premise. "I mean, environmental activists I know, and I know a handful," he offered, smiling, "hold the defense of the planet at the core of their credo. Their work has less to do with government and everything to do with bringing a halt to corporate greed and the wholesale destruction of the natural environment."

"Would you consider yourself a sympathizer, because you're sounding to me like one? And don't get me wrong, that works for the assignment we're offering you."

"Sympathizer for hire? That would read a little like *total sellout* in my annual Christmas form letter." Bret made quotation marks with both hands. "No thanks. I prefer to report the news and leave the news making to others."

A smile inflated to gradually bridge the expanse of Red's scruffy jawline. "I think we both know that's not entirely true. I've been following your reporting for years. In fact, you should be flattered to know your archived stuff on the Earth Liberation Front is required reading for anyone who becomes involved in this line of casework. I've been able to read *frustration* between the lines of your writing for quite some time." And this time, *he* made the quotation marks in the air. "I think that you believe in your heart that the sellout here happened a long, long time ago."

Rather than pause to give a debater an opening to rebut, Red launched into his close. "We're prepared to let you get your hands dirty again while keeping your reputation squeaky clean. Now back to our hunch, we tend to believe that the youth operatives that commit ninety-seven-point-eight percent of the eco-sabotage we see on our forests and lumber yards and housing developments and car dealerships is being orchestrated by a single puppeteer hiding out somewhere in the Pacific Northwest, likely in his late fifties or early sixties, a latter-day hippie, maybe even a contemporary of Ted Kaczynski if you will, who charismatically inspires young recruits who have the energy and flexibility and anti-establishment anger to traipse through the bramble-choked woods setting traps and leaving clues and calling cards everywhere between Yosemite and the Canadian border."

Bret didn't say anything out loud but there had always been this underground rumor of an almost mythical character through whom the flow of eco-intelligence and response was supposedly meted. The inside joke had been that this mystery guy's ill state of hygiene and wilder-bound elusiveness had more than once gotten him mistaken as Bigfoot. Bret didn't believe the legend personally. He felt if anything it helped ease the conscience for some if they could blame-shift under interrogation but he doubted any one person was actually calling the shots in the woods. Incidents occurred far too randomly to be the result of coordination. His neighbor, Anne, could probably offer a metaphysical equation to support this. He'd have to ask her about random theory.

Regional Bureau Chief Red Harvey turned from the window and continued his setup. "We've spent the last six months scrambling our assets around the region to support the insertion of our deepest probe yet."

"Please! All this penetration talk is getting me hot and ever so bothered. Make sure you add that to my file as it could prove useful during future manipulations." Bret thought this might get a chuckle, but it didn't. "Look, Chief Harvey, this isn't my cup of tea. Frankly, in light of world affairs I find it inconceivable that a little forest mischief even blips on your radar."

"We're prepared to offer you the book rights and to declassify everything you've experienced, once we pull you out. You'd have an exclusive from behind the lines of the war on domestic terror. We're handing you your first book but you have to earn it."

Bret was drunk on the thought for less than five seconds. "And who do you think wants the notoriety of having brought down those trying to raise human consciousness?"

"I hear you," Red returned to sit on the side of his desk top. "You use a pseudonym or we reinvent you in the witness protection program."

Feeling woozy again, he let a minute pass. Bret counted the number of framed certificates and diplomas on the wall opposite the window. Nine. "What's the Bureau gain from declassifying its trade anti-espionage secrets? I mean, isn't it the fear of the law that's supposed to keep the criminal element in check and all of us from plunging headlong into chaos?"

"Perhaps, but that's the deal we're prepared to offer. And here's the set-up. During the past six months, we've been leaving tags with your operative's signature all around the PNW and on the Internet."

"Tags?"

"Small-scale acts of vandalism with your distinct graffiti tag. Afterward, we boast about it on the web, giving GPS coordinates, sometimes photos of where the acts took place. Eventually, some months, perhaps a year from now, when you have web relationships firmly established with some of the more dedicated diehards in the movement, you'll give GPS coordinates to reveal your location."

"And where's that? My suite at the Vintage Plaza?"

"Once you sign on, we'll give you a series of GPS coordinates and a whack of used REI wilderness gear and a laptop with a satellite link, and drop you a day's hike from a remote cabin that will serve as your first base. The cabin's well provisioned and will be restocked via the same drop-off location for as long as you require it. Of course, we expect you to go in so deep that you drop off our radar completely. From there, you can take over your own vandalism and tagging until you develop a following. As long as we see the tag, we won't investigate and we won't close in, but you'll have to keep from getting caught by the lessers."

"Lessers?"

"Lessers…you know, security guards, county and state police. If they turn you, the book deal's off and in that event, you shouldn't count on us to come clean with our arrangements. The Bureau is very good at amnesia."

"And what about my job at the *Register-Guard*?"

"We've already made arrangements for your friend Martin at *The Oregonian* to ghost-write an article a week for you. He seemed grateful for the extra income as he has a first child on the way. You just need to tell your editor in Eugene that you'd like to reopen the Portland office and reduce your output to concentrate on a book deal you've just signed." Red reached for the red folder that, aside from its color, had no identifying labels, titles or codes. He handed the paper-clipped contents to Bret. The words *Contract to Publish* topped the legal paper–sized document.

"It's a standard industry binder. It details the conditions under which we will and which we won't publish your manuscript. I would like to suggest that you take this back to your suite at the Vintage Plaza and have a close look. Obviously, this can be the only written agreement between us, a copy of which you will keep in a safe deposit box at the main US National Bank a block from your hotel on Southwest Sixth Ave. The key to this box is attached to one of the back pages of your contract. You'll find your rather generous writer's advance in unmarked bills in this box. You're welcome to move all or part of it to your bank account to cover your automatic bill payments for an extended period."

Bret chuckled. "Unmarked bills? How *Untouchables*!"

"What can I say? We're historical romantics. I've written the telephone number for an attorney if you wish to review this with legal counsel."

"Your legal counsel, I presume."

"Answer—correct."

Bret didn't know whether to be grateful or exasperated. Going undercover was certainly a damn solid better plot than he'd been able to come up with on his own. How many times had he said to himself and to others, usually while drinking, that he'd rather be doing anything than spending his prime writing for the *Eugene*

Register-Guard? Still, the presumption by this FBI cheerleader that his life was so miserable, his career so dead-ended, that he'd jump for a rescue, well, Bret Meyer Brady still had his pride. The hell he did. "I'll do it."

WHEN HE PULLED AWAY FROM THE DOWNRIVER SIDE OF ICE HARBOR Dam six hours after he'd been forced by the emergency to request a trip variance, Ted DeHavlin had a jury-rigged filtration system and an oxygen-balanced front hold. He also had a stowaway sleeping on the floor of the wheelhouse and he was grateful for it. Sergio had saved the day, Ted's ass and at least several thousand juvie salmon. He'd earned his passage.

The day was breaking above the low canyon walls and the grass and sage carpet caught the light in a way that made the hills appear to be covered with felt. This reminded him of Teddy's preschool art projects, some of which hung about the walls of the wheelhouse.

Ted looked at his wristwatch. He was now going to arrive late at McNary Dam thanks to the mishap. He radioed ahead to learn he'd lost his reserved slot and would have to wait another forty-five minutes for an upstream bound Tidewater barge to clear before he could even enter the lock. In the meantime, Sergio, lying on top of his sleeping bag in his undershorts and that knappy Greenpeace tee, purr-snored in a fetal position on the bunk behind him. So much for the promise of company.

Among the details he was able to gather in the confined quarters of the wheelhouse a good fifty feet above the river's surface, such as the extent of gorilla-like hairiness on the chemist's legs and arms, the brand of underwear he wore which was either organic cotton or just plain dirty, and that his right—no his left—hand was splotched red with paint of some kind, Ted noticed a scar on his lower back just visible between the bottom of his T-shirt and the waistband of his shorts. The scar traveled around the side of his torso for a few inches. He wondered if he'd received or donated a kidney, maybe. It could be a knife wound he supposed, collected on any one of his journeys given his less than conventional means of traveling like a pirate. That was probably it. Ted turned back to the navigation at hand just as Sergio stirred, straightened out and rolled flat on his back.

When the slight snoring resumed, Ted glanced back. He could only imagine the kind of dream the kid was having; actually, he didn't have to imagine at all once his eyes adjusted to what they were seeing. There, in his shorts, the unmistakable outline of an erection shot like an arrow off to one side. Ted tried to look away but grew fascinated. Other than porn movies—and he could probably count on one hand the number of them from which he had gotten anything at all in the first place—he didn't have any experience with the mechanics of other men in an aroused state. Here he was, less than two feet away from a living, snoring man with a hard-on.

In another minute, fascinated wasn't all Ted DeHavlin had grown. Embarrassed and surprised by his own physical reaction, he turned away, reaching his hand into his own jeans to adjust himself out of an increasingly uncomfortable pinch. *Fuck*, he thought to himself. Why was this happening to him? He tried forcing images and thoughts of his wife, Samantha, into his brain so he could have a legitimate, hetero-excuse for the sudden concentration of pressure and awkwardness. He couldn't leave the wheelhouse. Not now, during this last stretch of the Snake River before he needed to maneuver the double barge into a left banking drift into the main stem of the Columbia.

When he glanced back to his stowaway, which he couldn't resist doing as though it were a line of unattended, forbidden cocaine in a room with nobody watching, Sergio's hand had traveled to his shorts to grip his member. Ted let slip out an exasperation of air.

Why in the fuck was this so hot? He was a father. He had only screwed women. And yet, Ted couldn't remember ever being so erect. In the next seconds, he monitored his heart beating by reading the pulse in his swollen pants. Sergio began rubbing himself. Ted pushed his own crotch into the instrument panel but could not look away.

Either the dream was intensifying or Sergio had subconsciously or otherwise realized he had hooked an audience. His red paint–stained hand migrated beneath the waistband of his boxer shorts and slowly, almost imperceptibly, went to work.

Glancing at his position in the channel and instantly recognizing the rise of the ridge off the starboard side, Ted automatically set the wheel and decreased his speed. He looked at his wristwatch and calculated in a flash that he'd merge into the Columbia in four and a half minutes. He looked back to the animated boxer shorts… he knew he could masturbate in half that time and relieve the pressure that he feared might otherwise cause him to blackout. Ted positioned himself sideways in the wheelhouse so he could keep an eye on his navigation and an eye on Sergio. His left hand was on the chrome wheel about the diameter of a barstool. His right hand popped the top buttons of his jeans to allow passage of his hand and wrist into his pants, where his touch caused the sensory nerves to synapse and crackle and short circuit the wiring of his more conservative conscience. He hadn't thought of Samantha once in the past ten minutes. Sergio was one hundred percent calling the shots in this fantasy and Ted could only oblige the moment.

Sergio's eyes fluttered a little as he set his jaw. Out of the top of his waistband, his working hand had liberated the top several inches of his dick, which seemed to be gasping for air. Ted noted the kid was uncircumcised and marveled at the extra skin that opened and closed around the end. Ted felt his face flush the remaining blood in his head down the drain to make him even harder, even larger. Emboldened by his ability to compare to Sergio's below-belt attributes, Ted's left hand brought his member into the open air and stared back and forth between the two erections that were most certainly making history in this particular wheelhouse.

Sergio bit his lower lip as his other hand stretched into service, completely lowering the boxer shorts below his balls.

Jesus, Ted thought. His eyes widened as he blew two cheeks of air through pierced lips. He took his hand off the wheel and popped the remaining buttons of his Levi's and worked his scrotum to hang his balls out of the open fly. He stared with pride, as he always did, at the equipment slipping in and out of his large hand. He'd never wondered what it would be like to be uncut like Sergio. He knew the glass smooth head of his own dick like a sculpture he'd been studying his whole life and with good reason.

When he next looked over to the man lying less than three feet away, Sergio's eyes were open through squinting eyelids. Ted was providing a show of his own, offering his passenger a profile view of everything he had going. Ted momentarily froze the slow pumping he had started but only until Sergio stepped up the task he had at hand. Ted knew that had there been a drop of blood left in his face, he would have used it to blush from embarrassment. Ted shifted his stance to prevent complete paralysis of his legs, which threatened to give out beneath him.

Sergio's eyebrows rose involuntarily, opening his eyes even wider. He took a larger bite of his lower lip and used his hand to accentuate, almost show off, the appendage he was most proud of in his life. Ted didn't know what to do but found himself pressing his thumb down through the red bristles of his pubic hair catching the morning light like optic fibers, to the top side of the base of his dick to provide a more perpendicular angle from which he might be studied, compared, admired.

Sergio popped up on one elbow, which brought his face within a foot of the barge captain's rod. Sergio's teeth let go of his lower lip. For the first second in hundreds, Ted thought of Samantha, who, repulsed by the thought, simply refused to give him head. As it was something he craved and something he couldn't do for himself, though try he had on plenty of these long river hauls, he found he had no restraints as he moved his groin closer to Sergio's face. Like a trout lunging for a mayfly that had skimmed the surface, Sergio gulped the head of Ted's dick and with some effort struggled to swallow the hook.

"Fuck!" Ted gasped aloud. Without abandoning the suction hold he had managed with the efficiency of a leech, Sergio sat on the edge of the low bunk and then kneeled on the floor of the wheelhouse before sending both his hands to wrestle down the denim and briefs in his way until he could firmly grasp the cheeks of Ted's pink ass. With this new leverage, everything Ted treasured in that moment disappeared beyond the teeth and gums and tonsils of another man. Ted's knees buckled but Sergio kept him from collapse.

Distraction aside, the requirements of navigation in the next two minutes needed to keep Ted from climaxing. With his dick exploring the depths of another man's throat, Ted maneuvered to line up with the navigation channel markers that would spill him into the world's thirty-seventh longest river. As the canyon opened to allow him new sightlines, Ted was relieved to see he would be competing with no other river traffic at this intersection. For a few seconds, Ted's eyes followed a yellow and white semi-truck likely hauling livestock along the narrow road that followed the contours of the winding canyon like a choker necklace. A corner of Ted's mouth lifted into a sly grin acknowledging that in the world of transport tedium, be it the same for truck drivers, solo pilots, ship captains, train engineers or even the clever overnight bus driver, all of whom relied on bad food and masturbation to pass the miles and the time that came along with them, his commute was being elevated in that moment to heights he'd never ascended or imagined before.

Sergio's eyes looked up from his work without compromising a technique he may have been perfecting on the spot. In that eye lock, when he realized he had the skipper's full attention, he slowly climbed his hands and his posture up the redhead's frame until their faces were centimeters apart and each could feel the panting breath of the other on their flesh. Ted felt himself tumbling into equal measures of panic and surrender that exploded like fireworks inside his eye sockets. It took his brain a second to realize that their dicks were touching, and in the instant of recognition that followed, Sergio pressed Ted's shoulders down, down, down until Ted was forced to his knees on the wood-planked floor. With the same hand that knocked off Ted's baseball cap, Sergio guided his hard-on to the red-whiskered bulls-eye that was Ted's mouth. Ted's teeth hadn't parted but Sergio thrust past them anyway, holding the side of Ted's head with the other hand.

"Come on, dude," the stowaway implored, not really waiting for a welcome mat.

Ted was struck by the taste and the warmth of Sergio inside his mouth. The sensation stunned him like he'd just plunged naked into ice water and was waiting for his nerve endings to dispatch the temperature to his waiting brain. In his impatience, Sergio thrust too deeply and Ted sputtered, jerking his head back and sending it crashing into the instrument console. With cat-like reflexes and the release of concussion, Ted bounced back with an open mouth, throat and mind and set about giving Sergio the same service he'd just received. All the while his own dick danced in spasms against Sergio's hairy leg. Ted was engaged in his first sexual experience with a man and it felt more charged than any sexual experience he'd had with anyone, ever. Sergio moaned with greater and greater amplification each time Ted allowed him to inch deeper and deeper. Soon, Ted's nose was probing the black pubic hair below Sergio's hairy navel, where it discovered whole new derivations of man scent, or was it animal, he couldn't decide. It made him feel drunk though and thirsty for more.

"Whoa, slow down, dude…ya gotta breathe," Sergio whispered. "Uh, the barge is sort of going crooked, too."

Ted pulled himself upright, wiping his mouth as he spun around to check the orientation of the barge in the channel. Sergio closed into an embrace behind him that bought his dick into contact with

Ted's bare ass cheeks. Threading his hairy forearms under Ted's extended arms and grabbing Ted's pecs, Sergio ground his manhood there, drawing an initial protest that Ted issued rather clumsily.

"Relax, relax," Sergio comforted him. "I'm not going anywhere with this, if that's what you're afraid of."

"I'm, uh…I'm not, uh."

"Shhh." Sergio nuzzled the back and side of Ted's neck with his nose and cheek.

Ted suddenly wondered in panic whether or not people could see inside the wheelhouse in the daylight from the road. There wasn't any traffic on the river and scarcely any on the roadway on the port side less than a quarter mile away on shore. Still, even in silhouette, someone might be able to make out two bodies in close proximity. *Fuck, it didn't matter*, he dismissed it in a second.

Sergio's hands cupped Ted's hard-on and balls from behind and ground himself into Ted's ass cheeks just to feel him squirm. When the barge captain didn't, and in fact seemed to respond with a barely perceptible tinge of encouragement, Sergio spit into his hand, smeared the saliva on his cock and with a few probing darts, found the entrance to Ted's world. There was a gasp, followed by another.

"Jesus!" Ted managed, dropping his chin to his chest and hinging slightly at the waist to smother the pain. Sergio repositioned his feet to take advantage of the new angle and then, slowly, he demonstrated how far he could disappear inside the man in his arms. He stretched his neck to clamp a bite on the fleshy back spot between Ted's neck and shoulder. There was a groan, but neither of them could tell who made it.

This pitched activity in the wheelhouse quickly consumed the next several river miles and with the McNary Dam now in sight, Ted grew increasingly anxious, just as Sergio was winding up for his big finale.

"You have to pull out, Dude. We're coming up on the next locks."

"No way, man! I'm about to blow."

"Fuck that!" Ted panicked. "Get out of me!" The two struggled in the cramped space and Sergio became adrenaline-aggressive. He wasn't about to lose anything he'd gained in the past five minutes and plowed even deeper, rougher. Ted continued to struggle but in an instant realized he was heading into his own orgasm with Sergio's hands working him and hanging onto him with gorilla strength.

The windows of the wheelhouse were fogging up and while navigation wasn't necessarily in jeopardy, even binocular-wearing shoreline observers could no longer make out what was happening on the barge in the middle of the river. The vibration of the wheelhouse beset by engines pumping river water in and out of the tanks could feel like the spin cycle of a Maytag but the two weren't finding anything to distract or disrupt them.

Ted's breath caught in his chest and for a second he could move it in neither direction. At the same time, Sergio issued a growl that originated in his scrotal sac and ballooned into a yell as it barreled through his body, exploding out of everything but maybe his belly button. Ted straightened his posture flying into an arch as semen lobbed into the air to polka-dot the instrument panel.

Panting like sled dogs, the two sweat-expired men surrendered all musculature control and collapsed into each other like Trade Center Towers in their own right though this merger left them standing. Ted felt like he needed to take the biggest crap in his life, that his bowels were overstuffed and that the pressure there could launch a surface-to-air missile. The problem with that was the missile in question was still lodged in the firing silo. Ted's face went cold flush and his ass contracted like a vise.

"Ow, ow!" Sergio protested. "Relax!"

"Dude, I—I..."

Sergio began to withdraw but it was like taking a stubborn nail out of wet wood. "You gotta let up," Sergio coached.

"But—" he was interrupted by a seismic fart he could not have stopped with fifty consecutive rows of cinderblocks cemented together, and the fart expelled and propelled Sergio against the rear wall of the wheelhouse, where he sort of crumpled into a laughing heap there.

"Don't worry about that," Sergio tried to comfort the virgin-no-more. "It's my fault, not yours."

Ted was suffocating in embarrassment and could not even turn around to face his aggressor. He clumsily pulled his shorts and pants up to his waist and with his shirt began frantically wiping the wheelhouse windows so he could see where the nearly 400-foot-long red-hulled steel vessel was heading. His eyes seized on the splatters of cum on the panel that had started to run. He diverted his shirt to frantically clean the console of evidence. He held the shirt up to stare at it. He couldn't wear that now. He tossed it in a corner with a bit more pent-up force than was probably necessary.

From around the captain's back, Sergio stretched his hand forward to dangle his green T-shirt as an offering. "Here, wear this. I'll grab another shirt from my pack and clean up."

With that, the stowaway slapped open the wheelhouse door and scrambled down the ladder. Ted watched him as he bounded shirtless and athletically across the deck of the aft barge, leaping between the tandem bumpers that held the two barges together, to disappear inside the pump and bunk room of the forward barge. A corner of Ted's mouth lifted into a grin as he tugged his arms through the T-shirt sleeves. With his ass still throbbing a pulse he could actually detect, he honestly didn't understand whether he'd just been violated or liberated.

FROM THE WINDOW ABOVE THE DESK IN ANNE'S BOOKSHELF-RINGED HOME office, she could see the kitchen window of her closest neighbor and only friend in the townhouse complex, a window that had been dark for over five weeks now. He had always seemed anxious as a caged parakeet to her, a man not at ease with the walls and circumstances that boxed him up like contents. She hadn't been terribly surprised that he'd grown bored with her. She was, after all, forty-six years older than he, overly expectant of others and stodgy-British to boot, three very ripe conditions for dismissal by anyone's accounting. It was the mechanics of his exile that Anne Martondale had not been able to decipher in the past however-many-weeks she'd been working the problem in her head. Had he really been away nine weeks already?

She lifted the cozy and poured a ribbon of Earl Grey from a pink teapot into a matching cup on saucer. With the other hand she moved her computer mouse to activate her monitor before rapidly typing the best decoding sequence ever invented on the keyboard: *www.google.com*. Where would she begin her search today? –Portland. Portland is where Bret said he was going to take a dual assignment for the *Register-Guard* and *The Oregonian*. She'd already followed this lead a half dozen times in the past month but she never stuck to any one path and always managed to collect something new that would fashion a twist on her latest theory. She adored research. In the latter third of her life, she'd embraced the realization that it should have been her calling, if only it had bloody called earlier.

In previous web searches, she'd bothered to read a few of the articles attributed to her neighbor's reporting on the newspaper's online edition known as *Oregon Live*, but she suspected from the start that articles were being filed for him by somebody else, somebody with a hastily schooled penchant for using contractions. She and Bret had logged many a candlelight supper discussing literature and a plethora of American shortcomings when it came to the English lexicon. And last year, or maybe it was the year before now that she thought about it again, she had actually challenged her comrade in literacy to make a New Year's resolution to not use contractions in spoken dialogue in an attempt to elevate his discourse. He had stuck to it, too, which is precisely why she knew something smelled off.

One night, she remembered it was at the very beginning of April, as he must have been cramming his life into a duffle bag, Bret had taken a break to pay her a rare late-night visit to share a sherry and say his good-byes. The sudden news took her so by surprise and wounded her so deeply that she hadn't heard half the explanation he'd offered her. She wished she had had her mini-Dictaphone recording that evening as she'd give anything to play back his explanation in search of new clues. It was how she deciphered most of her late-night rambling and disconnected thoughts. But he had also left her with a pale green index card. On it he had handwritten two email addresses with a blue Sharpie pen:

doel_84@hotmail.com
hanff_84@hotmail.com

He had asked that she attempt to contact him only at the first address and then only by writing from the second address. It had taken her but a few seconds to recognize his cleverness. Last winter, she had presented him a paperback copy of *84, Charing Cross Road*. She had confided to him in some flush of romance that the book reminded her greatly of the correspondence and suppers the two of them shared so intimately. He promised to read it but until that night she doubted he had ever made the time. The email addresses he presented her were nods to the novel and the main correspondents therein, namely Frank Doel and Helene Hanff. The sentiment was adorable. She promised to write often and in those first weeks she did, faithfully. Bret Meyer Brady, however, made no such promise, and hadn't responded to one of her letters.

Her insomnia had mutated into something altogether diabolical. She couldn't sleep at night when she needed to and she couldn't stay awake during critical daytime activities like housekeeping and *All My Children*. She'd wake from involuntary naps in the most unlikely of places: the car in the garage, on the toilet, in front of her computer, her hand still gripping the electric sweeper—and no increment of sherry seemed to get the problem under control—and in her advanced state of loneliness after the sudden departure of her favorite neighbor friend, she had experimented with this particular mood regulator quite liberally.

Speaking of American shortcomings, she could make out the droning of George Dubbya on CNN in the living room a vestibule away. *What on earth could it be now?* she wondered as she moved toward the telly like a doomed luna moth to a bug zapper. *–Another armadillo story of national importance?* She perched on the arm of the overstuffed orange chair.

> My fellow Americans, you no longer need someone like me to tell you that terrorists today can strike at any place, at any time, and with virtually any weapon. This is a permanent condition and these new threats require our country to design a new homeland security structure.

Well, he got the first part right —she said out loud, her habit of talking back to the television well honed by years of abandonment—*We no longer need someone like you.*

The United States faced an enormous threat during the Cold War. We created a national security strategy to deter and defeat the organized military forces of the Soviet bloc. We emerged victorious from this dangerous period in our history because we organized our national security institutions and prepared ourselves to meet the threat arrayed against us. The United States is under attack from a new kind of enemy – one that hopes to employ terror against innocent civilians to undermine their confidence in our institutions and our way of life. Once again we must organize and prepare ourselves to meet a new and dangerous threat.

Careful study of the current structure – coupled with the experience gained since last September 11 and new information we have learned about our enemies – has led me to conclude that our nation needs a more robust and unified homeland security structure. Today, I am recommending to Congress the establishment of a new cabinet level department, the Department of Homeland Security.

Anne's eyes rolled upward as she allowed herself to tumble most unladylike into the chair's intended design.

The mission of the Department of Homeland Security, as I envision it would be to:
- Prevent terrorist attacks within the United States;
- Reduce America's vulnerability to terrorism; and
- Minimize the damage and recover from attacks that do occur.

The Department of Homeland Security would mobilize and focus the resources of the federal government, state and local governments, the private sector, and the American people to accomplish its mission.

Anne Martondale awoke in her orange chair an indeterminate hour and some later listening to the subtle lilt of a BBC correspondent announcing that the UN had just launched an online ocean atlas. This was to be the insomniac's next clue revealed in the nonsensical way her days were strung together into a lopsided necklace of post-hypnotic suggestions. She moved automatically back to her computer to look up the ocean atlas site. The kitchen window across the way was as dark as it ever was.

NATALIE CHECKED HER PALM PILOT FOR THE DAY'S DATE. JUNE 13, 2002. *Shit!* It was her mother's birthday. She was on the *Cascades* commuter train about thirty minutes south of Olympia and without a wireless signal or she would have tapped out a birthday text message to her mother, who probably didn't expect much more from her youngest daughter anyway. The two had operated on a rather fragile level of détente since Natalie careened out of her twenties just as vengeful as she'd plowed into them. Maybe closer to Portland she'd catch a signal, she thought.

Scrolling through her inbox, it bugged her that she couldn't get Bret Brady to return even one of a half dozen voice and text messages she'd left him in the past week. She needed to ascertain whether he was heading to D.C. for the *House of Representatives Oversight Hearing on Eco-terrorism and Lawlessness on the National Forests.* She chuckled as she weighed the pretension packed into the overkill title of the congressional hearing. The truth was, if he was going, there wasn't much point in her making the trip too since his perceived journalistic expertise on the topic would trump her byline, even in her own newspaper. She assumed he wouldn't miss it, that this one-trick pony of a reporter couldn't afford not to be there, but still, it was an excuse to get him on the phone, maybe see what angle he was working. Depending, she supposed, on what Libre had to give her that made it *imperative she travel to Salem within the next twenty-four hours,* she might actually have something to dangle in front of the *Register-Guard* investigative reporter, for a change. It was tough to tell with Libre.

Getting a cab from the Amtrak station to the Oregon State Penitentiary had taken a fair bit longer than she'd imagined in her mind and allowed for in her schedule in order to be at the prison before the end of the visiting hours posted on the OSP website, a copy of which she'd printed off and tucked in her purse. If they were rigid about their visiting hours, her visit with Libre would be cut very short. She shook her head and grinned. *If they were rigid*—she played back her use of the subjunctive; it was a fucking state pen! An abbreviated visit with a prisoner serving twenty-two years suited her nerves just fine, though she knew Libre was harmless. She could be terribly brave and brazen by email or over the telephone but heading into the prison, she had butterflies now. Natalie fumbled through her purse for her compact and lipstick but became momentarily distracted by the papers there. She double-checked her information.

> *Visiting hours from 12:30* PM *to 3:45* PM *with the last escort between the visiting reception area and the visiting room at 3:15* PM.

Impatiently she asked the cabbie for the time and how much further to the prison. Libre was probably already pissed. She had attempted to schedule a professional visit variance as a credentialed member of the media but had been denied as she wasn't a doctor, dentist or lawyer. She continued to speed-glance down the visitor information sheet.

> *Appropriate Clothing:*
> - *A good rule to follow is to wear conservative, conventional clothing, something that is not suggestive or skimpy.*
> - *Visitors may **NOT** wear blue denim or any other clothing that is similar to inmate attire.*

- *Gang related clothing is not permitted.*
- *A visitor´s dress length or shorts cannot be shorter than two (2) inches above mid knee. Wrap around skirts, halter tops, see through clothing and hats are not permitted.*
- *All visitors must wear under garments. Women must wear a bra, but should not wear an underwire bra, as it may set off the metal detector.*
- *New visitors should bring an extra set of clothing just to be sure that they will be allowed into the institution. Visitors can store unused clothing in their vehicles or rent a locker for 25 cents.*
- *All visitors must walk through a metal detector. Avoid wearing metal as much as possible. Metal buttons, jewelry, underwire bras and many styles of dress shoes will trigger the metal detector.*

Whatever, she dismissed the rules, shoving them back into her purse. Nobody would tell her to wear a bra or conservative clothing for that matter and what in the hell is *not suggestive* anyway? Simply wearing clothes is suggestive if you'd rather be naked, she reasoned while hand ironing the crease in her beige dress pants.

Was this her first prison? She tried to remember. She hadn't seen Libre in person since his incarceration, though they'd chatted, phoned and generally all-around pen-palled pretty heavily since he went inside the system just days short of a year ago. What kind of reporter was she if a half dozen leads in her career hadn't taken her in search of a jailhouse confession before now? Was Libre planning to confess something to her? She was clearly in possession of more questions than answers when the taxi turned left off State Street and crawled at reduced speed toward the pinkish sandstone building that partly jutted out of a twenty-five-foot-high concrete wall that raced off in two directions for as far as she could see to encircle the twenty-two-acre complex. As they rounded the base of a guard tower standing alone in the middle of a parking area on the outside of the wall, Natalie got her first up-close glimpse of the Big House. It was a formidable building, maybe four stories tall and stuccoed pink like the flesh of a spring salmon.

On the other side of this rather pleasing architectural façade established in 1866, twenty-three hundred inmates, all of them men, were held in maximum custody in four cell blocks. Natalie felt her skin turn clammy. That was more people than lived in her hometown not far from Spokane in Eastern Washington. She paid the cab fare with a credit card since she next to never carried cash and asked the young cabbie if he could retrieve her in forty-five minutes for a fare to Portland International Airport. She practically could make out dollar signs in his brown eyes when he handed the receipt over the back of the front seat with a smile more eager than it was orthodontically pleasing. With a heave, she extracted herself and an overstuffed garment bag out of the back seat.

Natalie Wesson's stay at the luxuriously appointed Oregon State Pen would be brief by design and even briefer by her tardiness in arriving just as the afternoon visiting hour session was ticking to a close. Attempts to sweet-talk the guard overseeing the reception area were neutralized by one regulation after another. No, she could not get an extension because her train was late. No, there wasn't a locker large enough to hold her garment bag. No, they wouldn't hold the bag behind the guard counter, prompting her to race outside to implore the cabbie, who was having his lunch in the parking lot to ensure he wouldn't miss the fare she'd dangled, to hold her suitcase and engage the meter. No, she couldn't bring in the cookies she'd bought at a bakery because she never cooked. No, Prisoner #13797671 had not been waiting in the visiting area this entire time. No, she wouldn't, as a member of the media, be provided a tour of the facility beyond the escort to the visiting room. No, she wouldn't be allowed to take her camera past the metal detectors. No, she couldn't wear her intended blouse without buttoning closed the opening to the collar. No, it didn't matter that she considered her breasts not large enough to require a bra. Out to the taxi she sprinted again, this time to get a bra from her bag and put it on while cussing in the back seat, all the while playing to wide brown eyes stuck in the rearview mirror like a portrait in a frame.

What she didn't see of the penitentiary during her escort which wasn't a tour, down a long corridor and through three sets of gates, were the four cell blocks, two dormitories, the education department, library, infirmary, canteen, dining room, kitchen, five vocational training shops, the furniture factory, the metal shop, the upholstery shop, the state's third largest commercial laundry, the automotive repair and the in- and outdoor recreation areas.

"You have fifteen minutes," the male guard said abruptly after depositing her into a room with one long bank of tables segregated by low walls into a half dozen chambers. "You'll be in dock number four. You'll be permitted to engage your prisoner in a brief embrace including a kiss if that is the nature of your relationship and you will be allowed to hold hands on top of the table. It will be at my discretion to stop the visit at any time if I feel physical contact rules are being exploited or if I feel anyone is endangered, including me. Do you understand these regulations?"

Natalie nodded with a grin hoping to indicate she was amused by the pretense. Now that she was inside and a moment away from seeing the object of her affection at least on paper, the grin concealed that she was about to piss herself from nerves.

"I'll now go and retrieve the prisoner—that is if he wishes to proceed with the visit." The guard pointed to the corner of the ceiling with his chin. "You are under constant surveillance."

Natalie took a seat in dock number four but was immediately uncomfortable with the confinement of the walls and stood again, pushing the chair seat under the table. She surveyed the other walls of the room and, for the first moment since she'd entered the building, was seized with full recognition that she was inside a prison. "Fuck," she exclaimed, expiring all the air from her lungs.

Embarrassed, she smiled uneasily toward one of the eight or ten cameras suspended from the ceiling at varying angles. She was alone in the room; no other visitors or prisoners or guards, just cameras. She could feel her heart beating inside her blouse and now her bra. What if Libre didn't want to see her now that she was late? What if—

A buzzer sounded, causing her to jump. Her knees forgot their role in keeping her upright and she crumpled partway into the chair that now kept her standing. "Prisoner on the floor," came the words out of the speakers, followed by the squeaky sliding of the iron gate door opposite the door she had entered. The guard who had escorted her to the room entered first and Natalie couldn't tell if anyone followed until a man with a shaved head and a goatee appeared in the doorway. She'd never seen Libre without hair on his head though he had experimented with more variations of facial hair than any man she'd ever known. Then the prisoner smiled that square chin smile, revealing laugh lines and dimples that were as instantly recognizable as the climbing vine tattoo encircling his left forearm. The guard unlocked the wrist cuffs and tucked them in his belt. Libre moved toward her, wearing an oversized dark blue T-shirt and blue jeans with an orange Department of Corrections logo and the word INMATE stamped on the right leg above the knee. His arms opened and she let go of the panic grip she had on the chair back and took a step back from it.

"You made it after all," he said as he moved into her and imprisoned her even further in a hug that sent measurable voltage through her muscles and bones. Was she as starved for physical contact as a prisoner? She smelled Ivory soap and some product by Mennen when she nuzzled his neck, which is where her height reached on Prisoner Number 13797671, who stood at least a head and a half taller. He raised his hands to disappear into her red hair to hold her ears and head in a vise as he craned his neck for a kiss they had written and talked about for nearly all of the twelve months he'd been on the inside.

Natalie had never in her life felt more confined. In that instant she wanted to scream and dash flailing from the building. This was easily ten times worse than the feeling she got sometimes flying transatlantic when the wine or drugs wore off and she suddenly realized she was stuck inside a hollow tube hurtling through air so thin she wouldn't be able to breathe outside the tube, trapped in air so stale she began to hyperventilate inside the tube. She carried a quick-acting tranquilizer in her purse for just these anxiety attacks—a purse now locked up inside a twenty-five-cent pay locker a corridor and three locked gates away.

"I have a surprise for you," Libre whispered into a muff of red hair before pulling away from her. "But business first." He motioned for her to sit in the chair as he walked around the table to Dock Number Four on the prisoner side of the century-proofed arrangement. The guard leaned against the wall directly behind Libre, his arms crossed on his chest. Acting as though the guard were invisible to him, Libre reached across the table for Natalie's hand and pulled it toward him. "Thank you for visiting me. It's only taken a year to get you here."

"I know," she started but stopped herself. No use in going through the litany of excuses she'd trotted out before in her letters and phone calls. I'm sorry I couldn't get here earlier today. The train—"

"Doesn't matter," he interrupted her. "You're here now, sitting across from me with your hand in my hands." He kept smiling at her, unable to stop grinning. "You're off to Washington after this?"

"Later this evening, yes." She wanted to get back in control of her anxiety and the situation. "You've shaved your head," she stated the obvious.

"Gives inmates one less thing to grab hold of in the shower," he said with a suddenly straight face, before reverting right back into grin-mode. "I'm kidding—sort of."

Natalie was in no mood for prison humor while still stuck inside a prison, so she steered her way to a new subject. "Have we talked about a fellow named Bret Brady before," she asked, flipping her hair over her shoulder with the one hand that still enjoyed freedom of movement.

The grin vanished. "Bret Meyer Brady—the newspaper reporter from Eugene?"

Natalie nodded as she used the change in room chemistry to retract her hand. Libre leaned back in his chair and held his own hands as though his wrists were handcuffed.

"We first met in 1993 on Vancouver Island near a place called Tofino during a summer-long blockade against MacMillan Bloedel. I was young in the movement then, even impressionable, and in a field of outspoken female spokespeople, Meyer stood out as an activist and an intellectual. He had quite a reputation before he turned."

"Turned?"

"He was rounded up in that blockade as an instigator and hauled away with the other nine hundred that were arrested that summer. Because he was American and came from rich parents, he was ushered out of British Columbia with a warning and maybe some temporary travel restrictions. The next time our paths crossed was at a Ruckus training camp a few years later not far from Mt. St. Helens. By that time, Meyer had become really cynical and careless. He ended up taking the fall for some monkey-wrenching of logging equipment later that summer in the Gifford Pinchot National Forest and turned evidence to keep from going to jail or having a criminal record."

"And became a reporter to absolve himself of his sins, I suppose."

"Thing is, he was a reporter all along, even as far back as '93, he was working both sides of the equation doing freelance for magazines and a few papers. Nobody ever knew his real name at the time. We all have nicknames, you know—aliases to avoid the Freddies.

"The Freddies?"

"National forest cops—the feds. He even changed the order of his three names to shake folks off his writing tail. Might have worked when people searched the Internet or a library for Brady but all of us in the movement still know who he is, who he was, what he did. Bret Meyer Brady or Bret Brady Meyer or Bio-D-Grade doesn't matter. A snitch is a snitch and a traitor of the revolution. We've all wised up to trust next to no one."

"Biodegrade?"

"That was his alias in his day."

Natalie looked toward the ceiling, ever cognizant of the cameras. She looked at the guard standing behind Libre, the guard who had brought her to this room. She tried to imagine a time when Libre was free to walk through a forest or climb a tree, all the while trying to wrap her head around the truth that she could walk out of this room, into a forest or up a tree and he couldn't—not until the fucking Year 2024. She shook her head for it to make sense. It didn't.

"What is it?" he asked, leaning forward reaching again for her hand. His other hand disappeared under the table to undo his jeans. He had a hard-on that was cutting off the circulation to everything below his genitals. He'd stopped masturbating a year ago in his cell since he could never get away with it; he couldn't whack off in the toilet stalls during laundry detail or library time as none of the stalls had doors and now it was rare for a nightly dream not to leave him nursing a perpetual case of blue balls. He used to be quite the masturbator, too, relying on the activity to pass the time in tree sits and during target stakeouts.

He'd made it once before with the *Seattle Times* reporter for real and easily a thousand times since in his brain and in his dreams. She had been the last woman he'd had sex with and a prisoner tends to immortalize things like that, building altars and false promises to get him through the minutes, hours, days, weeks, months, years, decades, fuck! He'd gone a year without sex. Before he went on the inside and before having sex with Natalie Wesson propped up against the mud-caked wheel of a dump truck, he'd probably gone two or three years without sex of any kind but those had been his terms. These were not his terms so of course he craved everything he couldn't have. Holding her hand caused the cravings to become carnal. He began to manipulate his dick with the hand that had gone covert.

The guard behind him could have ordered both hands to the table as he certainly knew what was going on but they'd struck a deal on the way from the cell to the visiting room. The guard had half joked that he'd be tempted to allow the two to have conjugal relations in a side interrogation room just as long as he could watch or at the very least record it for later. In his words, Libre's visitor was "too fucking hot to be wasted on a prisoner." Libre had promised to make it worth the guard's while if they could get a little extra time together.

"Well, I've left a half dozen phone messages and a couple emails for Bret Brady and he hasn't bothered to return a one of them. So much for professional courtesy."

"Yeah?" Libre managed, already a bit breathless and biting his lower lip. "Maybe he's in Washington for the hearings. I imagine he wouldn't be happy with anything less than a front row seat at that circus. He still fancies himself a ringleader, you know." He fake-coughed so he could reach his hand to his mouth for some spit.

"Are you doing what I think you're doing?" Natalie suddenly asked him through a laugh more explosive than ladylike.

Libre smiled, showing his long teeth. "What do you think I'm doing?"

"Let me see it," she insisted, straightening her posture.

"You let me see something first," the prisoner bargained.

Natalie motioned with her eyes and forehead toward the guard standing behind him.

"He's more interested in watching me. Don't worry. Come on, Natalie Wesson. Remind me what I'm missing from the outside."

She tentatively raised a hand to rest over the top buttons of her blouse, at the base of her neck.

"That's it," he coached in a breathy whisper.

Natalie's eyes were on the guard as she unbuttoned one, then two buttons. She rested at a third but when she hadn't drawn his protest, she set her lips in a half grin and opened the blouse. The guard cleared his throat but didn't bother to speak. Natalie fixed her gaze at the guard's crotch as she reached inside her bra to liberate one breast and then the other. The guard was getting a boner. She could see the outline in his green regulation trousers. This was her scene too, she realized: a prisoner jacking off while his guard worked himself into a solid need to—she still had it. Libre's hand began carelessly knocking against the underside of the table. "Come on, your turn," she egged him.

Letting go of her hand, he pushed back from the table gently to show himself, all of himself out in the open, free as a jailbird about to cum. The guard moved to reposition himself at a new angle, drawing his billy club and holding it in front of him to rub on his swollen crotch. Maybe he was more into Libre than the visitor. Natalie decided not to take it personally, considering she wasn't able to take it at all, from either of them. Was this what it was like for a straight guy to fantasize making it with two women? These two were giving her a fine time. She'd forgotten how long and skinny Libre's dick was, not that she'd had a lot of time to study it and not that she hadn't confused this item in the catalog with three or four dozen conquests since. The guard's cock appeared to be nice and fat and getting fatter thanks to the club and thanks to Libre, who had no problem showing off to get off.

Natalie had one breast completely outside her blouse when she suddenly remembered the cameras, not that anyone else was the least bit shy beneath them. Just then, Libre's coaster reached the top of the track and he began convulsing in the seat as lob after lob after lob of liquid icing sugar hit his dark blue T-shirt. Natalie had split her allegiance between the prisoner and the guard, who bit his lower lip as he nearly broke the club like a stick of kindling he was bending over a knee, except that wasn't his knee. When he realized he was caught, he lowered the club with one hand and adjusted himself for full accentuation completely for her benefit. She couldn't help but grin her approval and consent.

"Get the train back in the station, Prisoner. Visiting time's up."

Libre quickly complied, a blush taking over his cheeks. He used the tail of his T-shirt to dab the obvious evidence before tucking the whole mess inside his waistband. "Just two more minutes," the prisoner claimed his part of the deal. He scooted the chair back under the table. "Thanks for that," he whispered across the table.

Natalie arranged herself back inside her blouse. She'd blush too, if it was part of her chemical make-up, but it wasn't.

"I have a letter for you to deliver to Congressman Scott McInnis. It is my testimony to the congressional hearing." Libre extracted an envelope from his back jeans pocket and pushed it across the table toward Natalie.

"I didn't think you were being asked to testify," she told him.

"Yeah, I address that in the letter too. Marmot will testify as the golden child of reform and he'll promise to never spread mischief in the forest again. If I knew I could get out of prison in six months for committing the same crime as another prisoner serving twenty-two and a half years, I'd work up quite a song-and-dance number for Congress too. This is my insurance policy just in case it slips Marmot's mind to mention the gross injustice of my prison sentence. The envelope's sealed but you can read it. In fact, it would be nice if you could make copies of it and get them to everyone at the hearing just in case McInnis doesn't allow it to be introduced. I could use a copy of it too. It's not like I have access to a Kinko's in here."

"Of course." Natalie put her hands on the envelope and pulled it to her side. "You'd like a copy to go to Marmot too, I take it?"

Libre nodded. "And it's really important to me that Bret Brady get a copy of this, since he's mentioned by all his names in this document."

"All his names—really?" The reporter picked up a whiff of a lead. "Anything I don't already know?"

The clearly aroused guard, who was no longer getting anything he could use to stoke the fire in his britches, moved away from the wall he'd been holding upright to re-cuff the prisoner for the escort back to his cell. Natalie watched the guard as he moved for outlines of his body as if his uniform were only a filter through which, thanks to an overactive imagination, she could see everything. "I'll be back for you in a minute. Just sit tight," the guard winked, having caught her watching him.

Libre walked around the table and leaned down to kiss Natalie on the cheek. "I'm sorry this visit seemed so one-sided. Hopefully the envelope will make this worth your while too." He paused, then whispered into her ear, "I'm wasting in here. Congress needs to know that."

"I'll do anything I can," she promised the prisoner.

Walking out of the room, he turned his head over his left shoulder. "Raise your fist and resist!"

Natalie gave an encouraging smile then waited but five seconds for the two to disappear down the corridor before opening the envelope to extract the contents.

S IXTEEN HOURS AND A COMPLETE MAKEOVER LATER, THE EQUIVALENT OF her body weight in photocopies bulging out the sides of her briefcase, Natalie Wesson took a vacant seat in the cavernous auditorium of the Longworth House Office Building just south of the U.S. Capitol. Lowering her Starbucks vente double-foam, no-fat latte by the lid to the floor next to her half-size-too-small black pump, the lid pried away from the rim to send the cup at an angle toward the marble floor. This dispatched a frothy caffeinated tsunami that broke against her nylon-trapped calf and ankle as she simultaneously and without the least bit of decorum for the hallowed place shrieked a very unladylike, *"Shit!"*

Heads and torsos spun to see what the commotion was all about and to assess whether or not they should flee from it given the yellow status on the new security threat color code system that indicated a significant threat of terrorist activity. Once it was determined that homeland security was under siege by a redheaded reporter dressed in black and looking more vulnerable than perhaps at any other point in her life, it was all hands on deck rushing to assist. Napkins and handkerchiefs flew to the latte lake washing across the floor like a biblical flood. Natalie thanked her rescuers with a smile and hand-outs from her brief case. Her attention-grabbing moment had even provoked an upward head jerk of recognition from Red Harvey, who was seated a few rows away. She smiled back at him wondering if the woman sitting next to him could be his wife.

Ice broken, she thought.

A gavel sounded. The Honorable Scott McInnis, a representative in Congress from the State of Colorado, according to the nameplate on the long horseshoe-arranged table in front of them, called the Subcommittee to order:

> Today the Subcommittee on Forests and Forest Health is conducting a hearing to explore the growing threat of eco-terrorism and lawlessness on our national forests. The hearing's principal focus will be on the violent and increasingly frequent attacks of environmental terrorist groups like the Earth Liberation Front and the Animal Liberation Front. However, we will also hear from a panel of witnesses focusing on the very real problem of timber theft and intimidation of Federal land managers on national forests. It is the opinion of the Chair of this Subcommittee that terrorism, no matter for what message, is unacceptable. It is not the proper way to send a message. I look forward to the important dialogue we are going to have today.

The congressman took a break in his opening comments to sip from a glass of water set like a prop in front of everyone seated behind shiny brass name plaques at the main table. Reporter Natalie Wesson scribbled notes and shorthand symbols onto a page in her tablet, thinking she reeked of spilled coffee. Fortunately, the coffee had cooled substantially during the four-block walk from the Starbucks on 7th Street NW. She passed by closer coffee shops to the Longworth House Office Building but they weren't Starbucks, and she was a Seattle gal, proud to carry the hometown flag. At the moment, she wasn't so eager to smell like the hometown flag but there she sat as though she'd been steeped in Sumatra Blend for the better part of the roasting season.

The blond Republican from the Rockies continued:

> For the better part of a decade, ELF and ALF and other rogue elements in the environmental movement have used brute force, intimidation and violence to promote an agenda that can only be described as radical. They attack Government buildings, homes, businesses and research labs with fire bombs, Molotov cocktails and timed-detonation devices. And I would urge any of you that would like, go ahead and take a look at the website. On the front of the web page it shows you how to use a detonation device. When it comes to the extensive violence on national forests, ELF's objective is as simple as it is unsettling, to create an overpowering aura of fear and anxiety that scares the American people off their forests or their right to use their forests. Today, some 10 years and many million of dollars in destruction after its emergence, the Earth Liberation Front has partially succeeded in achieving that objective in some parts of the country. People who legitimately work, live and play in these wild places now have no choice but to look over their shoulder in fear of a shadowy terror group like ELF.

At that exact moment, a man seated behind the redhead tapped her on the shoulder, causing her to violently jump in her seat. He motioned to the photocopies sticking out of her briefcase, the bolded title The Real Terrorists a bit too provocative to ignore, especially when others around him were paying much more attention to reading the copies they'd been handed for their roles in containing the hazardous coffee spill than they were to the fine young blond congressman conducting the hearing. Natalie handed him a handful of copies and motioned with raised eyebrows and a coy smile that he should distribute the extras down the row. He complied.

McMinnis introduced a brief video clip about ELF that appeared with a click on four large television screens positioned around the room. He continued to speak over the clip:

> What is ominous about the *ELFs* and *ALFs* of this world is the fact that every mainstream environmental organization I contacted in conjunction with this hearing, groups like the National Wildlife Federation, the Natural Resources Defense Council, the Sierra Club, the Wilderness Society, and many others, publicly condemned the acts of militant environmental groups. ELF's self-styled Robin-Hood mystique is under assault from every direction, even from the individuals who have spent their lives promoting environmental protection and stewardship. After the Vail fire in October 1998, a statement released by Greg Rosenburg, then spokesman for ELF, who has been subpoenaed to testify here today, warned America that quote—Elves are watching—unquote. Well, Mr. Rosenburg, I can tell you that today, when it comes to ELF and ALF, the FBI is watching, state and local law enforcement is watching, Congress is watching, the mainstream environmental groups are watching, and the public is now fully engaged in watching too.

He paused to take another dramatic sip from the water glass as the television screens went blank.

Natalie was bouncing a foot at the end of crossed legs. She noted that her media name badge clipped to the open collar of her blouse was exposing even more of her moderate cleavage than she had intended. Usually, this was an advantage with politicians but this appeared to be a particularly sour bunch. She had already received the nod of the home team politicos. Washington State representatives Inslee and Nethercutt both straightened in their giant wooden chairs considerably when she'd walked in and before she'd spilt her coffee. Though she'd voted for neither of them as they were outside her voting district—neither of them would have earned her vote anyway—they acted like she was a constituent and as a known reporter for the state's largest newspaper, this somehow made Natalie think they would be more accountable, more responsible. Still, she was more often embarrassed by them than not.

She had doodled the name Greg Rosenburg in the margin of her notes. Wasn't this the fellow Libre referred to as *Marmot*—wasn't he the co-defendant in the same trial as Libre—hadn't he plea-bargained for his life, cooperating with authorities, turning some minor evidence and giving a few names of people who might be of interest in ongoing investigations? For this, had not Marmot also bargained away the respect of his longtime comrade, now serving time as Prisoner No. 13797971 at OSP? Or was that a different *Greg*? Changing tactics, the reporter began using jagged points and angles in her doodle, which indicated she was getting angry with herself for not being able to keep the facts straight in her mind. Who was Greg Rosenburg? she repeatedly asked herself. Bret Meyer Brady could help straighten out the players and chronological jumble in her mind, but a systematic search of the suited crowd around the room did not yield many faces, hairlines, or postures she could recognize other than the monkeys hearing testimony. Where in the hell was Brady?

When they'd been at it for forty-five minutes, subcommittee chairman McInnis called a brief recess. Natalie rose, grabbing a handful of photocopies to distribute to the congressmen and Representative Hooley, the Democrat from Oregon who was the only woman on the subcommittee. She approached the politicians from Washington State first—the two men nearly tripped over each other to get to a face they both recognized as friendly.

"Gentlemen—good day for a hearing."

"Good as any," George R. Nethercutt said, extending his hand to grasp hers.

Natalie cleared her throat for the pitch. "I've just come from the Oregon State Penitentiary in Salem where I met briefly with Libre Salazar. He asked that I hand deliver his testimony to the subcommittee."

"Federal Express not good enough for Mr. Salazar?" Representative Jay Inslee asked with a smirk.

Nethercutt took a stapled copy of the document. "Libre wasn't asked to testify in this hearing. This subcommittee considers his case already closed."

"That doesn't mean that while he rots in prison for the next quarter century he doesn't have a perspective or information that this committee might learn from," Natalie turned defensive.

"Hmmm, a sympathizer in our midst," Inslee jabbed.

"Not at all," Natalie rifled back. "Unbiased as ever. It's just grossly apparent that the judicial system over-reacted in this particular case."

Nethercutt put a hand on the reporter's shoulder. "He should just be grateful that he was sentenced half a year before September 11th happened, otherwise, he'd probably be rotting for life right now." He took his hand back. "I have to take a leak. Excuse me."

Rep. Inslee followed behind him like a loyal schnauzer. Natalie didn't bother to mumble what she was thinking under her breath. She spotted the Oregon political delegation at the coffee station and approached for a full court press. "Representatives—Natalie Wesson, *Seattle Times*."

"Hello, Dear," Representative Darlene Hooley greeted her warmly. Together, along with Red Harvey's wife, they were the entirety of the female complement in an auditorium otherwise filled to the brim with testosterone. "We have met before, I believe."

Representative Walden scampered away to leave the two women to chat. Natalie racked her brain. "The Seattle WTO Riot Hearing?"

"The Columbia River Joint Fisheries Accord ceremony, if I'm not mistaken."

"You are not mistaken. You should be a reporter with a memory like that," Natalie said, doubting what qualified her to be a reporter at the moment. "Speaking of reporters, I haven't bumped into Bret Meyer Brady here yet," she said fishing.

"That is odd now that you mention it." The Congresswoman scanned the room. "Not like him to miss anything to do with eco-terrorism, is it?"

"Exactly. I'd hoped to compare some notes with him."

"And I should be reviewing my notes," the politician told her. "I speak next."

"Of course. It's nice seeing you. Oh—" she remembered her mission. "I've just come from OSP in Salem and Libre Salazar asked that I present a submission he'd like the subcommittee to consider as it deliberates."

"I see," she said, accepting a copy of the document. "We're really not supposed to consider any information that wasn't subpoenaed or given in person under oath."

"With all due respect, this prisoner is spending the next two decades of his life in your congressional district. Perhaps you could consider his circumstances the next time you speak with Governor Kitzhaber."

"Unless you know something I don't, it's not likely the Governor is about to seek out my opinion on anything, such are our differences. But I will read this. Thank you."

The gavel sounded and people shuffled back to their seats. Natalie hadn't distributed all of her copies but she'd been strategic. She'd target those wearing media badges with the remaining copies. She took one final look around the room before sitting. If Brady wasn't here, who was reporting for *The Oregonian* and the *Register-Guard*? She scanned the politicians behind name plaques. This was clearly all about the Pacific Northwest. The main papers in Oregon could not afford not to have someone covering this. And if they didn't have assets in the room, it would present an irresistible opportunity to snag a byline on the topic of eco-terrorism in one of Bret Meyer Brady's papers for a change. Scoop! She practically shouted aloud at the thought.

The Honorable Representative Darlene Hooley from the State of Oregon was introduced by the Chair. She reached to pull a stationary table microphone closer to her.

> Thank you, Mr. Chairman. It is very appropriate that we are gathered here today on the anniversary of a date in history that was a turning point in the administration of Abraham Lincoln, one of our country's greatest leaders. His career and the turbulent times he brought the Nation through exemplifies a need to foreswear violence in the name of political causes and abide by the rule of the law.

The congressman deliberately looked up from her speech to seek out the *Seattle Times* reporter with whom she'd just spoken.

> In the wake of an 1837 mob lynching of an abolitionist newspaper editor that took place 165 years ago, Lincoln urged his fellow Americans to let reverence for the law become the political religion of the Nation, to let legislators and judges chosen by the people, rather than lynch mobs motivated by passion and hatred, decide important issues. In the end Lincoln's philosophy was vindicated. Our Nation remains united and we are committed by the rule of law. But there is a minority of Americans who refuse to abide by this covenant. They believe the rule of law does not apply to them, and in the forests and communities of Oregon and the western United States, their actions are a rapidly growing problem.

Natalie was frantic in her note taking, so renewed with the prospect of scooping the region's newspapers that she failed to recognize the subtlety with which the congresswoman seemed to be rebuking her for suggesting that Libre Salazar was imprisoned unjustly in her congressional district or that his case should be opened for reconsideration.

She struggled to keep her concentration and her eyes open through the testimony of eight more elected representatives before the much anticipated and subpoenaed Greg Rosenburg took the oath after a lunch recess, swearing to tell the truth, as he stood next to his attorney at the solitary table facing the tribunal. But before this happened, the *soundbite* of the morning, the quote that framed the anticipation around Rosenburg's testimony, belonged to George Nethercutt, who spoke last before the break. He said, "In a recent magazine interview, Mr. Rosenburg, who we are about to hear from, showed his sympathy with the victims of September 11th, noting that 'anyone in their right mind would realize the United States had it coming.'" Natalie underlined each word in the quote at least three times since she had kind of felt the same way ever since the 2000 election.

At lunch, her search for Bret Meyer Brady became more systematic both in and outside the Longworth House Office Building. She double-tasked her noon hour by working to distribute the remaining photocopies of Libre's manifesto to anyone with a media badge. In this, she had learned during a brief exchange with a San Francisco reporter who thought he had seen a *Bret Brady* at the hearing during the morning session. This intensified her search. Could he be avoiding her?

Eureka! She spotted Greg Rosenburg talking to his attorney on the steps outside the building. Even as she approached, she could tell the two were engaged in a really intense pep talk—getting Rosenburg psyched up to deliver his testimony, she suspected. She walked right up to them anyway—reporter privilege.

The attorney shifted his posture like an offensive lineman

intercepting the sack of his quarterback. "I'm a friend," she offered deceitfully. When Rosenburg stretched his neck to see who she was, she thought to amend her claim. "I come from a friend." She reached around the lawyer to extend a copy of the prison essay to his client.

"You've seen Libre?" Rosenburg asked, like she'd been with a rock star or the Dali Lama.

"I've just come from OSP. He'd want you to have a copy of this. I'm a reporter from the *Seattle Times*." Rosenburg accepted the letter enthusiastically. She kept her hand out. "I'm Natalie Wesson."

A blush rose in the pale cheeks of the kid, who had to still be in his twenties and if he wasn't, then he must have just left them. "Ah, Libre's spoken of you, for sure."

Then it was Natalie's turn to blush. What was it with the male code to fuck and tell? She withdrew her hand.

"How is he? I haven't seen him in a year."

"He's healthy." She thought about that statement. "He's really healthy," she amended. "And still angry but growing more and more resigned, I think."

"Still greasing up the governor for a pardon?"

The attorney scoffed, knowing a snowman had better odds in a steam room.

"Averaging at least a letter a week, I understand. I get copied on most of them. Sometimes the message is on target; sometimes it's out to lunch. He hasn't done half bad in this piece of writing. I can't seem to get it introduced as testimony for him since he wasn't asked or subpoenaed to contribute."

"Yeah, I'm not sure how I drew the lucky straw."

"Because you quoted yourself in every press release coming out of the ELF office for half a decade, that's how," his attorney balked.

"ELF doesn't have an office," Rosenburg counseled his lawyer. "We are an autonomous collective, just like in Monty Python. How many times do I have to drill this into your head?"

"You said you haven't seen Libre in a year?"

"Yeah. We went in together but shortly after I got transferred to the Two Rivers Facility near Umatilla. Now that I'm out, I'm on a no-visit list at OSP. It sucks. I'd like to see him, discuss things, but he's been moved to max as part of a security threat group—SGP they call it. It's totally trumped."

"I have pretty good luck getting messages in and out and I'm still allowed to visit, so if I can help—"

"What? Trust a reporter?" Rosenburg laughed.

"And which do you think is the dirtier profession, a publicist or a reporter?" she referred to Rosenburg's years as the press officer for ELF.

"Same gutter, sucking up the same leaves," was Rosenburg's thoughtful response.

"Precisely. You can trust me," Natalie suggested.

His smile revealed he knew better than to trust anyone. "I should get back inside and get ready for my fifteen minutes of fame."

"I'll do what I can for you."

"Do whatever you can for the planet. Don't do it for me."

The teeth behind the beard revealed Rosenburg's blue blood upbringing. It was no mystery why he stuck to the press duties and got in front of the cameras every chance he could. He was really too pretty to pull off the whole tree sitter, never bathe, never shave routine. Natalie followed the two inside, checking out Rosenburg's ass. What was her attraction to prisoners and this jones she seemed to carry for rough trade?

Walking down the corridor toward the auditorium, Natalie collided with a guy charging out of the men's restroom. After the rather violent contact of their two bodies, once the two had a chance to step back from the impact, Natalie's eyes flashed to the media badge. *Bret Meyer Brady—The Register-Guard, The Oregonian.* Natalie squinted her eyes a little.

"I'm so sorry. Are you all right?" The man with eyes shocked wide blue behind partially frameless glasses continued to rub his wet hands on his pants.

"You may be sorry but you're not Bret Meyer Brady," she asserted.

His eyes weren't getting any smaller. "Busted," he confessed. "You're not going to turn me in are you?" She could tell he was reading her badge. "Yikes, *Seattle Times*—you might."

"What have you done with him?" she demanded to know. "He hasn't returned my phone calls or emails and now here you are posing as him."

"We should get inside or we'll miss Rosenburg's testimony."

"Seriously," she prodded as the two continued down the hall.

"His grandmother, or maybe it was his grandfather…one of them passed away. He's somewhere in the Midwest at a funeral."

With that they walked back into the auditorium, where proceedings had just started up again. It was odd to Natalie, that rather than sit with the woman he'd just mowed over, he waited for her to take her seat before diverting to the other side of the auditorium, very odd to her indeed.

McInnis was speaking:

> Our next witness has been subpoenaed to the Committee. It was with reluctance that we issued the subpoena, but the witness refused to appear in front of the Committee voluntarily. His response was that he had no desire to cooperate with the same state that is directly responsible for ongoing murder and exploitation of life both within this country and internationally. He has responded to the subpoena, and I would now call him to the stand. Mr. Rosenburg.

Greg rose with his attorney, who spoke first. "Mr. Chairman, I would ask your permission for me to sit next to my client, since he is the only person subpoenaed for this hearing and may require my representation. I would appreciate it."

"Counsel, it is my practice to have you—you may sit behind

your client, but I don't allow counsel to sit at the table with your client." The chairman was clearly flustered by the request.

"Very well. Thank you for considering my request." The attorney acquiesced and motioned his client to proceed.

"Mr. Rosenburg, please remain standing and raise your right hand. I would like to administer the oath. Do you solemnly swear or affirm that the testimony you are about to give is the truth, the whole truth and nothing but the truth, so help you God?"

"I do."

"Thank you, Mr. Rosenburg. You may be seated. You may begin with your opening statement at any time."

Rosenburg reached for the glass of water that had been set for him. He adjusted the table microphone to the elevation of his mouth. He cleared his throat.

Good afternoon. As Representative Hooley has set a precedent for referencing long dead presidents in this matter, I would like to quote Thomas Jefferson, who in 1776 wrote, "When a long train of abuses and usurpations, pursuing invariably the same object, evinces a design to reduce the people under absolute despotism, it is their right, it is their duty, to throw off such government, and to provide new guards for their future security. The oppressed should rebel, and they will continue to rebel and raise disturbance until their civil rights are fully restored to them and all partial distinctions, exclusions and incapacitations are removed."

H AZARD WOULD HAVE GONE INSANE—MAYBE DID GO INSANE AND CAME back from it—by now had it not been for his satellite connection to the Internet. That and his general orientation to the cabin that had been fully stocked to begin with and the daily, sometimes hourly explorations of the wonderful woods and mountain meadows he could reach by hike or motor bike, kept him in prime shape and aided his getting deeper into character. *Hazard*—that was his brand spanking new anarchist tag, his handle. He hadn't picked it, though he liked it and might have come up with that one by himself. His former tag, from a whole 'nother lifetime, had been too complicated, too hard to rattle off on a walkie-talkie, too long to spray paint or sign to emails sent anonymously from a roving IP address.

There had been no contact with anyone on the outside if you didn't count his new habit of wandering into a random chatroom or two on the nights he was too wound up to sleep. It had already been three months since he left that world. Now it was like he'd awakened from a coma to claim a completely different person's life and even though he remembered where he had come from, he wasn't permitted to have any connection to it. It was a bit like being a prisoner, he imagined. It must be what Libre Salazar wrestles with every single day. There's this world that you know—you've tasted it—full of friends and family, Starbucks and 7-11s, movie theaters, dance clubs, football games, cable television, music stores,

Dairy Queens, liquor stores and libraries, but you can't leave this place to go to any of them. He and Libre had both lost their freedoms, really. It had taken him ninety days, but he got that now. So to pass the time he invented new freedoms. From the ninetieth day forward, he would take whole new liberties and risks. Perhaps the biggest freedom of all, he had discovered, was no longer having to be the person you were.

Thanks to some bureau handiwork, Hazard was well on his way to becoming an anarchist legend in his own time. Agents had been trained, just as he had, to master his Hazard tag in all mediums—spray paint, blood, charcoal, feces, urine, sticks, rocks, deer bones, diesel tar—and they'd been leaving his mark on targets and small scale hits around the Pacific Northwest for months even before he could take over the caseload. He'd mastered his handheld Magellan GPS by devising far-ranging scavenger hunts on the motorbike that came with the one-room cabin, which was really just a shack with decent insulation. He could pretty much instantly convert any location into its horizontal and vertical axis point and then log that location on his laptop in a searchable database he'd created.

In ninety days, he'd become self-taught and pinpoint proficient in the high-tech sport of geocaching, managing to locate and scoop treasure left by others at specific locations revealed in webblogs and sites devoted to the pastime. He had so far collected a yellow barrel of monkeys from under a bridge at 46°19'47.38"N, 122°43'33.24"W, an old Ford truck key from the hollow of some tree roots in the last tree standing in a clearcut at 46°23'52.64"N, 122°31'30.87"W, a prom picture of a couple with '80s hair inside a ziplock bag under a sizable mound of rocks at 46°15'14.07"N, 123°00'45.10"W, and a miniature dragon carved from a piece of yew wood that had been left in the middle of an equally miniature pentagram made from moss arranged in a clearing at 46°03'21.85"N, 123°15'52.86"W—all within maybe forty miles of his cabin, which was located at 46°15'14.07"N, 122°59'51.93"W and all from clues he'd found first on the Internet. He later suspected these things had been planted for him on the Net by his handlers to get him used to his tech toys and to maneuvering the motorbike over logging roads.

And just to keep life in the sharpest possible perspective, he'd taken up smoking pot. It wouldn't have been something he would have sought out had it not been provided gratis along with the beater motorbike, the laptop, the Magellan, the solar-powered battery charger, the satellite internet dish, the case of red spray paint, and just because somebody had a sense of humor, the Etch A Sketch. He guessed it was part of the undercover ruse because nobody would suspect a pot smoker to be an agent working for the feds. Nobody.

And since it was the 4th of July, Hazard thought he might practice with a few of his homemade fireworks. Molotovs had never really been his specialty and his fingers were too big for detonation devices, so he liked to practice with low-grade explosives like gunpowder and some flammables. But since the Smokey Bear fire danger level had read Extremely High the last time he'd motored past the sign with the clever mascot deployed to put a soft fuzzy face to the U.S. Forest Service—just one more thing to distract the nation from the service actually being provided—he thought twice and took up some basic wiring drills testing the remote from an old garage door opener.

He'd been taught in his very early days of eco-activism—Hazard didn't use the word terrorism—that sometimes you could do the greatest amount of damage just by pissing in a gas tank so every time he came across a piece of logging or survey equipment, in he went with his own organic flair. He had penetrated more gas and diesel tanks than humans in this lifetime, not something you can really brag about, but Hazard was proud. He'd kept up this tradition, even during his reform period always amazed that companies left their assets unattended on weekends. He'd even come across chainsaws, just lying out in the open, which he of course immediately de-chained, amassing quite a hefty collection of what others called his chain-bling worn about his neck during particular fireside ceremonies and celebrations. Those were his younger days, when he could hold his bladder for three-quarters of a day just waiting to come across a pick-up or a logging truck, though you had to squat some to hit the hole in those tanks. He felt like a Timber Wolf marking his territory some days. Maybe his tag should have been Timber Wolf. Perhaps the next time I reinvent myself, he thought.

He quickly bored with the homework and dragged a pair of chairs outside the cabin to sunbathe. He loved sleeping during the day and the sun in this part of Washington State was a bonus any time of the year they could get it. Napping kept him much more alert and focused at night when the Internet signal was the strongest and his chances of networking with other activists was highest, especially for those embedded as deeply as he was. Summer was the busiest time for eco-freaks simply because the weather permitted them to go deep in the woods for strategic tree sits, monkey-wrenching or spiking. Autumn weather drove them out, back to urban centers, where the focus of activities would turn to car dealerships, government buildings and housing subdivisions.

So perennial was the cycle that the Freddies referred to the autumnal rains as the Douche Season and often waited at the junctions of main forestry roads for the impurities of the forest to get flushed out and into their custody long enough to ID and question them to fatten up their own searchable database. In spite of everything they thought they knew about eco-activists, they really only knew what the *eeks* let them know. Hardly anyone used main forestry road junctions anymore unless it was to leak counterinformation, and most diehards were equipped to delay their reentry into society until a full month after the first frost, long after the most sturdy of law enforcement asses had grown numb from the stakeout.

Hazard explored his naked body with his hands as the sun soaked through layer after layer of his flesh. His body fat had disappeared within the first thirty days thanks to a water, maple syrup and cayenne cleanse, and then push-ups and sit-ups revealed abdominal muscles on his hairless stomach that had been choked dormant in a sea of flab for pretty much the past five years of his desk-bound existence. He pulled his hair back from his face and ears with a hand. It should be shoulder length by Labor Day he guessed. Maybe it had been marijuana but he blamed the beard for driving him crazy and provoking the full body shave, legs, nuts, underarms and all, at the height of the cleanse. Well, not his head hair…it was in his contract to maintain a *viable hippie disguise* so as not to be recognized by anyone with whom he'd had contact pre-embedding. Freshly shaved and by a full moon he had dashed from the cabin that night as nude and as high as he was right now stretched between two chairs baking in the sun, in search of a creek to drown the lone out of his loneliness. He'd since built up an eddy with rocks in what had been aptly named Trickle Creek to create a pool for bathing and contemplating and spawning if ever a fish made it up this far to do the deed.

He dozed in and out of sleep under the broiler, flipping onto his stomach when he began to think his genitals were getting radiated. The smells of summer in the forest were intoxicating. Pine, Timothy weed, Syringa flowers, algae, decay of something that picked a lousy season to die, the garlic from last night's exquisite tofu stir fry pushing up through every pore. Then again, it might just be the dope.

After a munchie-driven, shirtless sprint by motorbike six miles into town to grab non-regulation rations at the Speedy Mart to get him through the cravings and paranoia that lay ahead, he sat down at the table inside the cabin to see if he might connect with other ex-patriots on this, the American Day of Arrogance.

Sort of amazed to have grabbed a signal in the middle of the day, he logged onto a couple of his more than a dozen hotmail accounts that he used on a rotation he'd devised according to the phases of the moon. Without really thinking, thanks due to the bowl he'd just incinerated, he'd logged onto the account he'd set up three months ago but never used to communicate with his townhouse neighbor, Anne. He didn't notice it until his laptop bleeped and a Messenger button on the toolbar flashed *Conversation…hanff_84* "Fuck!" he swore out loud. How covert was that if he could be busted by a widow shut-in? He opened the message window and tried to figure out what he should do, all the while chanting "Fuck! Fuck! Fuck!" She knew he was online. If he didn't answer her, it would only fuel her suspicions.

With his fingers in frozen poise above his laptop, he let out two great lungs of air like he'd been holding his smoke. He typed *Good Day, Miss Hanff*, pressed *send* and then held his breath again as the cursor blinked the same syncopation as his heart in that moment. The Messenger window indicated that *hanff_84* was writing a response.

I should hope you have been wrestling with the shame you must feel, Mr. Doel, for not letting me hear from you before now.

So far so good, he thought. At least she was sticking to their aliases that he'd based on *84, Charing Cross Road*.

"Come on Secret Agent Man," he coached himself aloud. "What story ya gonna feed her?" He began to type, in character, having read the classic novel cover to cover twice since going underground.

Miss Hanff, you are kind to inquire about my conscience. Indeed, too much time has passed since we last corresponded. –send.

Mr. Doel, where in Sam Hill are you?

Think, think. He opened *Expedia* in another Explorer window. *One would think, Miss Hanff, that you might employ your quantum physics and rely more on the connection of our souls to divine my location.* –send.

I fear, Mr. Doel, that you have mistaken science for mysticism and because of this I am uncertain whether I can continue this correspondence without causing great insult to my vocation. Using science, however, and a wise woman's intuition, I can posit where you are not and that would be writing for The Oregonian. *The clown that is ghost writing for you can string words together—mostly in contractions and clichés—but it does not pass for journalism, never mind writing.*

There was a pause. Hazard didn't know what to write next that wouldn't reveal another clue she could devote her insomnia to solving, but he also knew he needed to get her off *The Oregonian* scent or it would lead to more hooks he wouldn't be able to wiggle free from, not the way she was casting. He needed a diversion so he made one up on the spot.

Remember the sabbatical to India that I have been meaning to take all these years? –send.

Teachers and preachers take sabbaticals, my Dear. Journalists generally do not. And you have never once mentioned India to me. Do you now want me to believe you let the petunias wither and my loneliness blossom and proliferate in this high-summer heat because you've buggered off to India?

Yes! Yes, that's exactly what he wanted her to believe, but he didn't type that. *Well, Miss Hanff, you will be enchanted to learn that your loyal correspondent is at this moment finding his soul in one of the oldest cities in the world. –send.*

I will need another clue if you want me to solve this riddle, Mr. Doel. And I should tell you I'm running short on time. There is a web-lecture on quantum cryptography beginning in four minutes.

Beautiful, he thought. A chat deadline. *The city is known as one of the seven sacred cities in Hinduism and sits at the confluence of the Varuna and Assi rivers. –send.*

And you have just given away the mystery, Mr. Doel. Of course you are in Varanasi, are you not? In that case, you should know that Buddha gave his first sermon nearby in Sarnath. When will you be home?

Why Miss Hanff, I cannot return until I have achieved enlightenment. –send. As he sped-read through the Varanasi history section, he came up with a closing line to wrap up their chat and sent it too: *I plan to travel the Panch Kosi Road tomorrow. It is said that anyone who dies on this road while making his pilgrimage will go straight to heaven.*

While the petunias and I rot in this forsaken asphalt hell—on Stage Three water restrictions? If it is curry you wanted, we could have gone to the Brick Lane Curry House. Must now cut this short. I will insist that you email me within the week and answer all the questions I have asked in all the emails I have sent. In the meantime, please do not masquerade as a loyal correspondent. Regards…H. Hanff.

I promise to update you on the other end of the Panch Kosi. Faithfully yours, Frank Doel. –send.

He'd scarcely finished a very relieved exhale when his laptop chimed and a new conversation window began flashing along the bottom toolbar. It was Hooknose, another eco freak he'd encountered online a few weeks ago. He'd been waiting to connect with him again so to be sure he'd have no further interruptions, he closed out of all the windows he had opened under all the different hotmail accounts, and typed an anarchist greeting.

Happy Dependence Day, Hooknose. –send.

Yeah, we should really change that. Hazard, I've been thinking we need to step up the revolution. It's been a pussy of a summer in the woods.

Have anything in mind? –send.

I'm thinking the two of us should meet, sit down and come up with a plan to shift thinking…nothing that lowers flags around the country but something that inspires Greens to climb out of their tree sits and abandon tree spiking long enough to actually accomplish something radical.

Hazard thought the suggestion to meet may have come a bit too prematurely given how little they knew about each other. He decided to wave him off. *Maybe first don't you think we need to demonstrate to each other that we're both serious about changing things? I mean, we've only chatted a few times. I'm not used to partnering, truth be told. I have this thing with trusting.* –send.

There was a pause. *Hear that. You're right. We haven't even established our locations to each other yet. Tell you what, let's each vow that in the next 72 hours we will achieve the most radical acts of insurrection we can—something each of us can verify on the Web.*

Something that establishes us as blood brothers for the revolution. –send.

Exactly. Then, I'll reveal my longitudinal coordinates. You reveal your latitude and we'll make a date to meet at the intersection where we'll camp together for a week or two and figure out a way to convince Homo sapiens *to dismantle the system and rejoin Nature.*

Sounds like a manifesto in the making. Teddy-K would be proud. Count me in. –send.

So I'll catch you online, Hazard, around this time on the 7th?

Be stealth. Be lethal. –send.

39   44   42   121 47 4 **10 6** 46 30 53 116

HIS FRUSTRATION HAD BEEN MOUNTING, INTENSIFYING, NEARLY BOILING over for weeks now. He didn't know how many more times he could drive along the shackled rivers of the region without losing it in a clinically certifiable way. Something had to be done. He'd decided he wasn't going to take a chance on the courts and the enviro-activists and the promised new paradigms provoked by fears of global warming to get the dams off the rivers. Non-hierarchical structure, passive resistance and codes of nonviolence were crap and had failed. He just couldn't take a chance that any of these painfully molasses-slow processes would amount to anything in the end or succeed in removing even one dam during the remaining years of his lifetime.

Chewing on a piece of red rope, he realized there was really only one way to make sure a dam came down before he died and that was to take it down himself, even if it meant he died in the process. The questions were where, how and when. The subset of these questions included who to trust and who to involve. He'd need a physicist and he knew where to get one. He'd need a demolitions man with muscle and the ability to stand invisible in a crowd of fucking half-cocked Freddies. He'd been lately impressed with a rising superstar in the anarchist movement, someone who'd managed to tag every last one of the eight dams from Lewiston to Portland with brazen, blood-red spray paint no less—without getting busted. *Hazard* might be the man, if he was a man. Greyhound grinned around the licorice hanging from his mouth. Wouldn't that be the cougar's ass if Hazard turned out to be a she-anarchist? Now that would be something if a new phoenix for the cause was rising out of feminist ashes with balls tougher than any of them had. Then, maybe just then, something might fucking get accomplished, and yes, in his god-damned lifetime. He quick-chomped the rest of the rope and chewed with full cheeks spread in a smile.

Four hundred thirty-six miles, eight concrete motivators, twelve new passengers in four stops and a fucking corndog later that had been the mistake he'd known it would be—Greyhound had composed the bones and sinew of the new *fatwa* in his mind. He'd post it on the Internet in the coming days where it would gather flesh, stand erect and walk upright into the world to begin the process of returning the world to itself. It would be the single greatest achievement in the green anarchist movement since Man stupidly abandoned hunting and gathering. And he'd recruit and meticulously build a hand-selected dream cell to pull it off and even they wouldn't have a clue they were part of his eco-reckoning force—ERF—it would be a new day, new tactics, new outcomes and he would be revered as a mastermind on par with Osama bin Laden by historians who chose to make note of such things in the course of human reconstruction. Fuck, yes!

For two months, Ted had been *jonesing* for Sergio, not able to purge the fantasy of their encounter and his first ever same-sex experience from his brain or his crotch. Thinking about it, which he did at least a dozen times every day, easily twice as often when he was stuck on the river, he got instantly hard. He hadn't been able to function in any meaningful way with his wife, Samantha, who wanted a second child so badly she could taste the embryo that so far hadn't started growing in her belly.

He knew he was beyond obsession last week when he hoofed it across the Willamette River to the Portland State University campus to see if he could track down any scent of his supposed chemistry professor with the amazing body. That part of the story checked out when he'd inquired at the admissions office, posing as a former student trying to track down a favorite teacher. The girl in the admin office did a quick search of faculty on her computer and told him she didn't think Sergio Payne taught during summer session, but that they would know for certain up at Shattuck Hall or Science Building Two. His pants swelling with anticipation, he cut across the Southwest Park blocks and entered Science Building Two first, bounding up the stairs looking for a faculty office. All he found were empty classrooms in a building that seemed entirely abandoned, but still unlocked. On his way out, he stopped to take a leak in the men's restroom under the stairs and coming out, he collided with another man on his way in.

"Oh, Dude, I'm sorry," he instantly apologized for moving at the speed of a locomotive.

"I'm okay," the guy assured him. "No broken bones and I don't even know a lawyer anyway."

Ted smiled. "Say, you wouldn't happen to know Sergio Payne, a teacher here, would you?"

"Sergio? Sure, but he doesn't work on campus during the summer. I think he works spring and summer breaks inland; uh, where in the hell did he tell me he goes? A place called Orofino, I think. Maybe it's in Idaho?" he asked more than stated.

"Orofino? I know it! Thanks and again, I'm sorry for bashing into you."

"No worries, Man. Listen, if you run into Sergio, tell him Glenn said hi and to get his ass back here to carry his share of the faculty load."

Ted had only been able to smile, daydreaming as he did around the clock about once again taking his own share of that particular faculty load.

And that's what had taken Ted DeHavlin in the direction of Orofino, Idaho, about forty-five miles above Lewiston, not more than four days later. And who should he encounter hitchhiking on Highway 12 at the junction with Highway 95—but Sergio Payne, looking just as rustic and fit and determined as the last time he'd seen him. He slammed on the brakes of his orange pick-up and with his heart racing he rustled the general debris common to a four-year-old including an assortment of McDonald's Happy Meal toys, action figures and coloring books behind the seat, watching as the hiker jogged to catch up to his position. He quickly checked his hair and teeth in the mirror and leaned over to unlock the passenger door. This was too unbelievable to be happening. Ted could not contain his joy.

"Hop in, Stranger," he invited with a smile that his ears could almost not contain.

It took the renegade chemistry prof exactly eight seconds for his eyes to compare what he was seeing to the mental flash cards of the people he knew in his life to produce a name: "Ted, right?" The driver's enthusiasm told him he'd answered correctly. "How many times are you going to rescue me, Man?" He reached his hand out to shake but got pulled into a side bench embrace that nearly yanked him clean across the cab.

"Fuck, it is so great to see you," Ted gushed and kept on blubbering. "It's me that keeps getting rescued by you."

"What?" Sergio asked, trying to pull back to his side of the truck but finding resistance. "You don't look like you are in trouble now or in need of rescue."

"Fuck, kid. I haven't been able to stop thinking about you. I scarcely said three words to my wife and kid when I got back to Lewiston last night and here I am today, beating up the highway to see if I could find you again. I had no idea it would be this fucking easy."

Sergio crinkled his nose and eyes. "Really?" he managed. "And what made you look for me up this way?"

Uncharacteristically, Ted pulled him in for a kiss on the mouth.

"Whoa, Dude! I'm not like that, normally."

Shocked, Ted recovered with "I'm not like this normally either, but we seemed to get over that pretty nicely in the wheelhouse of my boat."

Sergio couldn't find argument with that logic so he darted in to give him a quick peck on the lips. He bounced back to the other side of the cab and put his seat belt on, shutting the door. "Are you good for a lift?"

"You mean a ride, don't you? Am I good for a ride? I sure am," he said eagerly, seductive-like, "but it's my turn to drive, isn't it?" Ted added, quite proud of his mastery of innuendo.

"Ted, I just need a lift to the Orofino city limits if you wouldn't mind. I can take it from there."

"Sure." Ted hadn't expected in a million years to be turned down. "Sure," he repeated, setting the stick shift into first and merging back onto the highway. A few miles of silence later, he offered how embarrassed he felt now.

"Don't sweat it, Ted. It was just a misunderstanding. I really appreciate the lift."

Ted couldn't keep his eyes from watering and Sergio couldn't help but notice them. Ted tried to be stoic but it was a tough look for redheads to pull off convincingly since they blushed so readily, especially if driven to emotional overload. Sergio bit his cheek. As carefree and unconnected to humanity as he tried really hard to act, he didn't like seeing somebody hurt and he didn't relish doing the hurting.

"Hey Ted, take that road up ahead on the left," He pointed. Ted sniffled and turned on his blinker, waiting for a truck loaded with woodchips to clear the opposite lane. The road went about a quarter mile up a ravine and dead-ended at a gate with a cattle-crossing grate. "Turn off the engine," he said undoing his own jeans.

"What are you doing?" Ted turned off the truck.

Sergio shoved his pants below his knees and his dick flopped somewhat aroused on the top of his thigh. He kneeled on the bench seat of the cab with some effort and turned away from Ted to offer him his ass in reciprocation so they could be even and move on. Ted couldn't help but let the dam of emotions burst and because he wanted it so badly, he tilted the steering column up and out of the way and lowered his pants and briefs. Using equal measures of spit and tears, he lubed his reddened rod and after a couple groans of protest, sunk it deep, then deeper into the ass of a traitor he never wanted to see again.

H AZARD HAD WASTED AN ENTIRE DAY BABYSITTING HIS PANIC TRYING TO come up with a target, poring over maps and hopscotching across the Worldwide Web looking for inspiration of any variety. He revisited his resume of forest-capades from a whole other life and systematically ruled out restriking any of those targets as he was too cautious back then. Even less than a decade later, those hits that once seemed major simply would not make a large enough splash to warrant a media sneeze after 9/11. To prove himself to Hooknose and the others who had to start taking notice if he were to slip credibly into their realm, this had to be bigger than tagging dams and pissing in gas tanks. He also needed to send a clear message to the chief of the Portland Joint Terrorism Task Force that he was firmly locked in position and that he didn't need some junior agent on overtime to do his spray painting for him anymore.

At the height of his self-doubting, there was a break in his fever. There it was practically jumping out at him in flashing neon off the Wal-Mart homepage. They'd opened a brand new *SuperCenter* not far from his former bioregion and it suddenly seemed to him like an opportune time to pay a visit to his Aunt Charlotte and Uncle Clarence in Coos Bay.

Hooknose had no problem with re-striking an old target,

especially when the first attempt hadn't even crippled their operation and possibly only managed to provoke an appendix to their emergency response plan. He'd gained much intelligence from his first foray inside the Agriculture Biotechnology Building on the University of Idaho campus in Moscow, where genetic engineering of plants and, one had to suspect, the experimental cloning of animals were earning a pedigree of note in the science world. Hooknose had walked around the three-story building at 604 Rayburn Street about thirty times when he realized what needed to be done and exactly how he'd go about it.

He'd learned from the Internet that the building had three stairwells, one each on the southeast, southwest and the northeast sides of the building, and one elevator located on the east side between the two stairwells. Offices were located on the west side of the building with the labs located on the east side. It was the labs he wanted to draw attention to with his action. That's where the radiation was used and the low-grade uranium isotopes most likely stored. He also knew the university had upgraded its interior fire suppression and alarm systems since the last incident. Striking during summer break meant the building wasn't staffed at capacity. Still, he would need to wait until later that evening when the last lights in the lab had been extinguished and he'd seen people leave the building. He set up an undetectable guard post about fifty yards directly east of the Ag Biotech Building in a few token trees planted decades ago around what was then the Forestry College.

What he hadn't accomplished in his first hit on the building last year, he wanted to make damn sure he accomplished this time. The public needed to know that radioactive materials were used inside this place, across the street from the Wallace Complex of dormitory buildings, which housed over 1,000 students during regular term, maybe half that census in the summer. Even a hoax bomb scare should provoke an evacuation of the lower campus quadrant and up the public awareness quotient.

He'd brought along in his shoulder pack a simple device made from a car battery, a couple of flashing LED lights and four laser pointers attached with duct tape. There were no explosives this time, as he couldn't chance hitting one of the locker boxes that stored the chemicals and radioactive stuff. This was merely a prop to provoke an evacuation and give the local authorities some practice in bomb assessment. For added effect, he also had two Molotovs corked and ready to deploy as window dressing on the outside of the building to add flame to the drama. To give the hit a local flavor, he'd retrieved the wine bottles from the bushes outside the Sigma Nu House, wearing gloves of course, thinking they might carry latent prints from a couple of the university's finer specimens.

His escape route had been planned and practiced to take him past a public payphone and into a maze of trails that ran through the heavily wooded campus arboretum. It was now just a matter of waiting for the last lights in the building to go dark. He checked his watch. It was coming up on midnight. Fucking scientists, he thought, rocking back on his elbows to wait them out.

Hazard had biked into Portland and stashed the motorcycle in the parking garage at *The Oregonian*, for which he'd long had the entrance code. He took a TriMet bus to the Greyhound station across from the train station in the Pearl District. Rubbing his sore ass from the bike commute as he boarded the bus, he was grateful to be off that thinly padded seat and to leave the driving to someone else. He had packed his laptop, several cans of spray paint, gloves and a change of dark clothes into his pack so when the gray-haired bus driver suggested he put the pack in the underneath carriage, he declined. "I need to keep my things with me. I have work to do," he smiled through a beard gone scraggly. The bus driver took his ticket and smiled back.

"Whatever you need," the driver said oddly. "We have the next six hours together."

This prompted Hazard to move toward the back of the bus. He didn't feel comfortable around people he suspected knew too much. Driving through the outskirts of Salem about an hour later, he thought of Libre Salazar, behind bars for getting caught doing what Hazard was now sanctioned to do, by the same government that had put Libre away for twenty-three years. Lady Justice was one fucked-up broad.

His pulse quickened enough that he noticed it as they entered Eugene. He knew it was wiser to stay on the bus than risk being recognized by someone whose path he'd crossed or in whose circle he'd traveled under some other guise either as a reporter or neighbor. The bus driver pulled into the station off Pearl Street and announced they'd be there for fifty minutes. He decided to take the risk. He knew of a grocery store just about two blocks away on East 10th and he still needed a few ingredients for his direct action recipe.

He'd only been inside the Station Market twice before, once to try cigarettes for the first and last time and once to buy condoms that he never ended up using. So much for optimism. Today was going to be another one item quick in and out. He knew precisely what he needed and he'd left enough room in his backpack for he guessed maybe twenty bags of Ore-Ida potato flakes, which the Station Market happened to have in stock. "For the Salvation Army food bank," he offered perhaps a bit too eagerly when the checker raised her eyebrows. At least it helped he'd picked something that certainly wasn't an ingredient in making crystal meth.

"How many bags ya got?" the checker asked.

"Eighteen," Hazard answered. She entered the price and a quantity of eighteen since she was too lazy to ring them in separately. Hazard knew there were twenty-four bags, but she paid little attention, seeing as it was for the Salvation Army and all. "I don't need a bag. Got one," he said hoisting the pack off his shoulder. He started cramming the bags inside the opened zipper before she could take time to count. He fished a crumpled twenty from his front pocket since he no longer carried a billfold or used plastic. Handing it to her, he noticed for like the first time in ten weeks how dirty and ragged his fingernails had gotten. He used to be so fastidious with his hands, clipping and filing and removing cuticles every other week. That's when he stared at his own hands on a keyboard eight, maybe ten hours a day. Now there were days spent in pristine boredom and inactivity, or more likely just stoned, that he didn't remember he had hands actually. A person really doesn't care what he looks like when there's nobody else around to notice or care. He was seeing his nails through the checker's eyes until he realized she was staring off somewhere else entirely as she waited for the cash drawer to open so she could make change.

He bee-lined it back to the bus and didn't really relax until he was settled back in his seat, this after walking past the wizened bus driver who stood guard outside eating a corndog. It wasn't long before the old man had finished his lunch on a stick. He wandered back inside the bus and down the aisle toward him, evidently to chat with his only passenger at the moment.

"So what's waiting in Coos Bay for you?"

"Visiting my aunt and uncle," Hazard answered without looking up.

"You sure you don't want me to throw that pack underneath so you'd have more room?"

"Nah, I sleep against it."

"Quite the security blanket, isn't it?"

Hazard hated small talk. He smiled and leaned into his potato flakes.

"You live in Portland, then?"

Was the guy hitting on him or what the fuck? "North of there some, across the river."

"You don't look like you have an office job. Mind if I ask what you do?"

"Yeah, really, I do mind."

"Hey, just shooting the breeze, killing time, trying to stay awake for the next part of this haul.

"Yeah, well I'd like to get to sleep while the bus isn't moving."

"Fair enough. Hey keep this in mind. If you're not working and you think you want to start, I might know of a gig or two up your way. Sleep on that, huh?"

Hazard opened the eyes he'd shut for effect half a minute earlier.

"What kind of gig?" He stopped the driver in his tracks halfway up the aisle. He could never stop being a curious reporter, no matter how bad he smelled or how long his hair got. The driver looked back and smiled, then continued to the front of the bus without answering him. Hazard thought about that offer as he shut his eyes for real and dozed off a few minutes later.

It was dark outside when he awoke, which told him he must have been asleep close to two hours. There was only one other passenger on the bus. He tried to get his bearings by looking out the window. It looked as though the ocean might be lurking out there since no other lights or landmarks were showing up. They must be on Highway 101, he thought. They should be coming up on Coos Bay pretty soon. He could see the bus driver watching him stir from his nap in his rearview mirror. It was creeping him out but he had other things to focus on as he began running through the drill he'd concocted on paper at the cabin and committed to memory.

"Hey, you got the time?" Hazard yelled to the front of the bus.

"All the time in the world," the old coot volleyed back with an audible chuckle. "It's ten to ten. We'll be there in fifteen." He raised the volume of his voice for an official announcement, which was overkill for two passengers. "Coos Bay in fifteen minutes."

The new, 185,000-square-foot Wal-Mart Supercenter #1880 on Newmark Avenue would close in another ten minutes. Hazard figured it would take an hour, maybe ninety minutes for the last of the employees to clear. That would give him plenty of time to case the place from the base he planned to set up in the adjacent wooded lot, which really made his first event on the new job too easy. A mega boxstore surrounded on two sides by woods? He couldn't have asked for an easier bull's-eye and he couldn't wait to post his first official ELF hit on the Earth Liberation Front website. He'd followed that site for journalistic leads for so long, it would be almost spiritual to create the news for a change. He needed this Wal-Mart action to cement his relations with Hooknose, shock his bureau handlers and inspire others to step up to fight against the full-press ecocide under way on the planet. Hey, he'd have to remember that sentiment…it would play well when he wrote the media release to accompany the ELF claim of responsibility email during the bus ride back to Portland in the morning. Did he just invent the word *ecocide*, he wondered?

The last lights in the Ag Biotech Building went dark, as best as Hooknose could tell from his post in the trees. He left his pack for another circumnavigation of the building to make sure the last person exited before he got to work. There she was, locking the building behind her. Hooknose was close enough to her to smile and say *hey there* as they passed on the sidewalk. At first, she smiled back, then instantly looked down to the ground. Hooknose was confident she would remember absolutely nothing about him. Someone who wasn't a science geek and the least bit sociable would have taken note of the lean man in the ratty long-sleeved Greenpeace T-shirt and camouflage cargo pants wearing gloves in July. She would be of no use to the campus police in another two hours.

Hooknose circled the target building once more before he returned to the cover of trees outside the old Forestry building. He could hear the dull beat of a party happening in one, maybe several, of the dorm rooms in the distance. *Summer students*, he thought, who'd likely fucked up during the previous semester, trying to make up their GPA so as not to jeopardize parental funding. There were no pedestrians on the sidewalks or streets. He monitored this for thirty minutes, thinking with each minute that passed that he could have done it and been gone by now. Suddenly, he heard a police or maybe a fire siren speeding off across town away from him. This was quickly joined by a new siren, perhaps an ambulance heading in the same direction. This was serendipity to have the city's limited assets deploying somewhere else. It was time to act.

Hooknose reached inside his pack and turned on each of the four laser pointer light sticks. He connected the LED lights to the battery and they began blinking spastically inside the black confines of the bag. He hoisted the pack on his chest, slipping his arms through the straps backwards. He could still hear the symphony of sirens but they were fading. His heart was throbbing between his ears when he lunged from the trees, a gasoline-filled wine bottle in each hand, a Bic lighter in his teeth. He could hear everything in that moment, crickets, the bass from a stereo, the fountain outside the entrance to the new library, his heart. Stopping short ten feet from the building, he set the bottles on the sidewalk with a clank. Reached into his marsupial pouch with both hands to retrieve the battery. With three strides he heaved the device through the window, which shattered brilliantly as the battery sailed inside the lab. An alarm sounded and a strobe light began flashing on the outside of the building.

Without pausing to admire his aim or strategy in using a battery that was heavy enough to break glass, Hooknose leapt back to his Molotovs, lit the rag on one and let the flame take hold before lobbing it against the brick building. The pop out-played the breaking glass. He was on his way out of the zone now. He tried lighting the second one, but he couldn't get a flame. He turned the bottle upside down to get some more fuel in the rag and tried again. Flames dancing in the landscaping twenty feet away were now illuminating his desperate attempt to deploy the second cocktail. It wouldn't light. In a decision made in the next split of a second, he heaved the bottle toward the flames. It burst and the flames multiplied very effectively.

Hooknose took off running into the darkness toward the old faculty building, through the trees and under the overhang of the University Classroom Building, up the steps three at a time above the roaring splash of the landscape water fountain, past the Art and Media Building, into the trees outside the Kiva auditorium, where he paused to rotate the pack onto his back, then, streaking past the radio and television broadcast building, he entered the arboretum and disappeared. He could hear new sirens now, as he fast-walked to catch his breath. When he emerged from the man-made forest, he began sprinting again, down the hill under the U of I water tower alongside the fence of the University President's residence, across the street to the payphone at the golf course. He took a gulp of air, dialed *64 then 911 and waited a second ring.

"Fire, police or ambulance?" the dispatcher asked.

"Bomb, Ag BioTech Building on campus." He slammed the earpiece on its hook and took off running down West Nez Perce Drive sticking to the shadows. The dispatcher, if she were trained properly, had just initiated a trace using *57 which she'd follow with *69. He'd blocked the latter using *64 to buy some extra time. Cutting between the Farm House Frat and another building he didn't know the purpose of, he caught the residential blocks of West Taylor and then West Lauder, before slowing to a walk as he crossed nonchalantly against the steady traffic of Highway 95 that dumped into downtown.

On the other side, he took up Styner Avenue, speed-walking to massage-nurse a side ache that had developed on his right abdomen. He checked his watch. It had taken less than half an hour to cover his four-mile escape route by foot. Where Styner Avenue met Highway 8, he retrieved his mountain bike and helmet, which he'd stashed under a footbridge that short-spanned a small creek. He washed any trace of gasoline from his hands in the creek and splashed some water on his face. He flipped on the rear and front strobe lights on the bike and began his long pedal out of town on the Troy Highway.

The layout was nearly exactly as he'd researched and committed to memory. Beginning at the front, Hazard circled the otherwise windowless Supercentre recording every detail as he searched for a way onto the roof. Returning to the front of the store, peering inside the only windows on either side of the quadruple set of entry doors, it occurred to him that even a single-person security force would require some overhead lighting just to get around the place. Aside from the red exit signs that lent a creepy *Friday the 13th* hue to giant fucking smiley faces advertising *everyday low prices*, the inside of this box was dark. There would be no sale prices tomorrow as Hazard forecasted a drastic dip in profits for at least forty-eight hours.

On the southeast corner of the building where the loading docks were positioned at a forty-five-degree angle under an overhang of the roof, a single Wal-Mart logo–ed semi-truck sat cold, backed against the building. Bingo! That was his way up. He slipped off his black and white Converse hightops so as not to leave tread marks on the windshield and in his socks, with his pack on, he climbed onto the hood of the truck and scrambled up the windshield to the roof of the cab. He steadied himself for the jump to the top of the trailer and made it in one try. He dashed along the roof of the truck toward the roof of the building. Halfway there he realized he had another six feet to overcome to get on top of the loading dock roof. Defeat was not an option and he began to run as fast as he could in socks on metal. He leapt at exactly the wrong time and might have even left a slight human stain on the side of the stuccoed wall. The smash knocked him backward on top of his potato flakes. Like a Hollywood stunt man crashing into a stack of empty cardboard boxes, he didn't feel the impact of his body bouncing back onto the truck in the least and this set him giggling. He'd have to try that again.

He grabbed his shoes from the pack and put them back on his feet. The tread of a Converse size-10 tennis shoe was not going to lead them back to him with any expediency. He was being too cautious again. He got up, tossed the backpack on top of the loading dock roof for a little incentive, backed up, raced forward, leapt again. This time his hands found the lip of the roof and he scrambled his legs up the side of the wall. He'd made the first roof, second if you counted the semi-truck. At least one more roof level lay ahead but he could see it had a caged metal ladder leading to it from the dock roof. He hadn't really stopped grinning since he first spotted the semi-truck. He tossed the backpack on his shoulders and climbed inside the ladder cage, wedging himself and the pack within the first three rungs. Okay, he hadn't thought that through completely. Maybe he needed to slow down and not act quite so cocky. But first, he needed to stop laughing and get unstuck.

A much more serious moment later, he was on top of the world and it was a white and vast canvas speckled with air circulation units, about thirty of them. The roof reflected enough work light from the low clouds ever-present on the coast and ever-passing overhead, soaked in the first light pollution they'd encountered in something like two thousand miles. Hazard half-walked, half-waltzed, half-shuffled to the center of the roof. The main Coos Bay police station was just two blocks away on NE Fifth, but without a helicopter tonight, they would have no inkling what was about to happen under their nose. He unpacked his bag of tricks and got to work on perhaps his most brilliant piece of work in twenty-eight years. Indeed, only navigating the birth canal might top this. Might.

Hazard was still grinning when his Uncle Clarence picked him up in his six-tire pick-up, oversized for hauling a fifth-wheel trailer up and down the coast of North America. His Aunt Charlotte, legally blind since the age of seven, had stayed behind to fix him something for supper once he got to the house out on Lone Rock Slough.

"Well, to what do we owe this surprise visit, young man?" His uncle was trying to figure out the reason his passenger had changed so much since the last time he'd seen him, only four years ago at a family reunion. He had other questions too, like why they'd never received a visit before now from a nephew who had lived two hours away for six years, but he held off asking too much. Didn't want to act too much like the boy's parents, who had always been over-suspicious and overprotective in his opinion.

"Well, I was bike camping with some friends south of here. We'd been at it for two weeks and they are in way better shape than I am. Then my bike starts falling apart and I decided I'm too old for this shit. I hitched into town on a whim you'd be willing to put me up for the night before I caught the bus home in the morning."

"You look like you've been camping for two months, Son. You'll have to clean yourself up before your aunt gets a look at you."

That's the way they talked too, always acting like she wasn't blind—hell, she acted like that too. She watched her hands as she peeled potatoes. She did her own shopping with Clarence following a distance behind, having pre-folded all her bills a certain way so she knew how much to pay at the checkout. And when his uncle suggested he clean up before his aunt got a look at him, Hazard knew she looked with her hands but saw with her soul. The least he could do was shave. It might be a wise idea to alter his appearance some anyway, given his antics earlier. "Sure, maybe you can let me sneak into the shower before supper. I hope she isn't going to the trouble of fixing lasagna for me. She knows her recipe has always been my favorite."

"Don't think you gave us enough notice this time. Maybe next time though. You know she can bake off a lasagna with no effort in our motor home? We can bring it to you in Eugene. Just give us an outlet to plug in our operation and we're cooking on all burners." His uncle struggled with a laugh that worked its way through lungs that had been seasoned by pipe and cigar and cigarette smoking for fifty years. He'd learned through his dad that his uncle had quit cold turkey a couple years back on the heels of something like his second triple bypass.

"How's your health, Clarence?" Hazard had long known the best way to avoid talking about something you didn't want to talk about was to flip the conversation to something you figured the other person didn't want to talk about either. He'd accidentally stumbled into this trap and shut down plenty of interviews that were just getting started. Silence could usually be guaranteed within one or two minutes, as was the case for the rest of their ride out to Lone Rock Slough.

The next morning, his belly bursting with more lasagna helpings than would have been doctor recommended, he climbed out of the cab of his uncle's pick-up. They'd been waved into a circuitous detour on their way to the Greyhound station by a fireman and an emergency response vehicle blocking the road on his uncle's chosen route down Newmark Avenue. He promised to visit soon and expressed his wish that everything was okay, referring to the emergency downtown. When he entered the bus terminal, there was a handwritten sign on the ticket window to buy tickets on the bus, cash only. Though he'd arrived in plenty of time before the scheduled 12:50 PM departure for Portland, he wandered outside. He rounded the back of the bus he took to be his as it was the only one in the lot at the time and ran smack into the bus driver—the same bus driver as yesterday, this time with licorice hanging out of his mouth instead of a corndog.

"Fucking Jesus," Hazard jumped back like he'd been electrocuted. "You scared the shit out of me."

"Best go change your pants before getting on my bus then, Stranger." The driver eyed him in a way that suggested his use of the word *stranger* was sarcasm.

"I'm sorry about that," Hazard offered. "I think I've had too much caffeine this morning."

"You look like you had a restful night, though."

"Yeah, visiting my aunt and uncle here. I haven't seen them in a few years. Good food, a pot of coffee to myself and some family stories, you know—not bad for an overnighter."

"Well you clean up well," the driver said. Hazard wondered again if the driver was interested in him for a purpose that didn't necessarily involve chauffeuring.

"Thanks," Hazard said uncomfortably. "My aunt's pretty picky about appearances."

"So, can I throw your bag underneath today?"

"No, I'm good," Hazard rifled back. "It says inside to buy my ticket on the bus."

"Yeah, the station manager is a paramedic and volunteer firefighter. I guess there's quite the situation downtown. They've shut down ten square blocks around the Wal-Mart."

"Oh yeah? Sniper?" Hazard tried to deflect suspicion.

"No, not this time," the driver was eager to share what little information he'd been able to gather. "The way I heard it there's a suspicious white powder of undetermined origin covering everything inside the store. They think it was introduced through the ventilation system on the roof. They have a hazmat team on its way from Eugene."

"Really? In little Coos Bay? Shit. My aunt and uncle probably shop there."

"I've got the news playing inside the bus on the TVs, if you want to hop on board. And don't worry about your ticket today. It's on me. We could be in the middle of another national crisis."

"Hey, thanks, Man. You're all right." Hazard smiled for the first time in two days.

As much as he wanted to race to get in front of a television, he acted like he had all the time in the world before ducking onboard when he thought the driver had looked away. When he'd gotten halfway down the aisle and turned around to see the bank of four televisions extending from the underside of the luggage rack down the right side of the bus, the coverage was from a helicopter hovering above the Wal-Mart and his handiwork. The feed was coming from CNN, for fuck's sake! Hazard couldn't remember feeling this much emotion over anything he'd written for any paper he'd reported for, which only confirmed his new theory that making the news was a much bigger adrenaline rush than reporting it. He might never go back. How often did an artist get this bird's-eye perspective of his work? There it was, from 300 feet off the ground, on four television screens: the white roof of the Coos Bay Wal-Mart Superstore, painted with giant red letters that spelled CORPORATE and GREED in reverse letters, followed by the word NOW. As one final embellishment, for the "O" in NOW the debuting eco-terrorist had substituted the biohazard symbol he had associated with his enviro-handle.

There wasn't any sound coming from the TVs so he couldn't tell if the reporters had deciphered the message and understood it to be *Reverse Corporate Greed Now!* He often wondered if readers "got him" when he was being especially clever. He knew his finer attributes were usually wasted on a pedantic society hopped up on NASCAR, *Monday Night Football* and really bad country music. He just couldn't take the collective ignorance personally.

H ER FAVORITE PERSON IN THE WORLD WASN'T IN INDIA. SHE HAD CONvinced herself of that. A quick visit to Expedia.com to see how she might get herself, hypothetically of course, to Varanasi, India, revealed that he'd copy-pasted that bit about the *Panch Kosi Road* directly from the webpage without editing. That, more than anything, had provoked her to leave the house, get into her Eddie Bauer Edition Jeep Cherokee and drive to Portland in a quest for the truth.

The Oregonian offices were a logical first stop except that she hadn't had an excellent Peet's coffee in so long, she drove directly to the spot she knew about downstairs at the Marriott Downtown between Washington and Alder Streets. Sipping gingerly on her Americano she was distracted by the television in the corner, where a small crowd had gathered. She moved herself two tables closer to the set. Ever since 9/11, which had defined *breaking story* television, you just didn't feel you could ignore a television set like the old days. She couldn't see the screen because of a sluggard who had taken a viewing position head-on as if the rest of the world didn't matter on either side of his giant melon head. But she could hear the reporter.

> Earlier in the day, a spokesman from the Coos Bay Police Department had released a statement that they were confused by the messaging painted on top of the Wal-Mart

Supercenter located downtown two blocks from police headquarters. We're now learning that thanks to a clever television viewer, they believe the intended message—with the words "corporate" and "greed" spelled backwards—is meant to be deciphered as Reverse Corporate Greed Now! We were told by an FBI agent arriving on the scene that the symbol used in place of an 'O' in the word "now" is reminiscent of a tag used earlier in the year to deface eight of the hydroelectric dams on the Snake and Columbia rivers. I should mention that we have been unable to confirm this at this time.

The FBI has taken over the investigation of this event from the Coos Bay Police Force as it has been deemed this strike carries terrorist overtones. As for the source of the unidentified white powder substance found to be covering the merchandise and floors of the store, a powder that has stumped authorities all day here, we have an unconfirmed report that initial lab testing has revealed a starch base that reminded one scientist of instant potato flakes. The shopping center remains sealed at this hour with nobody going in or out, and the morning shift employees, who discovered the store in a tampered state, remain hospitalized for observation.

A couple viewers lost interest or realized they were running late for work and peeled away from the television as the story was handed back to the in-studio anchor, who had been tossed this *Breaking News* segment.

In a related or unrelated story—we just don't know—officials at the University of Idaho in Moscow have reopened half of the campus after a bomb scare at the school's Agriculture Biotechnology Building forced the evacuation of five dormitory buildings and an on-campus apartment complex last night. The Building, in its short existence having just been opened and operational a year, has now been struck twice with acts of sabotage.

Last night, a homemade bomb-looking device, which turned out to be non-explosive in nature, was thrown through a window of the first floor laboratory. A small fire was burning beneath the window when fire and campus police arrived. One witness said they'd heard the building alarm and watched the fire for almost twenty minutes before anyone responded. Fire Chief Jim Howerton says the city's emergency response crews were on the other side of town responding to a domestic disturbance call when the bomb threat was phoned in by an anonymous caller from an on-campus pay telephone.

When we asked why half the campus was evacuated, it was learned that the building, which has been under scrutiny for its genetic plant engineering, also contains radioactive materials used in experimentation on plants and possibly on animals as well.

A posting on the Earth Liberation Front website this morning indicates that ELF is taking responsibility for this incident on the University of Idaho campus, they say, to raise public awareness around the use of radioactive materials in a residential setting and the consequences of genetically modifying the Natural world.

While it would be surprising to this reporter to learn that somebody in the Pacific Northwest had never heard of the Earth Liberation Front, just in case and for the record, ELF operates as a non-hierarchical, direct-action, under-ground movement whose autonomous members espouse anarchistic tenets and undertake a variety of vandalism and sabotage tactics in defense of the environment.

Since 1997 ELF cells have carried out dozens of actions that have resulted in close to $100 million in damages. This has earned ELF a spot on the FBI watchlist as a domestic terrorist group though it promotes itself as an international movement. There are no individual suspects in this bomb scare at this time and characteristic of ELF activities, nobody was injured by this action, but a Federal investigation is under way.

Anne turned away from the television as she drained the last of the smooth elixir from the cup. She wondered if her missing neighbor reporter was covering these stories. This was more than up his alley. It sat square in the middle of the street where he'd made his blooming career. So where was he? In a flash of brilliance, she thought to grab some Peet's whole bean to take home with her.

A while later, turning against the oncoming lane to pull into the underground parking structure at *The Oregonian* she was nearly sideswiped by a hippie on a motor bike who flew out of the garage like a bat being licked by the flames of Dante's *Inferno*. Once she'd grabbed hold of her nerve and parked the car, she had to smile. There was something about the hippie that had struck her oddly. Either he reminded her of her son studying abroad who really was a hippie or maybe it was just the way she automatically stereotyped any man with hair longer than her own as questionably degenerate. At any rate, she marched to the elevator and into the reception area of the newspaper and demanded in a way that only someone with a British accent could, to speak to staff reporter Martin Schooley. When asked what this was regarding, without missing a beat Anne Martondale said "his flagrant over-use of contractions and dreadfully droll run-on sentences."

NATALIE WESSON WAS NOT ABOUT TO LET THE TRAIL GROW COLD AND SHE figured if anyone could heat things up for her it was FBI Regional Bureau Chief Red Harvey. It didn't hurt the justification of the assignment in the least that in her books, he happened to be the sexiest middle-aged man alive. She had maintained an awkward crush on him since flushing him out of the eco-sagebrush like an English Pointer years ago. Every time she saw him or thought about him her heart pittered and pattered with nostalgia, not that she'd ever let on, all the while trying to come up with excuses to get into the same room with him. Even though she had long felt that two redheads together clashed, pretty much clashing with Red Harvey was all she could fantasize about and for a woman who managed to frame just about everything in fantasy, that was saying something.

On the train to Portland from Seattle, she played back his testimony before the Congressional Hearing on Eco-Terrorism just to hear his sexy gravel voice in her earphones.

> The way we're attacking the ELF issue is primarily through our Joint Terrorism Task Force, as we have 44 JTTFs now operating throughout the FBI's 56 field offices. With additional funding that we've recently received, we are pushing to get JTTFs in all 56 field offices by the end of this year. There have been a small number of arrests.

I know that's very frustrating to the public. It's very frustrating to us as well.

There are a few reasons why that happens, namely Constitutional guarantees. We walk a thin line between constitutionally guaranteed activities like freedom of expression, speech and the right to assemble and criminal activity, and we must make every effort not to step over that line and violate citizens' rights.

We have also learned, and everyone I believe is aware, that there's no defined hierarchal structure within the Earth Liberation Front. It's a very loose-knit group, a cell, persons, two, three, four get together, plan an act and do it, then disband after they claim it on the part of ELF. Without a defined hierarchical structure as you would find in La Cosa Nostra or some other organized crime activity, it becomes very, very difficult to get into the group and do routine investigations that we'd like to be undertaking at a more sophisticated level.

The major concern I have with this group is that they started out rather peaceful in their demonstrations to stop fox hunting in England or to protect habitat for the spotted owl in my part of the world, but over the course of time, splinter groups within the body have been frustrated with the lack of action or lack of intensity of action on the part of the main body, have split off and have taken more intense action, more violent action, if you will. This splintering has continued over the course of time and continues still. What we have seen in other civil disturbance areas is as time passes, those who become frustrated with the quote/unquote mainstream of these elements will take the next step.

If this continues and I have every reason to believe it will, then the violence that we've seen now is just a shadow of what's coming, and I think that's probably the most dangerous thing on our horizon and we are certainly putting a tremendous amount of effort into slowing this down and stopping it. The FBI has developed a strong response to the threats of domestic terrorism. The number of special agents dedicated to our counterterrorism programs grew by approximately 224 percent since fiscal year 1993. Cooperation among law enforcement agencies at all levels represents an important component of a comprehensive response to domestic terrorism. This cooperation is best illustrated by the JTTFs that are established in 44 cities across the nation, including the one I head in Portland, Oregon. These task forces are particularly well suited to responding to terrorism because they combine the national and international investigative resources of the FBI with the street-level expertise of local law enforcement agencies.

Law enforcement has a long way to go to adequately address the problem of eco-terrorism. Groups such as the Earth Liberation Front present unique challenges and the difficulty in investigating such groups, as I've mentioned, has thus far yielded few arrests. However, there are several ongoing investigations and these include the 10/14/2001 arson at the Bureau of Land Management wild horse and burro corral in Litchfield, California; the 7/20/2000 destruction of trees and damage to vehicles at the U.S. Forestry Science Laboratory in Rhinelander, Wisconsin; and the 11/29/1997 arson at the Bureau of Land Management Corral in my neck of the woods—Burns, Oregon.

The FBI and all of our federal, state and local law enforcement partners will continue to strive to address the difficult and unique challenges posed by eco-terrorists. Despite the recent focus on international terrorism, we remain fully cognizant of the full range of threats that confront the United States.

Natalie took the earphones out of her ears, as a flush of gratification swept through her body. She was on her way to pay a visit to the man behind the voice to see if she might use her behind to get that voice to help her find Bret Meyer Brady. It was the only tactic she used because it was the only tactic she knew worked on just about any man.

Red Harvey was not having a good day. His pet operative had struck a Coos Bay Wal-Mart overnight in a big way—much bigger than he'd authorized and much bigger than he would have predicted his activist- turned-reporter-turned-activist was prepared to go. After nine weeks not detecting a pulse from this guy, Red had a suspicion that had nagged him all morning long—that he might well have a sleeping rogue on his hands and on his payroll. He would spend the rest of the day trying to reel him back in just to establish a few parameters now that he had an idea of his capabilities. The most uncomfortable part of this was not informing his own bureau colleagues in the southern half of the state that this was an inside job. When he thought of the manpower and the costs both financially and from a public awareness—if not public panic—standpoint, he grew redder than was normal.

When his administrative assistant buzzed him to say there was a reporter there to see him, his first response was to wave it off as he would be giving no interviews today during an ongoing investigation, but when his assistant mentioned that the reporter was a *she* from the *Seattle Times* in almost an unspoken code that suggested he wouldn't want to miss this one, Red relented. "Fine. Send her down."

He jumped up from his desk to check himself in the mirror

hanging just inside the coat closet next to the window overlooking Tom McCall Park and Portland's Willamette River waterfront. *That tie doesn't go with that shirt,* he thought as he vowed to stop dressing in the dark so as not to wake his wife of almost a decade, who relished the extra forty-five minutes she smuggled out of bed each morning. He moved toward his closed office door and opened it just as the only-reporter-from-Seattle-it-could-possibly-be had started to knock.

"Oh, hi there," she said, twisting a bunch of her long, curly red hair in a hand she thought to extend to him in a staged greeting, just in case his co-workers were listening and of course they were. "I'm Natalie Wesson, *Seattle Times.* Thank you for agreeing to see me. I would have phoned first but with the incident in Coos Bay, I figured, well—" she trailed off.

"Red Harvey. My pleasure. Please, come in." He left the door open as was his practice when in a room alone with a female, a policy developed from personal experience good and bad.

Natalie walked straight to the window overlooking the river to give his *arrow* a chance to check out her *bull's eye* which she sported firmly, even athletically, inside her beige pleated dress slacks with the perfect batting record. She spun around to catch him in the act she figured he was committing, but he'd already sat behind his desk and was shuffling papers, faking obliviousness to her snake charming.

"I was there when you gave testimony at the Congressional Hearing last month."

"I, uh, saw you there," the bureau chief told her. He did, too. She had been the only other woman in the room aside from his wife and Congresswoman Hooley.

"I'm developing a theory and wanted to get your take on it," she strung him along.

"Let's hear it," he said, game for anything.

She moved from the window to take a seat on the other side of the desk from him. "I have a colleague in journalism who seems to have vanished. The stuff that's happened overnight in Coos Bay and over at the University of Idaho—that's the stuff that used to make him cream in his Dockers but he's nowhere to be found. I wonder if you might know him. His name's Bret Meyer Brady."

Game for anything but that. "I follow his work," Red admitted. "He usually can be counted on to get the facts right."

"My theory is this, and I appreciate your indulgence here, that he's now working for you as some kind of secret weapon in the war against domestic terrorists. Why else would he just disappear—walk away from a career that was just about to become mildly interesting? Unless," she proposed, "you found some way to make his life even more interesting."

"And that's your theory or that's your imagination, Miss— Wesson?"

"You of all people can call me Natalie," she offered, not yet prepared to shelve seduction.

"Look, the Federal Bureau of Investigation has hundreds of resources at our disposal from informants to undercover agents to surprisingly healthy and useful relationships with members of the media. While your theory is entirely plausible from a strategic and operational perspective, and while I wouldn't be at liberty to tell you if indeed your colleague was working for us, I can tell you that he is not. I might suggest if you truly think he has disappeared or in some way has met with foul play, that you contact the local authorities in Eugene to file a missing person report."

Showing her frustration, Natalie fumbled for a response. "Well, I guess you follow Bret Brady's reporting quite closely if you know where he has his residence."

"We're the FBI, Miss—Natalie. You might be surprised by what we know. For instance, I know that you paid a visit to our fine Oregon State Penitentiary on your way to the Congressional Hearing last month. I know you visited with the gold star arrest of my career while he jacked off under the table across from you. In fact, if you could give me twenty minutes I could probably get my assistant to rustle up the video footage. My day-to-day challenge rests with which knowledge to use and which knowledge to ignore. I like to think I've reached the status I have in the Bureau because I'm generally right about these things."

His assistant appeared in the doorway. "Pardon my intrusion. You now have a woman by the name of Anne Martondale, I think she said, waiting to see you."

"Have we suddenly started advertising our location on buses or something?" Red asked with one side of his face lifting into a grin. "Was there anything else I could do for you today, Natalie?"

"No," she said abruptly. "I appreciate you letting me run my hunch up the flagpole."

"Anytime. You might eventually come up with an angle we hadn't considered. Please be in touch." He rose to shake her hand. She completely missed the visual cue, having turned to leave at just that moment. He stuck his hand in his pants pocket and followed her out of the office and down the short hall to the front area. He'd decided to take his next visitor at the counter in the interest of minimizing the time he was losing with these interruptions. He watched the older woman who had taken a seat in the outer room as she sized up the reporter he'd escorted to the door. For some reason, he took the older woman's scorn as an indicator that she was thinking he might have been involved in some impropriety with the red-haired woman. He decided to interpret that as an indictment of how the reporter was dressed and not of any behavior he might be exhibiting. It's not that impropriety hadn't crossed his mind or his groin for that matter. "Safe travels, Miss Wesson."

He turned his attention to the woman he'd been told was waiting to see him. "I'm Red Harvey."

"Yes," the woman struggled to get out of the chair. "Pleased," then "I am Anne Martondale. I am up from Eugene attempting to unravel a bit of a mystery, you see."

Hearing the accent touched a soft spot and made the Chief think of his Gran—a history-steeped woman who had raised him decades earlier when his drugged-out mother had vanished apparently forever somewhere in the Midwestern prison system—before she got caught up in a foxtrot with dementia and had to be incarcerated herself.

"I live next door to a newspaper reporter, who worked until very recently for the *Eugene Register-Guard*. He first told me over three months ago he was taking a long-term joint reporting assignment with *The Oregonian* and that he'd be away for the spring and summer. I have just been there and they tell me he is not available today. What is even odder is that I had a bit of a wee chat with the lad on computer the other night and he claims to be in India now, of all places." She leaned her bosom across the counter, no small feat for her stature, and whispered. "I know he has some history on the other side of the law and I just got my head to wondering if, maybe, he had received some threats by people his reporting or testimony had, you know, caused damage to and that this might have sent him on the run. Because he helped your boys out in the past with information that led to your only high-profile arrests in something like a decade, I thought you might be in a position to help me be certain he is kept out of harm now."

Red hadn't really heard a thing the old woman had said after her opening sentence, so immersed was he in memories and voices from his childhood. But this also made the second inquiry about his not-so-secret special ops agent in less than three minutes. Perhaps he'd gravely underestimated the kid's connections to the world around him. When paired with the clearly out-of-bounds stunt last night in Coos Bay, the regional chief had reasons-galore to bring him in for questioning and possible realignment. If the Superstore had been his hit and his alone, he had gone recklessly beyond the instructions of remaining a semi-passive observer. It wasn't as though Harvey had the option to cancel the assignment since he had nothing else in the breadmaker and the public was lately coming unhinged over the proliferation of terrorism on the domestic front. At the very least, a review of undercover parameters was in order. With Homeland Security hogging the national agenda, he had a stubborn obligation to see if he might still groom a miracle breakthrough for his own team.

"Miss Martondale," he said placing his hand on hers as it seemed the thing to do if you wanted to pretend you were sincere. "If you could do me a giant favor and give your contact information and a description of your neighbor to my assistant, I'll put a couple of my guys on this right away. See what turns up, all right? Now, I hope you can understand that with last night's events in Coos Bay, I've got quite a few things to tend to at the moment. We will be in touch." He signaled his assistant to the counter to take over seeing the woman to the elevator as he disappeared down the hall to huddle behind his closed office door.

After a minute of recomposing, he retrieved his suit jacket and keys. He'd cross the river into Washington and take a little summer drive with the top down to pay a surprise visit of his own. But an hour and some later, when he got within a quarter mile of the hideout cabin just as far up the old logging road as he cared to take his new Saab, he had an uneasy feeling that agents sometimes get. Breaking a sweat as he hiked the rest of the way up the road, keeping to the shadows tossed by a margin of trees that had somehow escaped harvest in this clearcut landscape, he found the cabin graffiti tagged and abandoned. It was the spray painted symbol that straddled the jimmied front door and broken window that confirmed the reason for his tingling agent sense of unease. It was the same biohazard symbol as in the message on the roof of the Superstore.

THEY HADN'T BEEN ABLE TO AGREE AT FIRST WHERE TO THROW THE CELebration party and what was to be their first face-to-face meeting. Should they take the latitude of Hazard's cabin and the longitude of Hooknose's summer campsite or should they take the longitude of Hooknose's strike on the U of I campus and the latitude of the Wal-Mart in Coos Bay? Hazard had suggested they pick the exact midpoint between the two latest ELF strikes but it wasn't something they could readily configure with their GPS units. The marathon web chat between them had grown familiar and tiresome at the same time when Hooknose suggested they meet in the belly of the beast. *Where's that?* Hazard typed and hit *send*.

Weyerhauser corporate headquarters outside Seattle, twelve hours from now, had been the response. Hazard knew without being told that Weyerhauser—and MacMillan Bloedel before the takeover—had been singlehandedly responsible for the wholesale clearcutting of most of its 36 million acres of government-licensed forestlands in Oregon, Washington, British Columbia, and Alberta. He'd once reported in an article, incidentally under deadline and without fact-checking, that more trees and wildlife habitat in the past four decades had been obliterated by the whim and wielding of this megalithic corporate chainsaw than had been destroyed in all of human history preceding 1962. It had been one of those quotes that miraculously gathered moss and began popping up on websites and in journals around the country. The other quote he'd just sort of made up on the spot was that Weyerhauser's checkerboard handiwork across the once forest-carpeted landscape could be seen with a naked eye from space. It was probably true, he'd justified at the time.

Sure! Hazard had typed before signing out of their PGP-encrypted session to foil any eavesdroppers.

Stash your laptop. Don't bring it with you had been the final communiqué from Hooknose along with the rendezvous GPS coordinates of 47°18'04.77"N, 122°17'02.54"W.

Hazard removed a few nails from the floorboards and lowered the plastic-wrapped laptop computer to rest on an old stump that must have been left over from the original site clearing. But he didn't stop there. He destroyed any paper record or personal indication that he had even been there during the past twelve weeks and then finally, for added effect, he half-trashed the cabin to make it look unused in recent times. He'd always planned to ditch the bureau-sponsored digs to penetrate even deeper and more believably into the counterculture. Theirs was not a fixed roof society. If it wasn't neoprene, cedar branch lean-to or nylon, it might as well have been jail, especially during the summer months when *roughing it* under the stars simply wasn't.

Later, that night, as he fought numbness in his ass from the vibration of the motorbike that had been between his legs for over two hours, Hazard thought the impending meeting with Hooknose felt strangely like a love affair about to be consummated between two strangers in a pre-arranged marriage. The nerves had to be the same. He obsessed over trust establishing questions he feared Hooknose would ask, like *where did you come from* and *aren't you a little old to be taking up the defense of the planet?* Hazard couldn't know that the grossly ballooning notoriety of his Wal-Mart stunt, as news and photos of it continued to circle the globe by Internet through activist backchannels, would eclipse all doubts that Hooknose or anyone else might have had about the integrity of the ELF soldier that managed to pull that off two blocks from a police station, make world news and his point at the same time—all without hurting anyone. Hazard could have expected to get an audience with anyone in the movement as folks would have willingly made a pilgrimage for nothing more than a chance to offer him a high five and their respect, but that didn't cross his mind. He was already scheming his next move, which would need to be bolder if he was to escape the slippery slope that led him right back to the muck of obscurity where most activists were lucky to find any traction at all.

On a normal day, Hooknose usually had better luck hitchhiking than this. Twelve hours had seemed like a very conservative estimate, nearly twice as long as a straight drive would have taken him to reach the rendezvous point if he had a car or access to one, which he didn't. Truck drivers, whom he could normally count on and who one day should be given their due credit for their logistical role in social activism, must have been avoiding the heat of the day, which had topped one hundred degrees in the Valley before 10:00 AM.

He had wondered several times during the first two hours without a single promising set of brake lights if Ted was on the river. If he wasn't, Hooknose knew he would have dropped everything to drive him clean to Seattle, no questions asked. He actually disdained having that power over another human. Another hour later, fidgeting behind a highway speed limit sign that had kept the sun out of his eyes, he wasn't minding human controlling so much. If he knew how to contact the barge pilot, he'd do it. Ted would probably loan him his truck and probably wouldn't even mind if Hooknose borrowed it without asking, but he didn't know Ted's last name, his phone number or where in Lewiston he lived or parked his truck—unless he'd left it at the grain elevators.

With renewed vigor, Hooknose had a more immediate destination in mind and within twenty-five minutes he was walking down the gravel road from the frontage highway to the pier at the grain terminal, Ted's Ford pick-up practically sizzling dual holes in his sights. Hooknose knew how to hotwire just about any vehicle if it was unlocked but without a slim jim, which he didn't carry since it didn't have at least three other purposes, he would be out of luck. There was a second vehicle in the lot that indicated someone was likely inside the terminal trailer office so, confirming both doors on the pick-up were locked, he continued his momentum toward the trailer. He'd ask if Ted were contactable by radio or cellphone but as he began up the steps, a number of new clues jumped out at him to change the manner in which he'd read the situation.

From the porch, he could see the double barge fish transport vessel tied to the pier. He could hear the sound of a child giggling inside the trailer. He caught on the dry, stale air, a whiff of something floral that must have been perfume. In a heartbeat, he diverted his trajectory to hop off the end of the porch that had no railings just as the windowless trailer door slapped open and what must have been the components of Ted's family of three emerged single file like a red-headed trail of dust and ice left behind a ten-year-old comet hurtling through the universe. Hooknose flattened himself on the ground and half rolled under the porch hoping not to encounter a rattlesnake or much worse on the scale of his phobias, a spider. He could hear and see the exchange from his shadowed vantage.

"I'll be back on Sunday," Ted assured his wife while the boy jumped up and down as though the ground were molten lava burning off his feet instead of a dust trough dispatching a cloud that drifted under the porch to suffocate spies and spiders. "Remember to tell your brother that the spare key to the truck is duct taped to the engine block if he needs it for his landscaping project this week."

Hooknose smiled so widely in that moment that his whole mouth felt like the inside of a vacuum cleaner bag. He watched the adults embrace as the kid tugged on his father's hand. It couldn't have been jealously that he felt because he believed a trained scientist didn't feel, but as simple and perfect as Ted DeHavlin's life seemed to him in that almost Rockwellian snapshot, the storm clouds that were gathering in a world doomed—like the music in a movie nearing its climax—nearly broke every valve and chamber in the activist's green but well-meaning heart. What kind of world was that kid getting in the deal? Part of that answer was up to him and part of it, whether he knew it yet or not, was up to the kid's red-headed father. The option to remain complicit was no longer negotiable for any of them. He and Ted would have this conversation, just not today.

Hazard was initially confused when he tracked the GPS coordinates as far as he could get on pavement with the motorbike. He'd arrived at that point after dark, somewhere in the burbs between Federal Way and Auburn south of Seattle, and wasn't in the mood for bushwhacking, though that was clearly what lay before him if the handheld gizmo was working properly. It was a clear night with nearly a half moon and he was glad for that. He stashed the bike and his helmet on the treed side of Highway 18 and made sure what little chrome the stripped-down two-wheeler had was not going to reflect headlights or moonlight. He tossed his pack on the other side of a barbed wire fence and, using the post as a brace, got himself over the first barrier. He figured he needed to get another point and a half directly north of the spot where he was so he set off in that direction through a tangled combination of fir, spruce, salal and blackberry.

He had no idea if Hooknose had arrived before him or whether or not this might even be his fixed address, so he proceeded with some stealth, occasionally disturbed by a cuss word each time he snagged a blackberry barb in the flesh. Twenty minutes later, when he had reached the intersection point of the two axis coordinates and encountered nobody and nothing to confirm he'd been successful, he stubbornly set up his army green tent on the precise spot, crawled inside, stripped down to his briefs inside his sleeping bag and fiddled with the GPS unit some until he dozed off to sleep with the device resting on top of his stomach.

His series of early morning dreams was spoon-fed by new surroundings and a dose of fresh air laced with truck exhaust and the earth-rumbling vibrations of rush hour traffic from Interstate 5 and Highway 18, the junction of which was just under a mile away. Even before the day's sun had lent a measure of hue to the nylon roof of his tent, the urban forest came alive with the voices of birds and the engines of 747s laboring into the jet stream from nearby Sea-Tac Airport. Hazard's need to piss challenged his need to stay warm and was defeated for the better part of an hour, which allowed him to lapse back into a half-dream half-wake state.

When he finally emerged from the sleeping bag and then the tent flap, he wandered several barefoot paces to take his leak. His stream was strong enough to arc a good three feet away and raise steam from the carpet of pine needles. Hazard arched his back to see if he could reach even further when all of a sudden the target of his stream was joined by another piss stream that seemed to be coming from overhead. Hazard kind of stumbled backward a step in his attempt to look up into the trees and in the maneuver, peed on himself. Laughter fell down from the limbs as cusswords rose to the heavens.

"What the fuck?" Hazard expelled.

"G'morning, Brother!" It was another fifteen seconds before the piss fall was complete. Hazard had traced the stream to its source about thirty feet above his tent. A naked and rather hairy man held the trunk of the tree with one hand, and the trunk of his piss hose with the other.

"Fuck Jesus," Hazard was still waking up but could deduce though his fog that he had been joined in the night at the intersection of coordinates by his comrade, who had just baptized him with some residual droplets from his bladder. Still cussing under his breath, he reached inside his tent to grab his hooded sweatshirt and jeans, both of which he pulled on before the forest ape had lowered himself from his hanging tent. A jet passed overhead, making language pointless between them. They started out shaking hands but Hooknose suddenly pulled Hazard into a hug, patting him almost violently on the back before pushing out of the embrace to yell his greeting over the sounds of industry.

"Some wilderness sanctuary you've picked here," Hazard added once the engines gained a bit more distance.

"Shrinking around us more and more everyday, isn't it?" Hooknose looked toward the tent and then dove his still mostnaked body through the unzipped flaps. "Let's talk!" he shouted.

Hazard just stood there, barefoot in the pine needles. Seconds ticked by as his heart calmed down and the molecules of his shock dissipated into the waking forest. When he folded himself in half to enter the tent he found Hooknose snuggled inside his sleeping bag and propped up on one elbow. He wondered why he was intrigued instead of perturbed or put off by the thought of a strange man in his sleeping bag without any clothes on.

"Let's play Twenty Questions," Hazard suggested to break the ice that already lay scattered about them in shards.

"Sure," Hooknose agreed with more enthusiasm than anyone should have had that early in the morning.

Hazard realized in the silence that followed that he would need to initiate so he started off with an easy one: "Where were you born?"

"Coeur d'Alene."

"What is the ultimate deed you would do in defense of the environment?"

"Die."

"Are you an anarchist?"

"Of course." Hooknose held up a hand to indicate a score in the game and that he'd answered three questions so far.

"Should I keep going or do you want to ask me questions to catch up?" Hazard asked.

"No, I'm good, but that was your fourth question. Keep firing."

Hazard needed to bend his questions to be more open-ended.

He wouldn't learn much from yes and no responses. "Are you or are you not satisfied with the current level of eco-defense and why?"

"I'll answer that but so you know, you just asked three questions in one which makes seven down, thirteen to go after this. –No. Yes. And eco-defense has lost its original focus. Your stunt at Wal-Mart was brilliant but what did it have to do with eco-defense?"

"I'll answer that," Hazard smiled cleverly, "but then you'll be down to nineteen questions left. Box stores and pavement have chewed up more real estate in the past decade than all of industrialization in the entire previous century. The stormwater runoff from these impermeable surfaces chokes streams and rivers with car juices and redistributes and pollutes the natural hydrology."

"Did you just make up that statistic about the whole previous century?"

"Yes I did, and you're now down to eighteen questions."

"But you see my point? Your message to the public to reverse corporate greed had nothing to do with stormwater runoff."

"To answer your third question, I see your point. –Seventeen to go. Is it my turn?" Hazard asked, foolishly losing another of his opportunities, under his own rules.

" Be my guest," Hooknose invited, "but that was a question so you're down to twelve."

"Shit!" Hazard scolded himself. "What has been your most outrageous criminal activity so far?"

"Criminal by whose code?" Hooknose asked before he realized he had just wasted one of his remaining seventeen questions.

"U.S. Penal Code."

"Arson of a golf course country club pro-shop, I suppose. It caused the most damage. I tried to raise public awareness around the use of fertilizers and pesticides within a fragile watershed. I say I tried because the message got a little mixed up when NAELFPO's spokesman got in front of the cameras."

"You mean, Marmot got it wrong?"

"That's another question. I think you're down to nine questions left."

"Ten," Hazard clarified.

"Yeah, I mailed an announcement to the Portland office claiming responsibility on behalf of ELF but must not have included enough specifics. By the time Rosenburg, I mean, Marmot, did his research, he uncovered a golf course expansion plan that I didn't even know about, and that became the reason for the ELF action. It didn't matter in the end." Hooknose's hand, which had been propping up his head, disappeared inside the sleeping bag and seemed to be after an itch.

Hazard knew how to come up with the hard questions on the spot. He fired another one, number ten, as a matter of record. "If you had advance knowledge of 9/11, would you have stopped it?"

"Hell no!" Hooknose answered without hesitation. "What do you have to eat?"

"That, my new friend, is your fifth question." Hazard reached for his backpack and with hardly any effort at all, produced a breakfast of rice cakes, trail mix and half a Ritter Sport chocolate bar. In setting the table between them, which was the exposed edge of his sleeping pad that never seemed to stay in the one place he needed it—beneath his sleeping bag while he slept—he plopped down his Nalgene bottle of grape Kool-Aid without sugar. It was simple, not to mention economical, to add Kool-Aid packets to his water, the pureness and plainness of which he had never fully appreciated, ironically.

Stuffing a handful of trail mix in his mouth, Hooknose formulated his next question. He took a swig of the sour purple liquid, made a face and let the sleeping bag fall from his upper torso as he sat with his legs crossed inside the bag that had bunched up just above his waist. "If you suddenly found yourself alone with George W. Ambush, what would you do?"

Hazard really didn't need to think about his answer. He'd thought about this very question himself, lots. What true American hadn't? He often wondered whatever happened to the dubious art of assassination and what it would take to bring it back into vogue. "Well, of course I'd kill him to spare Humanity, but first, I'd humiliate him in a way like he's humiliating the United States; maybe post naked pictures of him on the Internet to show off his inadequacies, his own feces smeared all over his body. Yeah. Something like that."

Hooknose was suddenly nauseated and blamed it on the suggestion of seeing that idiot naked. "How will you know when you can trust me?"

"It's a judgment based on feeling. Don't worry. I'm getting there."

"How will I know that I can trust you?" Hooknose was burning up his allotment of questions quickly.

"I can't determine that for you."

Hooknose smiled, revealing the most un-anarchist-like teeth Hazard had ever seen. "Have you ever worked for the U.S. Government?"

Hazard showed his own dental assets. "I'm working for them now," he stated as matter of fact as he could, knowing his interrogator wouldn't believe him anyway. "You?"

"You're out of questions. I don't have to answer that."

"But we're playing Twenty Questions."

"And you've asked ten. I've asked nine with one to go. That makes twenty questions." Hooknose squinted one of his eyes and lifted one half of his smile into a thinking gesture. "Have you ever been naked with another man in the same sleeping bag?"

Hazard was sure the blood had just left his face much like how the ocean retreats just before a tsunami hits.

"Answer the question," Hooknose prodded.

"Not yet, I haven't."

"Well, nothing establishes trust faster than being naked together."

Wanting very much to change the subject, Hazard pressed for a review of the rules. "Playing Twenty Questions means we each get to ask twenty, not ten questions a piece. It's my game."

"Take off your shorts and climb in here with me, and I'll let you ask me ten more questions."

"It's a mummy bag, for Christ's sake. We wouldn't have room to inhale at the same time."

Hooknose's smile indicated that he wasn't going to back down, withdraw the question or lose any advantage he'd gained in the escalating game of wits between them. Hazard needed to be able to ask another ten questions. As it stood, he didn't have enough answers to file a news brief much less a full-blown exposé. He inhaled deeply, shoved his jeans down his legs and peeled off his hooded sweatshirt. With not nearly enough grace to avoid injury, Hazard clumsily threaded his feet and legs into the sleeping bag, past the initial logjam of his opponent's aroused nether region and hairy thighs until he was more or less face to face, peanut breath to peanut breath, with a man he was growing to revere. Growing became the operative word in the next minute as every nerve ending in his body registered the sensation of being man to man in a confined space.

"You've earned ten more questions," Hooknose said looking nearly cross-eyed into Hazard's eyes in their close proximity. Deeper down, inside the sleeping bag, he felt his friend swelling to press against him in exactly the right places.

"I can no longer think of anything I need to know about you," Hazard admitted. "I trust you."

Hooknose smiled, staring now at the lips that weren't more than an inch away from his own. His breathing deepened as absolutely everything intensified inside the mummy bag.

After twenty-eight years of experiencing what could only qualify as clinical androgyny, Hazard felt suddenly and animalistically sexual. It wasn't that he could be labeled a virgin as he'd experienced sex with others exactly twice before this: once with a woman and once with a man—though not in a sleeping bag, so he hadn't lied. He had emerged from that particular apples and oranges experiment convinced that he frankly preferred sex with himself, and then lived the next decade or so of his life accordingly faithful. Now, as he traced with the fingers from two hands the bridge of the crooked nose of the man whose nakedness threatened to extinguish him, he realized what he'd been missing just as tear tracks unfurled like welcome streamers over the topography of his cheeks. The greenness of the tent exaggerated the olive-ness of their complexions; the bluish veins plumbing the underskin bulged out as though they had been x-ray accentuated.

Hooknose cradled his nose and mouth near the Adam's apple of Hazard's neck and surfaced like a submarine toward the surface of his left ear where he whispered, "It is perfectly acceptable to want to fall in love with this moment but comrades mustn't fall in love with each other or they risk unpardonable infidelity to the cause."

"Was that Marx?"

"No. It *is* Hooknose—and he trusts you."

August 18, 2002
Elves Mount Tri-State Rampage
By Natalie Wesson

So far, in this Summer of 2002, Ecotage has become as common and scattered as the rains in the Pacific Northwest, as environmental activists, dubbed eco-terrorists, hopscotch haphazardly—or not so—across the counties in Oregon, Washington and Idaho with possibly related incidents now under investigation in Northern California and across the border in British Columbia.

The Earth Liberation Front has been active worldwide, mostly in England, since the 1970s and in the U.S. since the early 1980s. It is loosely organized around a rigid adherence to three operating guidelines: to inflict economic damage on those profiting from the destruction and exploitation of the natural environment; to reveal and educate the public on the atrocities committed against the earth and all species that populate it; and to take all necessary precautions against harming any animal, human and nonhuman.

Regional authorities seem baffled by the sudden escalation of activity in the past 16 weeks in the Pacific Northwest compared to last summer, which almost "amounted to a hiatus by statistical comparison" according to FBI Northwest Bureau Chief Red Harvey, speaking from his Portland office. Harvey admits that those who would resort to destruction of private and government property in defense of the planet are more than making up for any lost time.

The Summer of 2002 has been punctuated by the occasional development which never quite leads to the break in the string of cases that Homeland Security and the Joint Terrorism Task Force desperately need in order to demonstrate some measure of effectiveness in the war against domestic terror. Convinced that this summer's attacks were being coordinated by a single mastermind—despite the Earth Liberation Front's insistence that its activists operate independently and non-hierarchically—the FBI intercepted a series of emails that led them to suddenly clamp down on Oregon State Penitentiary prisoner Libre Salazar on June 13.

According to a former cellmate, Salazar, who is serving 22 years and 8 months under Oregon's controversial Mandatory Minimum Sentencing law for the arson of three vehicles, was rushed in his cell by four security guards who placed him in handcuffs and dragged him to "the Hole," where he is spending a total of 120 days in solitary confinement. Prison officials explained that Salazar had been advanced to the prison's Security Threat Group (STG) and needed to be isolated from the general population and the outside world. It has also been learned that in addition to the isolation and a no-contact gag order, Salazar has been slapped with a 21-day loss of privileges and has been further penalized 100 days of good behavior time. He is only eligible to earn a maximum reduced sentence of 15 months for good behavior during his entire 22-year incarceration. Prison officials and the FBI/JTTF have declined an opportunity to comment on the intercepted outbound emails and have declined requests by both this newspaper and representatives from Amnesty International to speak directly with Salazar, saying it is an internal matter in an open and ongoing investigation.

As the following chronology would indicate, in the first 60 days of Salazar's STG isolation, incidents of destruction to property and corporate assets claimed by ELF appear to have doubled over the number of incidents that occurred in the 60 days before Salazar was stripped of privileges and removed from gen-pop at OSP.

Chronology of Recent Earth Liberation Front Actions

August 12, 2002 – Bend, OR – The High Desert Museum outside of Bend was the site of an arson that destroyed the replica Lazinka Sawmill used to reenact practices of the logging industry in the last century. Lost in the fire was an authentic 48-inch saw blade from the 1950s that was believed to have ripped through millions of timber board feet during the heyday of the industry.

August 2, 2002 – Springfield, OR – Ignition wires were cut on 17 trucks and vehicles at the Springfield Gravel Mine. ELF later claimed responsibility, demanding a stop to gravel mining within the flood plains of all rivers in the state.

July 27, 2002 – Klamath Falls, OR – Incendiary devices were used after hours at the Home Depot to start a fire in the Redwood decking lumber to protest, as ELF later claimed, the logging of ancient Redwood forests.

July 10, 2002 – Auburn, WA – Members of ELF assumed responsibility for spiking trees throughout a demonstration forest directly adjacent to the world headquarters of Weyerhauser. Graffiti and broken windows caused several thousand dollars in damages.

July 6, 2002 – Moscow, ID –The Earth Liberation Front officially claimed responsibility for sabotaging the University of Idaho biotechnology building in opposition to genetic engineering. This is the second strike by ELF at the new biotech building.

July 6, 2002 – Coos Bay, OR – In an ELF-claimed act of vandalism targeting a Wal-Mart Supercenter, an unidentified white powder was introduced through roof ventilation units that confounded authorities before lab results revealed the powder to be harmless Ore-Ida potato flakes. Graffiti on the roof of the building called for the reversal of corporate greed and contained elements similar to the tags left on dams in April.

July 4, 2002 – McCall, ID – Over 250 shovel holes destroyed the fairways of the barely one-year-old Whitetail Golf Club. ELF claimed responsibility in opposition to the club's planned expansion into sensitive ponderosa pine forest habitat.

July 1, 2002 (Canada Day) – Abbotsford, BC – In an ELF suspected act of arson believed to be in protest of a proposed coal-fired generation plant that is rumored will increase British Columbia's greenhouse gas emissions from electricity production by almost 120%, a BC Hydro field office was burned to the ground. Damages were calculated around the $220,000 mark.

June 29, 2002 – Brookings, OR – The Highway 101 bridge spanning the Oregon-California border south of Brookings was vandalized with the red spray-painted words "Welcome to ELF-land."

June 17, 2002 – Ilwaco, WA – At least 11 vehicles were damaged by spiked 2 x 4s buried in the sand at the multiple entrances to Long Beach, a popular drive-on beach between Ilwaco and Grassy Island. ELF claimed responsibility to raise awareness that vehicles allowed onto the sensitive eco-system of an ocean beach could not be tolerated.

June 10, 2002 – Randale, WA – An anonymous group of individuals claimed responsibility for placing spikes in hundreds of trees in Units 5, 6 and 7 of the Upper Greenhorn Timber Sale in the Cowlitz Valley Ranger District located in the Gifford Pinchot National Forest.

June 1, 2002 – Clatskanie, OR – ELF burned an office and fleet of 13 trucks at Jefferson Poplar Farms in Clatskanie. Simultaneously, ELF destroyed the office of Professor Toby Bradshaw, who was believed to be advancing the genetic modification of plants and trees at the University of Washington. The combined estimated total in damages was reported to have been in excess of $3 million.

May 12, 2002 – Bonneville Dam, WA – An ELF-claimed series of graffiti tags resembling bull's eye targets were discovered in and around the navigational locks of each of the eight dams on the Snake and Columbia rivers between the Lower Granite Dam west of Clarkston and the Bonneville Dam east of Portland.

April 26, 2002 – Moses Lake, WA – A utility building belonging to the Columbia Basin Irrigation Project operated by BLM was destroyed in an early morning arson claimed by ELF. In a communiqué, ELF explained that the Columbia River has been sucked nearly dry since the 1930s and that the river basin must be restored.

April 14, 2002 – Nez Perce National Forest, Lewiston ID – ELF claimed responsibility for spiking trees throughout the Otter Wing Timber Sale in the Nez Perce National Forest.

August 27, 2001 – Susanville, CA – ELF took credit for the setting of timed incendiary devices at the Bureau of Land Management's (BLM) Litchfield Wild Horse and

Burro Facility. The resulting fire caused approximately $85,000 in damages when a barn was burnt to the ground. In addition, the group cut through four 60-foot sections of wooden fence on corrals holding more than 200 wild horses in an attempt to liberate them from BLM.

Anne Martondale lowered the newspaper to the surface of the Ethan Allen dining room table where she staged her daily morning tea and paper ritual. With its star reporter still MIA, the *Eugene Register-Guard* had lazily reprinted the Wesson article from the Sunday edition of the *Seattle Times*. From where she sat, she could see out the kitchen window to Bret Meyer Brady's townhouse, where new tenants with a two-year-old had been renting and generally driving her insane while they worked through the terrible twos for the past four months. She hadn't seen one blip from Bret in months. In fact, she hadn't learned anything new as to his whereabouts or activities since he'd lied to her about being in India. The new tenants stated they were dealing directly with a property management company who rented the townhouse to them completely furnished after they'd boxed up and removed for storage any personal effects of the townhouse owner. Fishy, that. Fishy, everything.

She was dogged by the only explanations that seemed plausible given that eco-terrorism had been ramping up ever since her favorite American—who had once been active in that movement— had vanished now over four months ago. He must have somehow gotten sucked back into the underground movement. Could Bret Meyer Brady be the regional coordinator or perhaps the mastermind of the Pacific Northwest cell of Elves? Or, even more likely, perhaps he had been injected into the eco underworld by the FBI to act as a covert plant to lead them to the real mastermind of this terrorist cell? That theory had legs when she remembered how dodgy that agent had been in Portland when she'd first inquired about her missing person.

She returned to the chronology of events listed in the newspaper.

Believing that nothing was random, she began to wonder if there was a pattern staring at her that she could decipher somehow? Was it mathematical? Geographical? Or was there something hiding in the chronology? The Angela Lansbury of Eugene, Oregon, needed maps and more information.

Chewing the last bits of cooked batter from the wooden stick, the driver wondered when he died if the surely staggering statistics of his lifetime would be revealed to him by archangels armed with calculators and cholesterol charts. Specifically, he would want to know how many corndogs he'd eaten and how many bus miles he'd driven during this particular incarnation.

He walked gingerly to the rest stop washroom and into a stall where he relieved his bowels in a symphony of squirts and pops. It was one of those days, more regularly occurring the older he got, when his hemorrhoids were flaring into a perfect storm. He'd carried in with him a section from his copy of the *Seattle Times* he hadn't yet had the chance to finish. He'd been working through the Sunday edition in installments he strung together between rest stops and the boarding of new passengers. He'd spotted the headline of the article he was dying to read sticking above the comics as he headed out of Umatilla and Irrigon. That was two hours ago. The suspense and his hemorrhoids had been killing him ever since.

The smells of newsprint and diarrhea commingled as the man's fifty-six-year-old heart began to thump rapidly in his chest. It had amused him that over the years, the authorities had gone back and forth like a grandfather clock pendulum between suspecting a ringleader—and—being perpetually frustrated by the continued randomness of the illegal strikes in the woods without a single individual on whom they could pin any accountability. Now, suspecting that Libre Salazar was calling the shots from his cell in the state pen at least gave them a person they should be able to keep track of despite how ludicrous their suspicion was. It was a public relations move at best; a need to assure the public that they were making progress, closing in on a target, any target. Libre could barely follow the shots, much less call them, which was precisely how he'd gotten himself into his current predicament, as far as he could tell.

The bus driver wiped his ass with a wince, drawing blood. He lubricated his index finger with spit and then holding his breath, systematically reinserted the offending polyps inside his asshole where they didn't hurt quite as badly. Corporate would try to force him into retirement in another year and a half and not that he'd ever give them that satisfaction, but he couldn't help daydreaming about hobbies that required standing positions, like golf and gardening and terrorism.

Ted would have liked to catch up on his sleep during the fifty minutes the complete lockage would take at Ice Harbor, but he'd gotten into a *Seattle Times* article that had been passed to him by an Army Corps staffer at McNary who, for the better part of the last year, had been trying to unravel the mystery of how somebody had gained access to the navigation locks of every dam between Lewiston and Portland. Ted's first thoughts had turned to the stowaway on his own boat in March, but his encounters with Sergio had dispelled the notion that he either carried a grudge or a torch for any particular agenda, least of which an environmental one. Until just a few months ago, the civilian public would have had easy access to just about any part of the navigation locks on each of the dams during regular visiting hours anyway. Now that surveillance cameras had been installed as part of the Homeland Security response, he imagined someone would have a tougher time avoiding detection, but he'd seen plenty of opportunities for someone to buck the system. He supposed the collective paranoia kept him more vigilant and that was a good thing.

The newspaper did get him thinking about Sergio again. As the weeks without any contact stacked end to end like empty box cars rattling through what was left of his memories, it had gotten easier to believe he'd managed to get over the stowaway. He hadn't. His wife was pregnant again so it wasn't as if he'd shut down completely. It was of some concern to Ted DeHavlin that to get and keep an erection these days, he had to be thinking about a man and the imaginary man no longer had to be Sergio. The ultrasound had already determined that he had sired another boy and when he'd brashly suggested that they name him Sergio, his wife couldn't figure out why they should give their child the name of a terrorist. Ted had wanted to debate the logic but with a smile only detectable by his conscience, he let it go. He had only known one Sergio in this lifetime and he wasn't yet willing to bet his life that she was wrong.

Red Harvey wondered if his undercover plant would be flattered out of hiding and into the open by the mimicry of Natalie Wesson's ELF reporting since she used the exact same set-up and chronological format that he'd made standard in his enviro-mischief reporting days. But then, Red Harvey wondered a lot about his undercover agent lately. His activist turned reporter turned activist had ditched both his company laptop and agency-provided hideout cabin, plus he hadn't made an ATM withdrawal or checked in with the Portland office since before the somewhat unauthorized Wal-Mart incident last month in Coos Bay. It wasn't unusual for assets that went deep to stay deep for a while, especially during the establishing phase, but all the activity getting attributed to the Earth Liberation Front in the past several months had convinced the bureau chief, more than ever before, that the incidents were being coordinated like never before.

Of course, he didn't suspect Libre Salazar of being anything but a model prisoner, but when the penitentiary intercepted the email

Libre had written to Bret Meyer Brady's old email address, and when the response email that Red himself had penned back provoked Salazar to reply with an email that quite personally invited Red Harvey to fuck himself and not expect the reporter to amount to anything undercover, Red figured he'd better tuck the prisoner away and out of Internet reach for a few months. It was clear from the article that the prisoner had already shared his counter-espionage theory with the *Seattle Times* reporter or more likely vice versa.

Red knew that agents surfaced when agents got into trouble. At least on this side of the States United, which had always been more civil when disobedient, agents' lives generally weren't at risk if they fucked up or their IDs got made. Still, a post card would have been nice.

The creep from the mailroom—and she still had never bothered to learn his real name even though she'd filed an employee complaint against him when her mail was occasionally delivered preopened—glided his cart toward her cubicle wearing his trademark shit-eating grin. She busied herself on Google to appear disinterested and unaffected. She was at the disadvantage since she knew he knew about her relationship with the inmate in Oregon but he couldn't admit he knew without admitting he'd opened and read one or more of her letters. The red-hot secret of the newsroom was protected by this code but it didn't mean it was a comfortable arrangement for either side. The mail creep occasionally floated a trial blackmail balloon suggesting he would be a better fuck than her prison fantasy, but it never got him anywhere and he always seemed genuinely surprised by this. But today, he either lacked the energy or his ego was too fragile to take a hit she would surely launch before he'd lifted his weapon from its holster. Instead, he lobbed the only envelope addressed to her, an oversized manila without bubble, without even making eye contact. Ignoring her might make her want him. It was a new theory he was testing out but she wasn't in a mood to give him any indication whether or not it was working. *Silly Bitch*, he thought as he wheeled away, pretending to be unaffected.

Natalie turned the envelope over to see the source. There was nothing but her name, the address of the newspaper, and CONFIDENTIAL written a half dozen times. Not even a cancelled postmark could tell her where it originated, which made her wonder how it made it into the paper's mail system in the first place...unless it originated from within the building. Maybe it arrived inside another envelope that had been opened then discarded. If she'd known the mail creep's name, she'd call him back for an explanation, but she didn't. Maybe it was from him. Maybe these were his blackmail demands at last. The envelope was sealed at least. She opened the flap. The contents amounted to two pieces of paper with computer printing that looked like it might have been spit out of a dot matrix. The font was unnecessarily large, maybe 14 or 16 point and either Verdana or Arial or Tahoma, she mixed those three up all the time. It wasn't Times New Roman, which normally ruled her profession. That was for sure. And the effect, though it wasn't initially obvious why, may have been to mimic an old typewriter.

August 19, 2002

Dear N. Wesson:

With the closure earlier this year of the North American Earth Liberation Front Press Office (NAELFPO) in Portland and no reliable means to issue our communiqués, we are sending this media release directly to you as an experiment to determine whether or not you would like to be used in this way in exchange for getting first crack at the important news ELF is making around the Pacific Northwest, the country and around the world.

We have been appreciative of your unbiased reporting over the years and have long detected a sympathetic undertone when reading your work between the lines. In the fine tradition of journalists like Bob Woodward and Carl Bernstein who were aided in their roles as information disseminators during Watergate (which occurred before most of us were born), we would like to aid you in our mutual objective to maintain accuracy and clarity and advance our cause.

On the enclosed piece of paper, we have included a number of ELF-claimed activities that we don't think you intentionally missed in your chronology but may not have been aware of at the time you went to press yesterday. We will do a much better job of keeping you personally apprised and in a timely fashion in the future; this is of course if you are willing to take on this role.

As an added incentive to make sure you stay tuned, please know that nothing to date has been random and an orchestra of elves is just now tuning up for a concert the likes of which the Pacific Northwest has never heard. We are offering you a reserved seat for the biggest show in the woods. You just need to find your way to the theater. We are prepared to provide you the clues.

Now, to fill in the blanks in your chronology, please update your readers with the following:

July 4, 2002 The floating intake grate of Lake Chelan Dam north of Wenatchee was damaged in a midnight explosion on Independence Day. The strike by ELF was timed to raise awareness around the 109 years that the Chelan River has been imprisoned by dams and the need for this river to be returned to its free-flowing independence.

July 7, 2002 The staged-for-tourism Old West shootout in the tourist town of Winthrop, Washington, was marred by the discovery of graffiti that had been spray-painted on many of the Old West building facades overnight. The clearly printed tags carried Old West themed messages such as "Proud Tradition of Land Raping" and "WANTED Dead or Alive: Last of the Untamed Places." One tag in particular seemed to claim responsibility for the act of vandalism: "It's ELF High Noon."

July 13, 2002 The Cascade Tunnel through Stevens Pass in northern Washington State, the longest railroad tunnel in the U.S. at 7.8 miles, was closed for nine hours yesterday as investigators combed the site for an alleged bomb that had been planted and set to detonate by trip wire, according to an anonymous message received by the Seattle office of Homeland Security. The bomb, according to the message, was placed to raise awareness of the transport of toxic chemicals by rail along the environmentally sensitive headwaters originating in the Cascade Mountains.

July 14, 2002 Concrete, Washington (Home of the Superior Portland Cement Company)—a four-story-tall and five-cylinder-wide concrete grain elevator at the entrance to the community that normally welcomes visitors with the message "Welcome to Concrete" was draped by a banner that read: "How the West was Dammed."

July 19, 2002 Seattle—a half-built 9,600-sq-ft, $3m house under construction close to Seattle was gutted by fire and left behind, draped on a front gate, was a crude message scrawled in spray paint on a sheet: *We found the missing forest! Forests burn, naturally!* it said. This is the latest in a series of so-called McMansion attacks that have happened all over the country but with particular regularity in the Pacific Northwest.

July 22, 2002 Hoh River, Olympic Peninsula, Washington—the proposed site of a wilderness camp expansion, high on the Hoh River, by Three Rivers Resort, Ltd., was redecorated overnight by forest fairies who pulled up survey posts, moved flagging tape and collected chainsaws and other equipment valued close to $5,000 into a cargo net that was found suspended fifty feet above the forest floor between trees in an ingenious manner that prevented workers from immediately recovering it. The Hoh River Rainforest is one of the largest and last remaining tracts of temperate coastal rainforest that is supposed to be protected from human exploitation. A tourism permit issued to Three Rivers Resort, Ltd., earlier this year by the National Park Service stunned environmentalists and members of the nearby Hoh River Tribe.

July 27, 2002 The Apex Mountain Resort near Penticton, B.C., was the target of environmental saboteurs who caused thousands of dollars in damages to water diversion equipment, pumps and piping. The resort annually diverts between 160 and 200 acre-feet of water from Nickel Plate Lake for snow-making purposes. The levels of water in this lake are to be maintained by International Treaty between the USA and Canada.

Correct this accounting, N. Wesson, and we believe you will be in a position to not only record history but be recorded as having played a role in making it.

ELF

LIBRE SAT NAKED ON THE FLOOR IN THE CORNER OF HIS CELL IN SOLITARY, rocking forward and then backward, watching his abdominal muscles bulge in the joke-of-a-light thrown from a 25-watt appliance bulb. The guards hadn't stripped him but to protest this unprovoked mistreatment, he'd shoved his jumpsuit through the food flap nine days ago. They didn't give it back. Prisoner #13797671 had been alternating between push-ups, naps, sit-ups and vocally amplified masturbation sessions ever since. His protest wasn't necessarily focused around a unified cause or demand, but it wasn't unnoticed either. The guard, who in the past year had made no bones about Libre being his favorite prisoner, had switched shifts and taken overtime to guard the Solitary cells. This was the same guard who hadn't returned his jumpsuit but knew how to operate the food flap like Pavlov's dog every time Libre began to moan rhythmically. Libre knew this guard was his savings account and he didn't hesitate to invest heavily.

Hooknose knew better than to phone Greyhound on his cell-phone but they had an emergency. Two nights earlier he and Hazard had spent too much time waiting for a security guard to duck indoors so they could cut through a fence not far from the Third Powerhouse to access the giant light projection lamps that normally lobbed kaleidoscopic colors onto the concrete screen that was once the world's largest cement project—now known as Grand Coulee Dam. Once they finally got inside the projection fence they waited nearly an hour for the lamps to cool after they'd been turned off for the night. By then it was after midnight, which hadn't left them much time. The two carefully applied decals to four of the six lamp lenses; black vinyl stencils they had cut with an Exacto knife so that the now well-known biohazard and target symbols that had long been their signatures could shine through the removed bits of the vinyl. The time-consuming part of this mission had been painting several layers of clear nail polish over the decals to encase them in Lucite to keep them from melting when the lights came back on and make them extra difficult to remove once discovered.

The reason the pair was in trouble now, nearly forty-eight hours later, stemmed from a disagreement that had escalated into an argument followed by a stalemate between them over whether or not it was safe to "hang out" another day. This had been Hazard's preference as he wanted to see the fruits of their labor when the lights came on the dam the next night. Hooknose had been much more practical in laying his argument that they needed to keep moving or they'd fall behind a rather ambitious schedule that included seven more targets on their geocache scavenger hunt before their rendezvous with another activist called Greyhound at 46°30'53"N, 116°17'48"W on the 27th of August. Apparently this was one day before an historically significant date for which the trio had been orchestrating every movement so that they could be in position to celebrate it in their own mischievous way.

But a development in the past twelve hours proved to be the biggest challenge the pair had faced in their nearly 45-day-long tag-team rampage. Security cameras below Grand Coulee had picked up some very grainy images that had been turned into modern-day WANTED posters distributed among local and state authorities: posters complete with their height, hair colors, facial hair characteristics, clothing and the fact that it had been two men working in tandem. They had spent the past forty-five minutes altering what they could of their images without going into a store for masquerade supplies, where they might have been identified or photographed.

Hazard had shaved his brown pony-tailed head completely bald. This hadn't been easy considering his hair had gotten to be eight or ten inches long and all he had was a Bic disposable razor in the bottom of his pack that he hadn't even used on his face in over a month. Hooknose shaved his face and with a pocketknife he cut his hair so that it would part on the side. This gave him a look as remarkably clean cut as a missionary or perhaps more apropos— the college professor that he was. It had made Hooknose sexy as hell to his comrade-currently-not-in-arms due to the argument, and Hazard longed to replicate the intimacy they had discovered in the sleeping bag on their first encounter.

As their circumstances conspired, they were stuck with lousy odds, camped outside Electric City in a ditch about two miles up a treed ravine from Highway 155. Hooknose was terrified to make a move by foot and had placed the rescue call to arrange a rubber tire intercept. As he waited for his personal Eco Angel to return the voicemail he'd left, as had been their established protocol for emergency contact, Hooknose grew more and more paranoid. Every dog bark and distant siren made him think authorities were closing in on their location. His face was awash in sweat in the August desert heat. He was all but despondent over the decision not to move under the cover of darkness before the sun had risen earlier in the day. It had been the sloppily cut fence that prompted Corps staff to review the surveillance tapes from the previous night. Neither vandal could be sure their whole sabotage had been discovered, but it had been a misstep not to have put that fence back together, something they couldn't afford to take if they wanted to keep moving freely.

The Eco Angel hadn't returned their call. It had been over half an hour that the two had been sitting in silence, Hooknose checking the signal on his cellphone every thirty seconds and Hazard scheming to somehow break the tension between them. They had squirmed naked in a sleeping bag six weeks ago when they'd first teamed up south of Seattle and even though neither of them had gotten off at the time Hazard had interpreted their first contact as sexual. To his budding homosexual lament, the two of them hadn't shared more than a tent and this lousy mission since.

Hazard wondered if Hooknose had only been burning off nervous energy back then while establishing a trust between them. He would have liked to help him burn off his nervous energy now, but there seemed no opening in the moment or his sleeping bag. It's like they had been using entirely different decoder rings ever since July 7. That and they'd been kept pretty task-oriented working through the never-ending list of coordinates they'd been sent by an ELF operative codenamed *Greyhound*. Hooknose had apparently spent time with this Greyhound in the woods of North Central Idaho, training and conspiring with this cream of the eco-sabotage crop, to hear Hooknose gush about it. As far as Hazard could tell, this ringleader was still an unsolved mystery and he was pretty sure he'd never crossed paths with the legend, neither as a foot soldier in the early days nor as a reporter covering the movement.

With bifocals crookedly perched on the tip of his bulbous nose, the pores of which had been pried wide by years of gin drinking and pot smoking before his doctor had handed down the ultimatum to kick habits or push up daisies, the fifty-six-year-old left a potato chip grease trail on his computer monitor as his finger traveled down the matrix of available driver routes he could take. He needed to get within a hundred miles or so to afford a detour that would allow him to *pax-snatch*, a code term he'd invented a year or so back whenever he needed to extract activist passengers from anywhere in the Pacific Northwest where situations had the potential of getting sticky.

The pair he needed to reach in the next twelve to twenty-four hours was currently a state away but by linking Portland to the Tri-Cities and the Tri-Cities to Spokane, then Spokane to Wenatchee he could get close but it would require the boys to move their position another 30 miles southeast of Grand Coulee to the town of Wilbur. There was that, and the small matter that he still needed to con another driver into letting him take his Spokane route and ideally trade him for the Portland to Seattle turnaround that he needed to unload in order to make all this happen. With his guts twisting again, he carried the mobile phone to the toilet where he phoned dispatch to get both his bowels and his wheels in motion.

Natalie had kept her part of the bargain. She'd printed the addendum she'd received nearly verbatim in the next day's edition.

The mailroom creep had made a grand detour through the press room to pass her desk with no mail and a knowing smirk that she couldn't source. Her intuition was screaming, DANGER, DANGER, but she knew she was dealing with a common man pig, a genus she was more than familiar with classifying and avoiding.

She'd done what the ELF operatives asked of her. Now she waited.

The day's sun was directly overhead with nothing and nobody casting a shadow anywhere. Hazard watched Hooknose watching everything else but him. The two waited.

The guard with the crush had indicated to Libre that administration was planning to return him to gen-pop sometime today. He had also returned his jumpsuit, which came through the food flap folded and smelling Downy fresh. Libre wondered not if but how many times the guard had tried on his prison issue wardrobe and drifted off to sleep naked in it. He wondered about that and he waited.

Anne took a mental break from *Physics and Philosophy: The Revolution in Modern Science* for a cup of tea. She hadn't been able to concentrate for love or science today. She'd been obsessing over her missing neighbor again. She went through spells. She hadn't had any communication from Brct since receiving his bluff travelogue from India nearly a month and a half ago. She should have called him on that but instead had sent a reply advising him not to miss the *Basant Panchami* Festival in Andhra Pradesh Province. She was such an enabler. And all she could do was stew and wait.

Red Harvey was one frustrated man on too many levels to know where the analysis should begin. He'd hit his professional peak during the first Clinton administration. Before that, he'd weathered the political pendulum toward the end of the first Bush Dynastic period but *9/11* less than a year ago had accelerated his career aging process one hundred fold and Bureau Life in this Golden Age of Bullshit was ridiculous and ludicrous and wholly unsatisfying. This month was turning out to be one of the most brazen periods of propaganda pandering he'd ever witnessed. August 1— *White House projects highest deficit ever.* August 2—*The Department of Homeland Security raises the terror alert at several large financial institutions in the New York City and Washington areas.*

It wasn't the national deficit or the financial institutions under *dire and imminent threat*; it was the general intelligence of Americans that was in danger of being re-engineered. It was no longer elitist to be an insider and these days he felt confined and imprisoned by his career, an inmate of the Bureau, serving his time—no better and no worse off than that poor fuck, Libre Salazar.

THE SUN STILL LOBBED THE LAST OF ITS STUBBORN REFLECTION ON THE reservoir's surface below the ravine, filtered through a haze of yellow onion harvest dust and a tapestry of heat waves you could weave with a naked eye. It had seemed too early to Hazard to be making a move but he didn't say so, since the two had made a day's ritual out of not speaking to each other. Their transport had been arranged but they needed to hoof it some twenty-eight miles southeast to get into the pick-up zone.

They'd been walking parallel to a banked railroad track that Hazard had been studying about a half a mile to their left. In his silent contemplation he daydreamed of hopping an open boxcar, something he'd never done, and taking this load off his feet, not the pack on his back so much but this whole scavenger hunt bullshit that didn't seem to be taking him anywhere particularly fast. If there were a method to the random madness they'd been exacting, it was escaping him faster than the original purpose for agreeing to get involved in the first place. He hadn't exactly come across anything revelatory or page turning as far as his book deal was concerned. So far, by his accounting, he'd been given the exclusive rights on a book that wouldn't sell, wouldn't inform, and certainly wouldn't justify the time he'd cut from his life, which, while he was being honest, hadn't been particularly captivating either. As the sun began to dip behind the hills and with every rock that made him stumble or break the cadence that their breakneck pace had established, he grew more and more frustrated and realized he needed to either provoke or be a part of something sensational, and soon. That, or he'd have to come to terms with the realization that writing for the *Register-Guard* may not have been so boring after all and perhaps he should stop dodging sagebrush and just get back to it.

Then, with his eyes following a hawk (or was it a vulture?), Hazard spotted a freight train in the distance over his left shoulder. Reflexively he spoke, words forcing their way past the mucus that comes from inactivity to make sounds. He cleared his throat and said it again. "There's a train we could jump if you're worried about time," he offered an option to his silent and hairy friend, who had stripped off his T-shirt a few miles back.

Hooknose looked toward the train, then to his companion, which only reminded him how much he preferred to travel solo, walked a few more dusty steps and then broke into a trot toward the tracks. Hazard wished he hadn't said anything. He was in no mood to run in this heat, but he jogged to catch up before breaking into more of a sprint taking the lead. The pair ran through a dry creek bed of a gully about 100 meters from the train track, staying low out of sight until the train's engines had passed them. Then like synchronized swimmers, the two bolted out of the desert and dashed to the tracks. It wasn't a box-car train. It seemed to be mostly top loader cars full of wood chips with no logical place to jump on, plus it was traveling faster than in any movie either of them had ever seen. Still, adrenaline propelled them forward. Hazard was the first to make contact with metal, grabbing a side pole that nearly wrenched his shoulder ball out of its joint. He was on. He secured a leg and an arm around the pole and reached out to Hooknose whose face revealed he was struggling.

"Throw me your pack!"

"Fuck!" Hooknose exploded, snatching the pack off his shoulders and lobbing it toward the train. Hazard picked it out of the air and shoved it behind him. Hooknose ran faster. Hazard's arm re-extended for the assist and in that instant, Hooknose vanished.

He'd twisted his ankle in a gopher hole and went down with a thud even he couldn't hear over the clanking of the train, launching an exclamation mark–shaped dust cloud.

Hazard's breath caught in his throat as his head flushed all the blood it contained. The train's whistle sounded somewhere in front of him. He could no longer see where Hooknose had gone down. He couldn't think rationally, only emotionally, as he jumped from the train, tucking into a roll to absorb the shock to his joints. They were a team, even though they hadn't been speaking to each other in the past twenty-four hours. Teams stick together, he thought, brushing the dust off his torso. Where did he come up with this shit, he wondered in the next second. *Teams stick together?* There were no teams in journalism. He didn't play organized sports. He'd never been in the armed forces.

Shaking the intruding masculine notion from his skull, he bounded into a half jog running against the direction of the train toward his injured comrade, fallen soldier, teammate. It wasn't until the last car lumbered past him and silence began to restore itself in the barren landscape that he remembered he'd jumped off the train without the other pack. His hiking boots skidded in the dirt as he turned to look back at the train now at least an eighth of a mile away. He didn't have to wonder if he'd fucked up. He knew it. From this distance, and he suspected even up close, every one of the woodchip cars looked identical and he didn't know if he had been on a car in the middle of the train or toward the front of it. Every second his mind scrambled to make sense of the situation, the train rambled another twenty track lengths away from him where he stood dumbfounded and dry heaving in the desert.

"Hook!" he yelled from panic as loud as he could. He raised his sunglasses, squinting his focus to detect movement. He began running along the tracks toward the spot he'd lost his partner. The longer Hazard ran the more amazed he was by the inconceivable distance he'd traveled on the train. Finally he spotted Hooknose red-faced and gasping in agony. He shed his backpack, letting it drop to the ground, as he crumpled to a skidding stop in the dirt next to him.

"You came back for me?" Hooknose sputtered.

"Of course I did, you lame ass!" Hazard propped his friend's back with his hand as Hooknose rose to sit so they could examine his ankle and assess their rotten luck.

"It's the left ankle but I don't think it's broken."

Hazard traced the hairy leg with both hands starting perhaps unnecessarily high on the thigh for an ankle injury. He caught Hook giving him a knowing roll of his eyes. The ankle was swollen but there weren't any bones sticking out of the skin. Hazard couldn't have dealt with that anyway, so it was a good thing. "Can we try to put some weight on it?"

"I don't think that's a good idea," Hooknose grimaced.

"Well, when I look at our fugitive options, we can try to walk out of here, wait for the next train or become vulture food."

"You didn't have to come back."

"Right." Hazard went to his backpack and extracted a T-shirt from the top, a shirt he'd likely worn several days in a row since he couldn't remember the last time he'd had cleaned clothes. He ripped the shirt into one long bandage and began gingerly but tightly wrapping the swollen ankle. He grabbed his water bottle and undid the cap, passing it to Hooknose. "Let's see if we have a cell signal out here." The words formed a sentence that fell out and into the air between them like rocks on glass. The cellphone would be in the pack he'd left on the train. Hazard held his breath.

"There's no signal out here," Hooknose proclaimed. End of discussion.

Another five minutes and the two were standing with considerable effort, Hooknose draping his arm and at least a third of his body weight over the shoulder of his mate. "I gotta piss," he stated.

Hazard looked at him and sensed a duty to give him a spot of privacy, though it wasn't what he wanted to do. He waited for the one-legged wonder to establish balance and took a step and faced away. Hooknose scanned the immediate terrain, taking out his dick. He spotted his target and directed his aim to fill the gopher hole that had very nearly taken him out of the game. As a terrorist smirk broke across his shaven face already showing a healthy shadow, Hooknose began to lose his balance. He hadn't stopped pissing but managed to get out just two words, "ah, shit," before toppling into Hazard, who had been ready and hoping for the catch and a chance to break his fall. He hadn't counted on getting pissed on, but then, beggars couldn't be that specific.

The two recovered after a good laugh and began hobbling along the tracks, fences between them apparently repaired. The ripe scent of perspiration and urine filled Hazard's nose with a debilitating rush. Hazard scooped up his pack as nonchalantly as he could and they struggled along for about a quarter mile, stopping frequently as the hissing and grunts indicated they should.

"Where's my gear?" Hooknose's demand suddenly pierced the membrane of silence with a double-edged saber.

Hazard thought of all the ways he could answer the question, settling perhaps just a tad too quickly on "my guess is Kennewick."

IF HAZARD THOUGHT HE'D BEEN GETTING THE SILENT TREATMENT AT GRAND Coulee, it had been a spirited dialogue with numerous inputs compared to the stone-cold détente between the three of them since their intercept outside the town limits of Wilbur, Washington. It didn't exactly help the conversation move along that the bus driver fed Hooknose a small fistful of Tylenol Codeine 3s after which he proceeded to verbally dismiss Hazard as a *complete idiot* for having left the backpack on the train—the entire inventory of which had been interrogated out of a quickly fading Hooknose:

- Disposable cellphone (without the battery, which Hazard carried separately as was standard protocol so the cell signal couldn't be tracked)
- Magellan handheld GPS
- Pocket knife
- Dirty shorts
- Hook's favorite ratty Greenpeace T-shirt
- Toothbrush and other minimal on-the-fly toiletries
- The mobile phone number for a river barge captain friend of his
- His treasured REI Kilo Plus Zero sleeping bag
- A quote by Henry Crow Dog that Hooknose had laminated himself at a Kinko's somewhere, handwritten by and given to him by Libre Salazar as he left the courtroom in Portland, Oregon, after being sentenced to 22 years, 8 months. The

quote, which even a drugged Hooknose could deliver by heart, was:

> I am preparing the sweat lodge for the Ghost Dance. —Not the old Ghost Dance, which was supposed to roll up the white's Earth and bring back the Indian Earth underneath, but a new-old spirit. It is like raindrops making a tiny brook, many drops making a stream, many streams making a mighty river bursting all dams. We are the first raindrops.

- And the last item he could remember, but didn't dare list off for Greyhound, was a ragged notebook of some, though not nearly all, of their assigned target coordinates (which he'd been specifically ordered never to keep in the first place).

They'd been traveling in silence just the three of them on the bus, for twenty minutes, Hazard figured maybe thirty miles, before the driver addressed him. Hooknose had drug-plunged into sleep in the last seat, which stretched the width of the bus save for the onboard bathroom, his badly twisted leg elevated on Hazard's backpack, Hazard's windbreaker holding in his body heat. Hazard had wandered back up the aisle to sit within listening range of the driver, should he choose to rip another piece off him. And he did.

"Do you even remember me from Coos Bay?" the driver asked so abruptly that it startled Hazard.

"Coos Bay?" Hazard played dumb, not something he ever pulled off well. He watched the driver watch him through the rear-view mirror, his eyes narrowing with impatience. "I take it you were my bus driver?"

"No, I was the clerk that sold you the case of Ore-Ida potato flakes," he deadpanned, knowing so much more than he should have about that particular operation. "Of course I was your bus driver."

Hazard couldn't remember the extent of their previous interaction but he could be pretty sure he hadn't confessed the details of his transgression to a complete stranger. "Well, thanks for the lift—I guess."

The driver was chewing gum with his mouth open, creating a smacking rhythm that matched the syncopation of the windshield wipers that were pressed into service as they passed Fairchild Air Force Base nearing the outskirts of Spokane. The gum was intended to take and keep his mind off his twisting intestines, innards that protested the introduction of what had been the latest in greasy, un-nutritional roadside cuisine. The driver had made a two-decade-long habit of eating behind the wheel out of boredom and he tended to junk-food binge out of nervousness and, of course, convenience since every other hour or so, he was making a stop at some hole along the highway. And he always paid for it. He was paying for it now.

"Look, there isn't anything about this little wrinkle in the plan that I am happy about, so I won't even pretend to be cordial with you," the driver groaned as his stomach launched into a particularly wrenching cramp.

"Yeah, I'd hate for you to have to make any effort, here," Hazard snapped back, suddenly feeling pissed. It wasn't his fault Hook twisted an ankle. He hadn't thrown Hook's pack on the train. And if anyone wanted to get technical about their arrangement, he wasn't Hook's keeper or guardian. "And I had the impression anyway that this plan was a tad organic at best. Strike when you can, where you can, and when it made sense. Random. You know? Anarchy and chaos at their most unpredictable."

"Random?" The driver looked at Hazard through his rearview mirror. "Like nobody is in control, calling the shots?"

"Well, are *you*? Is anybody?" Hazard watched billboards and highway exit signage whiz past the windshield in the high-beam–headlighted rain. "I've been traipsing all over the Pacific Northwest like a Mexican jumping bean these past few months and aside from a few inspired moments, it hasn't made a helluva lot of sense to me. Maybe I'm tired and I know the weather's about to change in another month. Maybe I'm getting older and I'm just not as cut out for espionage as I was earlier in my twenties. But Jesus, give me a break! I'd be a shitload more effective if I had an air-conditioned bus with suspension seating for my broken ass when it comes to schlepping mayhem across this territory."

"And just where do you think your targets come from?"

"Hooknose and I get to a place and we figure it out. We take a look around and see what's fucked up and we come up with a way to exploit it for publicity's sake."

"But where do you think the idea for the place comes from? You think you two are just drifting on the wind? Where'd you get the idea to hit a Wal-Mart in Coos Bay? You were fed information. You and Hooknose have been going places you were told to hit. I will give you credit for some of the ways you've left your calling card."

"The hell I've been fed information!" Hazard had to stop and think about this. He'd long cut communication ties to the agency that planted him headfirst in this mess. Early on at the cabin when he was running solo, he would chat with other eco-riddlers on Hotmail and get ideas, sure. That's how he linked up with Hooknose in the first place. After that, he mostly let Hook point out the direction they would head next. Yes, he knew about the notebook where Hooknose recorded GPS coordinates but it hadn't occurred to him until just this second that he might have been writing down the next set of coordinates and not simply recording the spot of the deed just done. "Wal-Mart in Coos Bay was my idea, mine alone."

"Was it?" the driver asked, raising his forehead to create more lines than could be found on a notebook page. "You weren't chatting online the week before with someone named *Greyhound*?" he emphasized. "Someone who mentioned what a big, fat corporate target a certain new Superstore would make?"

"Greyhound?" Hazard repeated out loud. "As in the racing dog?"

"Or, maybe more like as in the bus? Duh!"

"You were—? I mean, you're *Greyhound*?"

"Not very original, I suppose, given my profession."

"So that's why you can just swoop in and pick us up in the official middle of nowhere?"

"Genius. Like I said, I'll give you credit for some of your calling cards. I don't think I would have thought to use Ore-Ida Potato Flakes."

"So you're running this show then?"

"More or less."

"Which is it?"

"Well, you really can't *run* an autonomous collective of eco-terrorists."

"What collective? I'm getting the sense that it's only Hooknose and me stirring up the shit anymore. The only hits I hear or read about are ours."

The driver held his tongue between his teeth waiting for a cramp to pass. There were times he came so close to shitting his pants that it became a battle of mind over fecal matter. The irony was never lost on him that he was driving a *Honey Bucket* on wheels but the kind of explosive movements he had would have rendered seats seventeen and back uninhabitable without full-face respirators or open-able windows. "I'm going to hit this truck stop." He signaled to pull off Interstate 90. With the bus in park, but left idling, he rifled through a side pocket and produced a day-old *Seattle Times*. "You're not the only two making headlines. I'll be right back. Mind the wheels." He slapped the newspaper into the chest of his passenger. "Where do these egos come from," he mumbled as he descended the stairs with his butt cheeks clenched so tightly it was a struggle to chart forward progress.

Natalie felt used. No wonder Bret Meyer Brady from the *Eugene Register-Guard* specialized in eco-terrorism stories all those years; he never had to write anything, she thought out loud. Easiest assignment in North America covering the Earth Liberation Front since everything came packaged completely scripted and ready to drop into 8 point Times New Roman with ½" left/right margins. She let the opened newspaper crumple into her lap. She was sick of being a one-trick pony. This wasn't journalism. It was plagiarism.

The manila-colored envelope caught her eye sticking out of a stack of papers. She extracted it to examine it more closely. Just like the times before, this envelope didn't have a postmark either. The ELF press release had arrived on her desk in this skin, addressed to her attention, seemingly without having gone through a postal or delivery service. Had it been couriered, she wondered? There was one little creep who should have the answer. Natalie rose from her desk, straightened her blouse and prepared to descend into the bowels of the oppressive Art Deco four-story concrete building— four stories if you counted the basement level with the truck loading bays—that occupied the entire block on John Street.

The further she got from her reporter's cubicle, the fewer faces she discovered she could actually recognize. If it weren't for the press credential tags that everyone wore around their necks or on key fobs, everyone could be a terrorist these days. When she reached the basement, she had to pass through a metal detector identical to the unit at the main entrance one floor up through which she came and went everyday. She recognized *Black Charlie*, the security guard who normally held down the desk upstairs. Referring to him in her mind as Black Charlie wasn't racist, she always needed to remind herself. With 2,500 employees and a 24% mixed-culture hiring ratio at the Seattle Times, there was a *Latino Charlie*, an *Asian Charlie*, an *East Asian Charlie*, a *Bosnian Charlie*—which Natalie sometimes confused with the *Croatian Charlie*—and there was at least one *Native American Charlie*.

"And what brings you to hell?" Black Charlie asked the reporter in heels.

"The Devil," she responded. "Charlie, you must know the name of the mailroom creep."

The security guard issued a belly laugh. "Child, you must mean *Earl*, the bearded fellow...doesn't shower that often?"

"Earl. Thanks, Charlie." Natalie Wesson passed through the metal detector without anything out of the ordinary being detected and as she continued walking, she knew that if she turned her head around, she'd bust Charlie doing nothing out of the ordinary, too—which meant he was probably staring at her ass. She hastened to follow the directional signs to the mailroom lest she get lost in the labyrinth of cubicles and half walls conspiring to ensnare her in the webby stickiness of the basement. It smelled like a locker room down there; testosterone practically condensed on the fluorescent bulbs of the suspended lighting overhead. And in the same instant it repulsed her, in some Jodi-Foster-on-a-pinball-machine sort of way, it turned her on, definitely.

"Whoa, to what do I owe this wet dream?" the mailroom creep watched her approach. "Are you lost in my fantasy? Can I help with directions?" The smile under his beard nearly revealed that a really attractive man could be lurking behind the mane just waiting to be transformed through the grooming magic of an Oprah Before and After Valentine's episode. But she wasn't falling for it. He was still a creep.

"Your name's Earl?"

"Is it the future Mrs. Earl that's asking?"

Natalie rolled her eyes. "Look. You've delivered three envelopes to me now in the past couple months and none of them have postmarks or delivery routing stickers. I figured you'd be smart enough to know how they were getting into the building."

The mailroom creep looked above the cubicle walls to confirm they were alone and out of earshot. "And I figured you'd be smart enough to one day figure out your way down here to the basement where maybe you planned to take me just like you took that lockdowned tree hugger. Would it help if I were tied to the postage meter?" Again, with that smile of his that almost disarmed her.

"I'm not interested, Sasquatch. I just want to know where these Earth Liberation Front press releases keep coming from and I thought you might have a hunch."

"Oh I have a hunch, Miss Wesson." He grabbed his crotch and held it in a way that proved he had the goods. "I have a hunch," he repeated. "And you know you want my hunch."

"Don't you know there's no such thing as a Free Hunch? You want something from me. I want something from you."

"Hell, I assumed these envelopes were coming straight from the Oregon State Pen. Isn't your boyfriend coordinating this orchestra-in-the-woods from there?"

Natalie started to speak but the word caught in her throat as she scrambled to disprove the theory. "Nah," she remembered. "All outbound mail is stamped *Inmate Mail – Oregon Department of Corrections.* They do that to stigmatize prisoners and prevent them from communicating to the outside world with any anonymity."

"I did not know that. So, it comes from someplace else then."

"But you did know that. In the past, you've delivered my mail from the prison already opened. I filed a complaint against you, remember? There was supposedly an investigation?"

"That proved nothing."

"Except you've shared snide remarks with me in the past, information you would have only known had you read the contents of some of my mail."

"Or heard a rumor about the contents from someone else who read them…can't pin that on me, I'm afraid."

"Maybe *you're* the one writing the press releases. It's probably no coincidence you have the disheveled look of one of those disenfranchised forest fuckers."

"You mean that same look your Libre Salazar has? The look that makes you moist? Come on! You gots to give me some of dat." Again with that killer smile.

"You know, in a strange way, you do make me want to bathe, shave and delouse you. I can admit that, I suppose."

"At last, we're getting someplace!"

"And you can admit you've been reading my mail, even if you haven't been writing some of it."

"You take off your clothes and prove to me you're not wearing a wire except the kind that makes those breasts so perky, and you'd be surprised what I'd confess."

"You are such a typical pig. You don't even try to wander from the stereotype in case you'd miss a chance to feed." She turned to leave, bracing her hand on the counter so as to not lose her balance on dramatic heels. Under her hand, it caught her eye: the INCOMING MAIL logbook, itself a three-ring binder holding a sheaf of tabled sheets that recorded the receipt of what appeared to be every incoming piece of mail. "What do we have here?" she asked rhetorically. "More specifically, can you show me where my last two ELF press releases were recorded? Yes, I think I would like to see how your truly baffling mailroom system works."

"I'd have to know what dates you received the releases to show you in the log. If it didn't have a return address, despite your personal theories to the contrary, I wouldn't know the contents of an unmarked envelope that happened to contain a press release."

"I didn't say the envelopes didn't have return addresses," Natalie stated, growing confident in the reliability of her snare to trap the elusive and horny dweeb-pig. "The last envelope I received was yesterday. The one before that was two weeks ago on the 12th or 13th."

"Well, let's have a look." The mailroom creep put his calloused hand on top of Natalie's and turned the book in such a way that she turned with it to fold inside his body. With his arms creating a jail cell, he held her against the counter with his body and, looking over her shoulder, flipped a few pages in the book. He tucked his head against her neck to smell the shampoo in her hair. "Of course, there is always the possibility that the envelopes weren't external," he whispered directly into her ear. "In other words, maybe they were carried into the building and placed on your desk by somebody on the inside." With that, he gently thrust his pelvis forward where it made contact with the small of her back. "Someone who violated your personal space."

While her inner feminist was busting an ovary for allowing him to exert his dominance like that, the creep's breathing and perhaps even more potentially the beast that lurked beneath it—including, in no small way, the asset suddenly poking her in the back—*had* reminded her of her incarcerated Libre. She faced it. It had been a while since anyone had given a shit about her personal space: violating it, consecrating it, or *otherwise-ing* it. Repulsive and jaw dropping as it would sound when she recounted the dingy mailroom fantasy to her girlfriends over fat-free lattes at some point later in the week, she was getting off on the attention and she wouldn't mind if he tried to pull this particular bunny out of the hat. Since she hadn't screamed, recoiled or made any attempt to get out of his squeeze, he pressed forward. Natalie Wesson pressed too. "Are you the one writing the releases for ELF?" The question sort of fell out of her mouth, probably since being blunt seemed to be the established theme for engagement between them.

"Would that advance matters between us, if you could think of us on the same team?" He nuzzled his nose into her neck and the bristles from his beard dispatched a nervous lightning synapse of goose bumps that shot from a spot between the blades of her shoulders to the nipples of her breasts.

What could she gain from this arrangement, she wondered, besides sure-to-be-clumsy stand-up sex against a damp concrete basement wall? Could the mailroom creep, for instance, confirm a theory of hers that her prison boyfriend was an ELF mastermind—something he denied even to her—still coordinating every Molotov cocktail and graffiti tag deployed in the Western States and all for the love of *Mother Earth*? Or could the mailroom creep who was pressing an erection into her back like a gun in a botched kidnapping get her access to the underground movement she hadn't been able to expose by clawing randomly in the dirt? "I know what's in this for you, but what's in it for me? I mean, we have sex. You get off. You brag about it to your subterranean co-nerds and I'm painted unflattering colors with an industrial size sleazy brush."

"Here's the deal I propose. Yes, we have sex and then I pass along a major clue I've been asked to deliver to you personally." He switched sides of her head to whisper in the other ear. "I know what you're thinking. You would have been happy just having sex with me without the inducements. Look at it this way. Think of the clue as the icing that doesn't require birth control."

"Yet another violation of my personal space? I see." The clue, she figured, couldn't be coming from Libre as he wouldn't have trusted the creep not to have tried something as lame as bargaining sex into the exchange. If the creep was writing the media releases, he was receiving intelligence. Maybe he'd stumbled across something he hadn't put in a release. Maybe *he* was the ELF mastermind. "As fine a specimen as you clearly are," she said, as she reached her hand behind her back to assess the instrument of negotiation, "I'm afraid I need more and I need it upfront or we have no deal."

The mailroom creep started to sputter something then held his words, just as the reporter vised her hand around his nuts unmercifully.

"Okay, okay." He breathed rapidly through his mouth. "Your nemesis from the *Eugene Register-Guard*—Bret Meyer Brady—he's turned, crossed over. Please let go of the family," he whimpered.

"What proof do you have of that?" She turned her body to face him, hand still vise-clamping the sudden cooperation right out of him.

"These releases from ELF, they used to get funneled direct to Brady. Then, a few four months ago, I get a message from Libre that the routing has changed and now everything is supposed to go to you."

Just then, another employee's head and torso rounded a corner of the half wall to pass them on his way to the restroom. Natalie released her hand and the creep took one step back.

"I started wondering what happened to Brady." He continued talking without the threat of torture. "I knew he'd been a reformer, that he used to do the stunts he was reporting on, so I imagined he'd either been lured back into espionage or he'd been recruited to help the authorities smoke the insurgents out of the woods."

"Well which is it, do you think?" Natalie wondered if she were off the hook sexually and in the next moment seemed disappointed that she might be. The creep was actually pretty cute up close and by the informal measurements just taken, an Everest to be conquered. Maybe if she started flirting again...

"I happened to be in the general vicinity of Eugene this past weekend, and I took a drive past Brady's house. It is easy enough to find, so I got out, walked up to the front door and rang the doorbell. There was no mail in his mailbox and the lawn was freshly mowed. Of course, there was no answer at his house, but as sure as his doorbell must have been wired to his neighbor's place, out pokes the head of this little old lady, maybe in her seventies, asking if I'm a friend of Bret's. *I am*, I told her, *except I think he's been abducted 'cause I haven't heard from him in several months.* Then she says, taking me very seriously, *I've thought the same thing, that somebody has brainwashed him and taken him away from me. But I can't get the authorities to believe my story.* So I drew closer and asked which authorities she had spoken to and what they had said, and she says *the FBI, of course. Like I'd trust the CIA*, she confided like I'd know better." He chuckled, showing dimples and surprisingly the whitest, straightest teeth.

Natalie assumed a more relaxed posture and wondered what had happened to all that wonderful sexual tension that had been spreading between them like Philadelphia cream cheese that had sat too long at room temperature. "And did she, do you think…go to the FBI?" she asked him.

"Did she ever. Said she'd tried to speak to an agent named Harvey in Portland but that he had dismissed her…how did she put it…*as some kind of menopausal kook with a boy crush.*"

"You're good with quotes and memory. Ever thought of being a reporter?" she asked genuinely.

"Who has the time, what with this grueling mail run and my nationally syndicated column? I can't exactly take on another odd job."

"Syndicated?" Natalie tucked hair behind her ear and leaned forward in astonishment she wasn't exactly doing a very good job of hiding.

"You don't even know my name, do you?"

"I knew it once. I filed a complaint against you, remember?"

"I remember," he emphasized. "But do you?"

She didn't. Game over. Black Charlie had just told her his first name but she didn't register it. His inquisitive expression collapsed on a frame of cartilage and bone. *Self-absorbed bitch*, he thought, before shuffling his feet and re-tucking his shirt. "I need to finish the afternoon mail run. It's been nice chatting…and squirming," he thought to add.

"I'll see you around," he said walking away from her, "not that you're likely to notice."

Natalie sure noticed his fine bubble ass walking away in khakis and wondered how in the hell she had failed to see the mailroom creep as a sexual object before today. "Syndication," she said out loud, recognizing she'd misread a book by its cover. She had her research and an apology cut out for her.

ER KNEES WERE SWOLLEN, SHE HAD A SHINGLES FLARE-UP ON HER LEFT ankle, a headache right behind the eyes and she found she needed to crack her knuckles to relieve the pressure from the joints in her hands. Anymore, every second of every minute served notice that she was aging by every second of every minute. It was altogether depressing and she lacked the motivation to do what she could—which she had already rationalized was nothing anyway— to overcome or outsmart it. String Theory, in the end, had proved most things in life are tied to something sad or debilitating and are entirely unavoidable.

Fuck it, don't fight it had become her new battle cry, except now, nobody was listening. Somewhere along her journey, she'd forgotten how to interact with or seek out humans. She was missing her only friend in the world who had completely made-up some whole different life to escape her contagious misery. And in moments of illumination that happened maybe once every 86,399 seconds, Anne Martondale forced herself to smile through the pain and to be grateful for all her blessings, because that's what a good Christian woman would do, and it tickled her to no end to realize there were crackpots like that in the world, much more profoundly fucked up than she was. That, a solid bowel movement and the daily newspaper were just about the only activities that gave her pleasure. This dismal realization, too, added to her depression, especially on days like this morning where she tackled all three pleasures at once and then had the rest of her day to face rather anticlimactically.

There had been a side article on the front page of her *Register-Guard* taken from the AP wire listing another string of ELF activities. She'd made a habit of snipping these to save for her neighbor, for whenever he decided to come home from his fake India trip. The newspaper writer seemed to be struggling between the lines for a theory that explained why the number of reported eco-vandal hits had quadrupled this summer compared to last, which amused Anne Martondale.

Was she the only one paying attention? Was it not obvious to everyone why some would find it necessary to act out their frustrations like a Passion Play in the woods of the Pacific Northwest? This escalation was a direct causal consequence of being ignored, handcuffed, imprisoned, devalued, beaten down, dehumanized, and lied to.

Not even three years ago, the grossly mishandled WTO protests in Seattle had been allowed to pus and fester without resolve or apology. Then came 9/11 and the machinations of *George W. Backwards,* what with his attention and IQ deficits, too busy tilting at terrorists and vanquishing evil doers to realize his country was on fire. All the while, it had been an intensifying coal-hot anger that bulged into a demonic dome in the crust of civility these past two years that was now prying open steam vents and pressure fissures all along the *Left Coast* fault line.

Sure, these new eco-hits brought major damage and substantial disruption to commerce. These acts gave the general march of imperialism plenty to trip over and were probably causing a viral blip on the Homeland Security Spyware, but it was nothing compared to the correction that needed to happen to restore balance to the thievery and thuggery of the *Bushies* that had pinched the pendulum to keep it from swinging back.

It amused her. Perhaps it was because she was British, which gave her almost passport permission to pretend she was immune to the malignant idiocy propagating from the White House like a plague. More likely it was because she knew if Bret were here, it would amuse him too. Her reporter-neighbor simply could not get enough of these stories recounting Samson-like victories over Goliath-size rapists of the earth, that maybe he had gone off someplace to write his own. In his void, some WASP of a female reporter was penning them now for the *Seattle Times*. Anne had never cared much for female writing given its propensity for serif-fonts, flowery prose and cannon-ball dotted i's filled in with smiley faces, because the world was just that—cheery. *Oh Buddha*, how she missed her Bret.

There was always the Magic Box, *and thank Al Gore for it!* She praised with arthritic hands in the air, as she moved from the toilet to her writing desk, completely forgetting to flush her blessings.

It had been a while since she'd checked the Hotmail account that Bret had created expressly for them to communicate while he was away. He'd only used it once as far as she could tell, and even then, she'd been the one to initiate a chat when she discovered him to be online. He hadn't bothered to contact her since and that was one month, two weeks, and two—or was it three days ago? She always lost track of the count on Tuesdays for some reason.

She typed in her username: *hanff_84*, followed by her password: *ChCROSSRd*. Bret had instructed her that the password was case sensitive and it had taken some practice for her to be able to navigate the lower and upper case sequence, but she mastered it. It was no surprise to her today that there was nothing in her inbox and even less a shock to find she had no friends online. She had no friends, period. Looking at her hands poised above the keyboard she rolled her wrists over to ponder what earthly force had kept her from hacking at them with a straight edge years ago.

She stared at the computer screen without blinking until her vision blurred and then she logged out. The sign-in screen returned, prompting for her password. She cleared the user name and typed in *doel_84*. She wondered if Bret had used the same password for his Hotmail account. It had never occurred to her to attempt to sign-in as him to see if this provided clues to where he was or what he was doing.

She typed in her password. The computer cleared her wrong attempt. She straightened her posture. Simple deduction suggested to her that Bret must have used a password that had its origins in the book she had given him. He'd set up her account that way. His own email address was derived from *84, Charing Cross Road. Oh, goodie, a hunt*, she thought, perking right up. *Come on, Magic Box!*

She warmed her hands together as though she were about to toss a pair of dice. In the password spot, she entered *Marks&Co*, the name of the bookshop located at 84 Charing Cross Road in London from where the main character and the book's author—an American writer named Helene Hanff—ordered her references and literature from a British bookseller named Frank Doel. It was their twenty-year correspondence that had reminded Anne of her spirited exchanges with Bret. She tapped the enter key. Error message. Of course she shouldn't have expected success with a first try. He'd always made access to the thing she wanted most, which was his company, more difficult for her than that. She exhausted a couple more variations on the theme: *Marks_&_Co*; *Marks_&_Company*; *Marksandco*; *Marksandcompany*; *Marks*; returning errors with each try. She switched themes: *Helene*; *Hanff*; *HH*. Nothing. *Frank*; *FDP*.

This wasn't working, she conceded. The mad scientist within needed to be more systematic and less random with her elimination process. She walked across the room to her wall-to-wall bookshelves and extracted the thin first edition hardback volume, published by Grossman in 1970—four years before the object of her platonic affection and the subject of her frantic search now had been born. She was convinced that Bret Meyer Brady was far too clever not to have fashioned a password from the book. He was anally tidy, that way.

In order to quench the hunt, she detoured to the stove to start the teapot. Waiting for the water to boil, she began going through the book page by page tapping any word or combination of words that jumped out as potential passwords: *QuillerCouch*; *YorkshirePudding*; *GroilerBible* from page 38; *Nylons*; *WaltonsLives* from page 47; *TinnedHam*; *TristramShandy*. Then just as her eyes lit on *CommonReader*, the name of Virginia Woolf's novel cited on page 84, the kettle whistled. She tended to the water and while the tea bag steeped, she wandered back to the computer. *That little devil,* she thought. Of course the password would be on page 84, a nod to the title she'd taken the effort to share with him. Confidently, she typed the words *CommonReader* and pushed *Enter*.

Celebrate Jesus, Mohammad and Buddha! She was in. Anne Martondale had officially become a hacker.

"Ted De-Hav-lin," he must have repeated his own name three times. It wasn't his first experience with customer tech support. When he first got his fancy watch a year ago, he had spent several hours on the phone—to India he presumed by the accents on the other end of the line—calibrating everything from the barometer to the Pacific Time Zone. While this was his first onboard laptop, getting it to integrate with or even to recognize his Army Corps–issued Magellan Maestro 3140 GPS Navigation equipment was proving a challenge larger than a dozen techs had been able to overcome. He recited the Service Tag number from the sticker on the bottom of the computer with an obviously stern and frustrated syncopation. It seemed he needed to start from the beginning every time he got transferred to a new agent and he wondered why his information didn't transfer along with him. He was about to bring up that question too, when he started receiving a second call from a "private number" on his cellphone. He asked the tech to hold while he alternated between calls. "Ted, here."

The male caller identified himself with a soft voice.

"Sergio! Man, I've been trying so hard to reach you. Hold on one second. Let me dump this other call." Suddenly it didn't matter how long he'd just spent trying to resolve technical issues or if the damn computer ever worked. He'd been trying to track down his one-time stowaway and, if he was honest with himself, his constant daydream obsession for months now. "Sergio, how have you been?

I'm having computer issues that I bet you could fix for me if you were here right now." There was silence. He hadn't managed to get the call back. He jabbed a button again to reach him. "Sergio?" he asked frantically.

"No sir, this is Baptist with tech support," the accented voice sang on the other end. He jabbed the phone button again. "Sergio?"

Silence. *Shit!* He'd lost the call. He'd lost both of them, actually. The number had been listed as private so he couldn't hit redial. He'd wait for Sergio to phone back. He would surely phone right back. He'd gone to the effort to call in the first place, right?

For twenty minutes, Ted kept the line clear, but Sergio did not phone back, causing him to wonder whether he'd even heard the caller correctly or if he just wanted it so badly to be Sergio that he'd convinced himself it had been him. Ted had spent the last few months trying to coach his heart out of the man crush he'd gotten himself into but he couldn't get the imagery or the sensation out of his brain or his ass, which he must have clutched a half dozen times a day when he was on the river. He had never doubted his masculinity or his sexual wiring in thirty-three years and suddenly, he questioned everything, absolutely everything except his feelings for the hairy kid in a Greenpeace T-shirt who had taken him by surprise when he took him from behind.

With Samantha pregnant with his second child, Teddy Jr.'s sister-to-be, there was no expectation of and virtually no meaningful way to have sex at home. This had happened before when she was pregnant with Teddy Jr. Ted hadn't understood back then that it wasn't his fault or that it wasn't because he suddenly repulsed his wife. He'd stewed about that, though, letting it strike a major blow to his self-confidence, and it wasn't until this pregnancy six years later that she had taken the time to explain to him that because of the internal squeezes, cramps and pressures on her systems, the physical pressure of having sex was just too uncomfortable for her.

Samantha still had no interest in treating him to oral sex, which would have at least given them an option to counter this anticipated vaginal closure policy of hers. It was the same with anal sex except Ted hadn't desired it. She hadn't offered it. It simply wasn't on the table. Sex with his wife had always been mechanical, like riding a bull really. If he managed to stay mounted for eight seconds, while she squirmed to buck him off, he just might get his rocks off. She'd express-trained him to climax quickly. He'd made a contest out of it too when he masturbated alone, using his fancy watch to shatter previous all-time-bests. But, because he worried that maybe one day, he wouldn't want sex to be over quite so quickly, he also began to time his endurance sessions, especially between the long stretches between the dams.

Then, onto his ship and into his life wandered Sergio, the first man to stir interest inside his jeans since his teenage exploration years. Sex with this man had been altogether mind blowing. Ted hadn't wanted it to end—never mind quickly—but, no matter how much he had tried to hold onto his orgasm with white knuckles wrapped around the edge of the wheelhouse dashboard, the forceful prod of Sergio's long, slender man-piece drumming on his prostate gland, a body part he'd never even known was in his inventory, had him immaculately dowsing the instrument panel without having touched his own instrument.

The new training drills since that encounter were marathon by nature and involved staving off the orgasm until his whole body just about caved in. He couldn't wait for an opportunity to field- and Sergio-test his new skills.

He checked his cellphone wondering why Sergio hadn't phoned back yet. A light that he hadn't noticed earlier was flashing, indicating he had a message. He used the speed dial to access his voice-mail and in that instant braced himself for disappointment in case the message was tech-support related. It wasn't.

"Ted—hey there! It's Sergio. Look, uh, I'm in a bit of trouble and seem to have screwed up my ankle pretty bad. I can't really talk now because I'm on a bus, but I need to get back to Portland, get my leg looked at. I'm hoping you are in the vicinity and can help me out. Shit, I hope you remember who

I am…a few months back, you know, the guy in the Greenpeace T-shirt… saved your fish once. Anyway. I should be in Lewiston sometime tomorrow morning and I'll try to reach you again then."

With a huge grin, Ted thought to himself: *saved my fish?* It was more like *saved my life*.

HAZARD LOOKED UP FROM THE NEWSPAPER, ADJUSTING HIS HEAD SO that his ear could zero in on the sound of a man's voice speaking in what sounded almost like a whisper if not deliberately hushed tones. In the darkness of the bus that had been left idling at an irritating, vibrational hum, he had trouble making out the sounds. He looked toward the back of the bus where Hooknose's propped leg stuck out into the aisle. From where he was sitting, it seemed his injured comrade hadn't budged. Still, Hazard stood up and slowly began moving toward the sound of the voice, which seemed to be coming from behind him. Then the sound ended.

After a brief pause, he continued walking to the back of the bus as an excuse to check on his partner. Tenderly, he reached his hand toward the front of Hooknose's head to check for fever. The injured man stirred and issued a bit of a purr, indicating he wasn't resisting the caring touch, which more likely pointed to the pain-killers rather than Hooknose's willingness to forgive him. Hazard thought he might have seen the light of a cellphone fade under the windbreaker that he'd draped over Hooknose when they'd boarded the bus an hour ago, but that couldn't be since Hooknose had listed the cellphone as part of the inventory lost in the backpack that hadn't disembarked from the train when Hazard did. He supposed it could have also been the service station overhead lights reflecting off the plastic of the windbreaker.

Hazard couldn't remember who had had the cellphone last.

Hooknose had phoned in the pick-up request several hours ago, but that was before the incident with the train. Had the battery been given back to him to be put away in his pack, which was now the only backpack that remained between them or had Hooknose held onto it and only said it went missing on the back of the train? And if Hooknose had been phoning someone, who was he contacting?

In the couple of months they had been together, he hadn't been able to decipher who Hooknose might have been coordinating with besides him, but had seen him on the phone maybe a half dozen times. Once, behind his partner's back, he had been able to hit redial before the battery had been removed and in that instance, the call had been answered by *Oregon Corrections*. Hazard had presumed that call had been to Libre Salazar. He hadn't really thought about that call since. In fact, he hadn't been that much of an investigator and hadn't even checked in with his own handler since jettisoning his laptop months ago.

If the FBI hauled him in at this point, he wasn't really sure he had any information that would be helpful in moving their stagnant investigation along. It wasn't that he hadn't been paying attention as much as he hadn't come across anything particularly plot turning or juicy. Facts revealed, this wasn't a glamorous or even an exciting life. Trudging through woods and urban alleys in clothes you've worn unwashed for days doesn't inspire a following or enough interest to lead to anything conclusive anyway. What Hazard had been discovering in the past months was that Hazard was depressed because Hazard was bored. It hadn't turned out to be nearly as exciting as he'd over-romanticized it and now he was a good decade older than the last time he'd foregone antiperspirant in defense of the planet. He stroked his stubbled-out face on his way back to the front of the bus to check for the phone battery in his backpack, which turned out not to be in there. Hazard ached for a shave and a shower and some escape hatch out of this magic trick, this clever box that he'd fashioned for himself, that defiantly now would not give up its seams or hinges.

He plopped down in his seat and, grabbing the newspaper, he wrapped his face tightly in it so the smell of newsprint could invade his body and reality-snap him back to life. On his second deep inhalation, he simultaneously felt and heard the driver mount the bus. He gradually lowered his papier-mâché disguise and began reading the front-page story he'd been handed earlier:

There Appears to be No Slowing Down, Stopping or Capturing Those Dedicated to the Earth's Liberation this Summer

Seattle—While news from the woods these past few weeks is being loudly made across the border in a remote rainforest on the West Coast of Vancouver Island where hundreds of eco-activists have returned to the site where nearly 1,000 of them were arrested a decade earlier by the Canadian government for blockading logging roads, there are some quiet newsmakers keeping the anti-corporation fires stoked and smoldering all around the Pacific Northwest, this month.

August 1, 2002—Ellensburg, WA Nearly two dozen giant inflatable pool toys in the shapes of fish were suspended from power lines with a banner reading "FISH OUT OF WATER" above Manastash Creek near Ellensburg. Water Wars in the West between local farmers and environmentalists have escalated with farmers demanding more water for irrigation while environmentalists scream for the protection of threatened fish, calling for the screening of water diversion pipes, the elimination of passage barriers and the restoration of stream flows to support species.

August 2, 2002—Yakima, WA The Building Industry

Association of Washington had partnered with the Federal Bureau of Investigation to offer a $100,000 reward for the arrest and conviction of Earth Liberation Front (ELF) terrorists burning down homes in Washington State. BIAW advertised its $100,000 reward for the capture and conviction of ELF eco-terrorists with a large billboard on Interstate 12 near the Yakima city limits. The billboard featuring the image of a gutted home was adorned with a banner sash over the weekend that read: You Build It with Old Growth, We'll Burn It with New Fire—ELF

August 6, 2002—Richland, WA An oversized cardboard cutout depicting a tombstone was attached to the fence near the main gates to Area B of the nuclear complex. The tombstone read: HERE LIES 100,000,000 GALLONS OF ATOMIC WASTE BURIED IN THE 1950s IN CONTAINERS WHOSE KNOWN LIFE IS 30-40 YEARS. PLUTONIUM 239 HAS A HALF LIFE OF 25,000 YEARS AND WILL BE RADIOACTIVE FOR A PERIOD OF SOME 250,000 YEARS. THESE TANKS HAVE ALREADY LEAKED MORE THAN A MILLION GALLONS OF HIGHLY RADIOACTIVE WASTE. JACK RABBITS HERE SHIT "HOT" PELLETS AND THE COYOTES THAT EAT THEM DIE OF RADIATION POSISONING. HOW CAN ANY OF US R.I.P?

August 8, 2002—Spokane WA The USA Pavilion structure, left over from World Expo '74, had a nimble visitor in the pre-dawn hours who scaled the skeleton structure to attach and unfurl a 100-foot-long vertical banner from the top that read: "Aerosol Fluorocarbons Have Made Earth a Pavilion Without Skin." It is not yet apparent if this act was intended to coincide with the arrival today of a panel of judges from *Communities in Bloom, International* that was to have adjudicated Riverfront Park for a prestigious contest. An anonymous tip phoned into the fire department suggested the approach to the banner was booby-trapped. This delayed the banner's removal until late in the afternoon, long after the judges had toured and left the vicinity.

August 8, 2002—Walla Walla, WA The imprisoned eco-activist who goes by the name *Britta Water* (being held at the Washington State Penitentiary pending the trial to determine her role in the Seattle/University of Washington arson on May 21, 2001, that destroyed the Center for Urban Horticulture) learned today that her prison time has just been extended by five years, even if she is found innocent of the arson. Water, in a press conference she had given in July, had said her conscience would compel her to "wring the neck of President George W. like the chicken he is," if she ever found herself alone in a room with the man. The U.S. Department of Homeland Security has chosen to view her statement as a credible threat against the life of a sitting president and has charged Water with contravening the *Threat Statute US Code Title 18, Part 1, Chapter 41, Sec. 871*. It is not yet known if Water will also be fined the $250,000 that can accompany the incarceration for this offense.

August 12, 2002—WSU Grizzly Bear Research Station, Pullman, WA In a graphic move, protestors tethered the carcasses of a coyote and a juvenile white tail deer, apparent road kill victims, to the outer cage of the grizzly bear pen with words spray painted on a blood-stained sheet: This is not predatory behavior. End Grizzlies in captivity NOW!

August 18, 2002—Grand Coulee Dam, WA Eco-saboteurs infiltrated the facility housing the elaborate light and multi-media show projected nightly on the concrete face of this dam. Instead of the usual whimsical play of colors and animated mascots, last night's post-dusk show featured images of biohazards, skulls and fish bones, swastikas, target bull's eyes, and upside down pentagrams forming "a disturbing light collage that seemed to hail the end of environmental days," according to an ELF spokesperson, claiming responsibility for the attack on behalf of the Earth Liberation Front.

Hazard checked the date on his watch in the quickly fading light from the gas station as the bus pulled clumsily back onto the highway. It was the twentieth of August. With less than a week to go before the scheduled rendezvous with their handler somewhere in the Idaho panhandle, it seemed to him that the remaining targets on their hit-list had already been hit. He lowered the newspaper in confusion.

"I'm not sure I get it," he played dumb to the driver who had been watching him in the rearview mirror. "Are we being retired?" When the driver didn't answer right away, Hazard continued to formulate his latest theory out loud. "It's just that according to our work orders, we had another two to three weeks of work that seems to have been completed for us." Hazard had figured the driver for the Handler. It didn't take a genius to figure out that if a cellphone could make an empty 64-passenger Greyhound bus materialize in the sagebrush desert, the driver was part of a scheme larger than a couple coordinates on a map.

The driver turned on the dome light above his head, which cast an ominous spotlight directly on top of his uniform cap. Between the brim of the hat and the shadow from his nose, there was no way the man could be identified, at least not from where Hazard sat. "I'll be quick about this since we begin picking up fares in another five miles," the driver spoke, clearing his throat around the words. "We were running out of time and our intelligence in the woods is starting to indicate that the *Freddies* might be moving in, thanks in no small part to your cameo on the surveillance cams at the dam the other night." He stretched a corndog behind his seat as an offering.

"I'll assume this isn't vegan?" Hazard ventured with a raised eyebrow, far too hungry to refuse anything at this point anyway.

"Dubbya is getting agitated since he can't turn up WMDs that didn't exist in the first place never mind spooking out a single ter-rorist to substantiate his War on Terror, so he's directed *Homeland Scrutiny* to empty the woods and fill the jails with dissenters…" he took another bite of the corndog in his hand, "…at least until his polling improves." After taking one final bite the driver cleaned the stick by drawing the batter bits between his teeth. "Things will be clearer once you read my response to your email. But in the mean-time, we need to pull you two out of circulation for a week to get ready for the finale and make sure the dogs lose your scent."

"The finale?" Hazard posed. *What email?* he wondered.

"Yes, the finale on August 28th and we are the first raindrops."

39 44 42   121 47 4 **10 10 11** 46 3

T HE FIRST TIME SHE'D HACKED IN, IT HAD TAKEN ANNE A FEW MINUTES TO realize Bret's inbox was mostly full of unopened messages from her. While that hurt her a bit, that wasn't what she was looking for today. The last time she was in, she had discovered a rather curious email forwarded to Bret from a *hooknose@hotmail.com* that had originally been sent by a *greyhound@hotmail.com*; curious because it contained a six column, forty-four line spreadsheet of numbers that at first and even second glance she hadn't been able to decipher.

39	44	42	121	47	41
40	25	12	120	44	19
40	54	39	124	05	06
42	00	19	124	12	37
42	12	16	121	42	36
43	21	35	124	07	52
44	33	15	123	15	69
43	58	42	121	20	28
46	10	50	123	37	25
45	38	39	121	56	27
46	19	50	124	03	60
46	07	53	121	52	42
47	18	77	122	17	54
47	34	18	122	14	13
47	56	43	124	11	23

49	10	58	122	53	25
49	30	06	119	34	57
48	32	12	121	45	30
47	44	47	121	05	09
48	28	32	120	10	48
47	50	05	120	00	48
47	27	46	120	33	43
47	57	22	118	58	57
46	59	59	120	29	10
47	10	33	119	57	54
46	36	19	120	28	60
46	27	18	119	30	55
47	39	14	117	25	86
46	4	49	118	21	39
46	43	44	117	8	6
46	43	44	117	00	51
45	51	01	115	16	49
44	49	16	115	28	32
46	30	53	116	17	48

On a frustration-driven whim, after three sleepless nights and a bout of constipation that bound her cellulite-pocked ass cheeks like Super Glue, Anne, posing as Bret, composed an email reply, which she'd sent to "Hooknose" and "Greyhound," hoping to bait one of them for another clue. Hers was a one-line hook: *Einstein asserted that nothing is truly random so what is the un-randomness of these numbers, truly?*

Today, top of the inbox, was a response from Greyhound.

Even though I know you aren't who you are pretending to be, I can recognize it's time we became a little less subtle with the authorities, assuming that is who you represent, if we are to make this at all interesting. See if this helps:

39	44	42	121	47	41
40	25	12	120	44	19
40	54	39	124	05	06
42	00	19	124	12	37
42	12	16	121	42	36
43	21	35	124	07	52
44	33	15	123	15	69
43	58	42	121	20	28
46	10	50	123	37	25
45	38	39	121	56	27
46	19	50	124	03	60
46	07	53	121	52	42
47	18	77	122	17	54
47	34	18	122	14	13
47	56	43	124	11	23
49	10	58	122	53	25
49	30	06	119	34	57
48	32	12	121	45	30
47	44	47	121	05	09
48	28	32	120	10	48
47	50	05	120	00	48
47	27	46	120	33	43
47	57	22	118	58	57
46	59	59	120	29	10
47	10	33	119	57	54
46	36	19	120	28	60
46	27	18	119	30	55
47	39	14	117	25	86

46	4	49	118	21	39
46	43	44	117	8	6
46	43	44	117	00	51
45	51	01	115	16	49
44	49	16	115	28	32
46	30	53	116	17	48

Same numbers, same sequence, but with interruptions this time, which must indicate an inter-relationship between the numbers in a set, she deduced. She stared herself into a headache not realizing that day had passed into night outside the lace-curtained windows of her suburban Eugene home. She rose from her desk and the monitor to re-fire the teapot but diverted to the washroom to first evacuate the tea she was already carrying. Maybe she needed to break down and start collecting cats, she thought, so pathetic was her house arrest. She emerged from the *loo* and took a squinting look about the cluttered place. Cats. Those, and her neighbor, Bret, were all that were missing.

While Anne waited for the harmonious half-notes of her RushGideon Berkshire Whistling Tea Kettle to sing, she wondered what would come up if she simply Googled the first line of numbers. The Magic Box had always delivered the goods in the past. Why not now? Without sitting down, she arched over her keyboard and typed *39 44 42 121 47 41* into the search line of her browser. Enter. The first return was a Google Map with Chinese names and icons. Anne zoomed out on the map to realize she was looking at a position on the map determined by the numbers, which in this case were acting as global coordinates. She sat down. Where in the world was this, exactly, she wondered. The little red balloon with the letter A was sitting in the Liaodong Peninsula in the Liaoning Province of northeastern China, an area Westerners would recognize as Southeast Manchuria. Well, what in the hell did this have anything to do with the price of tea in China, she thought, smiling at the cleverness of her gifted brain, just as the kettle answered the riddle from the stove.

Reaching into her tea cupboard, she selected a jasmine green loose-leaf tea, loading some into her tea ball to set the mood for her treasure hunt through China. She returned to her desk noting that two dried, white jasmine flowers had escaped the strainer to float on the surface of her cup like lanterns or swans in an imperial garden. She blew them about as she waited for her tea to cool.

She loaded the next set of numbers in the first series into the Google search bar. It returned gibberish and no map. She scrunched up her brow and tilted her head sideways hoping the hunt wasn't over before it really became interesting. She entered the third set of numbers: *40 54 39 124 05 06*. Bingo! Another map with a red balloon positioned north and east of her first return, this one in the same province in China.

She took a quick sip of tea sucking up a jasmine flower. She chewed it between her front teeth, releasing the bitter fragrance into her salivating mouth. And then it occurred to her that her neighbor might have been in India after all, just as an earlier email of his claimed he was, but on his clandestine way to Manchuria. She zoomed in on the Google Terrain Map, her conspiratorial mind almost expecting to see revealed a tented and tattered Al Qaeda training camp in the dusty foothills of this rugged no-man's land, but it wasn't.

After repeatedly zooming in and out, east then west, switching from map to satellite to terrain views and recognizing that it was nauseating her, she clicked on a few more buttons to reveal Panoramio photos speckling the map. She clicked a few around the red balloon with the letter A; still no terrorist training camp. She back-paged on Google to the first map she had stumbled upon. Clicking the pictures around that balloon revealed photos of a Mundoro Maoling Gold Mining Project. That might be of interest, she thought, so she Googled it: a global exploration, development and investment company. Sounded very Halliburton, she surmised.

How in the world could her neighbor have gotten swept up in this sort of activity?

She spit a green tea leaf back into her cup and lifted her right ass cheek off the chair to release some sudden abdominal pressure. She would pop down to the University of Oregon bookstore in the morning, get herself a poster size map of China, plot what she could and then drive her theory up to Portland and the office of that quick-to-dismiss Federal Bureau Chief Red Harvey.

I T WAS PRISONER #13797671'S THIRTIETH BIRTHDAY. PRISON CELEBRA-tions, as they were, weren't particularly festive affairs, and those that marked anniversary dates usually only served to remind the inmates how much time they had left inside or how old they would be when they finally became out-mates. Libre Salazar would be fifty-one years old and would have spent half his life in this penitentiary by the time the Year 2024 crawled around. His mood on this day couldn't help but deflect that despair back into the Universe making it an even darker vacuum of space than it normally felt like. His leggy reporter friend from Seattle was inbound and that usually lifted his spirits, at least the one that still counted, he thought as he adjusted himself in his prison issue pants, but something told him today was going to get a whole lot uglier before it was over.

Lately, Libre's pipeline to the outside world was getting clogged and the traffic flowing through it was becoming more and more prone to static and interference. For starters, there was the get-together last week that was really more of an interrogation by that Freddie Bureau Fuck—Harvey—that gave him an uneasy feeling that he was being constantly monitored and might be provoking another stint in isolation unless he backed right off the wires. He was counting on Natalie today to get a crucial message out to his puppets to signal the commencement of *Operation Douche Bag*. He would have handled it himself if his phone and Internet privileges hadn't been revoked again after he was accused of being less than cordial and gentlemanly during the Freddie Tea Party last week.

What the fuck did he know about a couple guys going by the underground code names of *Hazard* and *Hooknose* anyway? *Fuck all*, and that's exactly what he told Harvey, too. Guys who were going by names weren't likely from ELF ranks anyway so he really couldn't be bothered. But this message of his just had to get out of the Oregon State Pen today so that it could get picked up by the one man in the woods who was certifiably crazy enough to guarantee the plan could be carried out, just as Libre had masterminded it. Still, he was nervous. In the past few weeks, there had been some second-guessing, slip-ups and insubordination issues with the kook he had entrusted to tip the first domino, leaving him to wonder if there was any integrity left at all in their autonomous collective of pranksters, arsonists, saboteurs and thieves.

And on this day in particular, when a birth certificate and a handful of fellow inmates insisted he acknowledge the three decades already behind him when all he wanted to do was set into motion an unstoppable plan that would play out in the weeks ahead, it was extraordinarily difficult to strap on a party hat, sing songs and eat stale prison cake.

The real reason to celebrate was approaching like a tidal wave.

39 44 42   121 47 4 **10 10 13** 46 3

THE CORNDOG HE'D PURCHASED BUT THEN HAD SECOND THOUGHTS ABOUT ingesting steamed up an oblong patch of windshield above the dashboard. He hadn't been so much as bothered by appetite for at least the past three days while his insides flipped then flopped like they were being worked over by an internal taffy-pulling machine. This was the worst it had been so far and he knew this because he no longer even had the runs, something he'd lived with daily for the worst half of the last year. He wasn't hungry. He wasn't necessarily bloated. It didn't feel like constipation really. He simply hadn't passed anything more substantial than a rank fart in days. Sitting all day and staring out at a landscape on a route he could have driven blindfolded gave the bus driver lots of time to focus on what his bowels were and more recently *weren't* doing.

The bus edged back onto the highway and was under way for the 119-mile leg to Umatilla. The driver was always grateful when he could time this desolate stretch for after dark. His stomach growled suddenly, causing him to press and straighten his back against the beaded seat cover; it was more of a roar that prompted him to wonder if maybe the first few rows of passengers might have heard. Still, the corndog sat untouched, unsavored on the dash. He dimmed the overhead lights, which always prompted a half dozen reading lights to click on like stars to irritate the handful of passengers who really preferred to sleep through the diesel and body-odor-ed drudgery that was bus travel.

The driver had every reason to believe this would be his last scheduled trip. He hadn't bothered to inform his long-time employer that more than calling it quits, he had plans to take the company with him when he went. It was time, more than anything else. It no longer mattered about the details and the calendar that had been constructed by an idle and unconnected man with nothing but a scheme and time on his hands. That punk with a brain and a vendetta couldn't anymore know what it was like at the frontlines of this new movement than the driver with a suddenly horrendous stomach ache could comprehend losing his freedom, ever. And yet, it was the loss of freedom for rivers all over the Pacific Northwest that had brought the two strangers together—in spirit, in momentum and a commitment to a singular deed—eighteen months ago. His fifty-six, almost fifty-seven-year-life, his beliefs, corporate greed, government complicity, Man's arrogance, the latter-day foot soldiers his charisma had attracted, and the rot in his gut would all culminate in a moment that was about to detonate in the hills of North Central Idaho. It was his destiny to become the fuse for the one great ka-boom that would liberate the Columbia River Basin for generations of salmon yet to spawn.

Just then, as he'd topped sixty miles per hour, his intestines kinked in a cramp so severe, it caused him to lurch the twelve-ton boxcar onto the right shoulder. He over-corrected, crossing the center lane, as a few passengers gasped out loud. "Coyote," the driver lied and yelled over his right shoulder, slowing the bus down by twenty miles per hour. The first cramp was followed by a second one just as bad that he tried to hold his breath through, but when it wouldn't pass, he polka-dotted the windshield with spit as the blood rushed from his face, threatening to take his consciousness down the drain with it. His eyes flooded as he was certain to crap his pants or pass out from the pain.

He stopped the bus on the shoulder, punching on the hazard lights. He unfastened his seat belt, took a giant breath and turned to dash past twenty-two passengers for the onboard washroom at the rear of the bus. Those beneath reading lights looked up in astonishment at the profusely ailing driver streaking past them like a gaseous comet. When he reached the back of the bus, he found the washroom latch locked. He banged on the flimsy door, expelling his lungs. "This is the driver! This is an emergency!" A teenage boy, who had been masturbating out of boredom on the other side, freed the latch and exited the washroom, adjusting and concealing himself in his jeans as he returned to his seat. The door slammed shut as a cry of agony shook the windows and rattled the luggage rack overhead.

He hadn't even gotten his pants completely down when the first explosion plastered the underside of the raised toilet seat. He clenched his butt cheeks as tightly as he could to get into a better position in the vertical shoebox but ended up sitting in his own shit. A third wave simply dropped out of him as though his asshole were a dump truck on full incline. His rude cement more than half filled the tiny bowl, displacing what little water there was and rendering a flush certainly impeded if not impossible. Sweat gushed from his pores while Armageddon spewed not at all quietly from his ass. He could hear laughing and a few protesting shouts on the other side of the aluminum-trimmed cardboard door now, and his own gasps of fouled air were shallow and measured.

While his stomach and bowels continued to conveyor belt a substantial portion of his body mass right out of him, an angelic calm began to return to his quaking body as the driver experienced the most soul-levitating wave of euphoria he had ever known. It was as though he had been holding back the North Fork and the Snake and the Salmon and the Clearwater and the Lochsa and the Bitterroot and the Columbia and the John Day and the Deschutes and the Rogue and the Selway and the Willamette and the Pend Oreille and the Skagit and the Cowlitz and the White and the McKenzie and the North Santiam rivers behind a stubborn plug of concrete and log jam that finally, metaphorically, prophetically and otherwise gave way.

Now, more certain of his destiny than he had ever been, he slowly raised to a trembling half squat to assess the disaster he had just birthed. As he'd feared, shit had exploded everywhere including his shorts and shirttail. The stench was so absolutely morbid that it provoked vomit to back up in his throat. Still lightheaded in this new asphyxia, he leaned heavily on the sink, mindful that the bus was still running, that he was still on the side of Highway 84 with twenty-two passengers and that a good part of his gray polyester professional outlook was mired in his own feces. What a way to mark his last trip as a career bus driver, he gritted his teeth, suddenly noticing something in his shit on the back of the toilet seat. *What the hell*, he whispered, still trying to limit the number of times he had to inhale. There, in the brown plaster, was something the size of a whole grape. He never ate grapes because that's where raisins came from and he despised them. As he got closer and clamped down his jaws even harder, he noticed more of the things.

There was the sound of a fist banging on the other side of the door. "You want someone to call 911?" asked a man's muffled voice. "Jesus, that is rank!" the voice followed as laughs broke out among the passengers.

"Out in a minute. Thanks for your patience. I'm all right," the driver lied to buy some time. Just then, his gag reflexed a threat it might add to the masterpiece. He coughed but managed to choke it back—whatever *it* was. That was some fucked-up shit, he thought, examining the stuff and wondering how he might preserve a sample. He counted a half dozen of the translucent grape looking pod thingies before the whole nasty scene freaked him right out of the bathroom where he'd left his uniform shirt and soiled underwear behind. The driver in a tank top double locked the door from the outside with a pass-key that could also unlock the luggage compartment, the diesel hatch, and the engine trunk, without needing to remove the main key from the bus ignition. Passengers that may have been seated in the blast zone near the washroom had moved out of the noxious fumes and into the aisle where they covered their mouths with hands and shirt sleeves.

"The bathroom will remain out of order for the remainder of the trip," he announced the obvious to a few snickers and groans. "I will be increasing the number of roadside stops between here and Spokane for those in need of facilities. Greyhound apologizes for the inconvenience," he added sarcastically, taking his seat behind the wheel.

For the next 165 miles, the driver didn't think about anything else but those pods in his shit at the back of the bus, pods that had come out of his body, pods identical to others that had to still be inside him. This was right out of *Alien* and it obsessed him without end. When he finally reached the bus and train depot in Spokane and the passengers had departed, he returned to the back of the bus and with a corndog stick, flicked as many of the pods into a ziplock sandwich bag as he could manage before his nerves and madly thumping heart forced his retreat.

It would be another forty-eight hours of pacing before he could shit again.

And then, more pods.

Fuck!

T HEY'D BEEN RESTLESS IF NOT AMICABLE CAPTIVES OF THE ONE-ROOM cabin thanks to a persistent rain that hammered the tin roof most of the afternoon. Hazard and Hooknose had grown sick of playing cards and second guessing the reason they had been dropped here to wait by a bus driver codenamed Greyhound, a crusty fart of a man who had appeared out of nowhere to pluck them from the desert then had disappeared just as efficiently. Before leaving, however, the driver with no medical training beyond occupational first aid had determined Hooknose didn't have a broken ankle though it was perhaps badly sprained.

Perhaps was of no consolation to Hooknose now as he gritted his way through the small talk and the pain, either of which could have killed him stealthily in the next minute to come and he would not have been at all surprised by the outcome. His hastily hatched plan to make it to Lewiston to time an intercept rescue by his barge pilot had fallen through once he discovered the cellphone he had concealed from Hazard had been removed from his pants pocket while he was asleep or out of it with pain. The driver, who he suspected had his phone, after having first indicated he would be taking them to his house in Lewiston to lay low a spell, proceeded to travel another thirty miles up the Clearwater River to deposit them at this remote cabin. Though Hooknose had toyed with the possibility of walking out of the woods leaning his bad side on Hazard, his ankle barely allowed him to reach the outhouse behind the cabin. He knew where they were and he also knew it was about a seven-mile hump to reach the town of Orofino. He could do it on a bike no problem as it was all downhill, but even that meant a two-and-a-half-mile hike from the cabin in the woods above the reservoir to where his bike was still locked up in the employee break room at the dam's visitor center.

How he'd managed to end back up at Dworshak Dam where he'd worked during the past three summer breaks as a tour guide and custodian before taking a leave this summer to, well, *travel* around the Pacific Northwest, shouldn't have been as big a mystery as he made it out to be. He was tied to Greyhound, had been for three years, though he hadn't confessed this rather familiar acquaintance to Hazard. He was tied to Greyhound and for some reason, Greyhound was tied to Dworshak. In the beginning the old coot had just been a person of interest, but that was in the months before Hooknose had been shown the old abandoned mine.

When he'd first been hired by the U.S. Army Corps to work at the dam's visitor center, his employment a favor and a cover arranged for him by his real employer, he'd rented this cabin from the driver. Then, maybe once or twice a month when the driver showed up he'd help him unload boxes and crates from a bus and into the mineshaft. The driver would enrapture the young chemistry teacher with truly inspirational stories of activist uprisings and general monkey-wrenching, like in 1929 when a group of homesteaders got together in Central Oregon to do something about a dam that had been built by the Oregon Fish Commission across the lower reaches of the Alsea River. The back-asswards reason for the dam, as the Driver told the story, was to capture spawning salmon in a healthy river to harvest their eggs in order to seed dead rivers above other dams. *When the citizens couldn't get their heads around the need for the dam and they couldn't get the government to remove the thing, they sent a raft of dynamite downstream and removed it for them.*

Hooknose was pretty sure this was the driver's favorite story since he'd told it to him more than once, and each time he'd be sure to add his personal footnote that the more simple a plan is, the more beautiful its execution. *Remember that*, he'd say.

Hooknose looked out the four-paned window in the direction of the mineshaft. When he had gotten up the nerve to ask what was in the boxes they were packing in there, the driver told him he'd scored a coup on eBay for a whole shipment of surplus Army rations that had been destined for troops heading to Iraq. Somehow the skids had missed connections with the requisition ship in Bremerton or some such thing.

"Care for some Top Ramen?" Hazard had asked innocently enough, but the two words between them had grown into something akin to a personal insult since they'd eaten so much of the cardboard shit these past two months. "Far as I can see with my gourmet eye, it's the only thing edible in this place unless one of us is prepared to walk out for supplies. Oh, wait," Hazard interjected when Hook pulled his face. "You can't walk, can you?"

"I could shock you with what I might be able to do if we're stuck here together much longer."

Now it was Hazard who pulled the face. "I can't tell from your tone, Sir, if it's the *here* or the *together* you find more unbearable?"

There was a silence next that seemed to beg for one of them to fill in the blanks, but when stubbornness prevailed, Hazard left the cabin through the front door to stand on the porch.

Rain poured off the roof wherever it wanted to and a shroud of fog had lowered like a venetian blind into the trees on the hill that continued to steeply rise above the cabin. The surface of the lake, not more than an eighth of a mile below, was a choppy gray mood ring trying to imitate obsidian. Hazard was thinking he may have finally had enough of this experiment. The seasons were changing. Tension between Hooknose and him had risen to form the outermost layers of their skins. Coordinates for eco-tage had stopped coming in and with no apparent direction, no food, and no energy or passion to push on, Hazard was feeling very ready to become Bret Meyer Brady, all of a sudden. His blue eyes narrowed into determined headlights that would show his soul the way out of this darkness.

The cabin door creaked open behind him and Hazard's body concealed the start it gave him. When he didn't turn around, a barely audible voice beckoned.

"Hey—I'm sorry," Hooknose managed, arms folded across his compact wrestler's chest, shifting from one foot to the other.

Hazard turned around slowly and saw instantly that his companion had watery green eyes behind overgrown bangs that broadcast an inner crumbling he might not have otherwise chosen to reveal.

"What's up with you?" Hazard whispered, his missing passion and direction all at once flooding back into him with a *whooosh*. His arms betrayed his rough stucco façade and reached out. Hooknose took a step to be inside them. Hazard was taller by a head and found it easy to fold himself around his friend like a big, stinky manila envelope. He cocked his head to nest it in the hair of the man he had shared time with but nothing else. Neither really knew a thing about the other, aside from sleeping habits, but their embrace was at once familiar and comfortable. Most telling for two men of the woods, it wasn't brief. When Hooknose moved first, it wasn't to retreat but to liberate his crossed arms to reach them around Hazard. He craned his neck to bring his face to the man he had never intended to hurt.

"We should talk," he said with the soft, resigned voice of a man not just hopped up on painkillers, but about to reveal the way through the jumbled maze that was his soul. Hazard's own water table approached the surface and now his eyes filled as they looked into the window of new opportunity that Hooknose was offering. Their faces touched, then their lips. Mouths parted. Tongues rushed in. Hearts pounded a Morse code that both of them understood: anything they had to talk about, including the Top Ramen, would wait.

Hazard steered his comrade back inside the cabin and gingerly backed him onto the platform where they'd already spent two nights cocooned in sleeping bags side by side on top of a thick chunk of foam maybe the width of a queen size bed. With Hooknose looking up as Hazard climbed over the top of his wrapped ankle, the two took a moment in time to stop moving, to stop thinking, to stop avoiding what was about to come next.

"I haven't showered in a week," Hooknose rushed to discount the goods.

"And I have?" Hazard rifled back, lowering himself down on top of the crowning bulge inside the camouflage pants that had always made his partner's ass so easy to hike behind. If this had been a cartoon, there would have been a spreading ground ripple explosion like from an atomic bomb blast when Hazard's swollen goods made contact with the dome rising from Hooknose. Neither of them could have been bothered with analyzing from where this spontaneous homosexuality was springing though each of them knew they had been pumping this dry well since the day they'd met in the woods off the highway south of Seattle. It had taken them this long to wear down the bravado and un-cinch the armor that hung about their vulnerabilities on custom-made suspenders. Evidently it also took painkillers, physical exhaustion and the threat of dehydrated noodles. Hazard was surprised they hadn't stumbled upon the secret recipe before now but didn't let it deter him from the banquet.

"Am I squishing you in a bad way?" Hazard asked, kissing his mouth.

"I think I need to elevate my leg," Hooknose answered. Hazard raised his body providing enough clearance for Hook to rotate 180 degrees, placing his leg on a pillow by Hazard's head, and his face in Hazard's crotch.

"Is that better, then?" Hazard asked with a laugh as he roughly unfastened the camouflage hardware that had been brought to eye level.

"Much." Hooknose was suddenly a man of even fewer words than normal and Hazard's back arched involuntarily. The two devoured each other whole while the rain continued a suspense-building drum roll on the tin overhead.

Coming to the surface for air, Hazard propped on one elbow. "I had no idea you were gay."

Hooknose took his mouth off Hazard's dick and looked up the length of Hazard's torso to his eyes. "I'm not. I'm an anarchist. By definition I cannot conform to any established label, thought or category you or anyone else thinks they can use to define me."

"Well, long live anarchy."

Hooknose licked his smiling lips and returned to the greater cause.

When each of the men had made offerings to the gods that they had become, the talk and lo, the confessions they'd held off, tumbled out of their mouths like an unstoppable rockslide.

"I'm a chemistry professor at Portland State."

"I'm a newspaper reporter in Eugene."

"My real name is Sergio."

"I'm Bret."

"If I don't get to Portland by next Monday, I could lose my tenure."

"I've already lost my job and I'm way too old for this shit."

"Ha! Maybe we can be unemployed and homeless together."

"Uh, isn't that we've been these past two months?"

"To be honest, when I fucked up my leg, I was seriously thinking about chucking this gig."

"And now?"

"Well, now–" Sergio started then stopped, turning his head to face Bret. "Now that you and I, uh, understand each other better, I could probably be sweet-talked into sticking it out a while longer."

Bret grabbed Sergio's softening erection. "You better be more careful what you stick out around me."

"Well, now that I know where your talents really shine, I will for sure be taking greater advantage of your skill set."

"And you thought I was only handy with a compass."

"Uh, no I didn't. You've gotten us lost more than once."

"Hey, this place isn't my fault. You're the one who called in this four-star favor. I was happy seeing the country by rail."

"Yeah, that plan worked out really well for us, too. Okay, I need to level and tell you I've been here before, to this cabin, I mean. I worked the past three summers at the visitor center at the dam about two miles down the reservoir from here. This cabin is where I lived each summer."

"Really?" Bret climbed on top of Sergio to straddle him at the waist and pinned his arms at the wrists with his hands, suggesting that torture might be imminent.

"I've known Greyhound for the three years I've been up here. I figured him to be harmless but he's been at this sly fox and Freddy game at least a decade longer than us now and I've had this feeling lately that he is up to something bigger than I've given him credit for. Claims he once met the Unabomber in person, you know?"

"No, I didn't know. I still can't believe this is your cabin; that you've been home—not to mention been a rather lousy host—this whole time. Tell me, how far to a grocery store then? We need to get real food into us if we're going to build up your strength to walk out of here."

"Or have sex again?"

"And that too."

"It's not my cabin. It's Greyhound's. We're a little more than seven miles from Orofino where there's an IGA and maybe an Excell Foods."

"IGA?"

"Independent Grocers Association, I think. There are junk food vending machines at the visitor center and that's only a couple miles from here. Hey, wait!" Sergio tried to sit up but Bret forced him back into submission. "I just remembered that Greyhound has been hoarding Army rations in an old mineshaft not far from the cabin."

"Army rations? What in the hell for?"

"The coming civil war? Who knows in that conspiracy-twisted brain of his? But if you follow the trail behind the outhouse for about a quarter mile, you'll see a patch of pine trees above it to your left. The trees sort of half-ass conceal the entrance to the mine, if you weren't looking for it, I suppose."

"Oh, so I'm going?" Bret smiled. "We're done here, then?"

"Dude, I just heard and felt your stomach growl so I know you're as hungry as I am. Besides," his eyebrows disappeared into his bangs, "my le-e-e-g," he said about as pathetically as a war amputee coming out of anesthesia.

Bret rose off his prisoner, holding his hands away palms up. "You weren't nearly as fragile five minutes ago. I'll go check out the mine. If I'm not back in thirty minutes, you'll need to buck up, hobble out and find me."

"That seems fair," Hooknose said.

"No, it doesn't," Hazard replied, pulling back on his pants. He tossed on a rubberized rain slicker and left the cabin, pulling the stubborn front door closed behind him.

The rain hadn't let up and rivulets poured off the hill and onto the trail. Hazard could see his breath when he exhaled, which told him more than anything else that Autumn, invited or not, was testing out the welcome mat. Stopping off at the outhouse to relieve his post-sex bladder, he caught himself smiling at the conquest that had just happened inside, and it mattered not a bit to him if he were the conqueror or the conquered. All of a sudden, it felt as though he had a purpose again and that the past two months hadn't been a jerk-off jaunt for nothing. More than this, after the sting of the past week of silence between them since the train incident, it was good to feel close to a human again, like they were in *this*—whatever it was—together.

In his elation, Bret walked right past the clump of trees he was supposed to have been watching for and had to double back once he figured he'd gone too far. Rain was getting inside his jacket at the back of his neck to remind him of the comforts of the desk job he'd traded for this. Could he even consider this *working* since he wasn't exactly making a living, he wondered as he took in two giant lungs full of the rain and the pine trees and the Indian paintbrush. He flexed his wrists and sort of missed the onset of carpal tunnel that he used to bitch about in the coffee room while making a selection at the vending machine. He hadn't been to or checked an ATM machine in nearly a hundred fifty days to even know if he was still tethered to reality. He hadn't turned fuck-all over to the Freddies either and they might not be blamed for cutting him loose or worse, forgetting about him all together.

Just as he was sizing up his abandonment, the tip of his boot caught a rock in the trail and he launched ahead of himself. The word "shit!" involuntarily shot from his mouth as he shook the suck of his sour luck from a rightly stubbed toe. The rain intensified, if that was even possible, prompting him to half jog a dozen swollen strides straight up the hill to duck into the trees, launching a raven from his roost.

Out of the weather, he raised his boot to massage his toe while he took a look around. The entrance to the mine was conspicuous now as though he'd been escorted into the holding area to await the start of the next Ghost Town Mine Tour departing at the top of the hour. Extracting from his pants back pocket the flashlight that Hooknose had advised he take with him, he trained the beam into the darkness, where several railroad ties had been stacked and upended to suggest unadvisable passage. Those weren't nearly as effective as the spider and cobwebs that caught the light and caused Hazard's heart to thump madly.

It was the threat of Top Ramen that drove him beyond the entrance to the chilly tunnel before he had time to talk himself out of it. Within four or five yards, he encountered a ratty orange tarp curtain behind which he found the entire circumference of the mine plugged by a wall of plastic-strapped, waxy cardboard boxes with giant green stenciled letters: US ARMY. He stepped on the edge of a pallet and stretched onto his toes—one of them newly tenderized—to see if he could determine how far back the supplies went. He couldn't. He grabbed a box and decided he could carry two.

As he emerged from the mine he could hear the rain outside the trees and thought he might minimize the number of times he'd need to repeat this soggy hunting and gathering mission. He set the boxes down and hopped back inside the mine. With his heart drumming out a nervous rhythm, he figured if he could move enough supplies into the cabin now, the two of them could hole up, staying dry, warm, cozy and intimate for a couple more days, maybe a week if they had to, he supposed. It wasn't like Hook was covering any great distances on that leg anytime soon, he thought as he removed two more boxes off the top row of the very precise stacks laid to overlap each other like bricks. *Sergio*, he tried, saying the name out loud a couple times while he moved boxes. It would take some getting used to.

Back outside the mine, where he was stacking his grocery store, he wondered how much food was in one of these boxes to gauge if he should go back in for more. He popped the flaps on a box to find a packing slip listing the contents of each of the twelve smaller ration boxes:

> Entrees: Bacon Omelet and Beans, Chicken Tikka Masala Rice, Cream of Tomato Soup, Chocolate Pudding in chocolate sauce. Tuna in light mayo. Pack also contains: Oatmeal Block, Fruit and Oat Snack Bar, Golden Oat Snack Bar, Fruit-filled Cookies, brown digestive crackers, 1 chocolate bar, hard candy, brewers yeast, jam, dried fruit, instant coffee, instant black tea, beverage whitener, sugar, hot chocolate, isotonic drink, Tabasco Sauce, chewing gum, waterproof matches, water purification tablets, paper tissues.

He opened the flap on another box to see if the entrees varied. They didn't. He could see how a cave full of the same rations could quickly become the next Top Ramen. He went for two more boxes inside the mine, but when he removed the sixth box from the top of the stack, he could see in the flashlight beam that the contents of the mine changed beyond that. *What the Hell?*

R ED HARVEY'S OFFICE WASN'T A SPRAWLING AFFAIR BUT THE CORNER windows overlooking the riverfront park and the mirror tiles on an opposite wall—original decor from when the building was built in the '70s—offered the illusion that it was. He slipped into melancholy each year when kids went back to school and leaves began changing in the Rose City. It was sort of a post–Labor Day BBQ depression that hit him every year. With his colon contending with more red meat than a lioness lands in a Kalahari summer, the season of root vegetables and squash was upon him. He would slip into blood withdrawal and function in a semi-vegetative state until April when he would false-start the season with a garden party grill fest that would surely get rained out.

His bureau mate, Rich, poked his head through the open door. "There's an old bat packing what looks like an AK-47 Missile Launcher out here asking to see you. You in?" He couldn't maintain a neutral face anywhere close to office professional.

"She's not an ex-girlfriend, is she?" Red Harvey looked away from the window to his junior colleague.

"Even taking into consideration your vast and very liberal taste in women, I would have to infer she is not an ex-girlfriend."

The bureau chief moved toward the door. "And she cleared the metal detector downstairs?"

"Apparently."

Red rounded the corner just as Anne looked up from a notebook she had brought along. "Ms. Martondale. What can I do for you?"

"You know my name. That is just too creepy," she said rising from a chair.

"Well, we aren't the FBI for nothing."

Anne was about to make a 9/11 wisecrack, but thought better of it wondering if it were still a Bushie-decreed federal offense to reference the government's shortcomings. She patted the poster tube with the homemade string strap slung over her right shoulder. "I'd like to show you something. It will only take a moment of your time."

She was already walking past him toward his office when he thought to say, "Come in, please."

"My visit today concerns what I'm sure must be your round-the-clock investigation into the disappearance of my neighbor, Bret Meyer Brady," she said, moving a few things out of the way on his desktop.

"Go on," he replied with a hand over his mouth to conceal the grin he couldn't otherwise control.

"I managed to intercept an email that wasn't intended for me and wouldn't you know it was encoded. But I of course broke the code."

"Of course," he nodded. She shot him a look indicating he would be wise not to patronize her. "I mean a woman your age is probably very good at Sudoku and word searches. Puzzles are what you do, right?"

She extracted a laminated map from the poster tube and unrolled it on top of the desk, using his things to weight down the corners. He drew closer to see that he was looking at a map of the People's Republic of China pocked with a bunch of adhesive yellow dots.

"Well, let me stop you right there, Ms. Martondale. This is clearly outside my jurisdiction. The Central Intelligence Agency handles intel of an international nature. I could perhaps give you a referral—"

The woman, a good thirty years his senior, looked up from her map in astonishment. "You're telling me you're off the case? That you don't care about my missing neighbor or want to see the coded email or hear about the Mundoro Maoling Gold Cartel?"

His hand flew involuntarily to his mouth just as his parting lips and narrowing eyes were about to betray the secret agent man image he so needed to pull off in that moment. "I'm certain your findings and theories will be of immense import to Interpol. Maybe I can refer…"

She cut him off at the knees. "From what I gather, aside from that Salazar character you put away in Eugene, your career, Mr. Harvey, hasn't exactly lit up the commendation board. And these past couple of years, the Bureau seems to be full of chiefs like you who wouldn't know a lead if it were barb-wire-cinched around their empty scrotums. I'm here to tell you," she drummed the map of China with her index finger, "something major is about to go down and I wouldn't be a-tall surprised if it bears the autograph of *Al Qaeda*." She whispered the last six words and closed her eyes a count just for dramatic pause.

The agent who had introduced the old woman's arrival appeared again in the doorway, as though he had been instructed to interrupt at the two-minute mark. "Pardon me, Red. Natalie Wesson is here for her appointment with you."

Red Harvey knew that the reporter from Seattle didn't have an appointment and Anne Martondale knew that name, but from where? She dispatched her brain into a deduction, analysis, and dismantling drill. Whenever she linked one free association to another and eliminated the detritus, she could usually connect the dots and get the answer she was seeking. *That's it!* She suddenly lost all other train of thought. Staring at her map of Red China and the yellow dots she had affixed there, it occurred to her she might try connecting the dots. In the next instant she was rolling up her map and shoving it back in the tube. This was a discovery and a break in her case she wasn't about to share with someone not intelligent enough to take her seriously. She was out of there.

Leaving Harvey's office while he sputtered something drippy

and cynical like *thanks for stopping by*, she spotted that long-legged reporter from Seattle she'd glimpsed during her previous FBI visit. *Natalie Wesson*, her brain fired with the flashcard she'd been thumbing her cerebral catalogs to find. The reporter looked at her with an uncertain familiarity of her own. Anne Martondale gave her a tip of her head as if to nonverbally indicate there might be new power in the sisterhood; she was onto something big. The reporter registered a glance of intuition that communicated back that Anne should lurk behind; she would be brief here. Anne winked as she passed under the bureau insignia on the wall and crossed the tiny reception area for her exit. In the hallway on the other side, she quickly scanned the elevator landing to locate the two corner cameras. Nonchalantly, she pressed the button to retrieve the elevator. When it arrived, she stepped inside.

Natalie followed the agent into his office, taking note of the middle age spread his ass seemed to be taking on, and were those *Dockers*? Like that non-fashion choice helped matters one bit, she thought to herself.

"My visit won't come as a surprise."

"Why's that? Your Libre Lover land in solitary again?"

The reporter took the liberty of closing the agent's office door behind them, creating a bit of a slam. "It's his birthday, you ass. Nobody gets that treatment on his birthday. What did he do this time? Flip off a guard?" She shoved his stapler and tape dispenser away from the edge of the desk so she could prop her hands on it to lean forward into his space. "You and I both know you're running a social experiment here 'cause you have time to kill and this guinea pig ain't going nowhere, thanks to you."

"Look, Ms. Wesson. If you're trying to build a case for *cruelty against animals*, fly at it." He rearranged the office supplies on his desk. "I don't run the state pen. I just handle guest reservations."

"Not according to one of the more sympathetic guards who says Salazar is in solitary under FBI orders."

"I can't begin to presume which assets you deploy to gain the cooperation and confidence of guards and prisoners," he looked directly at the tops of the very breasts she was trying to use against him now, "but I assure you, we are a bit more sophisticated, not to mention professional, at the Bureau."

The reporter yanked down the front of her dress with two fists, freeing her assets, as he'd referred to them. "There was a time these sealed your cooperation too, Chief Harvey, but in all fairness that was before 9/11 when you weren't so goddamn uptight!"

"They're still lovely, Natalie. But we've changed—hell, the whole world's changed in these past two years. For instance, federal agents don't *do it* for you anymore while apparently convicts serving near life-sentences do."

"You chose to get old while you were still young and you can't pin that on me or my breasts," she said, tucking them back inside a black dress that featured random geometric patterns in white. "But you're wrong to punish him to get back at me. You knew I would be coming down to visit him on his birthday. You knew I would head straight here once I found out you'd cut him off from the outside world. So you got me here. What in the hell do you want from me?"

The chief lifted a corner of his mouth into a grin he probably shouldn't have revealed.

"You bastard!" she nearly squealed once she realized she'd been played.

"Look," he decided to level with her. "You'll remember what I was doing when we first met?"

"Whimpering and masturbating on the floor in the corner of a gas station restroom?" She walked to the window and stared down at the lunch hour picnickers in the park.

"Before that," he prompted.

"You were undercover in the Enviro movement. You were getting ready to betray the only friend you ever really had. And then you met me." She turned back to face him.

"I was doing my job. You were doing your job. Salazar, I suppose, was doing his job. We all believed in what we were doing."

"Your point—?"

"I haven't believed since."

In the silence between them that followed like winter after fall, Natalie wondered if he might be holding her responsible somehow. She'd used sex for information all those years ago. Not much had changed about her tactics since, now that she'd been reminded about it. But she'd never had real feelings for the bearded woodland bunny—furry and cute that he may have once been. Plain and immovable, Red Harvey had always stood between a reporter and the real story she was trying to get at and that was Libre Salazar. He maintained that role even now, which was why she was here in this office in the first place and not blowing the birthday boy, which had clearly been her modus operandi when she chose the dress she was wearing. Harvey was like some demonic regulator that turned the tap when it suited him and wrenched it tight when it suited him even more.

"I've lost an undercover agent. I think he's gone rogue," he blurted out something entirely different from the confession she had been angling her shield to deflect back into the universe. "My hunch is he would talk to you before he did something stupidly dangerous, and I wondered if—you know—he's been in contact?"

"Who in the hell are you referring to and why would he talk to me over anyone else?" She could feel the burn of his trained observer eyes x-raying straight through her dress and fleshy parts. She silently asked herself the same question and nearly instantly an answer flashed on her frontal screen: The Mailroom Creep. Of course! He had always had the answers and the letters and the media releases. He knew too much to not have been on the inside and now it made perfect sense that he hadn't found his way inside by accident. He had been injected through the bureau syringe like an air bubble that would worm its way through the capillaries, veins and arteries until it reached the central nervous branch of the operation.

"He's made contact already then. That's what I suspected."

"I didn't say anything," the reporter protested. "I don't even know who you're talking about," she added.

The agent lifted the second corner of his mouth to display a two-point grin indicating he'd gotten all he needed from this particular transaction, unless of course, she wanted to polish his hardware like in the old days.

"I need to see about making an earlier train," she said suddenly. "If you'll excuse me."

"Excuse you? Are you needing forgiveness, Natalie?"

"Don't we all?" She moved toward the door, opened it and then left the room without looking back.

In the next half-moment, Rich stood in the doorframe and asked what that was all about. Red tried to cover by claiming *nothing out of the ordinary*.

"Well, speaking of out of the ordinary," his assistant primed, "you might be interested to know that Anne Martondale has been riding the elevator for the past ten minutes."

H AZARD BURST INTO THE CABIN DOOR LIKE HE'D BEEN CHASED BY A mountain lion, out of breath, full of adrenaline, and panicked into disbelief by what he'd discovered in the mineshaft. With breaking news to deliver, the reporter scanned the one-room cabin only to register anticlimactically that his audience had vanished. With the sudden break in the weather and assuming Hooknose must have hobbled off to the outhouse, he called water into the basin through the mile-long feeder hose that had its source high on the mountain above the cabin. He filled a glass and emptied it twice. His eyes locked a focus on the stack of Army rations he'd set on the countertop, while his brain spiraled through a dozen theories he tried to wrangle into rationality.

Behind the decoy rations stacked floor to ceiling three rows deep, the mine appeared to be crammed with wooden case after case after case of dynamite; not the cartoon variety of paper towel–sized red tubes wrapped in duct tape, but bundles of seven sticks each secured with two straps of wire, the tube in the center pierced with rubber-wrapped silver cable that looked like the hose end of a bicycle tire pump. While he downed the last of his second glass of water, he studied the sample sitting on top of the Army rations he had brought back from the mine. He didn't know much about dynamite except what he'd learned in high school chemistry, mainly and ironically that it was discovered in the mid 1800s by accident by Alfred Nobel, for whom the Nobel Peace Prize was named.

Bret was slow to formulate the reasons why so much dynamite might be stockpiled there, in the northern panhandle of Idaho, and he was slow to realize that Hooknose wasn't in the outhouse and he wasn't coming back to the cabin that afternoon. The sun was raising steam off the hillside. Birds chirped and cawed. He had been abandoned, left behind in the mountain hideout of a madman. It didn't feel like the right thing to take off looking for his eco-mate in case he was coming back, but it didn't make sense to stay a sitting duck if Hooknose had met with foul play, especially if Greyhound were about to return any second to discover he'd been snooping around in his mineshaft.

Scavenging around the small cabin for clues, he realized his own pack was missing along with the replacement cellphone Greyhound had provided them. The battery was dead anyway since they hadn't been near an electrical outlet in weeks; ironic that, given that less than a mile away a hydro-electric dam generated something like 2 million megawatt hours a year, Sergio had mentioned. The duo had been reduced to living out of his pack after losing the other one on the train and Hazard took its disappearance from the cabin as an indication that Hooknose had left on his own volition, though that betrayed him, even more so after the two had just exposed their largest vulnerabilities to each other.

In that lonely moment, Bret Meyer Brady thought that perhaps his renegade run had just come to a very dead end. Not only was he out of cash, but his emergency debit card that he had sewn under a Canadian Flag patch on the underside of his pack, something he hadn't used since before Coos Bay, was among the missing things he'd grown to rely upon for insurance these past many months. He walked to the side view mirror hanging above the sink, thinking it must have come off a passenger bus, given its size and the cabin's owner. He grabbed his beard in his right hand and tried to remember what his own face looked like underneath. With nothing more to lose than his anonymity, into a rubber plugged sink he poured hot water from the copper teapot that seemed to live atop the wood stove. He worked a sliver of bar soap into lather and not knowing whose dull disposable razor he was using, he began hacking at the thick brown hairs that tugged stubbornly before giving into the blade. Nicking his face with nearly every other pass, his mind wandered into a fantasy that Hooknose had just gone to a store to fill the pack with the things they'd told each other they'd been craving—dark chocolate with hazelnuts, goat cheese, cold IPA microbrew, movie theater popcorn, fresh berry cobbler ala mode, and feather pillows—and that he was surely on his way back to the cabin with his surprise booty right now.

T ED HAD TO FORCE HIMSELF TO HOLD STILL. HE WAS SUPPOSED TO HAVE left the grain terminal twenty-four hours ago and had faked a mechanical problem to buy more time. He was already under a ton of pressure from his expectant wife to get this trip on the river and over with in case she went into early labor. He wished he were a superball that could bounce off the grain elevators in every direction looking for Sergio, who'd said he was hurt and in trouble. He didn't know anyplace else to look and wait for him but here. This is where they met the first time. Except on the river, the elevators and that fluke encounter outside Orofino were the only places they'd ever been together, he reasoned. It made sense to Ted that Sergio would have to know to return to the one place he'd expect to find him, and that was at work on the river, right?

Even from across the quarter-mile-wide slack water river, he could have spotted the barge from almost any viewpoint in Lewiston to know that he was sitting right there, waiting. Where in the hell was he then? He grabbed a fist full of red hair on the back of his head with one hand and stared at the watch on the wrist of the other hand that palmed a cellphone he willed with all his might to vibrate. For the sixth or seventh time since he'd received the cryptic distress call, Ted bargained he'd wait another two hours before he absolutely needed to pull ropes and get underway.

Leaning against a grain silo about four times his height, Ted DeHavlin allowed his knees to slowly buckle and his back to slide down the corrugated ridges as the weight of his world pushed his shoulders down, down. He was about to become a father for the second time but rather than celebrate their mother his wife, he was losing the balance of his shit because some guy who had fucked him in the ass had run off with his heart. A hand rose to cover his mouth as one tear and then another escaped from hidden springs beneath aviator sunglasses. There, in a shadow that stretched across the railroad tracks and made for the centerline of the old highway beyond, he sort of fell apart. When he heard a truck leave the highway and hit the gravel before crossing the tracks behind him, he immediately started putting himself back together again. He looked up with a jolt of anticipation. It was his brother-in-law's pick-up. He quickly wiped his cheeks with the back of his dusty hand. The pick-up launched more dust and the cloud rumbled toward him even after the truck had stopped. In the brown-out, he heard a truck door open. When he stopped rubbing his eyes and the air cleared he saw his four-year-old racing toward him where he sat on the ground. He opened his arms and legs to receive the red-headed bullet.

"Daddy! Daddy! I passed"—and impact.

The father embraced his son, then moved him back a bit so he could look into his face. "Passed what, Teddy?"

"Salamanders," he shouted, waving a piece of paper with a blue foil seal affixed to it. "I can put my head under and blow bubbles and I can jump in by myself," he boasted. There was the sound of a second truck door and his brother-in-law approached.

"Samantha had me bring him down just in case you were still here. He couldn't wait to tell you."

Ted removed the ball cap his son would wear to bed if it were allowed and ruffled his red hair. "I am very proud of you, Teddy."

"Dad, you promised!" he sang.

"What did I promise?" Ted Sr. asked his son, playing dumb.

"That I could come with you if I passed swim lessons, and I passed!"

Ted looked at his brother-in-law as he raised his eyebrows. "Sam packed him a suitcase and said she could really use the down time to prepare for his little sister, if it was all right with you." The brother-in-law produced the suitcase and held it in front of his beer belly.

Ted looked at his son, who seemed to be holding his breath for the verdict. When the boy's cheeks grew more red than usual, Ted caved. "Well, let's get these fishes on their way. All Salamanders aboard!" he called.

It was more or less a double-crossing even though a verbal contract between driver and hitchhiker was usually loose at best, subject to change—certainly. He had specifically asked to be taken to the barge dock opposite downtown Lewiston and with a nod of her head the driver had accepted the contract. But then he had to go and pull up his pant leg in the front seat of the car to examine his ankle, in front of the driver who just happened to be the only available nurse on-call in the Valley that particular afternoon. She took one glance and gravely announced, "Oh, that's not good," and voided their contract on the spot. "We're taking that straight to the hospital."

He knew the twisted ankle, already looking pretty bad, could not have been helped by the hike from the cabin and then the bike ride into Orofino. As they left Highway 95 to cross the Clearwater River Memorial Bridge into Lewiston, Sergio craned his neck to the right to confirm that Ted and his barge were still there. He'd plug in his dead phone at the hospital while he waited for a doctor and try to reach him again. The ankle needed to be looked at but it was imperative he get to Portland in the next forty-eight hours. The river was the most anonymous way to cover that distance and he couldn't risk pavement as Greyhound would surely come after him to safeguard the mission.

All he could smell was shit. He'd drained the foam soap dispenser and sandpapered his skin absolutely bare in spots with the brown paper he kept cranking out of the machine above the running taps of the sink. In his embarrassment and shock, he'd ordered everyone off the bus at the station. He had no passengers continuing on anyway, but he wasn't terribly diplomatic about their departure, tossing bags out of the bins like a gopher hell-bent on excavation. His insides twisting and scheming all the while, he needed to focus. He needed to stay on track.

He grabbed a wad of toilet paper and held it to his twitching asshole. He pulled it away and wasn't at all surprised by the quantity of blood there. He would have been even more panicked than he was if there weren't some sign of the apocalypse that had been unleashed there. His guts cramped and he folded in half at the waist, his head in his arms on the edge of the sink waiting for it to pass. "Fuck!" He spit the word and some phlegm into the bowl. As he straightened against the pain he could see the sweat on his forehead and around his eyes. Having pods in his shit wasn't good, but it couldn't stop what was coming. He pulled up his pants and zipped up his windbreaker. It no longer mattered what the lab had to tell him about the ziplocked madness he'd just provided them for testing. He wouldn't bother to follow through with the blood-work they'd just ordered for him either. It wouldn't make any difference in the ending of his story.

He just needed to get out of this hospital fast.

It was only a matter of miles after they left Portland for Seattle that one of them would make a reference to *Thelma and Louise* and so it was, round about Kelso, that Natalie brought it up as an awkward silence breaker. Anne Martondale had never seen the movie so the reference would have been lost had Natalie not taken pains to paraphrase the plot and strike the parallels.

While assessing her star qualities in the rearview mirror, Anne the driver asked Natalie her car-pooling partner if she saw her more as Geena Davis or Susan Sarandon. If she'd seen the movie, the question wouldn't have been necessary, Natalie thought to herself, as vestiges of Angela Lansbury, Judy Dench and Maggie Smith vied for the more appropriate actress comparison statuette. Meanwhile, the driver attempted to smooth out the wrinkles in her neck by stretching her chin toward the sunroof, prompting Natalie to think perhaps she should have just stuck with her plan to take the train back to Seattle.

"So you were talking about a theory as to Brady's disappearance or his whereabouts and you couldn't get the FBI to buy into it. Wanna try your pitch on me?"

"On or off the record?" Anne cocked her head and waited for the answer. "I may be one bitter ol' blister of a broad, but I wasn't born yesterday."

"Well, it's up to you I suppose. Why don't we start off the record. If I think you have something, I may ask if we can switch it up. Fair?"

"Switch it up? You mean go on the record then."

"Yes, but only…" she trailed off. For the love of Pete, why was she putting herself through this when she could have been on the train, plugged into her iPod and unplugged from the drudgery of this world?

Anne shifted from one butt cheek to another and cracked her knuckles beyond the steering wheel as she drove up Interstate 5 using her wrists. "I don't know if it is illegal or not, but I hacked into Bret's hotmail account and intercepted a couple coded emails. I then broke the code, which probably *is* illegal," she accepted culpability but seemed pleased to brag about it. "You would have to comprehend the Theorems of Random Probability to appreciate my process." She didn't even try to make that sound less condescending. She knew her intelligence quotient. "But basically," she continued, "using both discreet and continuous random variables to support a statistical outcome, what I uncovered was a series of global positioning coordinates; you know, like 39, 44, 32, and 121, 47, 41. You're thinking *just numbers*, right? Of course you are, Dear. But when I feed that string into Google, it returns a gold mine site in the Liaoning Province in China."

Natalie was sure that was a dig at her intelligence. "It sounds to me like all I would need to comprehend is how to do a Google search, but okay, I'll play. China?"

"The People's Republic, Darling. In the email I decoded, there are thirty-four of these number strings in eight groupings, all corresponding to remote Manchurian outposts in China. I've plotted them on the map that is in the tube in the back seat. It's what I showed Secret Agent Man Harvey in Portland and why I'm headed to the Seattle office of the CIA.

"What would Bret Meyer Brady be doing in China?"

"Precisely!"

Just then, in Natalie's mental Academy Awards Show, Angela had edged out Judy and Maggie for the recasting of *Thelma and Louise* in real time.

The two swapped all the information each of them had on the missing reporter, even delving into some assorted side topics, and before they knew it, they'd passed the exit for Sea-Tac Airport and the Space Needle was coming into view just beyond the Columbia Tower. Natalie had decided she wanted to run Anne's China map theory past the one person she could think of who would indicate if they were on the wrong track. She had Anne drive them straight to the *Seattle Times* office.

"She's with me, Charlie," she told the security guard, flashing her badge as the two breezed through the metal detector.

While Anne waited for her purse and mail tube to come out of the x-ray machine on the conveyor, she thought at last she was being taken seriously instead of just getting taken. She knew that what she'd uncovered was bigger than the *Eugene Register-Guard*. It was bigger than the Portland FBI office. Maybe now she would get somewhere.

Mindful of the apparent age of her cohort, the two took the elevator to the basement that Natalie would normally have accessed by the stairwell. They hurried through the subterranean labyrinth that clanged with mechanization in the middle of the production day. The Mailroom Creep wasn't there. He was probably upstairs urine-marking the legs of her desk.

"Anne, why don't you spread out the map on this table and I'll go find my—uh, my co-worker."

"I could make short use of your water closet if you've got one. Traveler's bladder," she added, underscoring the urgency.

"Oh, of course! How thoughtless. Come with me." When Natalie spun around to lead the elderly woman to the loo, she turned straight into a stationary and immovable Mailroom Creep.

"Hello there," he said lecherously, reeking of something garlic he must have fed on recently.

"I was just—"

"Is this your mother, Miss Wesson? No, wait—your older sister maybe?"

His flattery was just as pus-ridden as his charm, she thought. "She's an associate of mine. We came down here to show you something that I'm hoping you can help us interpret." The mailroom creep tilted his head like he was trying to make sense of the human language she was using.

"Hey, sorry you didn't get to see Loverboy again. Rotten luck you've been having lately, huh?"

'How do you kn—?" She self-regulated. It didn't matter how he knew everything he always seemed to know. Well, it mattered. She debated her conscience. She just couldn't let it matter this instant. "Listen. My uh—associate has a map here she'd like to show us to support a most interesting theory of hers regarding the disappearance of a reporter named Bret Meyer Brady."

The Mailroom Creep laughed. "Brady hasn't disappeared, Ms. Wesson. He maybe just doesn't want you to know where he's gone, but I assure you he is alive and he's doing quite well, actually."

"By whose account, young man?" Anne stepped forward.

"Let's have a look at your map, Miss Lansbury."

The trio stepped back to the table where she removed the map from the tube and displayed her wares.

"It's a map of China," he stated the obvious.

"Well, I'm relieved to have that confirmed," Anne said with her out-loud voice instead of sticking with the one in her head. The Mailroom Creep looked up, a bit astonished by her directness. "These yellow dots here correspond to coordinates I, uh, *acquired*." She was back to self-editing. "Marking locations," she continued a bit more cautiously, "that I have reason to believe are gold mines—perhaps active, some perhaps still developmental."

Natalie could get lost in a map, so fascinated was she with topography and deciphering access to places far away. She leaned in much closer to the *basement dweller* than her strictly enforced no-creep zone would have normally tolerated. She was drawn to the map like a paper clip to a magnet and she willed her brain to parachute into the terrain below not even realizing her nemesis was taking advantage of the proximity to nostril vacuum the last essence of shampoo molecules from her hair.

"With a Level B Clearance, I bet pounds to shillings I could link the Mundoro Maoling Gold Mining Project here," she tapped the map with an arthritic index finger, "to something on Halliburton letterhead in less than a half dozen keystrokes."

"Where did you say you got your coordinates from?" he slyly asked the older of the two women.

"She didn't say." Natalie detected a trap and by interrupting, she succeeded in nudging her colleague just beyond the reach of its hinged, bone-crushing jaws.

"Okay, well might I have a look at what the coordinates looked like when you acquired them?" He knew enough about Natalie

Wesson to know she wouldn't have taken an interest in an old woman with a penchant for China if she didn't think there was something embedded in the relationship for her. Reporters were like parasites symbiotically seeking hosts. It's just that he had a feeling this particular odd couple was headed for the wrong watering hole.

The two ladies looked at each other, communicating in that secret silent language that could only be shared between Beings with Ovaries. He shrugged his shoulders, flinging his own non-verbal cue that it didn't matter much to him whether they shared it or not, but that it likely mattered to them. They caved. The older woman rustled through her backpack to extract a spiral-bound notebook she'd probably purchased at five for a dollar and had to rubber band shut to contain the scraps of loose paper and notes she'd shoved in there. She extracted a full sheet of paper but used her hand, not all that quickly, to attempt to conceal that the source of her information was an email printout. He took one look at the page and realized their error.

"What do you know about the Planet Earth?" he asked succinctly, but they took it as a riddle and he could tell by their faces they were both trying to unscramble the trick from the question. "Let me break it down. How many hemispheres does the planet have?"

"Northern and Southern," Anne answered. "Separated by the Equator."

He grinned under his beard. "You're right and you're wrong." He took a pen from his ear and flipped her spiral notebook over, drawing a circle on the back of it. "Here's your Equator, more or less." His line was crooked, but it soon wouldn't matter. "Geographers divide the Earth into two hemispheres, north and south, but they also divide the Earth along the Greenwich-Dateline meridians into Eastern and Western hemispheres. The problem is you can't refer to four hemispheres at once since there would be overlapping regions and besides, the word hemisphere means two halves. The exact coordinates you have here appear on the planet in two different hemispheres, in this case, the Eastern and Western."

"What does that have to do with the price of Halliburton Gold in China?" the reporter asked.

"Well, depending on what treasure you two happen to be hunting, your coordinates could be pointing to the opposite side of the planet. In other words, to locales a little closer to home, in the Western Hemisphere."

This revelation did not sit well with Anne, who felt she should have known better. She wanted to slink out of the basement and get to the public library, fast. She wasn't at all subtle about her defeat as she rolled up her bum steer map and clumsily rubber-banded her notebook. "Well, thank you," she said curtly. "Miss Wesson," she tipped her head and turned to leave.

"Anne. Wait." Natalie lipped the words *thank you* to the Mailroom Creep, familiarly wrapping her hand around his forearm before chasing after her eccentric little friend.

He rubbed his arm where the reporter's hand had been and he wondered how long it would be before she made two important connections: that they had met before when he testified before the Senate Subcommittee and that the inmate she took for genius was not the mastermind she should be sexually manipulating for intel if she truly wanted a break in her investigation. In another few days, the whole cat and horny mouse gig wouldn't matter anymore anyway, he reasoned with his bruised libido. After August 28th, the world will have changed, Marmot could shave, clean up and go back to the utterly nondescript business of being Greg Rosenburg, while others took the fall for him—again.

39   44   42   121 47 4 **10 10 18** 46 3

B RET RECOGNIZED THAT HE WAS PACING WITH INDECISION. THE CABIN walls were closing in with every minute that ticked audibly by on the *Westclox* glow-in-the-dark travel clock sitting in a sea of dust on the windowsill. He remembered what his father had always told him: *Deciding not to make a decision is still a decision.* As that pontifical voice finished echoing around in his skull, he bolted out the cabin door, which slammed back with a whack.

He didn't think twice about which way he should start heading. Hooknose hadn't escaped in the direction of the mineshaft or he would have seen or heard him so there was no point retracing those steps. This bloodhound, he thought to himself, wasn't going to risk being intercepted on the gravel road that ran behind the cabin and down into town. Bret galloped into a fairly athletic jog over the rough terrain, all the while hoping to pick up a familiar scent. Given how rarely he and his eco-comrade had been provided the chance to shower in the past half year, scents were both readable and distinctive.

In just under fifteen minutes at that pace, Bret topped a low ridge. There in the near distance, postcard framed between a couple clumps of deep orange Indian paintbrush, loomed the largest concrete structure he thought he'd ever seen, and because it looked so out of place straddling a canyon that had been cut by a river that no longer existed, it startled his sensibilities, bringing him to a clumsy stop on the path. He expelled a half lung of air in one burst of emotion that could only be described as disgust.

He trotted the next ten minutes along a divergent path that drew him closer to the place where it seemed the shoreline, the lake and his escape all ended at a mile-wide wall that shot another 40 feet straight up in the air. The sun had been ducking in and out of clouds but now it shone on the concrete behemoth in front of him like a prison searchlight that had zeroed in on an escaped Manhattan skyscraper that might have thought it could escape detection if it lay sideways and still in this canyon. Bret hopped off the trail and with a couple rather athletic leaps pounced onto a sidewalk that led right up to the visitor center on the dam's western wedge, crammed by gravity and the pressure of a backed-up reservoir behind it into the mountain wall. Raising a hand to shield his eyes from the sun, Bret surveyed the dam deck that stretched to and disappeared somewhere on the other side of the canyon.

When he pivoted back toward the parking area he saw and at the same time heard a Greyhound passenger bus crescendo into a full park stop. Instinctively, he slipped behind the visitor center entrance sign to more covertly spy over the top of it. His heart thumped madly, like when he'd scored the undiscoverable spot of the summer in Hide and Seek. As his streak of luck had been lately, the bus door folded in half to slap open and Greyhound struggled through it holding his gut with two hands looking as though his water were about to break. Quite obviously mobility affected, the driver moved toward the visitor center with considerable difficulty. Bret could see a second bus occupant now in the doorway and with a squint could tell it was his AWOL sidekick. With Greyhound closing the distance between the bus and the visitor center entrance, Bret slipped inside, spotted a half-formed group beyond the information desk and, like a chameleon, blended into the middle of it. He watched covertly as the bus driver knocked over a stanchion he didn't pause to set upright before disappearing around a wall marked with washroom icon signage.

Bret's quandary multiplied. He could either make a dash out to the bus to confer with Sergio, who may have crossed back to the enemy side of what was about to become a dynamite-reinforced battle line, or he could make his getaway and reach Harvey to deliver his intel, whatever in the hell that amounted to—when in reality after five months undercover, he still didn't really know shit.

Bret reached up to feel the raised letters of a government bronzed plaque on the wall next to where he stood trying to blend into the background: *Help protect this delicate environment for future generations*. He sprayed the sign with an explosive burst of laughter at the irony and the audacity of the thing given the irrevocable damage to the environment this dam must have caused. The folks around him didn't seem to appreciate his perspective and they shuffled uneasily like they were awaiting the start of something.

"My name is John Clifford Hopkins and I will be your Dworshak Dam tour guide today."

"*JC?*" Bret found himself speaking out loud, as he turned his head slightly to match the source of the voice. For the second time in as many minutes, Bret managed to raise the ire of the hushed and rapt focus of the group of sixteen or twenty whose core he had used as camouflage and who he now understood had assembled to hear the presentation and take the guided tour.

"Oh my god!" the absurdly tall guide in the U.S. Army Corps uniform broke character. "Bret Meyer—I haven't seen you since Commencement Day!"

Bret broke into a smile, more from the joy of hearing his name spoken aloud after nearly eight months of denial, but also a great measure due to suddenly recognizing his teen-hood friend with whom he'd spent his formative years fooling around. By a fluke based more on popularity than grade point average, the two had been named co-valedictorians by the faculty at Corvallis High. *Go Spartans*, Bret thought as an amused smile swept across his face.

"I'm sorry about that," the guide apologized to the rest of his tour group. "Sometimes the world gets a bit smaller in this job."

The six-foot-six Army Corps spokesman telescoped his thirty-seven inch arm over a couple tourists to squeeze the shoulder and neck of the man that had squeezed more than a few of his own body parts in their common if not ancient past. "Like I said," he smiled through a blush at Bret and continued, "on behalf of the U.S. Army Corps of Engineers, I'd like to welcome you to Dworshak Dam. In the next forty-five minutes, as we walk through the dam, I am going to tell you a little bit about why it was built, how it was constructed, what some of the benefits are, and what you will be seeing as we go along. But first, some interesting facts about the dam."

Bret augmented his vigilance into a three-way split between the washroom, the familiarly handsome tour guide and the bus parked outside. Hooknose was no longer in his sightlines. He turned back in time to watch a man leave the washroom, clearly in some sort of sensory distress by the pained look on his face and the rather demonstrative gasp he took for fresh air. Bret took this to indicate the bus driver still inside had likely not yet recovered from his intestinal woes.

The group began to move in one clump down a flight of wide stairs as if it were being drawn by a string tied to JC, whose bluish-green eyes and single-dimpled smile—as Bret became alarmingly aware—happened to be features even more noteworthy than his height. So was he now officially turning gay he wondered or was it just becoming official that he always had been? Bret shuffled to keep up. He needed to disappear to keep from getting spotted by Greyhound and since he no longer understood, if he ever knew in the first place, which side Hooknose was playing for, it seemed an appropriate time to go solo again, like those early days in the cabin in the mountains above Kelso. Bret knew that what he needed most right now was time to think and plan and to formulate his next move. As he watched his teen-hood friend smiling back at him, now a more-than-full-grown man who was blatantly ignoring the rest of his tour ducklings to reconnect with him, Bret also couldn't help wondering whom his next move might include.

Without taking his blue-green gaze off of Bret as he unlocked the set of double glass doors one level below the main center entrance, Dworshak Dam Tour Guide John Clifford Hopkins responded automatically as though an internal "play" button had been pressed. "At 717 feet tall, Dworshak Dam is the highest straight-axis concrete gravity dam in the Western Hemisphere. That would take 110 me's standing end to end," he fake-giggled at his own ad lib, a joke that quickly singled out the non-English speakers in the group. JC next flicked a set of light switches just inside the open doors that chain illuminated a bank of fluorescents along a linoleum-lined corridor that narrowed in the distance further than the eye could see. "We are now about to walk through the dam inside what we call the 1603 Gallery. This corridor runs the length of the dam at nearly three-quarters of a mile and is 1,603 feet above mean sea level." The group walked through the doors and sensed an instant decrease in temperature. The guide closed the doors and relocked the group inside the dam. Bret felt he was finally invisible, safe, but the feeling didn't last and was quickly replaced by the oppressive weight of the obstruction that constipated this canyon and held back Nature.

"The U.S. Army Corps of Engineers began construction on Dworshak in 1966. It cost $312 million and took six years to complete. That meant pouring concrete nonstop for four and a half years, twenty-four hours a day, seven days a week. Using thirteen million tons of concrete, there is twice as much weight in Dworshak Dam as in Cheops' Great Pyramid in El Giza, Egypt. Another way to think about this is that it would take the same amount of concrete to build a sidewalk three feet wide that wraps around the Earth… three…times," he syncopated the last words for added emphasis. "The reservoir created by this dam is 3,453,000 acre-feet and fifty-four miles long extending deep into the Bitterroot Mountains, making it the largest lake by surface area in all of Idaho. It flooded a series of mountain valleys covering over 50,000 acres of land that had been prime elk habitat."

"Not to mention destroying the river," a young college-age woman spoke what Bret was thinking.

JC smiled to reveal he was not proud of the more dastardly facts of the project. "Yes. One way to look at this project is that the U.S. Army Corps of Engineers destroyed the North Fork of the Clearwater River with this dam—the habitat, the elk and fish, but hey—they turned around and acquired 5,000 more acres of land for elk management and spent $21 million to build the largest steelhead fish hatchery in the world, just a few miles downriver from here. Sure, this costs taxpayers about a million dollars a year to operate and recreate what Nature was doing for free, but it's important to understand—in addition to what was lost—what was gained by this project. This is a hydroelectric dam that was originally intended for flood control. The total power output from the dam is 380,000 kilowatts or roughly 2 million megawatt hours of electricity produced every year."

The group followed their guide down the corridor until looking back they could no longer see the doors from which they'd entered. This was about as mind-boggling as the amount of water being held back by what now seemed a relatively small amount of cement. Every couple hundred feet a series of three windows on the downriver side of the structure provided the best indication of how high the dam rose above the original level of the river below them, and the group would crowd at the windows, gasp and step back, almost as predictably as the tour script that continued rolling out of the guide's mouth.

"I mentioned flood control and that is one of Dworshak Dam's primary functions. In the fifty years before construction, the North Fork of the Clearwater River flooded thirty-eight times, affecting downstream communities almost every other year."

"Yeah, communities that maybe shouldn't have been built in a flood plain in the first place," said the same young lady.

"You're certainly going to keep me on my toes during this tour, aren't you?" The official spokesperson for the USACE smiled a somewhat preemptive warning, though personally he couldn't agree with her perspective more.

"Just saying," she added.

"Hydroelectric power is the other important function of Dworshak Dam. Three large pipes, or penstocks, channel water from the reservoir to turbines in the powerhouse just about seventy stories below us. We will be taking an elevator to the powerhouse now." JC inserted a key to unlock the elevator that was waiting for them. He held open the doors as everyone filed inside. Bret, being the last to enter the crowded car, intentionally brushed by his friend in the process, making physical contact in about a dozen places. JC made a barely audible purr that brought a satisfied smirk to Bret's face as he leaned against the elevator wall in full flirt mode.

The elevator doors opened and the group spilled out into the 1005 Gallery. Bret lingered to catch a minute with JC.

"You here visiting? Are you sticking around for a bit?" he asked a couple questions at once.

"It's complicated," Bret said. "Maybe we can talk after this; after you're off work."

"No, of course!" JC reached out to pinch-massage Bret's closest shoulder as the two left the elevator. "We will move into the powerhouse next but I wanted to point out that where we stand right now there is just twenty-five feet of concrete that separates us from the reservoir."

"That would be less than four of you," the female university student calculated aloud, trying to win back the handsome guide's favor.

JC chuckled. "The gauges you will see along this corridor measure the water pressure against the bedrock at the base of the dam. Regular readings are taken off these gauges to establish benchmarks and trends for analysis." The guide braced himself for the question that always followed the explanation of the gauges at this precise moment on every tour. He had experimented with altering the script to see if the question could be avoided, but his scientific study conclusive, it could not.

"I have a question," said one of the middle-aged know-it-alls in the mostly in-state crowd, a man who had a beer belly, probably hadn't completed high school and was most likely staying in a fifth-wheel trailer guzzling Coors beer by the case lot in the Big Eddy Campground for the week. He didn't technically have a question at all. He just wanted others to know that he knew something that maybe they didn't because that would make him seem smarter than, clearly, he was. "They ever fix that crack in the thing?"

And bingo, the guide thought to himself, trying really hard not to roll his eyes. "That crack in the thing, as you so technically put it, became apparent in June of 1980, seven years after the project was completed, when a leak was discovered. And at 236 feet long spewing about 7700 gallons per minute, it wasn't a small crack. That's about enough water to fill an Olympic size swimming pool every hour and a half. The crack was discovered on the reservoir side of the dam and water from the leak was spraying past the Powerhouse and into the river below the dam."

"That must have been an *oh, shit!* moment," someone chose that timing to launch their comedy routine. Bret rolled his eyes so JC wouldn't have to.

"In an attempt to intercept the crack and relieve the pressure, the U.S. Army Corps of Engineers drilled seventy holes into the dam and then lowered a large sheet of plastic, like a shower curtain. This reduced the flow through the crack by about half. Later, they used a patch of cement, volcanic ash from Mt. St. Helens of all things and some sawdust, which brought the flow down to an acceptable level. And that seems to have held up pretty well for the past twenty years."

"But dams won't last forever." The college girl felt it her duty to remind the group of the perils of messing with Nature.

"You're right," JC wrestled to regain control of his tour group, which unfortunately didn't include any children in the bunch, as this usually tended to self-moderate the doomsaying. "Dams have failed." He steered the group down the corridor as he talked. "Here, as a matter of fact, in Southern Idaho in 1976, the Teton Dam collapsed, killing eleven people. It was an earthen dam, meaning it was made from stacked rock and dirt. Concrete dams like this one have a much better record of lasting. Still, in 1928 near Los Angeles, the St. Francis, a concrete curve axis dam, failed killing over 400 people, which reminds engineers and operators to be vigilant and use safeguards to remediate risks to the populations downstream. Fixing the *Dwor-Crack*, as it came to be known, is exactly what I'm talking about." He exhaled, holding open the door to the Assembly Bay. "Now, let's talk about turbine generators."

Thirty minutes later when the tour was over and the group emerged from the elevator at the North Tower and onto the open deck to return across the dam at its own unguided pace back to the visitor center, Bret held back to reconnect with his old friend. The two men bent forward at the waist and rested elbows on the railing and with forearms touching, surveyed the downriver course from this remarkable vantage that once exclusively belonged to hawks and eagles.

"It's been a decade, Man. I can't believe I'm standing here with you." JC wagged his head from side to side, took off his wide-brim Army Corps hat and ran a hand through his hair that used to be the color of late summer wheat, but now looked darker to Bret or maybe just older, if hair can look older. "Last I heard, you were still reporting for the *Eugene Register-Guard*."

"I was, JC. I still am, I suppose. I'm on a sabbatical."

"You chose to take your sabbatical in Orofino, Idaho?" the guide asked incredulously. "What? You couldn't have saved up another fifty bucks to really splurge in Spokane?"

Bret pushed into his giant friend. "I told you earlier, it's complicated." JC shoved back, and because Bret's leg happened to be tucked around one of the railing posts, the force knocked him off his balance. At that height on the edge of a cement cliff seventy stories above certain death, whether he bounced or got tangled in the 500,000-volt transmission lines coming out of the roof of the powerhouse like a marionette, was enough to provoke a Last Rites express prayer. "Jesus!" he managed. And just when he might have tipped over and onto the deck of the dam, an impressive pair of 37-inch-long arms snatched his shoulders and kept him righted a few seconds before pulling him into an embrace.

"Hey don't worry. Some kids dropped a cat off here a while back and it survived. Made the papers when the kids got juvie detention and the cat got adopted out as a legend. You can see how the dam flares out a bit after the initial drop?" He pointed out past the railing and over the edge, one arm still holding tightly to his friend. "Say," JC cocked his head some to look Bret square in the eyes. "You grew into one handsome man. You feel as great to me as you ever did."

"And you grew into a giant, JC, while I was obviously not paying attention." The two pulled apart, realizing at the same time the embrace might have lasted too long.

"You were saying your situation is complicated. How?"

"Well, I took this sort of investigative reporter job that led me here where I was—well, I guess double-crossed sums it up." Bret was being as honest as he thought he could be. "I could really use a phone and maybe a place to stay tonight."

"Sure, no problem, Bret. Hey listen, I live with this girlfriend of mine. It's just a dinky one-bedroom kitchenette affair with a sofa but we're used to having friends find me and then crash a night or two when it occurs to them how fucking in the very middle of nowhere this is."

The two began walking back toward the visitor center. "And you don't know what complicated is until you have to spend six days every week deflecting rednecks and environmentalists without offending anyone."

"Yes, nicely handled back there," Bret commended.

"Well, they're just lucky they had me today and not this guide that was working here the past couple summers. Now, that one was a truly obsessed motherfucker when it came to the crack in this hunk of concrete. He easily freaked out more tourists than—hell I don't know—a rogue grizzly bear attack. It wasn't just the crack, either. He'd pore over structural deformation surveys and try to *Chicken-Little* me over the increase of seepage flows under the left abutment that he said were a clear indication that fill material was being eroded from bedrock fractures in the mountain.

"I was stuck being his roommate two summers in a row and toward the end, I tried to take the brunt of it so he wouldn't bounce his apocalyptic theories off the really gullible rednecks and environmentalists. But when the Brainy Little Shit began looking into the ramifications of a complete Dworshak Dam failure on the towns and cities downriver, like Lewiston and Clarkston, and began predicting catastrophic probabilities and widespread casualties, well that just got a bit too sick for me and I started tuning him out. It cost him his job in the end, but he didn't care much about the work anyway as it was only a summer gig until he could head back into the classroom each September."

Just then, the math started coming together for Bret as he remembered Hooknose saying he had worked a few summers as a tour guide and that he taught chemistry or was it physics at Portland State. Simultaneously he thought about the mineshaft full of dynamite and the events of the past few months that seemed to be locomotive propelling them to this environmentally twisted set of coordinates on the globe. Shit! After all these months thinking he had nothing to go on, and even less to show for it, he suddenly realized he might just be standing on top of a 13-million-ton epicenter of what was to come.

"What became of that guy?" Bret asked and stopped walking.

"Beats me, honestly. Shortly after the Corps let him go, there was almost immediately this very curious and coincidental act of sabotage on the main transmission lines. Someone took a 22-rifle and shot up thirty-five transmission tower insulators, knocking the dam's powerhouse offline and taking the transmission lines out of service for nineteen hours until a bypass could be rigged and the insulators replaced. I didn't say anything to anyone even when a $5,000 reward got posted but I kinda couldn't help suspecting my ol' roommate who used to conjecture how easy it would be to take out Dworshak." JC scrunched up his face to indicate that perhaps he should have turned in his roommate a summer ago.

"Just as likely some redneck cowboys from town out target shooting, don't you think?" Bret didn't believe for a second that it wasn't Hooknose.

"Damn lucky rednecks then. Had those insulators completely failed, the line could have fallen and the second it touched the ground, people, cows, elk—anything standing in the area—could have been killed by the electricity traveling through the ground. It was a damn stupid stunt and it cost Bonneville Power something like $150,000 in lost power generation."

Bret raised his eyebrows but didn't say anything. The sun felt amazing on his face and arms after spending the past hour in the refrigerated concrete bunker. JC looked in three different directions and then smiled.

"Wanna know something crazy?"

Bret nodded.

"Right here, where we are standing, is directly over the crack. Freaky, huh?"

Natalie had lost track of the number of Starbucks runs she'd made in the past four hours since Anne Martondale had installed herself as the newest, apparently permanent fixture of the Seattle Public Library. Natalie was beginning to think that only when the last book got moved to the new Central Library under construction at 1000 Fourth Avenue would her new research assistant be unseated. Just then the gray-haired woman raised her head from the maps and spoke, not to order a replenishment of the green tea lattes that seemed to have been fueling her, but to say that it was time to "bring the car around, Louise. I can put the rest of these pieces together on the road."

"And which road would that be, Thelma?" She hadn't the heart to tell her that she had the names backwards, at least from her perspective of the characters in the film, anyway.

"East on I-90 for now. I should be able to update our route by Ellensburg."

After months that became years yearning for a career-making break like this, Red Harvey wasn't sure what he should do first. Since it had been the very beginning of the assignment almost five months ago when the two of them had last spoken, the regional bureau chief only vaguely remembered the voice of the amateur agent he had inserted in the woods. The brief call that had just been transferred to him by the junior agent in the outer office caught him off guard and didn't allow for enough time to go through the usual agent verification protocol. The chief couldn't remember if he'd even bothered to review the protocol with the former newspaper reporter, as there had been such a rush to get him planted. It was maybe one or two sentences into the less than cryptic phone call that he signaled Rich, by throwing a stapler down the hallway outside his office, to start a trace.

In his haze, Red was sure of a few things he had heard. Brady had gotten out and wanted to stay out. He had named a major target and predicted the date of an attack that looked like it was timed to coincide with the first anniversary of September 11, 2001. He looked at his desk calendar. It was August 26, which meant every asset and agency would need to be scrambled in the next few days and moved into position within the week to intercept the cell before this strike could be allowed to happen. It was a huge gamble that a bunch of forest monkeys could actually pull off something of this magnitude anyway, making this particular lead phoned in from Area Code 208 even more incredible in the first place. Given that he didn't yet have real names, plausible motives or evidence beyond circumstantial that he could really act on, he had no choice but to send his agent back into the thick of things. It was the only way to get better intel, he figured, and one of the best ways to learn when the optimum moment would be for them to move in. Brady had said that if he went back to the cabin there would be no guarantee he'd be able to get information back out and that in reality, he was worried he might not make it out either.

Rich popped his head inside the chief's office handing him the results of the trace. It had been a payphone outside a grocery store in Orofino, Idaho. A quick Internet search confirmed that not only was Dworshak Dam less than ten miles away from this payphone but that it was also #17 on the latest release of the Joint Terrorism Task Force's Hot Target Threat List (JTTF/HTTL). Scrolling down the page of the fifty most vulnerable targets in the United States, Harvey had to chuckle. Along with nuclear power plants, this dam like most dams of significant size also happened to be classified as an installation containing dangerous forces that could consequently render severe losses among civilian populations. In theory, this meant that it was *extra*-forbidden by International Humanitarian Law to attack it. Since 9/11, Red Harvey had held fast to a personal belief that these types of lists, which always got leaked to the Internet, and the attendant legislative deterrents usually proved no impediment whatsoever and were more often used as a government certification program or their stamp of approval, practically highlighting with searchlights where terrorist cells might want to spend their hard-earned jihads and fatwas.

He stared at the new page he'd turned to in his daily log where he had scribbled the day's date, August 26, and then double underlined a heading that read *Timeline/Next Steps*. Tapping the eraser end of his pencil on the journal page he realized that perhaps he wasn't quite the list-maker his government was. *Use your training*, he self-coached. *Think!* At least he knew for the first time in many months where his embedded agent was, or more accurately, where he was four minutes ago when he'd made the call. He knew there were at least two other male suspects involved, one considerably older. The plan appeared on the low-tech end of the spectrum if dynamite was the only explosive in their arsenal. *Typical*, Harvey thought of forest monkeys, for decades the masters of little splashes in very big ponds.

Just then, hollering down the hall at his junior agent at the same time, three words came to him and he didn't hesitate to write them under the heading:

Get on scene!

Hazard burst into the cabin causing its occupants to lurch out of their skins. He'd been psyching himself up for this re-entry since his friend, John Clifford, had dropped him off at the visitor center a half hour earlier. It's not at all what he wanted to be doing but he'd been practically ordered back undercover by the Portland Bureau Chief. The head-clearing night away from the cabin, and his first shower in he-couldn't-remember-how-many-days, had given him time for reflection. And in his shampoo-and-soap–frenzied high, when Bret was being honest with himself, he realized that while he probably had enough firsthand material to fake a story, what he still lacked was the plot on which everything turned, the hook that would help him sell it to a mass reality-addicted audience no longer fazed by fiction. What he had so far would barely pass as a beneath-the-fold, B-section exposé that so far revealed little more than when he'd started this. No. The FBI wasn't the only one who needed more here.

He and JC had stayed up the whole night talking and catching up and while Bret hadn't been specific about the story he was following in North Central Idaho just outside Orofino, he had been able to convey a between-the-lines urgency along with maybe a measure of danger sufficient to prompt his high school friend to insist he borrow his cellphone for the week. JC would use his girlfriend's cell and play back-up if Bret signaled a need for assistance and even if, by week's end, he didn't signal at all.

"Fucking Hell!" Greyhound wailed, before doubling over in pain, the physical momentum of which he couldn't correct before falling onto the floor.

"Jesus Hazard Christ!" Hooknose exploded once his lungs had managed to find the air that had been knocked out of them. "Where've you been?"

Greyhound hadn't righted himself from behind the ratty couch where he'd disappeared but his groans gave away his hiding place. Hazard took maybe a half-dozen steps toward him and stopped short when he reached the outer boundary of a stench that might have been trademarked Sulfuric Acid, that is if it smelled better.

It was Hazard's turn to curse. "What fucking died in here?"

Hooknose was up with considerable effort and hobbling in the direction of the stench. "Greyhound's guts are rotting out. Here. Help me get him up."

The notion that these two gimps were capable of mass destruction seemed suddenly comical to Hazard. He was flush with embarrassment for having put the FBI on high alert. What in the hell had he come back for? To play nurse to these two?

Hooknose and Hazard helped Greyhound to the sofa. The older man's stomach was grotesquely distended and his skin was the color...well, the color of nothing, it was so gray. No question this close that the bus driver was the source of the sour gas stench. Hazard glared into the eyes of his eco-lover turned traitor watching them narrow as if to say, *what did I do?* And in their nonverbal conversation, the old man let out a squealer of a fart so toxic that soon everyone's eyes began to water.

"He's got these pod-worm-things in his stomach," Hooknose explained. "I could show you some samples he's collected if you wanted to see what I mean."

"No thanks, *friend*," Hazard answered back, stressing the sarcasm and betrayal he felt by the sudden abandonment in the middle of their first real emotional and passionate breakthrough since they'd met. Hooknose had vanished, but then he had returned, and sporting a fancy new walking cast. Observed details were arriving quickly now and Hazard's brain scrambled to process them. They half-set and half-dropped the sick codger on the sofa and rushed outside onto the porch for fresh air and privacy.

"I went out looking for you yesterday and when I couldn't find you I ended up taking the dam tour where I ran into an old friend from high school." Hazard wiped the pine needles off the porch railing and anchored one of his ass cheeks on it. "He offered me a shower and a sofa-bed at his place in town last night." The confession poured out of him as though his guilt were a pitcher. "I was about to chuck this gig and start the journey home, wherever the fuck that is anymore, but this morning I had a change of heart and figured I'd better check back here for you one more time."

"Who's this friend?" Hooknose switched to interrogation mode so abruptly Hazard had to smile at the jealousy that must have shoved the question onto the center of the porch between them.

"His name is John Clifford." Hazard could see the recognition flash across his mate's face. "That's right. Of course you two must know each other. He's a guide at the dam, works for the Corps."

"You two fool around last night?" Hooknose looked off disinterested into the woods but his countermeasures weren't working very well. Hazard was confused that Hooknose would feel this way as he had the oddest ways of showing it to him before now.

"He has a girlfriend now," Hazard responded, realizing as he said it that it was going to come across as though that was the only thing that had kept them off each other. But at the same time, the question-slash-accusation also told him that Hooknose must have known firsthand that JC was capable of fooling around with a guy, or he wouldn't have asked it. *So of course—the two of them had sexual history!* Hazard formulated the depth of their obvious connection and simultaneously experienced a wave of his own jealousy that broke against his legs, nearly sweeping the two of them off the porch. What an insecure pair of unlikely dancers the two of them made, stumbling over their feet even when they weren't moving. "What's going on here?" Hazard deflected.

"You mean with us or *here*, here?" Hooknose raised his red-cheeked face to look him square in the eye. Hazard could see that he was hurt and possibly on the verge of something emotional. He sort of wanted to hold out to see what might be revealed but instead he sprung to defend their masculine honor and gave him an out if he needed one.

"No, I mean here, with Greyhound?"

"Dumb luck on my part." Hazard wiped the corner of one of his eyes with the palm of a hand. "When I limped out of here yesterday, it was for good. I was in a lot of pain. I wasn't thinking straight and in that haze I decided I'd had enough. I was headed back to Seattle or Portland depending on where I could catch a lift. Didn't matter as I have friends in both places." He took a moment to let the sting of abandonment sink beneath the first layers of Hazard's skin. "But then the first ride I got on the way out of Orofino was with this nurse on a crusade. She took one look at my ankle and drove me straight to St. Joseph Hospital in Lewiston. I was already feeling lousy from the pain and shitty for walking out on you."

Well, that helps a little, Hazard thought to himself. "But you're back."

"*That's* my dumb luck. Walking out of the ER, I run smack into Greyhound, who's there cause he's shitting out his guts and doesn't know why. He's in no shape to drive and because I'm caught out of bounds with my shorts down around my casted ankle, I needed to think fast even if I couldn't think smart."

"And that's the only reason you're back?" Hazard instantly hated how pathetically wounded that sounded.

"I'm curious, too…aside from being unlucky, I mean."

Hazard raised an eyebrow in hope, but it was misguided. Hooknose led them off the porch and away from the cabin so they could have some privacy.

"He's planning a big move, if you want to know what I think. I figure whatever the hell alien bacteria that's eating him from the inside out is driving him mad and my guess is he's about to kick it."

"I don't suppose that cave shoved full of dynamite comes into play, does it?"

"If I'm right and he's going out, might as well be with a bang." Hooknose thought this through a moment. "You know, I wouldn't put it past him to float down the reservoir from here on a raft full of dynamite, just like they did on the Alsea River in Oregon back in the '30s. Ignite the whole mess just as the raft bumps into Dworshak. He never shuts up about that Alsea, too."

"You think that would do it? Take the dam out, I mean?"

Hooknose chuckled. "Leave a pothole maybe. There's six million cubic yards of concrete driving a double wedge into that canyon. Dworshak isn't budging, my friend."

"What if he aimed the raft for the crack?"

Hooknose stopped walking and looked into the tops of some ponderosa trees ahead on the trail. "What do you know about the crack?" he asked, turning back slowly.

"I took the tour, Sherlock. Duh!"

"Right," Hooknose answered. "Well, back in the day, it was thought the crack was a real Achilles heel, but I don't know. Dynamite on the reservoir surface isn't going to have a lot of impact 250 feet below the waterline where the crack begins, beyond maybe sending a couple dozen small mouth bass with blown-out gills to the top. Now perhaps if he could position his dynamite inside the dam, somewhere between the *1005* and *1603 Galleries,* at just the right point on the reservoir side of the dam, well that and the crack working against each other just might blow things wide open."

"Yeah but how's he get dynamite inside the dam?"

"Who's saying it isn't already there?" It was Greyhound's raspy and strained voice that asked the question behind them.

Hooknose was visibly startled but Hazard was feeling particularly bold, having called in their position and with help certainly on the way within the week. Without missing a beat, he asked, "What is your plan here anyway, Old Man?"

The bus driver doubled over, holding his seemingly pregnant stomach with both arms. When he could straighten even slightly, more than a minute had passed with Hooknose looking to Hazard, Hazard looking back at him and then the two of them watching helpless at a man in horrible discomfort. Hazard couldn't help thinking that things weren't going to end well for the older man and just when he formed the thought that the almighty Federal Bureau of Investigation was going to rescue his double-agent ass in the knick of time, the cellphone he'd forgotten was in his cargo pants pocket—the very one he'd forgotten to check to make certain the ringer was off—began ringing.

The hobbled bus driver straightened fluidly into the posture of a twenty-five-year-old as though he'd just been touched by the healing hands of Jesus Christ. He scrunched his forehead and cocked his ear to zero in on the source of the forbidden device. "Who in the hell has a battery in their cellphone? You idiot!" He lunged at Hazard with alarming agility for a man whose intestines had reportedly granny knotted about his colon.

"Shit, it's me! I totally forgot." Hazard plunged a hand into his side pocket to silence the ringing, but his hand got caught in the tight opening on the extraction and the still ringing phone slipped out of his hand sideways to land in the dirt closer to Hooknose than Greyhound. Hooknose stepped to the left to shuffle the phone toward the old man.

"Where did you pick up a cellphone?" Hooknose snorted like a bull about to charge something red.

"JC loaned me—" he started to say.

"Hello?" Greyhound answered the ringing phone. "I said no cellphones period. This is *green-ops* now. We paddle the river-to-be at *cuatro ante meridiem* on eight-two-eight." He rifled off a riddled rant without taking a breath and then heaved the phone off the side of the hill. The exertion left him winded and doubled over again. The other two listened for the splash as the phone disappeared into the lake.

Hazard's heart was thumping. He didn't know what would happen next. Nobody was talking. Nobody moved. Greyhound looked like he was squeezing his asshole to keep his guts in. Hooknose knew what the riddle meant but wasn't saying. Hazard had heard the clue but didn't understand it and already found he couldn't remember all its parts. He knew that the call coming in on the borrowed cell must have been from the only person who knew he was carrying it. Or it could have been a call *for* JC from someone who didn't know he'd loaned his phone. But Greyhound wouldn't have given those instructions to a stranger. So JC wasn't exactly a stranger to this plot just like he wasn't a stranger to Hooknose, which would explain how dynamite might have found its way inside Dworshak Dam as the old man had suggested. The rapidly expanding scope of this operation had a sudden mid-air collision with Bret's command of reality and the realization that he might not get surgically extracted in time. He was left with two questions. Could he stop what was coming? And, for the good of the river and the species in it, should he?

Prisoner No. 13797671 stared out the window of the prison library and couldn't think of a time that he had felt more abandoned. He half-chuckled out loud at how ludicrous that was. And that analysis included the shafting by his so-called friends who'd blown up whole SUV sales lots alongside him but let him alone take the fall while they slipped back into real world shadows where they masqueraded as college chemistry professors, *Seattle Times* research assistants and hydroelectric dam tour guides.

They hadn't managed to drift even ten minutes away from the dock or escape the long afternoon shadows of the grain elevators before the first of half a dozen warning lights flashed onto the dashboard to indicate critically low DO levels in the aft tank. This seemed to always happen whenever they pushed the barge occupancy limitations and over-pumped fingerlings into the tanks. The Corps did this toward the end of summer to reduce the number of fish they had to hold at the hatchery near Orofino over winter. For the largest steelhead hatchery in the world, it was still only designed for 420,000 pounds of steelhead smolt and 100,000 pounds of resident fish annually. The surplus, in years when there was one, needed to be evacuated downriver below the dams. The egg harvest from the returning salmon had been uncharacteristically high this year, so Ted shouldn't have been at all surprised to be dealing with this. He just would have preferred to have an issue-free float with Teddy Jr. aboard.

He reversed the engines and maneuvered to back the tandem barges along the dock where he could decide what needed to be done. His options could well include having Samantha drive down from the Orchards to retrieve their son, but he didn't dare tell that to the ball-capped redhead standing on his tiptoes trying to take in everything in his daddy's world.

"Pull over, Thelma," Anne commanded. "I have something you'll need to see to believe."

The sound of her passenger's voice startled Natalie's eyes open. Her lids had only fallen a second or two during this never-ending straight stretch of Washington Highway 26. In temperatures that had to be topping one hundred degrees, the smell of rotting onions from a harvest under way had filled the car and her nostrils for what had seemed like hours. Checking the car's dashboard clock, she was forced to accept that it had only been forty-five minutes since they'd changed drivers at a town called Vantage during a rest-stop on the east bank of the Columbia River. "What?" she asked, trying to act as though she hadn't drifted off so soon into her shift.

"I said pull over," Anne repeated. "You have to see this."

Natalie drifted onto the gravel shoulder and watched as the landscape in her rearview mirror got obliterated in a plume of superheated onion dust. Anne was halfway out of the car before Natalie had set the brake and turned on the hazard lights. Natalie opened her door. The heat raced inside to embrace and immobilize her. She raised a hand to her forehead and wiped the perspiration there into her hair. Her mission-obsessed passenger was spreading out her giant map on the hood of the car. When Natalie's eyes adjusted to the glare of the sun off the paper, she could see red dots had been applied all over this map of the Pacific Northwest, just as she had first done with her misdirected map of China.

"This is a map of the same coordinates applied in our hemisphere." Anne set the stage for her big reveal. "Here is a chronology of environmental terrorist hits perpetrated by the Earth Liberation Front, as reported by you in the *Seattle Times*." Anne passed her accomplice photocopies of articles that she had pulled off the Internet at the Seattle Public Library. This was followed by her next piece of evidence. "Here is the string of coordinates that I intercepted in Bret Meyer Brady's hotmail account. I've written the names of the cities or towns where the ELF attacks occurred next to the corresponding coordinates on this page."

"Nicely done," Natalie had to admit.

"But that didn't solve the puzzle. See how the list of coordinates is grouped in this list?" She pointed to the page with the eraser end of the pencil that had been in her mouth.

40	54	39	124	05	06	Fortuna
39	44	42	121	47	41	Chico
40	25	12	120	44	19	Susanville
42	00	19	124	12	37	Brookings
43	21	35	124	07	52	Coos Bay
42	12	16	121	42	36	Klamath Falls
44	33	15	123	15	69	Springfield
43	58	42	121	20	28	Bend
46	10	50	123	37	25	Clatskanie

"See this break between Brookings and Coos Bay? Well, I've checked and it doesn't correlate to a break in the chronology or the type of mischief that took place so I had to figure out why these coordinates had been grouped the way they are."

"And?" Natalie jerked back a hand that had been placed on bare, hot car metal to support her lean.

"Watch this. Read me the names of the cities in the first coordinate grouping."

Natalie took the notebook from Anne just as a semi-truck loaded with chickens or pigs or some other unholy aroma category thundered past them at seventy miles per hour. Anne sputtered until the dust had thinned out and she could breathe again.

"Fortuna, Chico, Susanville..." Anne was tracing a blue marker line between the dots as the locations were read out. "Brookings." There was a blue rectangle on the map situated in Northern California.

"Okay, next set."

Natalie looked back to the notebook. "Coos Bay...Klamath Falls...Springfield...Bend...Clatskanie, or however you pronounce that." Anne had left a blue *W* straddling the western end of the State of Oregon.

"Next group."

Natalie felt like a contestant on the *Wheel of Fortune* trying to solve the puzzle. She broke her stare-down with the map to read the next set of place names. "Bonneville...Ilwaco...Auburn... Randale." Natalie didn't know what to make of this new shape exactly. The *W* from the previous grouping had given her the idea this was going to be a word spelling game. This shape was very roughly a triangle, maybe.

Anne seemed also perplexed. "Let's move on. Next group," she chirped.

"Seattle...Hoh River...Abbotsford." Anne's blue marker paused in the middle of the Olympic Peninsula as she recognized with momentary paralysis the spot where her family's plane had gone down. "There, outside of Vancouver," Natalie aided her. The blue line traveled across the border into Canada. "Okay, next group is a longer one. Penticton...Concrete...Stevens Pass...Winthrop... Chelan and Wenatchee." That blue line looked like a block-style *S* to Natalie. She and Anne hovered over the map. The *W* and the *S* suggested to them both that they might still be onto something bigger than dots on the map. They forged ahead. "Grand Coulee… Ellensburg. Hey, we were just there." Anne lifted the blue marker off the page.

"Go on."

"Moses Lake…Yakima." The two of them took a moment and tried to make sense of the two somewhat parallel lines this grouping created in the center of Washington State. Natalie lowered her head to look closer, raising her sunglasses to her forehead. "If you use the blue line that is already here," she pointed to the Columbia River, "we'd have an *H*."

"Brilliant!" Anne exclaimed, maybe giving the investigative reporter her first real point of credit since the two had teamed up.

"Next comes Richland…Spokane…Walla Walla." There was an upside down *V* in blue left on the page.

"And following your legend, if we use the pre-existing blue line of the Snake River, we get an *A*. The map is definitely trying to spell out something."

"Okay, there are four places left to link and one set of coordinates you've left blank. Pullman…McCall…Moscow…Lewiston… and this last set of six numbers." Anne had created a *Y* on the map reaching into Idaho.

"I'm embarrassed to say I ran out of office supplies. I'm one dot short." The two looked at each other and grinned at their fallibility. "But if I had a dot, I think it would be right about here, in the vicinity of Orofino." She drew a circle in the lower panhandle of Idaho and colored it in blue.

"That would make this a *K*, then."

The two stared at the map in the sun on the hood of the car at the edge of an onion field, willing the blue lines to jump out at them in a word or a location they could recognize. Anne was the first to sound out the last half of the word. *"R-S-H-A-K?"*

"**I** DON'T GIVE A FUCK IF IT'S RECRUIT RUSH WEEKEND. I'M COMMAN-deering the Idaho National Guard Base in Lewiston indefi-nitely. You get anyone who isn't an officer above the rank of pea-shooter the hell off the grounds by the time I get there." Red Harvey couldn't believe the attitude and resistance he was getting from agencies that were supposed to have learned and matured since 9/11. This was his situation to call as the Incident Commander. He'd planted the agent undercover. He'd handheld the process through every development and he was the one that the tip had been called into, end of discussion. The JTTF protocol had been written to establish just such hierarchy and eliminate inter-agency competition for the commanding spotlight.

"Can you believe that? Attitude from the *Idaho* National Guard." Harvey made idle chat with his chopper pilot who was doing his level best to stay professionally out of the fray. They'd been in the air less than twenty minutes and the FBI bureau chief had hogged the secure channel radio since they'd wheeled-out of an unmarked hanger belonging to the KC-35 Oregon Wing of the U.S. Air Force based at the Portland airport. "Are you able to put me down at their HQ?"

"We can have a look when we get there," the pilot said. "I

currently only have clearance to land at Nez Perce County Airport, which is about six miles from there."

"Your clearance is about to change—" Harvey craned his neck and struggled in his full body restraint belt to read the nametag on the jumpsuit of the pilot next to him "—Master Sergeant Antoni. It seems the only air support I can get out of Lewiston is a bi-wing crop duster. Looks like you're stuck with me for the next week while I assess this situation."

The pilot held his lips together very tightly so as not to reveal a grin at the crop duster comment. He looked down at the Hood River above the spot where it emptied into the reservoir of the Columbia River backed up behind Bonneville Dam. "Will be my pleasure, sir."

"Do you know the Lewiston area then?"

"I grew up in Grangeville, about an hour and some south of there."

"Is that right? Know anything about Orofino?

"State mental hospital is there. So's Dworshak, but I guess you already knew that."

"Think we could take a quick high-altitude detour up that way before we kiss the pavement in Lewiston?"

"I can take you in at 8,000 depending on clouds. That's roughly a mile above the surface of the reservoir. That's usually high enough to avoid visual or auditory detection by human eyes and ears. You wanna see it any lower, you should check to see if you could borrow that bi-plane you mentioned." The pilot checked his high-tech wristwatch. "I can have you over the target in another fifteen minutes."

"Let's not refer to it as a *target* quite yet, if you don't mind."

"Apologies, Sir."

In the awkward hours that had followed the cellphone fuck-up,

Hazard had kicked himself metaphorically raw for being so stupid. While it raised the tension in their little work camp, knowing that JC had turned also gave him one fewer person he could trust to bail him out of this mess.

After they had strung up a giant camouflage tarp from the trees at the shoreline to twin lodge pole pine posts stuck into the end of the oversize dock, Greyhound—sitting gingerly on a ratty lawn chair under the tarp—supervised a two-man supply line that ferried the cases of dynamite from the cave to where they were stacked around him in a specific, honeycomb configuration on the dock. Like a master weaver, the old man paced himself, between cramps and sphincter spasms, to connect fuses to electronic wires and boxes together.

After the second load from the cave had been delivered to the dock in silence and they were out of earshot of the old man, Hazard covertly tried to coax rudimentary communication from his one-time partner.

"Shut the hell up!" had been the snapped response and none too covertly just to be sure the old man had heard the reprimand. "I'm thinking," he whispered more softly under his breath. And with that, Hooknose staggered his already limping pace during the next couple trips to be coming from the cave when Hazard started back up from the dock and when they passed each other somewhere near the middle, eye contact must have been under penalty of instant annihilation, because it didn't happen.

As he traipsed up and down the forested and occasionally grassy slope, Bret began formulating his options trying to gauge odds on whether there was any chance he could make a break for it and if he did, his probability for succeeding. It looked as though the clouds that dragged like pillows along the tops of the hills that ringed the reservoir were about to unload a downpour at any minute. If he leveraged the confusion that a sudden change in the weather might bring, he had a chance, he supposed. Neither of his captors, if he could call them that, were in any shape to stop him if he bolted up a hillside turned to mud but then nothing told him they wouldn't just move the clock ahead and, with JC hustled into position, attempt to blow the dam before he could reach help in time to stop them anyway.

He'd lost track of the trips and the escape plans he'd made from the cave to the dock and still he could see no indication of how far into the mine the arsenal extended. As the dock began to fill to capacity, Bret heard what he thought must have been a distant motorboat. He stopped to listen. Maybe it was JC coming to pick up the dynamite they'd been staging for him.

"Hey! Nobody move a muscle!" Greyhound shouted up the hill at them as the motor sounds grew louder and began to reverberate off the rocky slopes above them.

Bret inched to the edge of a clearing in the trees for a better view of the reservoir to spot the boat he was sure was approaching just as a helicopter buzzed around the cliff face behind him and raced past several hundred feet overhead at a speed that suggested it was either being chased or it was late getting to where it was headed. In a thwacking streak that shook the trees it was gone in the direction of the dam but when he tilted his head to aim his ear, the sound didn't seem to disappear entirely. His brain scrambled.

Was the chopper coming back?

Was this his rescuer?

Was one helicopter an appropriate Post 9/11 response to a terror threat?

And then—

Was Greyhound actually capable of blowing Dworshak Dam to smithereens?

Or was he going to crap himself to death before his shit could hit the fan?

Was the writer inside this undercover agent really going to pull a book out of this?

Was Hooknose really thinking?

"Snap out of it, turd face." Hooknose jutted out his shoulder when the two passed on the path just to knock Hazard off balance and out of his apparent daydream. "Greyhound says it's time to bring the bus around. Come on."

Hazard stood there a bit dumbfounded, perhaps from the physical attack or maybe it was from his astonishment that they were communicating again. At any rate, Hooknose looked back and signaled with his head for him to follow. He did. It wasn't until they neared the cabin that Hooknose quickened his limp to pull alongside Hazard to speak as they continued walking. "Look, I don't know about you, but I didn't sign up for this. Hold on." He placed an arm on Hazard's shoulder and lifted his casted leg off the ground. "Fuck! This sucks!"

"Just take a breath. Tell me what you're thinking, please—" he implored.

"I'm thinking I really need to make a run for it but this leg is killing my chances."

"Well let's go together then. I can help you move along faster than if you go it alone. It's not like he's in any shape to come chasing after us. We're still a team, right?" There was silence between them. Hooknose began limp walking again. Hazard took a half-dozen strides to catch up to him. "What gives, Hook?"

"I just think it's time we went our separate ways."

"What?" Hazard fired back.

"Look, I'm not in this like you are."

"What do you mean, *this*?"

"It was just sex to fight the monotony, blow off steam, you know?" He could tell his comment had stung. "Look. There's somebody else in my life that I have feelings for; somebody I should be with right now."

Hazard stopped walking and Hooknose turned around. "It's not like I'm in love with you, Serg, if that's what you're thinking." When Bret said the words, he wasn't betraying either of them. It wasn't love—not that Bret Meyer Brady had anything in his life he could verify that against—but he did have strong feelings of affection and loyalty for this man he'd spent the last couple of months with and certainly the sex had taken these feelings to a different level.

"I don't know what I'm thinking, Man. This," he gestured widely with both arms, "is about to turn fucking ugly and go so far beyond the monkey-wrenching we've been up to this past half year. Do I think Greyhound can actually blow this dam out of the canyon? No, of course I don't, but he's aiming straight for the Achilles heel and believes he can weaken the integrity of the structure along the patched vertical crack. I'm the one that put that fucking idea in the ol' cuck's head."

"Yeah, JC mentioned you had been rather crack obsessed the past few summers."

"It's not just the two-hundred-foot crack but the whole seepage problem under the western abutment that has more than just me obsessing. I promise you that. That whole end where the crack is located is practically poised to ride on a lubricated slope of granite with the slightest nudge. Greyhound is about to become that nudge."

"Let's keep moving," Bret suggested, briefly taking Sergio by the elbow.

"I can manage," he said pulling away.

Bret acted as though this indifference wasn't carving into him like an Exacto knife. "And what about this person you have feelings for?" He was deliberate with his gender neutrality and bracing for the revelation his inquiry provoked.

"That's just it. I have this feeling he's on the river somewhere downstream from this mother-fucking reservoir and she's about to take out everything in her path."

"So we get the hell out of here and warn the authorities so they can stop that from happening."

"No!" Hooknose stopped, spinning around to make his point very clear. "The dam has to go. I'll light the fuse myself just as soon as I make sure he's safe. That's why I have to go it alone and you have to cover for me until I can get back here. This dam doesn't belong here. The river behind this fucker needs to be freed." He pointed in the direction of the dam.

"Jesus, Hook! Why didn't you warn this guy before now?"

"I tried to reach him the other day when I walked out of here, but what did I do instead? I somehow fucking managed to walk right into Greyhound at the hospital in Lewiston. I've had the sweetest damn streak of luck lately."

"And just how do you expect me to cover for you with Greyhound? What guarantee do I even have that you're coming back? No way, Man! I'm out of here too. We both know where this is headed and he's going to do what he has to do whether we're here or not." Hazard strode past this traitor on the trail and quickly outpaced him as he headed straight for the cabin.

"You don't even know where the key to the bus is," Hooknose hollered after him.

"I'll walk out. I have two legs that work!" As tantrums go, this wasn't his most elevated exchange intellectually, but he saw his break, both from his partner of two months and for freedom from this whole twisted mess about to go sideways, and he was taking it.

Up ahead on the trail the screen door of the cabin shot open and slammed against the outer wall. At the same time, Hazard tripped on a tree root and tumbled onto the path. "Fuck!" was the only word he could form as the air flew out of his lungs.

"Smooth move, Ex-Lax!" JC lobbed from the porch. Hazard came up on one leg and then the other, brushing the dirt off his cargo pants. Hooknose caught up from behind him on the trail and stood frozen to assess this new obstacle he hadn't factored into his escape plan. "What's up, old friends? You don't call. You don't write? What gives?" JC had to bend his neck to avoid hitting his head on a cross beam as he stepped off the porch into the sun. "You're just in time to give us a hand with the fertilizer drums," he advised as he raised a hand over his eyes to block the sun that had just come out from between the clouds. As Hazard was processing what JC meant by *us*, a second man appeared in the open doorway of the cabin. He was shorter than JC, though most people were, but roughly the same age that all of them seemed to have in common.

"Marmot—" Hooknose acknowledged his old colleague as he continued moving toward the cabin where the two embraced in a robust back-patting hug.

Hazard kept thinking this whole mess was spiraling down, down, down. Their numbers had just doubled and with every ten minutes that passed, things got more and more unbelievably complicated. Now fertilizer? They weren't just going for the Achilles heel. They planned to obliterate the whole goddamn leg. Nobody and nothing would be escaping now.

The two women with a combined age pushing 100 years had been on the road for nearly twelve of the last twenty-four hours when the car's brakes slammed them to a stop before easing up for a fifty-yard dust-belching-reverse against oncoming traffic along the shoulder of Highway 12. When the brakes engaged again, and Anne had placed the Jeep Cherokee Eddie Bauer Edition in park with the hazard lights flashing, the two women were staring with their jaws dropped open at a green highway sign as big as their car. There, in four-inch reflective white letters was the impossible scramble of consonants and vowels of the word they'd been trying to puzzle solve:

D W O R S H A K Dam
and *D W O R S H A K National Fish Hatchery*
NEXT EXIT

It was the only thing he could think of that had the remotest chance of appeasing the four-year-old bundle of disappointment that sat buckled up and pouting in the front seat of the pick-up. Their maiden voyage together had been scrapped by a plugged inductor valve that couldn't be fixed until a replacement part arrived by *Federal Express Overnight*. And by then the Captain would have been delayed nearly thirty-six hours and couldn't possibly hope to make up for lost time *and* babysit his obsessively curious son. As it was, dead in the water and lashed to the docks at the grain elevators, Ted Sr. had no choice but to flush a quarter million juvie steelhead trout into the predator-rich slack water above the Lower Granite Dam just miles from what would have been the confluence of the Clearwater and Snake rivers if it wasn't just another reservoir. It would have been another matter entirely if the little fingerlings had been given a chance in the wild, which penned up slack water was not, but he'd also been told that nearly seventy-five percent of his cargo this summer had been afflicted by a hatchery-caused infectious hematopoietic necrosis problem that had nearly halted production and jeopardized the anadromous program at the Dworshak National Hatchery, the very place that he and his son were field tripping this morning to see.

Driving up Highway 12, all Ted kept thinking was *how do you explain such catastrophic fuck-ups to the public, much less to a four-year-old about to inherit rivers and oceans without fish?*

Master Sergeant David Antoni had only been lying down maybe ten minutes on the cot in the empty barrack quarters he'd been assigned by a civilian staffer at the Idaho National Guard Compound when there was a knock on the door. He popped off the cot like he'd been cannon-fired, sure it was somebody there to tell him he couldn't park the copter on the drill field. He snatched his airman's hat, adjusting it over his crewcut as he opened the door. "Yes sir!"

There were two men in Levis and matching navy blue ATF windbreakers with yellow block lettering. "We understand you just brought in FBI Chief Red Harvey." Each of the men flipped the covers on their credential badges like synchronized swimmers.

"I am the Air Force pilot assigned to his transport detail, yes."

"We'd like to take a look at the area around Dworshak Dam and apparently you are the only air support in the Valley, that is if you're not counting a crop duster."

The Air Force pilot couldn't contain his grin upon hearing the punch line for a second time in the same day. "I'm sorry, sir." He apologized for the facial breach. "I have been assigned to Chief Harvey and I would need his authorization or orders from Oregon Air Command to—"

"I appreciate your position and respect the chain of command, but Incident Command has passed from the FBI to Alcohol, Tobacco and Firearms to coordinate surveillance and ascertain threat response operations from this point forward." He lifted his sunglasses to his forehead to make direct eye contact with the green-eyed airman. "Once again, we'd like to see the area around Dworshak Dam, if you'd be so kind to fire up your bird."

The middle finger on the airman's right hand twitched involuntarily from where it was concealed behind his back. "I will file request for a flight path and altitude clearance from Fairchild Base in Spokane. We should be underway in five to eight minutes, Sir."

"Thank you, Airman."

Master Sergeant Antoni saluted, stepping backward into the room to fetch his sunglasses. With his eyes disappearing into teepee'd eyebrows he paused a moment to determine if he needed to empty his bladder before this milk run. He decided instead to use the time to see if he could find the FBI chief in case he hadn't gotten the memo explaining that he'd been relieved.

Sergio hadn't anticipated the decision to move the attack ahead by a day, but he also hadn't realized that Marmot had been the one calling the shots all along from a cover job he'd been holding as a mail clerk and research assistant at the *Seattle Times* newspaper building. All this time, he'd alternated between Libre in the Oregon State Pen and Greyhound as the two lead contestants in *The Mastermind is Right*. In the end, he'd been satisfied that Greyhound was the mastermind who was building up to one final swansong he'd probably die fucking up in order to end his three-decade run as a hellion in the woods. That's the way the now-rancid and rotting older man had pitched the simply asinine plan to him over a year ago when the summer tour guide had convinced the hippie in the cabin to take him in under his wing in exchange for intel on Dworshak's many vulnerabilities.

Sure, he'd thought silently to himself, *send your sentimental raft of dynamite down to bump against 13 million tons of concrete. If they could patch a crack nearly a football field long, surely they could fix the nuisance pockmark your dynamite might make in the side of the thing.* He'd never really taken the man or his threat seriously and never bothered to stop or even really encourage him. That's when Hooknose had believed Greyhound was alone in this, before he realized there was enough dynamite stockpiled to overload the dock plus a passenger bus and a half, and before forty-eight thousand dollars of Monsanto high-grade ammonium nitrate rolled up to the cabin on the hillside overlooking the lake that shouldn't be there.

In the minutes that followed the activist reunion on the cabin porch, with that unlucky streak of his at full flare, he'd gone and drawn the short straw in the mission. It was now his role to drive this packed bus to tuck it just west of the powerhouse control rooms in a blind spot between the base of the dam and the area of the powerhouse known as Assembly Bay, while JC distracted the Duty Engineer away from the array of camera monitors that would have otherwise captured his approach. Then he was to use his passkey to slip inside the dam through an Assembly Bay Door, where he would join up with JC and the two of them would take the elevator to the 1603 Gallery to take refuge in the very back of the visitor center, which would double as their safety bunker.

Fuck that noise! Hooknose stammered behind the wheel at a stop sign at the bottom of the hill, turning away from the service road that led back up the tailrace to the base of the dam to instead cross the bridge into Ahsahka heading toward Orofino. It was the very nearly empty parking lot at the fish hatchery that caught his eye and struck him as possibly the safest place to ditch a bus loaded with dynamite and fertilizer. With the bus in park and the engine turned off, he spotted an earlier model Ford pick-up truck with a hatchery logo on the side nicely masked by some pine trees growing in a land-scaped parking median. The driver had probably wisely expected the trees would keep the truck shaded until early afternoon.

How considerate, Hooknose thought, as a whole new plan unfurled in front of him. He needed to find Ted to get him off the river, just in case Greyhound's plan succeeded, even without the fertilizer bus bomb wedged behind the powerhouse. The truck would be a cinch to hotwire. It was simply a matter of locating the starter relay under the hood not far from the battery. Then, following the positive cable coming off the battery to a small round cylinder nearby, all he'd have to do is connect the wire coming out of that cylinder to the wire off the starter relay and *voila*!

But first, he needed to try one more time to reach Ted on his cellphone. He'd last tried when he had been at the hospital in Lewiston a few days before while getting the cast on his ankle, but all he had gotten was a wrong number message. He was afraid he'd memorized it incorrectly or maybe he had just been transposing a couple numbers. Just then, he remembered a payphone on the wall outside the public entryway to the fish hatchery visitor center. He'd used it once before to get JC to pick him up there when the inner tube on his bike tire had blown on his way back from the IGA completely loaded down with two packs full of canned goods, one on his back and one on his front.

He decided to take an extra minute in his new plan to try using that phone to see if he could reach Ted one more time before having to race down the highway to Lewiston to see if the fish barge was at the docks.

The number you have reached is disconnected...

He slammed the payphone with the end of the receiver and the force he used caused the plastic housing to bounce back, striking him in the forehead above his left eye. "Fuck!" He dropped the phone to dangle on the end of its cable. His offending hand tried to massage the pain out of the spot where a hard lump was already forming. There were really only two other phone numbers he had committed to memory since he traveled without anything that could trace him back to, well, anyone. Even the notebook where he would enter the coordinates he'd get from Greyhound that went missing with the backpack on a freight train going who knows where—back when this string of rotten luck first began threading beads of worry—contained nothing to link or identify him. Of the two numbers in his head that he knew he remembered, one was Greyhound's and the other he hadn't used in over a year. With the luck he wasn't having, it wasn't a bad idea to see if he could still count on reinforcements. He gingerly raised the phone ear and mouthpiece back to his throbbing temple and punched the numbers in sequence. He counted the rings as he thought about what he would say.

"Yeah, hello. Listen carefully. There is an attack planned on a hydroelectric dam in North Central Idaho. The dam is called Dworshak—you look up the spelling," he snapped indignantly. At that moment a helicopter buzzed by not very far overhead drowning out the next bit of conversation. Hooknose leaned out from under the overhang to see it heading up the mile-long tailrace toward the dam, the top of which he could make out through the trees where he stood fidgeting from one leg to the casted other. "Get people out of low-lying areas and off the river!" He rushed out the last part and hung up the phone, all of a sudden realizing he was in a lousy position.

As Anne approached the uniformed workers behind the visitor center desk she dialed way up the level of *Helene Hanff–like* persistence she would need to employ in order to extract what she wanted to know about the dam's security and whether it could possibly be considered a target. Using her own measure of proper British reserve couldn't hurt so she pasted on a tea-stained smile at the last minute and leaned onto the guestbook.

"Welcome to Dworshak Dam," the perky young miss behind the counter parroted for probably the three hundredth time that afternoon.

"Hello, Dear," Anne added an optimistic upward lilt to her accent.

"Oh, where are you from? You must sign our guest book. We haven't had many foreign visitors today."

Anne couldn't judge which smile must have seemed faker. "I'm seriously considering this dam tour of yours, but I have some concerns about how safe it is—you know, from terrorists," she whispered the last bit.

The not terribly polished summer student employee let her smile down and swallowed uncomfortably. "I don't get that question often," she confessed. "I can tell you we have security cameras everywhere and all of us are trained to, you know—be on the lookout." The attendant could tell that her explanation wasn't comforting the visitor's anxiety. "Say, come around here." She motioned for the sweet woman who reminded her so much of Angela Lansbury from *Bedknobs and Broomsticks* to join her behind the desk.

Anne edged her way around the prominent piece of furniture and stepped up onto the dais. Beneath the counter she could see a semi-circular display of closed circuit television monitors. "Oh, I see what you mean."

The employee felt suddenly comfortable as though it were *bring your grandmother to work day*. "You see, there is truly nothing to worry about." Another visitor approached the desk. "Here, you try—" she motioned toward the new visitor with her chin.

"Welcome to Dworshak Dam," Anne said most professionally, the fake smile still plastered to her face. "Won't you sign our guest book?" she moved the open book toward the rotund man in the Budweiser T-shirt.

"When's the next tour of this place start?" The visitor had elevated grunts to language to Anne's amazement. Still, out of curiosity she had to lean over to see if the hunched-over Neanderthal's knuckles dragged on the ground as she presumed they must.

"You mean to ask when *does* the next tour begin?" Anne Martondale could not fake tolerance for ill schooling when she had none.

The paid employee took over, pointing to a desktop white board with the day's remaining tour times conspicuously posted in block-style letters. Anne's attention drifted back to the television monitors where she spotted a rather lanky uniformed man jogging the length of a long hallway. She grabbed the arm of her trainer and pointed with her other hand to the monitor just as the desk phone began to ring. The young lady picked up the phone and after a moment, uttered an awkward "Oh—" before placing the phone back in its cradle. "Excuse me," she directed her comment to the woman she'd invited inside her space. She lifted a desktop microphone to the level of her mouth and her little cracking voice spilled out of speakers positioned all over the triangular-shaped concrete and glass structure. "Ladies and Gentlemen, I'm afraid I've just been informed we will be offering no more tours of Dworshak Dam this afternoon. I apologize for this."

"Ah, Jeezus Ethel!" the round little man said in a raised, exasperated voice that was clearly amplified for others to hear.

"I'm sorry about this," the employee said but only to Anne.

The running man had disappeared on the monitor.

Ted and the miniature version of the original, Teddy Jr., pulled their orange pick-up into the hatchery parking lot where the driver instantly spied a shaded spot on the far side of a parked tour bus as the noon-day temperature climbed.

Red Harvey was livid. He had heard the chopper taking off but he had also been in the middle of a colossal crap and couldn't pull out of the mission at hand fast enough to find out what the hell was going on with his assigned helicopter. The weekend base clerk described the two men in ATF jackets that had left with his pilot, which was enough to provoke a heated call to the ATF Seattle Field Division demanding that they stand down and return his pilot and helicopter immediately at the risk of jeopardizing *his* operation.

The middle-aged clerk, who had been called in to work from a less than inspiring family reunion on his wife's side to lend the impression that the Idaho National Guard, as its mission suggested, was *there to protect, preserve and defend the lives, property and individual liberties of the citizens of Idaho*, busied himself with a stack of files so as also to lend the impression he wasn't eavesdropping.

"Do I seriously have to remind you that during *Operation Backfire* from 1996 to 2001, it was the Federal Bureau of Investigation that learned that members of ELF had two weapons caches and that both caches were buried in Tillamook County, Oregon? What do you mean ATF has always maintained there was a third cache? There was no third cache. Look, we grilled our suspects more-than-thoroughly, if you know what I mean. We asked them all about the dynamite, the hexamine tablets, the ample supply of Kel-Tec ammunition, two AK-47s, a mini-14 rifle, and the Glock 9mm semiautomatic pistol that were recovered *by the FBI*," the wound-up bureau chief emphasized with pause and special syncopation. "They said repeatedly that there were only those two caches and that they were meant for survival after Y2K, not for terrorism or assassinations. It was the FBI that saw to it these past five years that eleven members of the ELF have been indicted for conspiracy to attack federal land and animal management sites, private meat-packing plants, housing developments, lumber facilities, and car dealerships. This is why the FBI has jurisdiction here, my friend." Harvey and the clerk locked eyes and Harvey raised his eyebrows and winked, which was to say he just told them who was boss. "I don't know anything about a recovered backpack, no." He turned away from the clerk and walked as far toward the window as the telephone cord allowed him to travel. "You're telling me ATF has undercover on this and you just heard from your asset who called in from a payphone at the Dworshak Fish Hatchery?" Regional Chief Harvey lowered the phone to muffle it against his nervously tapping leg. He looked back at the clerk.

"Can you grab the fastest transport truck you've got and get me anyone on base ready to mobilize in ten minutes?"

The clerk dropped the files on the desk. "Yes sir!"

It was like an Agatha Christie stage play: *And then there were two.* Marmot and Hazard had been locked in nonverbal standoff in the trees by the shore below the mineshaft ever since JC had left to help Greyhound change into a set of clothes he hadn't already shat in before moving into their positions. The second pass of the helicopter had left Marmot agitated and pacing. Finally he broke the silence between them.

"I know who you are," he said, stopping to look him in the eyes.

Deciding just exactly how he wanted to play this, Hazard set his chin. "And you're Greg Rosenburg," he said with more confidence than he actually possessed in that moment.

"Always the reporter," his sudden adversary conceded and confirmed at the same time.

"And always the reporter manipulator," Bret gave credit where it was due. He didn't know whether to shake his hand or break it for spoon-feeding him from his bottomless trough of eco-bullshit all these years. "You'll have to pardon me. My guilt has been worn thin these past nine months. I don't carry the same torch for the anarchist environmental movement like maybe I used to. This attack, if you pull it off, crosses any line I might have once defended."

"*Me* pardon *you*? We're neither of us here for redemption, Meyer." He chuckled when he saw the reaction using his real last name had evoked. "We are far too egotistical and selfish for something so noble and fleeting as that. Reserve me my place in History and I'll die happy for the cause. Don't waste my time with esoterics."

"Well, let me leave you to it, then. This isn't my cause."

"Quit shapeshifting, you coward! This *is* your cause. Stick with it for once." He walked upslope a few steps to be face to face. "How else can you close your eyes on the world at night without knowing you'd done your part to save it?"

"What's my part, Greg? You've always told me what I was supposed to write, what role I need to play. Tell me. What's my part in this?"

Rosenburg reached behind his back to pull a handgun from his waistband. "Recognizing that I may not be as persuasive as I used to be when it comes to directing a performance from the raw clay of your cowardice, I'll spell it out for you, Meyer."

"Fuck me." Bret stepped backward toward the water. "This isn't what the Earth Liberation Front stands for. This is your own fucked-up manifesto."

"Fuck you? You fucked all of us by turning Freddie when our backs were turned. Not even they trust you. Come on! One helicopter?" He pointed the gun to the sky toward the dam. "Is that all the arsenal your credibility can draw? After today, we'll all be taken a lot more seriously. Move!" He shoved the agent with the blown cover toward the dock at the waterline. Without taking his eyes or the gun off him, he unlashed one and then the other of the two lines holding the tarp to the trees. "Get onto the dock!"

Hazard's heel caught on a rock jutting out of the ground and he sailed backward to land on his ass. The fall had hyper-extended one of his wrists and the pain rifled up his arm to flush the blood from behind his face. He felt like vomiting but it passed in the next instant.

"I said get your ass on the dock, or should I say the S.S. *Alsea?*" As Bret moved onto the platform, rubbing the sting from his wrist, Rosenburg dropped a thirty-horsepower motor between two flanges attached to one end of the dock. He pulled the ripcord and the motor sputtered until it settled into a steady hum.

"Your task is simple," he said as he prodded his reluctant volunteer toward the motor side of the dock by waving the end of the semi-automatic handgun. You steer the S.S. *Alsea* nice and slow down the reservoir aiming directly for the spot on the dam where you'll shortly see Greyhound's tour bus parked on the deck. When you get to the safety buoys about fifty feet out from the dam, use these bolt cutters to cut the line so you can motor right up to the concrete below the bus."

As he gave the final instructions, Rosenburg released one pin at a time that had been all that was holding the dock—or rather what was about to become his raft of dynamite—to the solid rock escarpment of that part of the lakeshore. "And just so you know, me and my *persuasion,*" he raised the gun in the air, "will be following you the whole way along the shore. And if you doubt my aim never underestimate how fast your asshole can become Ground Zero."

At that moment he extracted a remote control device from his cargo pants and pointed it at him. "You get the S.S. *Alsea* to the spot at the dam like I've asked you to, cut the motor and I'll give you a clear ten minutes to swim to shore where you can scramble into the woods to run from your own shadow the rest of your days. Knowing you, though, you'll likely write about my life story, because my life is infinitely more purposeful than yours, and claim it as your own. Either way, we both stand to get what we want out of this, so play nice."

With that, Marmot christened the S.S. *Alsea* with a shove off from his worn Timberland boot.

Hooknose had gunned the fish hatchery pick-up at least thirty miles above the posted speed limit all the way into Lewiston. Had he been stopped by a state patrolman he would have just spilled his guts about the attack about to happen anyway and probably get a light and siren escort to wherever it was he was headed. As he reached the outskirts of town he did see two Idaho State Patrol cars on his left closing the highway to traffic in the opposite direction. Another mile and a half further and he encountered a snarl of honking traffic that seemed to be fleeing the lower valley up the mountain toward Moscow. Tuning the hatchery truck radio from station to station, all he could get was emergency broadcast messaging urging residents and visitors in low-lying areas to seek altitude away from the rivers either in the Orchards or up the hill toward Moscow and Pullman. His phoned-in tip had worked!

He edged the truck onto the left shoulder to get around the cars that had stopped moving and made it another mile before even the shoulder became impassably clogged by the first mass exodus he'd ever witnessed in his life. This wouldn't do. He was still a good five miles from the docks at the grain elevators and he couldn't make that distance on his leg. He inched along hugging the guardrail and the bumpers in front of him so tightly he feared he might get wedged. Then, up ahead he could see where there was a break in the guardrail that might allow him to scrape through onto the grass strip that divided the four lanes of traffic. When an eternity seemed as though it might have passed, he finally stomped on the gas pedal to shoot through the opening with clearance on either side and that momentum carried him flying through the grass where he picked up speed until traffic on both sides of him became a blur of streaking colors. "Whoo-hoo!" he hollered out the rolled-down windows of the truck like he'd just won the lottery. By the time he approached the first obstacle in his way, which happened to be the main support structure for the overpass that lifted traffic from downtown onto the steep grade of a highway leading out of the Valley toward Moscow, he could see the grain elevators in the distance. He'd walk it now. He really had no other choice. He was boxed in by guardrails and the support column.

He'd no sooner closed the door and started limp-walking toward the lane of traffic to his left, when a motorcycle horn began sounding. He looked over his left shoulder to see a state patrolman on motorbike waving at him as he slowly edged through oncoming traffic with his lights flashing. Expecting to be chastised and possibly ticketed for his hasty parking job, Sergio was shocked when the officer offered him a lift out of this zone. It was time his luck changed, though it took some maneuvering to get his casted leg to swing over the back of the motorbike.

"Where to?" the trooper asked.

"I'm coming from Dworshak Hatchery. I need to check on my fish barge pilot at the grain elevators up ahead to make sure he's not on the river. Then I need to go to wherever the Department of Alcohol, Tobacco and Firearms has set up their field reconnaissance office for this operation."

"No problem. That would be the Idaho National Guard compound but we'll swing by the grain elevators on the way."

Sergio Payne could not remember the last time he'd smiled. He hoped there would be a legitimate reason for the one on his face now.

Greyhound longed for one moment of bliss that he knew was coming when he no longer had to clench his bowels to keep his insides from spewing out. For several days, the spasms had ceased to arrive in breath-holding cramps he knew would pass if he could just out-clench them, like when the pods first began emerging.

Since returning to the cabin with Hooknose after he was last seen at the hospital, his gut had been wracked by one single knotting, twisting, excruciating cramp without end. He hadn't eaten or slept in at least three days and it didn't matter how much water he took in, none of it came out of his dick but all of it came out his ass.

With every ounce of strength he had remaining he cranked the steering wheel of the loaded bus with all its windows tinfoiled from the inside. He was down to his last exertions on this planet as he turned hard left to drive his rig past the visitor center. He got to the ridiculously over-built cage of a gate that had been added to the dam deck after 9/11 and according to the carefully orchestrated plan he was able to nudge it open with the nose of the bus and a series of slight accelerations. When the entire bus had cleared the gate, and with the gate on a backward swing, Greyhound tossed the rig in reverse and using his side mirrors, which he viewed through slits in the tinfoil, popped the gate hard to wedge it closed behind him.

He proceeded a distance of about three city blocks toward the midpoint of the deck span, where he had the greatest amount of clearance to initiate a four-point turn to orient the bus back toward the direction it had just traveled along a strip of concrete scarcely wider than it was long. He traveled back toward the visitor center and to the best of his limited vision, stopped the bus at an angle on a precise spot that faced up-reservoir. He turned off the engine and listened to the wind. In the eerie silence, he looked into the rearview passenger mirror and marveled at what had to be the most gratifying moment he'd ever experienced in his thirty-year career with a completely full bus.

He lowered the tinfoil flap in front of the driver's seat to conceal from the inside anything that might be taken for a target when looking through a high-powered rifle scope from the outside and then he moved with some effort over dynamite to assume his post in the control seat three rows back from the front of the bus. He lifted the tinfoil flap at his new location and pressed his head to the slit of daylight. A massive and glimmering expanse of Dworshak Reservoir stretched from one edge of his field of vision to the other. He managed a grin as he spotted the S.S. *Alsea* nearly at the buoy line directly in front of his position. In that moment of supreme accomplishment of planning and coordination—assuming that the second bus was tucked out of sight behind the powerhouse 700 feet below him and that the insurance policy of explosives they'd packed into the 1005 Gallery managed to fire by remote timer traveling through all this concrete—he forgot his sphincter for quite possibly the first time in months. His pants and shorts filled with warm ooze that tumbled out of him like molten lava.

His grin widened because he didn't give one fuck-all.

The pilot knew he should have peed before leaving the field in Lewiston the first time but his newly self-appointed special ops boss had been antsy to leave. In the end, it had been the fuel gauge as much as his bladder that signaled an imminent need to return to base roughly thirty minutes ago. All the while he'd been monitoring military radio traffic and knew that fighters had just been scrambled from Fairchild and that the airspace around Dworshak and Orofino had been closed. But as he flew his aircraft back toward Dworshak for the third time, the passenger list had changed once again to now include the head ATF field agent as well as an Army Delta Force–trained sharpshooter who had rendezvoused with them at Nez Perce County Airport while they refueled and an ATF undercover agent in a leg cast who had just been delivered to the National Guard base and was considered an invaluable information asset to the ATF.

Everyone on board had craned their necks to see the immobilizing chaos that was taking place on the streets leading in and out of lower Lewiston. If there had been an emergency evacuation plan, it was hard to see how it was working for them, at least from the air. Sergio Payne was looking out his oval-shaped window and confirming for the second time in the past hour that the fish transport barge was still alongside the docks at the grain elevators. While that didn't tell him where Ted was, it told him where he wasn't, which was almost more valuable intelligence since it meant he'd be safe. For now, he could concentrate on the task of saving other lives—and more importantly if he got to work it both ways— restoring a river.

As the chopper neared the drop zone that had been selected based upon intelligence ATF Agent Payne was providing, Airman Antoni found himself piloting a flying gong show. There seemed to be a lot of spotlight hogging going on between ATF, the Army who had loaned the sharpshooter, the FBI chief who had origi- nally brought the helicopter and its pilot into this cluster, and the U.S. Army Corps of Engineers, who were the latest to weigh in on the pushy side of things after commencing a full-scale evacua- tion of the dam including the powerhouse and visitor center, which was going—more or less—according to the dusty emergency plan someone had just referenced.

But it was the usurped FBI chief who probably had the largest ax to grind who somehow managed to acquisition an Army trans- port truck along with sixteen Idaho National Guarders who helped him secure a rather sophisticated satellite relay communication patch to the ATF agent in charge who was still twenty minutes away on board the chopper—all from his field base unpacking like a well-provisioned picnic basket at the Big Eddy Marina about two miles beyond the dam. It was his cadre of Guards organizing the evacuation from the visitor center that were earning their Weekend Warrior stipends, shuttling evacuees up the road and out of harm's way a fair distance above the dam.

Anne had made the decision that she would be immovable and,

once decided, no amount of physics—quantum, meta or otherwise—could possibly budge her from underneath the visitor center desk where she and her road-weary accomplice had wedged themselves out of sight. The women could hear the deadbolts of doors being locked and then there was silence. Anne positioned herself where she could view the surveillance monitors and still not raise her head above the profile of the desk. There was not a speck of human movement to be seen but an overactive spider working its web seemed to be hamming it up in front of the camera on Monitor 6. Natalie pointed with an exquisitely sculpted urban nail to the screen that showed a beat-up Greyhound bus on the deck of the dam. *Hostages*, thought Anne Martondale as she pressed her back flat against the inside of the reception desk. *This can not end well*, she predicted.

It had been all Bret could do to maintain control of the mobilized dock and keep it heading in a relatively straight line. Every ten or twenty seconds, he could spot Rosenburg walking through the trees as he played over and over in his head the flimsy bargain that had been thrust upon him. Water tumbled over the edges of the platform on all the sides he could see from his position where he had a death grip on the rudder stick of the outboard motor, giving the navigator the suspicion that he was riding too low in the water. If he could figure out what was giving it buoyancy, he might puncture it on the off chance you couldn't detonate wet dynamite.

When he rounded the last triangle of land jutting into the reservoir that precipitated a righthand veering turn to line up a straight shot for the dam, he became instantly nauseated and puked up the remains of a granola bar eaten in haste about forty minutes earlier. He dipped his hand into the water and brought it to his face. Fishy. It tasted green, trapped. He stared at the hindrance of concrete that rose out of the water directly in front of him. He saw the bus parked on the deck. Over the sputtering of the motor he heard a helicopter in the distance but the sun was in his eyes and he couldn't see it in the sky even with a free hand above his brow. One thought sprung into his brain. He might kill or kiss Red Harvey if he ever saw him again.

Greyhound thought he could hear a helicopter as wind whistled through the cracks in the old bus around the foiled windows. He could see the raft now almost to the buoy line. He set the electronic detonator box on a fertilizer barrel next to him to rise to a better viewing position through the inch-wide slit of tinfoil. He felt a warm squish in his pants, like he needed to be reminded he was sitting in his own feces. "Fuck!" he announced to the most crowded bus he'd ever chauffeured.

"You can't stop what's coming."

"What the hell's that supposed to mean?" The ATF agent in charge barked over his shoulder into the back seat of the chopper.

Sergio leaned forward, taking off his headset to speak in a louder than normal voice. "By now, he has a bus full of fertilizer on the dam's deck, a stash of TNT off one of the main corridors inside the dam that were smuggled in one stick at a time by a rogue employee, and a raft stacked with dynamite floating down the reservoir to bump into the dam at precisely the same moment as the other stuff detonates by remote control. Look!" he pointed ahead and out the front windows to the glint of a bus in the sun sitting right where he'd said it would be about a mile and a half away from their position as they swung high and left into the canyon. "With one helicopter, we can't stop this."

"Take us over high and wide," the agent yelled into his headset microphone, startling the airman to jerk the controls into a steep climb before banking east.

"In my opinion," the pilot offered, craning his neck as they passed the dam and headed over the area of the reservoir known as Bruce's Eddy, "the scrambled jets that should be entering this airspace inside another five minutes could missile lift that bus five feet in the air with one rocket and knock it splat into the reservoir with a second."

"There's the raft!" Sergio yelled, cutting off the pilot. He twisted in his seat to keep his eyes on the floating reference, remembering in an instant that it had been Hazard who had drawn the S.S. *Alsea* short stick. He had made it to the buoy line, which must mean Marmot had kept him on a short leash. Sergio made sure that the slight grin that lifted up in one corner of his mouth wasn't visible to any of his fellow passengers. They were certainly too late and couldn't stop the rebirth of the North Fork of the Clearwater River now. All he could hope for was that everyone he cared about in this operation would get to high ground and stay safe.

Rosenburg pounded on the locked glass door leading into the visitor center from the observation deck on the reservoir side of the cement structure. A lanky, uniformed JC, who had been glued to the front window watching the raft as it neared the outside markers, jumped at the loud pounding and went to unlock the door.

"What the fuck happened here? How are we supposed to blend in with the tourists if the place is fucking empty?"

"The Corps panicked and evacuated the whole place. Even the powerhouse got handed off to master controllers at Bonneville. This installation is officially abandoned."

"Where's Hooknose?" Marmot demanded.

"No-show," said the uniformed giant. "I waited as long as I

could. Maybe his old key didn't work. Too bad. So sad for Sergio. Fuck him," JC decreed with a jilted lover's leer.

As the two surveyed the playing field, in the distance, first one then the second spillway tainter valve was remotely manipulated wide open, sending foamy white water tumbling out of the gated chutes. They rushed to different windows using their arms on the glass to guide their movements leftward. "Look!" Marmot pointed to the twin spillways of the dam where three jet streams of water gushed, shooting straight out of the concrete like water cannons.

"Bonneville is releasing as much water as they can through the three regulating outlet intakes in advance of an event," JC explained, never quite able to turn off his inner tour guide. As he spoke, frothy white curtains of water began to unfurl near the top of the dam to fill the channels of the spillways. When this new cascade of water reached the three cannon spouts, it was like a guillotine had sliced three fingers free from a hand, leaving three nubs behind for the thousands of gallons of water to cascade over and around. JC chuckled.

"What's so funny?" Marmot asked.

"Wasting water this way has got to be killing the Bonneville bean counters since it doesn't run through the turbines, meaning they aren't making money."

"You gotta love the irony that they're thinking about this instead of what they should be worried about and that's losing their whole damn dirty money maker when this thing blows and the salmon swim free."

Natalie and Anne had locked each other into a stare-down in their position hiding under the reception desk from where they could hear every word of this dialogue. Natalie's face suddenly screwed into a thirty-something question mark as her head tilted to the right. One of the voices reminded her of somebody and her brain scrambled through a database of lovers and family and friends and colleagues.

"I expect they'll open the 1,700-foot-long diversion tunnel next to take as much reservoir pressure off the dam as they can." It was JC's turn to point to a location a bit farther downstream just as his theory got proven. A column of water about the size of a single-story building began to tumble out of a hole in the mountain less than an eighth of a mile below the dam and grew in size like a motivated erection until it stretched out parallel to the surface of the river that appeared through the miracle of plumbing to form the tailrace.

"How long do we have before their efforts begin to hurt our maximum impact?"

There it was again; so distinct, the pronunciation just so, the accent remarkable and yet to Natalie, neither geographically or contextually place-able.

JC expelled air quickly and dramatically. "Hardly! At most, the Regulated Outlets can only spit out fifty thousand cubic feet per second and the spillways together, maybe 150,000 CFS? I don't know what the discharge would be for the diversion tunnel but with three million *acre*-feet of water backed up behind this fucker, the tub water isn't going down very fast."

"Well, you know that Greyhound wants his moment on *CNN Headline News* and if we don't give Anderson Cooper time to find his way to bum-fuck Idaho, this mission won't go down as planned."

Natalie's eyes grew large with recognition as she deployed her own hand to stop the gasp coming out of her mouth. That voice belonged to the mailroom creep!

"Hey, check it out!" JC turned their attention to the reservoir side of the dam as he moved along the windows with his finger pointing from the end of an enormously long arm.

Hazard dipped the bolt cutters into the water, with trembling everything, to cut the buoy cable line. His heart rate had grown speedily reckless in the minutes before he reached the warning boundary designed to keep errant logs and boats from getting caught up in currents that tended to form near the intake gates. He was aware of a helicopter now. He could pick up the vibrations of its rotors bouncing off his eardrums. The sun glared straight into his eyes from where it ricocheted off the side of the battered bus above him on the dam deck. He struggled with the cable. It was thicker than the planners probably imagined it would be. The biceps in his arms cramped. He retracted the two handles and rested the heavy iron pincer end on the raft to muster new determination.

He'd lost track of Marmot in the trees and the sunspots on his watery green eyes made focus labored and not particularly useful. But he remembered the deal and didn't have an option beyond a life or death cliché to doubt it. He needed to cut this cable, motor the *Alsea* to the cement wall, cut the motor and swim for his life. But as he returned the cutters to the water and willed the pincers to slice through the cable bundle one metal strand at a time, his mind began to exaggerate what his sun-blinded eyes were sure were whirlpools forming on the water's surface inside the protected area, the area into which he was supposed to navigate five thousand pounds of dynamite. Sweat stung his eyes and his arms were violently shaking from prolonged exertion. He struggled to find focus on something other than the demonic water and as he muscled through the last couple strands of cabling, another bundle of wires suddenly willed the dripping bolt cutters out of the reservoir, up over his head, where they caught the sun and tossed flying mirrors onto the shaded concrete fortress before him.

With a surgeon's precision, he plunged the pincers into the center of the dynamite stacks and holding the breath he hadn't taken, poised the open jaws of the cutter to clamp around the braid of wires that led to a control box on the deck of the raft. In that moment, Bret Meyer Brady—no—it was *Bret Brady Meyer* who forgot the environment and the trees and the rivers and the species and the ozone and the acid rain and the Monsantos and the World Trade Organization and Global Warming and the *Exxon Valdez* and clenching his teeth together, thought only about humanity—the souls downstream—and he sunk the cutters into the thick tangle of wires that was the carotid artery of the S.S. *Alsea*.

"What the fuck's Brady doing?" Marmot yelled so loudly into the glass of the visitor center window that his own voice hurt his ears. Clanking the pistol against the glass as he moved hand over hand to his left along the room to the door that led out to a viewing platform and a staircase, to the dam deck, Rosenburg strung together a most impressive necklace of profanities that sent Anne's tweezered eyebrows into her bangs. She was certain he'd said *Brady*—her Brady. She just knew it! Her certainty brought her legs back under as she rose to stand behind the reception desk in plain sight, had anyone been looking her way. She spotted the tall guy in the U.S. Army Corps uniform and, conjuring up her most affected Angela Lansbury accent and charm to date, said to him, "I don't suppose you can tell me what's happening here, can you? I've just come from the loo, you see." The clever old bat smiled all *Bedknobs and Broomsticks*–like.

JC spun around with a tour guide's start and took two steps toward her. "Ma'am, we're in the middle of a situation here. It's *terrorists*," he loud-whispered, pointing toward the dam.

Anne Martondale took several steps away from the reception desk so that his approach didn't compromise the reporter's hiding place. "Terrorists?" she asked with a soprano's intonation that originated far past her eyebrows and bangs.

He moved nervously and awkwardly now, amplified by his gangly stature. "It seems they've taken over the dam and powerhouse. We've just evacuated the center. You should have heard the announcements."

As he moved closer like a cat circling a robin too busy extracting an earthworm from the ground to notice, she counter-moved away and toward the bank of plate glass. She did this of course to avoid capture and so she could see why the other bloke was still screaming his vulgar head off outside as he moved along the railing of the two-lane-wide deck that separated the reservoir from open air.

It took several more seconds before he could release his locked jaws to celebrate that absolutely nothing had happened when he severed the wires. Nothing but silence followed until it didn't and was replaced by the shouts of a lunatic he couldn't make out but seemed to be running toward his position at this spot in the reservoir on the deck of the dam above him. Just then a couple of tinny plunks echoed like a piano being played beneath the murky water beneath him as the last of the cable strands snapped under pressure from the floats and anchors that had held this taut position for decades.

When the two ends of the cable leaped backward in two directions dragging buoys and giant strands of suspended algae blooms with them, Bret felt the S.S. *Alsea* begin to drift inside the danger zone. He swallowed funny as though his heart had just head-on collided with a gulp in the tunnel of his esophagus, and with the shore-side cable still pulling away from him like a giant hooked fish making its getaway, Hazard launched a two-footed leap and dove into the icy reservoir in an attempt to pounce on the cable that could keep him from getting sucked into the bowels of the monolith where he would surely be pulverized by the turbines. His aim was misguided as he quickly surfaced holding onto a buoy that had become unthreaded.

Gasping and sputtering, he watched as the cable retreated away from him as though it was a serpent being power-winch retracted, leaving behind suddenly autonomous buoys that in their new freedom, unmistakably began drifting toward the drain in this bottomless bathtub that would suck them all under. His ears were full of water. He couldn't hear the helicopter or the shouting from the deck or the splashing of his own panicked and thrashing arms that began windmilling their way toward the trees he could make out through water-stung eyes an unfathomable distance away.

Airman Antoni brought the chopper in fast and low, tipping the nose steeply upward as the Army sharpshooter slid his door open, lowered his special eye goggles, and bailed out of the air machine when the pavement got close enough.

"Hey!" Sergio yelled into his headphone microphone. "Put me down too! I can be more help on the ground than I am in here!" He was undoing his belt harness when the ATF agent reached his arm back to hold him in place. "I want out!" he screamed, as the airman pulled the chopper in a gravitation-defying maneuver to clear a frontline of ponderosa trees like a pea out of a slingshot. The pilot banked a hard right back toward Orofino. Sergio craned his neck to watch the sniper hustle through the post-noon shadows and under the overhang and windows of the visitor center. "Where are we going?" Sergio Payne demanded to know.

"We need to clear this air corridor. We have fighters coming in just about—" he looked at his fancy pilot watch, "—eighty seconds from now," the pilot said forcefully. "Don't worry. I'll get you a front row seat," he added, showing a smile as he turned his head to the side to indicate he was addressing his remaining backseat passenger. Within seconds the chopper was hovering a mile and some below the dam, roughly twenty stories directly above the fish hatchery, just about as safely *front row* as you could get. Sergio's heart was thumping in time with the *whoosh, whoosh, whoosh* of the twin rotors on the other side of the thin aluminum skin that surrounded him and to which his body had been faithfully strapped in half a dozen constraint points.

For a grotesquely dehydrated man who'd given over every drop of moisture he'd conserved in the past five weeks to the diarrhea factory, Greyhound was sweating enormously. He had underestimated how miserable it would be waiting in this roaster oven on wheels in August with the windows foiled and rolled up and the air off, and in the years of envisioning this plan, he hadn't counted on the death-stench that emanated from his pants and every pore of his body. He lifted slightly out of his droopy drawers and peering through the slit in the tinfoil, he could tell the *Alsea* had breached the buoy line but from his angle he could not tell it had done so without a navigator. So appropriately, he thought, that he should squish back down in his own cold shit to contemplate his last five minutes of life on this pretty messed up planet. His shorts filled with pods wriggling with intestinal worms became metaphor. There was poetry all around him. His five senses danced in the muck of it.

He closed his eyes to make peace with Mother Earth but in the next seconds any peace he'd conjured was shattered by the thunder and vibration of what had to be jets, one after the other, shaking the bus as they rocketed past in a show of reconnaissance or intimidation. They'd be back but they'd be too late, Greyhound reckoned as he moved the four-switch detonation box to rest between his two meaty hands on top of the fertilizer barrel.

There were suddenly and unmistakably three gunshots fired. The second pierced the windshield sending a few chards of glass and tinfoil rattling through the bus around him. When Greyhound raised his ducked melon-shaped head, he spied the hole in the windshield at just about the height his own head would have reached had he been in the driver's chair behind the wheel. He began rolling with laughter that couldn't be helped. He had out-smarted the Freddie Fuckers every step of the way!

Flailing for the end of the cable that he would use to pull himself hand over hand to shore, Bret discovered a cable without buoys didn't float and wasn't where it should have been. He had begun swimming like a spastic madman and seemed to be making no progress in closing the distance to the shore. The shocking temperature of the water, the tsunami of adrenaline that inebriated reason, and the racket of his own splashing should have masked what he was sure felt like a muted thud ripping like an arrowhead into the back of his left thigh, but it didn't. His leg seized up like a wet towel being wrung out and any motion, forward or otherwise, ceased.

Bret had the sensation of sinking because he was. His aching arm reached a hand to the back of his thigh as the last gasp of breath he'd taken expired in his chest. His back arched in agony as a finger disappeared inside his flesh and shredded muscle. At the same time his other leg came in contact with the mucky bottom of the reservoir. He must have made it further toward shore than he had realized or a shoal had revealed its mystery. He used his good leg, now that he'd confirmed he had a good and a bad, to launch off the bottom and rocket his empty lungs back to the surface for refueling.

When he broke into the atmosphere there were so many things happening around him that his senses were all at once swamped and began shutting down. Water plugged his ears and stung his eyes blind. He couldn't feel his legs, either good or bad, below his waist. His mouth filled from the back with the taste of mercury fillings as his stomach heaved and heaved in a convulsive tug-of-war with his lungs. Great gasps of life escaped his bluish lips but were instantly recalled before they dared get away for good and this rapid mouth venting bypassed his nose, which if it could smell would only pick up fear traces that he might be quite possibly dying somehow.

In his state of total senselessness, the seasoned reporter, finally endowed with the breaking story of his career, couldn't have understood or gathered the facts piling up around him. He couldn't have known that a Delta Force sharpshooter had just dropped the eco-lunatic known as Marmot onto the dam deck with a shot to each of his legs. He couldn't have verified it had been Marmot who had been shooting bullets from a revolver aimed into the water at him. He couldn't see or hear the tandem fighter jets that had just made their synchronized 180° turns over the rolling fields of the

Camas Prairie maybe twenty miles southwest of there and were now supersonically bee-lining their way back.

The reporter was clueless that the U.S. Army Corps of Engineers' master controllers at Bonneville Power had started to flood the 1005 Gallery inside the dam reacting to intel provided by a double-agent who had also been his eco-comrade and occasional-when-it-suited-him lover these past two months. Nor could Bret know that a suddenly flustered, dehydrated and hypoglycemic bus driver sitting in his own feces and with violently trembling hands had just pushed the first of four detonation box plungers.

Sergio needed to pee and was getting antsy just sitting there, strapped to that vibrating seat welded to a metal bubble held defiantly aloft by spinning blades. His eyes scanned ground-ward from the dam to the hatchery and that's when absolutely everything seemed to suddenly start moving through unpasteurized honey.

Ted Sr. emerged from the fish hatchery double doors grinning with pride and satisfaction, Little Teddy's hand in his, feeling vindicated for the botched maiden voyage of his little sailor. Teddy Jr. bounced up and down yelping for a chocolate milkshake to add like a cherry to the excitement of having just fed hundreds of baby fish for the first time. The little redhead in the Cincinnati Reds ballcap air-skipped with giant leaps across the parking lot, suspended at the end of his father's long flexing arm as they neared their orange Ford pick-up.

Sergio's two fists flew to the plastic inner window as his mouth opened to issue a scream that was muffled by the honey and the rotors. Simultaneously and directly below, he saw the father and son, the orange pick-up named *Bruce*, the battered bus he'd ditched in an empty parking lot less than four hours ago and then an explosion of such blinding and pressure-displacing magnitude it lurched the helicopter sideways and violently downward at an angle from its position in the sky. Amid the hybrid profanity-praying of the ATF agent in charge and the *Mayday*-ing of the pilot who struggled to control the fuselage that seemed to be counter-spinning independent of the rotors and the gravitational force that had suspended three stomachs high up into three ribcages, Sergio had forgotten to breathe.

Even before the ringing in his ears had stopped and before he had opened his eyes to see what had just happened, he'd felt the bionic squeeze of a four-year-old hand around his index finger. Spitting leaves and pine needles from his mouth, Ted raised his head and spied his crumpled *Mini-me* a few feet away, his arm stretching out to hold his finger, the two of them sprawled end to end on the cushion of orange bark mulch in the landscaped median that had been their landing pad. They must have looked like that Michelangelo scene on the ceiling of the Sistine Chapel where God's finger touches Adam's, Ted Sr. thought.

"That wasn't funny," Teddy Jr. said, slowly sitting up, as though his dad had just played a surprise joke on him like he was always doing.

Greyhound couldn't understand why he hadn't been rocked by an explosion. He pushed the button again with his head tilted and ear straining. This plunger was supposed to have detonated the bus parked behind the powerhouse. He was certain he was going to be able to hear and feel the rumble of it even inside the bus sixty stories on top of the dam. He panicked thinking that maybe now none of the buttons would work, that perhaps he'd calculated the ranges incorrectly or misjudged the signal-jamming capability of all this concrete. He raised and looked out the slit in the tinfoil. He could no longer see the barge, which was a good sign to him that it was either in place or hopefully close enough to do the dirty work. Just then his bowels seized in a wrenching cramp that surely must have pushed the already flowing sweat more quickly out of thousands of pores, since he was drenched. It was time. He'd heard the gunshots. He knew that every second he waited gave the authorities more options to thwart the plan. "Remember the Alsea!" he screamed, channeling the agony of the cramp through his lungs and out his mouth as he pressed the second button.

Bret didn't have time to reach the shore as the bargain had promised. He didn't have time to submerge or protect his head from flying debris when the dock he thought he'd sabotaged and abandoned exploded behind him. The force of the blast, which he'd never know was only half the force intended given the number of wires and fuses he'd been able to sever, first sucked him violently backward but then drove him like a snowplow blade forward just as violently. His arms struggled against the tow and then the shove and because his legs were weights that did the opposite of propel—whatever that was—he was just a chunk of helpless, fleshy, bleeding flotsam. Still, he was flailing, swallowing more reservoir than his body could hold and unable to focus on a horizon that wasn't concrete, when a second explosion from deep beneath him vacuum-packed the water tightly around his shape before giant bubbles rose under him and tossed him about like a Jell-O–filled sock puppet on a sea of popping beach balls.

"Just get me air, now!" the cherry-faced ATF agent in charge yelled into his headset microphone that was sitting crooked on his head still not recovered from the barely death-escaping jolt from the sky. "Knock the bus the fuck—off—that—dam!"

In the back seat behind the pilot, glued against the cabin door window, Sergio had moved his fists into open hand blinders on either side of his tear-streaked face as he waited for a break in the column of black smoke for any sign at all of the only life he had cared about in his three years undercover. Neither his own life nor one minute of his covert mission would have mattered a damn if that six-foot-three-redheaded-barge-pilot-of-his didn't walk out of that smoke.

Natalie had felt the more-subtle rumble of the first explosion she had heard in the distance, but it was the second one much closer that had brought her scalp above the profile of the surveillance monitors she'd been scanning from her hiding place beneath the reception desk. She heard Anne scream "It's Bret!" as the older woman broke free from the sheltering arms of the very tall uniformed tour guide who had folded half his body over her when the window view they'd been watching had flashed from glistening blue reservoir to flames that now billowed and churned orange and fire white.

Anne Martondale yanked open the glass door to the deck with more force than should have been packed into her slightly hunched over frame. She had reached the mid-point of the outdoor viewing platform when a third explosion tossed her horizontal and sent her skidding to an abrasive stop on the roughly scored and slip-resistant concrete floor.

Before the screen went white then black, Natalie's intuition had returned her gaze to watch the No. 4 television monitor labeled *1005*. For several minutes, this camera had been showing water gushing from overhead sprinkler plumbing and from pipes and valves spaced in exact intervals that spit fountains onto the flooding floor of the long hallway quickly becoming a canal. With this third explosion, over half of the monitors had flashed black.

Anne had started to raise her scuffed face and arms off the cheese grater where she'd landed when the thunder of the first fighter jet cleared the deck and banked left over the smoldering reservoir. In that instant a fourth explosion so close perforated an eardrum and smashed her head down into the concrete, breaking glasses that had managed to stay on her head through the three explosions prior.

JC had ducked his head when he saw the fighter jet enter his peripheral field of vision. When he looked up, the bus, which had been deflecting sun arrows off the windshield to refract and dance on the concrete walls and ceiling inside the visitor center, had disappeared from the deck of the dam. A second fighter jet materialized in thin air streaking through the jet trail left by the first and as it banked steep right after releasing its ordnance, the glass in the windows before the giant tour guide shattered and rained to the ground as the levitated Greyhound—bus and driver—exploded in giant chunks in midair.

It had taken a gratuitous flash of his cock and balls, but a privileged Libre Salazar stood face to screen watching *CNN Headline Breaking News* on the library television in a state of diabolic trance. His stalker-guard pressed a hard-on into the corner of the desk as he too leaned a crazy angle forward ostensibly toward the television, though even more toward his favorite prisoner—#13797671. Without reporter credentials on the scene, CNN scrambled to broadcast one grainy Google-downloaded image of Dworshak Dam after another as an inset corner picture first showed the State of Illinois but within fifteen seconds had been clumsily changed to the *State of Idaho*. The unfortunate audio came from a redneck-sounding tourist who spoke in backwater jibberish by cellphone from a holding area where evacuees from the DAM UNDER ATTACK, as the screen had been chromotronned in yellow block letters, were being held. One explosion after another had provoked a limited repertoire of cuss words but the tourist was doing his level fourth-grade best under the very tense circumstances.

Natalie Wesson pulled the hair and a small chard of embedded glass out of her face, took a moment to gather herself, inadvertently smearing blood like eye shadow above her left eye, cleared her throat and picked up the headset from the reception desk telephone. There was a dial tone and she silently thanked the *Jesus of Lucky Breaks*.

"What City and Town Please?"

"Atlanta, Georgia. *CNN*."

Libre felt the guard's hot breath on his neck, but he didn't let it bother him. Once you accept being a caged animal for the amusement of the masses, you didn't let anything bother you anymore. Blue-eyed Anderson Cooper was abruptly framed by an awkward camera transition away from the looped images to the live studio and tried to recover a perplexed face that had been buried in the centerfold of an atlas of the United States—indivisible, with liberty and justice for all.

"Oh, thank goodness," the popular anchor was anxious to elevate the discourse. *"We now have on the line a* Seattle Times *newspaper reporter, who apparently is reporting for CNN from inside the Visitor Center at this DAM UNDER ATTACK."*

"That's right, Anderson. I'm Natalie Wesson, investigative reporter for the *Seattle Times* newspaper."

"YES! Baby! You made it!" Libre yelled, embracing both sides of the television with his arms.

"Anderson, I'm standing behind the reception desk at the Dworshak Dam visitor center in North-Central Idaho looking through the frames of giant plate glass windows that just moments ago were shattered by the reverberations of twin fighter jets and a fifth massive explosion to occur at this facility since this insurgence began about forty-five minutes ago. There is black smoke rising from the reservoir behind the dam where burning debris is floating everywhere. There are flames and smoke pouring out of the front half of a disintegrated passenger bus that has quite literally fallen out of the sky to land teetering on the downriver side of a hand railing. This railing, which to me looks badly damaged from here, is all that appears to be holding this charred and burning piece of wreckage from careening down the nearly seventy-story-tall dam face."

When Libre stepped back from the television to allow his watering eyes to refocus, he bumped into the arms of his guard, who tactically had moved closer when it looked as though the television might have been in danger of being vandalized. The guard's hands grasped Libre at the biceps and held him firmly in place as he buried his nose into the nape of the prisoner's neck and nudged so slightly his other baton into the orange jumpsuited hills of his prisoner's buttocks. Libre shrugged his whole body like a housefly had just landed on him. The guard in love stepped backward one step.

"At this time and from this vantage point, I cannot tell how badly damaged the dam structure is, but water continues to tumble down the spillway and at this time the reservoir is still being held back by this nearly thirty-five-year-old dam." Natalie stretched the telephone as far as the cord would allow and then even further stretching the coil out of the headset cord to check on the tour guide, badly bleeding and just rising off the floor. "I am joined by a tour guide for the U.S. Army Corps of Engineers who stayed behind after this facility was safely evacuated. I should tell you, Anderson, since we don't have a camera with us, that this employee is badly injured by the flying glass but appears able and willing to provide us some perspective on what is unfolding here."

Not willing or able to be identified by anyone, JC took the phone that was being handed to him and with a sharp twist and tug of his body, ripped the phone cord out of the housing in the wall behind the reception desk just as a sixth explosion flashed on the dam deck, then sounded with a one-second travel delay. The handrail and the large chunk of bus wreckage that had snagged on it were blasted off the side of the dam to cartwheel down its straight-axis face toward the 500,000-volt transmission lines and the powerhouse.

Libre took a step forward as Anderson Cooper tried to sound-check the telephone connection with his newly deputized reporter on the scene following what sounded like the start of an explosion. The two of them, Libre and Anderson, called for *Natalie* at the same time. The television screen in the Oregon State Penitentiary outside Salem flatlined black and the lights and air-handling units in the prison library dimmed and whirled down to nearly off for several seconds reminiscent of a rolling brownout. Both Libre and the guard cocked their heads to listen. Then, in that next instant, before the prison's generators had kicked in and before the controllers at Bonneville Power could switch the grid to auxiliary, the guard, Prisoner #13797671 and much of the Pacific Northwest were suspended in a blackout that didn't roll.

*A*FTER TEN YEARS OF SECOND THOUGHTS, A STRING OF FALSE PREGNANCIES *including the first that had rushed them to the altar and the last that had nearly ended in divorce, Ted's four-year-old—not to mention, the Portland cement of their marriage—Teddy Jr., sat between them in the front seat of the orange pick-up as it bounded down the familiar gravel road toward the river. It all but destroyed Ted the father to have to leave on these twelve-day trips. Being away from home for a week to two weeks at a time had worked when he and Samantha had been having problems instead of children. Now that he had a son, being a journeyman for the Corps had mutated from a job he loved into one he loathed.*

Teddy Jr., sunburned and shirtless in Oshkosh overalls with a Cincinnati Reds baseball cap, squirmed under the seat belt between them. He knew what the black nylon bag in the back of the truck meant. He knew his Dad was leaving again. Except when he showed up ten or twelve days later, leaving was pretty much all that his Dad ever did. He looked out from under his red bangs through blondish eyelashes at Ted Sr. as if to say, even at four years old, that he knew he was getting the raw end of this deal being stuck at home with Mom. His dad ruffled his hair. "Learn to swim this summer, and you can come with me, Son."

His child's green eyes widened and for what had to be the first second in forty-eight months, he stopped squirming. "I will learn to swim," he said. "I sure will."

Bret Meyer Brady swallowed for the first time in a dozen para-graphs. He gave a coy wink to Anne Martondale perched on the edge of her chair in the front row. Then he closed his eyes and lowered his head a fraction of a second until the anxious readers around the even-more-than-usually crowded Powell's Bookstore began to applaud his doubts of ever becoming a published author into complete remission.

MICHAEL SCOTT CURNES is also the author of *VAL*. His writing has appeared in *The Globe and Mail*, *Writing the West Coast: In Love with Place*, and *The Clean Water Act Owner's Manual, Second Edition*. He attributes his enthusiasm for free-flowing, wild and scenic rivers to his PNW upbringing and his whitewater and canoe-obsessed father. He drew inspiration for this novel during volunteer and professional engagements as a board director for The Friends of Clayoquot Sound (Tofino, B.C.) and as a development and communications specialist for River Network (Portland, Oregon). He now lives in Vancouver, British Columbia.

* 9 7 8 1 7 7 7 2 9 8 8 2 1 *